Praise for *USA TODAY* bestselling author Marie Ferrarella

"Ferrarella delivers a fabulous couple. Wonderful storytelling expertly delivers both lighthearted and tragic story details."

–*RT Book Reviews* on *Her Red-Carpet Romance*

"An easy-read modern romance with a creditable and self-possessed heroine to steal your heart."

—*Fresh Fiction* on *Mendoza's Secret Fortune*

"She has a genuine knack for keeping the reader interested and involved in the characters and their emotional feelings."

—*Fresh Fiction* on *His Forever Valentine*

"Expert storytelling moves the book along at a steady pace. A solidly crafted plot makes it quite entertaining."

—*RT Book Reviews* on *Cavanaugh Fortune*

"Master storyteller Ferrarella has a magical way of spinning feel-good romances that readers can lose themselves in, and her latest is no exception."

–*RT Book Reviews* on *The Cowboy and the Lady*

DR. FORGET-ME-NOT

BY
MARIE FERRARELLA

First Published in Great Britain 2016
By Mills & Boon, an imprint of HarperCollins*Publishers*
1 London Bridge Street, London, SE1 9GF

ISBN: 978-0-263-91960-8

23-0216

Our policy is to use papers that are natural, renewable and recyclable products and made from wood grown in sustainable forests.The logging and manufacturing processes conform to the legal environmental regulations of the country of origin.

Printed and bound in Spain
by CPI, Barcelona

USA TODAY bestselling and RITA® Award–winning author **Marie Ferrarella** has written more than two hundred and fifty books for Mills & Boon, some under the name Marie Nicole. Her romances are beloved by fans worldwide. Visit her website, www.marieferrarella.com.

To
Nancy Parodi Neubert,
And
Friendships
That go back to the
3rd Grade

Prologue

"You haven't finally decided to sell that beautiful house of yours and downsize to something a little smaller and more modern, now have you?"

It wasn't really a question. Maizie Connors, sitting opposite the attractive woman in Jack's Hideaway, Bedford's newest trendy restaurant, knew better than to think that Charlotte, a woman she had known for close to forty years, would ever sell the house she loved so much. When she'd taken the unexpected call from her old friend that morning, Maizie had suspected something was up, but she'd instinctively known it had nothing to do with Charlotte making use of Maizie's successful real estate business.

"What?" Charlotte asked. Sitting ramrod straight, doing her best to appear cheerful, Charlotte Stewart was caught off guard by the question. She also felt somewhat embarrassed, not just because of the deception she'd allowed to continue, but because of the real reason for her getting in contact with Maizie in the first place. She cleared her throat and stalled for time. Trying to get her thoughts together in order to find the right words. So far, they had frustratingly managed to elude her. "Oh, no, I haven't," she confessed, then added in a sincere moment of truth, "I don't think I'll ever sell that house. It's where all the good memories are."

Maizie smiled, nodding her head knowingly. Unlike Charlotte, who had gone stylishly gray, Maizie's short bob was a light golden blond, the same color it had been when she'd first met her late husband all those years ago.

"I didn't think so. So, Charlotte," she asked, getting comfortable, "what's this lunch *really* about?"

To be honest, Maizie was fairly certain she knew the answer to her question. As a successful Realtor, she had started her agency after her husband passed away years ago. It did a brisk business; but these days, she was just as accustomed to getting calls from people who sought her services for the business that she ran on the side as she was from people who wanted to either buy or sell houses.

Maizie, along with her two lifelong best friends, had an aptitude for making matches.

Lasting matches.

When Charlotte called, asking to see her over lunch, the woman had murmured something about needing advice and alluded to it being about selling her house. Surprised—since Maizie knew how attached her friend was to the only place she had ever called home once Charlotte's late husband had slipped a ring on her finger, Maizie had played along until after appetizers had been ordered.

When Charlotte now made no reply to her question, Maizie leaned forward over the small table and placed her hand over her friend's.

"We've been friends for almost forty years, Charlotte, you can tell me. No matter what it is, at my age, I've heard it before."

Charlotte continued to look uncomfortable. "I don't know where to start."

Maizie's smile was warm, encouraging. "Just jump right in and I'll try to keep up."

"It's Mitchell," Charlotte finally blurted out, referring to her only child.

Again, Maizie was fairly certain she knew what was coming, but she approached the subject slowly, not wanting to make her friend nervous enough to abruptly change her mind and table the subject.

Guessing at the true reason for this impromptu meeting, Maizie was well aware that the subject the other woman was attempting to broach was not an easy one for some mothers. Although genuinely concerned, mothers like Charlotte didn't want to be seen as meddling, which was only a cut above words like *controlling*, *calculating* and *interfering*. No true mother wanted that label.

"Ah, how is Dr. Mitch these days?" Maizie asked, her blue eyes sparkling with humor.

The word escaped Charlotte's lips before she could think to prevent it. "Lonely."

"Is he?" Maizie asked with keen interest. She loved matching up people with their dream homes.

She loved matching people up with their dream soul mates even more. The former came with a commission, the latter was priceless to her, even if the service itself was free.

"Except he doesn't know it yet," Charlotte hurriedly qualified.

Maizie was nothing if not patience personified. "Explain," she requested.

"He'd really be annoyed if he knew I was saying this," Charlotte interjected hesitantly.

"Then we won't tell him," Maizie assured her pleasantly. None of the protagonists in the matches she and her friends had undertaken ever knew that their "meetings" had been orchestrated. Things worked out far more naturally that way. "But you're going to have to give me a little more to work with here."

Charlotte took a deep breath and forged ahead, knowing that if she lost her nerve, if she told Maizie "never mind" and just left, the problem would only continue. And most likely get worse. She loved her son far too much to let that happen. He deserved to have a full life.

"Mitchell is a fantastic surgeon," she said by way of an introduction to the crux of the matter.

Maizie nodded. "Like his father." She was rewarded with a grateful smile from her friend.

"But he lacks Matthew's gift for getting along with people." Charlotte hesitated for a moment, knowing that wasn't specific enough. She tried again. "He just doesn't *connect*."

"With his patients?" Maizie asked, quietly urging her friend on. She vaguely remembered Charlotte's son as a quiet, intense young man.

"With anybody." Charlotte sighed as she leaned forward over the table toward Maizie. "He's brilliant, handsome and you couldn't ask for a better surgeon—or a better son," she tacked on.

"But...?" Maizie asked, fully aware that the word was waiting in the wings.

"But I'm never going to have any grandchildren." Charlotte appeared distressed at the words she had just blurted out. "I know it sounds trivial—"

Maizie quickly cut her off. "Trust me, I understand perfectly. I was in your shoes once. So were some of my friends. Sometimes, you can't just sit back and wait for the planets to align themselves. Sometimes, you have to drag those planets into place yourself," Maizie told her with a wink. And then Maizie got down to business. "As far as you know, has Mitchell ever been seriously involved with anyone?"

"I *do* know." Charlotte prided herself on the fact that she had the kind of relationship with Mitch where her son actually *talked* to her. "And he hasn't. I once watched a young woman all but throw herself at him at a party—it was a fund raiser for his hospital," she interjected. "Anyway, Mitchell had absolutely no idea that she was doing it." Charlotte pressed her lips together as she shook her head, recalling the incident. "I'm beginning to think things are hopeless."

Maizie was always at her best when faced with a challenge. A string of successes had only bolstered her confidence in her knack—as well as Celia's and Theresa's—for bringing the right people together.

"Never hopeless," Maizie assured her. "Let me ask around and see what I can do." She patted Charlotte's hand and repeated, "Never hopeless." And then she grinned. “Now we can order,” she declared since her agenda had come into focus. “I don’t know about you, Charlotte, but I’m suddenly starved.”

Chapter One

She was doing her best to get lost in other people's lives.

Melanie McAdams knew she should be grateful for the fact that she was in a position to help them—which was what she was doing here at the Bedford Rescue Mission, a homeless shelter where single mothers could come with their children and remain as long as needed. The women were encouraged to attempt to stitch together a better life for themselves and their children. Melanie had been volunteering here for almost three years now—and when, nine months ago, her own life had suddenly fallen apart, she'd taken a leave from her job and volunteered at the shelter full-time.

But today, nothing seemed to be working. Today, trying to make a difference in these people's lives wasn't enough to keep the dark thoughts from the past from infiltrating her mind and haunting her.

Because today was nine months to the day when the somber black car had come down her street and stopped in front of her house—the house she and Jeremy had planned to share. Nine months to the day when she'd opened her front door to find a chaplain and army lieutenant John Walters standing on her doorstep, coming to solemnly tell her that her whole world had just been blown up.

Coming to tell her that Jeremy Williams, her high school sweetheart, her fiancé, her *world*, wasn't coming back to her.

Ever.

No matter how good she was, no matter how hard she prayed, he wasn't coming back.

Except in a coffin.

Melanie gave up trying to stack the children's books on the side table in one of the shelter's two common rooms. They just kept sliding and falling on the floor.

When did it stop? Melanie silently demanded. When did it stop hurting like this? When did the pain fade into the background instead of being the first thing she was aware of every morning and the last thing that she was aware of every night? When did it stop chewing bits and pieces out of her every day?

Four days, she thought now. Four days, that was how long Jeremy had had left. Four days and he would have been out of harm's way once and for all. His tour of duty would have been over.

Four days and he would have been back in her arms, back in her life, taking vows and marrying her.

But it might as well have been four hundred years. It hadn't happened.

Wasn't going to happen.

Because Jeremy was now in a cold grave instead of her warm bed.

"Are you okay, Miss Melody?" the small, high-pitched voice asked.

Trying to collect herself as best she could, Melanie turned around to look down into the face of the little girl who had asked the question. The small, concerned face and older-than-her-years green eyes belonged to April O'Neill, a beautiful, bright five-year-old who, along with her seven-year-old brother, Jimmy, and her mother, Brenda, had been here at the shelter for a little over a month. Prior to that, they had been living on the streets in a nearby city for longer than their mother had been willing to admit.

Initially, when April had first made the mistake and called her Melody, Melanie had made an attempt to correct her. But after three more attempts, all without success, she'd given up.

She'd grown to like the name April called her and had more than a little affection for the small family who had been through so much through no real fault of their own. It was an all too familiar story. A widow, Brenda had lost her job and, after failing to pay the rent for two months, she and her children had been evicted.

With no husband in the picture and no family anywhere to speak of, the street became their home until a police officer took pity on them, loaded them into the back of his squad car and drove them over to the shelter.

Melanie told herself to focus on their problems and the problems of the other homeless women and single mothers who were under the shelter's roof. Their situations were fixable, hers was not.

Melanie forced herself to smile at April. "I'm fine, honey."

April appeared unconvinced. Her small face puckered up, as if she was trying to reconcile two different thoughts. "But your eye is leaking, like Mama's does sometimes when she's thinking sad thoughts, or about Daddy."

"Dust," Melanie told her, saying the first thing that occurred to her. "There's dust in the air and I've got allergies. It makes my eyes…leak sometimes," she said, using April's word for it and hoping that would be enough for the little girl.

April was sharper than she'd been at her age, Melanie discovered.

"Oh. You can take a pill," the little girl advised her. "The lady on TV says you can take a pill to make your all-er-gee go away," she concluded solemnly, carefully pronouncing the all-important word.

April made her smile despite the heaviness she felt on her chest. Melanie slipped her arm around the very small shoulders, giving the little girl a quick hug.

"I'll have to try that," she promised. "Now, why did you come looking for me?" she asked, diverting the conversation away from her and back to April.

April's expression became even more solemn as she stated the reason for her search. "Mama says that Jimmy's sick again."

Melanie did a quick calculation in her head. That made three times in the past six weeks. There was no doubt about it. Jimmy O'Neill was a sickly boy. His time on the street had done nothing to improve that.

"Same thing?" she asked April.

The blond head bobbed up and down with alacrity. "He's coughing and sneezing and Mama says he shouldn't be around other kids or they'll get sick, too."

"Smart lady," Melanie agreed.

As she started to walk to the communal quarters that the women and their children all shared, April slipped her hand through hers. The small fingers tightened around hers as if she was silently taking on the role of guide despite the fact that she and her family had only been at the shelter a short time.

"I think Jimmy needs a doctor," April confided, her eyes meeting Melanie's.

"Even smarter lady," Melanie commented under her breath.

The comment might have been quiet, but April had heard her and went on talking as if they were two equals, having a conversation. "But we don't have any money and Jimmy feels too sick to go to the hospital place. Besides, Mama doesn't like asking for free stuff," April confided solemnly.

Melanie nodded. "Your mama's got pride," she told the little girl. "But sometimes, people have to forget about their pride if it means trying to help someone they love."

April eyed her knowingly. "You mean like Jimmy?"

"Exactly like Jimmy."

Turning a corner, she pushed open the oversize door that led into one of the three large communal rooms that accommodated as many families as could be fit into it without violating any of the fire department's safety regulations. Polly, the woman who ran the shelter, referred to the rooms as dorms, attempting to create a more positive image for the women who found themselves staying here.

The room that April had brought her to was largely empty except for the very worried-looking, small, dark-haired woman sitting on the bed all the way over in the corner. The object of her concern was the rather fragile-looking red-haired little boy sitting up and leaning against her.

The boy was coughing. It was the kind of cough that fed on itself, growing a little worse with each pass and giving no sign of letting up unless some kind of action was taken. Sometimes, it took something as minor as a drink of water to alleviate the cough, other times, prescription cough medicine was called for.

Melanie gave the simplest remedy a try first.

Looking down at the little girl who was still holding her hand, she said, "April, why don't you go to the kitchen and ask Miss Theresa to give you a glass of water for your brother?"

April, eager to help, uncoupled herself from Melanie's hand and immediately ran off to the kitchen.

As April took off, Melanie turned her attention to Jimmy's mother. "He really should see a doctor," she gently suggested.

Worn and tired way beyond her years, Brenda O'Neill raised her head proudly and replied, "We'll manage, thank you. It's not the first time he's had this cough and it won't be the last," she said with assurance. "It comes and goes. Some children are like that."

"True," Melanie agreed. She wasn't here to argue, just to comfort. "But it would be better if it went—

permanently." She knew the woman was proud, but she'd meant what she'd said to April. Sometimes pride needed to take a backseat to doing what was best for someone you loved. "Look, I know that money's a problem, Brenda." She thought of the newly erected, state-of-the-art hospital that was less than seven miles away from the shelter. "I'll pay for the visit."

The expression on Jimmy's mother's face was defiant and Melanie could see the woman withdrawing and closing herself off.

"He'll be all right," Brenda insisted. "Kids get sick all the time."

Melanie sighed. She couldn't exactly kidnap the boy and whisk him off to the ER, not without his mother's express consent. "Can't argue with that," Melanie agreed.

"I brought water," April announced, returning. "And Miss Theresa, too." She glanced over her shoulder as if to make sure that the woman was still behind her. "She was afraid I'd spill it, but I wouldn't," she told Melanie in what the little girl thought passed for a whisper. It didn't.

Theresa Manetti gave the glass of water to Jimmy. "There you go. Maybe this'll help." She smiled at the boy. "And if it doesn't, I might have something else that will."

Brenda looked at the older woman and she squared her shoulders. "I've already had this discussion with that lady," she waved her hand at Melanie. "We can't afford a doctor. Jimmy'll be fine in a couple of days," she insisted, perhaps just a little too strongly, as if trying to convince herself as well as the women she was talking to.

Theresa nodded. A mother of two herself, she fully sympathized with what Jimmy's mother was going through. But she didn't volunteer her time, her crew and the meals she personally prepared before coming here just to stand idly by if there was something she could do. Luckily, after her conversation with Maizie yesterday, there was. It was also, hopefully, killing two birds with one stone—or, as she preferred thinking of it, spreading as much good as possible.

"Good to know, dear," she said to Brenda, patting the woman's shoulder. "But maybe you might want to have Dr. Mitch take a look at him anyway."

"Dr. Mitch?" Melanie asked. This was the first reference she'd heard to that name. Was the volunteer chef referring to a personal physician she intended to call?

"Sorry, that's what my friend calls him," Theresa apologized. "His full name is Dr. Mitchell Stewart and he's a general surgeon associated with Bedford Memorial Hospital—right down the road," she added for Brenda's benefit. "He's been doing rather well these past couple of years and according to mutual sources, he wants to give a little back to the community. When I told Polly about it," she said, referring to Polly French, the director of the shelter, "she immediately placed a call to his office and asked him to volunteer a few hours here whenever he could." She moved aside the hair that was hanging in April's eyes, fondly remembering when she used to do the same thing with her own daughter. "He'll be here tomorrow. I'm spreading the word."

Brenda still looked somewhat suspicious of the whole thing. "We don't need any charity."

"Seems to me that it'll be you being charitable to him," Theresa pointed out diplomatically. "If the man wants to do something good, I say let him." Theresa turned her attention to Jimmy who had mercifully stopped coughing, at least for now. "What about you, Jimmy? What d'you say?"

Jimmy looked up at her with hesitant, watery eyes. "He won't stick me with a needle, will he?"

"I don't think he's planning on that," Theresa replied honestly. "He just wants to do what's best for you."

"Then okay," the boy replied, then qualified one more time, "as long as he doesn't stick me."

Theresa smiled at Brenda. "Born negotiator, that one. Sounds a lot like my son did at that age. He's a lawyer now," Theresa added proudly. "Who knows, yours might become one, too."

The hopeless look on Brenda's face said she didn't agree, but wasn't up to arguing the point.

Theresa gently squeezed the woman's shoulder. "It'll get better, dear. Even when you feel like you've hit bottom and there's no way back up to the surface, it'll get better," Theresa promised.

For her part, Theresa was remembering how she'd felt when her husband had died suddenly of a heart attack. At first, she had been convinced that she couldn't even go on breathing—but she had. She not only went on breathing, but she'd gone on to form and run a successful catering business. Life was nothing if not full of possibilities—as long as you left yourself open to them, Theresa thought.

The last part of her sentence was directed more

toward Melanie than to the young mother she was initially addressing.

"I'd better get back to getting dinner set up," Theresa said, beginning to walk away.

Melanie followed in her wake. "Are you really getting a doctor to come to the shelter?" she asked.

It was hard for her to believe and harder for her to contain her excitement. This was just what some of the children—not to mention some of the women—needed, to be examined by a real doctor.

"Not me, personally," she told Melanie, "but I have a friend who has a friend—the upshot is, yes, there is a doctor coming here tomorrow."

"Photo op?" Melanie guessed. This was the Golden State and a lot of things were done here for more than a straightforward reason. It seemed like everyone thrived on publicity for one reason or another. "Don't get me wrong," she said quickly, "some of these people really need to be seen by a doctor, but if this is just some kind of publicity stunt so that some doctor can drum up goodwill and get people to come to his state-of-the-art new clinic, or buy his new skin cream, or whatever, I don't want to see Brenda and her son being used."

Sympathy flooded Theresa's eyes. She had to restrain herself to keep from hugging Melanie. "Oh honey, what happened to you to make you so suspicious and defensive?"

She was *not* about to talk about Jeremy, or any other part of her life. Besides, that had nothing to do with this.

"This isn't about me," Melanie retorted, then caught hold of her temper. This wasn't like her. She was going to have watch that. "This is about them." She waved her hand toward where they had left Brenda and her children. "I don't want them being used."

"They won't be," Theresa assured her kindly. "This doctor really does see the need to give back a little to the community." That was the story Maizie and the doctor's mother, Charlotte, had told her they'd agreed upon. "He's a very decent sort," she added.

Melanie looked at her, confused. "I thought you said you didn't know him."

"I don't," Theresa readily admitted. "But I know the woman who knows his mother and Maizie would never recommend anyone—even a doctor—who was just out for himself." Theresa paused for a moment as little things began to fall into place in her mind. She had the perfect approach, she thought suddenly, pleased with herself.

"Dr. Mitch is a little...*stiff*, I hear, for lack of a better word. I hate to ask, but maybe you can stick around a little longer, act as a guide his first day here. Show him the ropes."

Melanie would have thought that Polly, the director who was bringing him on board, would be much better suited for the job than she was. "I don't know anything about medicine."

"No, but you know people," Theresa was quick to point out, playing up Melanie's strengths, "and the ones around here seem to trust you a lot."

Melanie shrugged. She didn't know if that was exactly accurate. She was just a familiar face for them. "They're just desperate..." she allowed, not wanting to take any undue credit.

Theresa laughed, nodding. "Aren't we all, one way or another?" This was the perfect point to just retreat, before Melanie could think of any further objections to her interacting with Mitch on a one-to-one basis. So Theresa did. "I really do need to get back to the kitchen to get things set up and ready or dinner is going to be late," she told Melanie.

About to leave, Theresa hesitated. It wasn't just small sad faces that got to her. She'd been infinitely aware of the sadness in Melanie's eyes from the first moment she'd been introduced to the volunteer.

Coming closer to Melanie, she lowered her voice so that only Melanie could hear her. "But I just wanted to tell you that should you ever need to talk—or maybe just need a friendly ear—I'm here at the shelter every other week." She knew she was telling Melanie something that she already knew. "And when I'm not—"

Digging into the pocket of her apron, Theresa extracted one of her business cards. Taking a pen out of the other pocket, she quickly wrote something on the back of the card, then held the same card out to Melanie.

"Here."

Melanie glanced at the front of the card. "Thank you, but I don't think I'm going to be having any parties that'll need catering any time soon."

Theresa didn't bother wasting time telling the young woman that she wasn't offering her catering service, but her services as a sympathetic listener. "That's my private number on the back. If I'm not home, leave a message."

Melanie didn't believe in pouring out her heart and burdening people, especially if they were all but strangers. "But we don't really know each other," she protested, looking at the card.

"That's what phone calls are for," Theresa told her. "To change that." She paused for a moment, as if debating whether or not to say something further. "I know what it feels like to lose someone you love."

Melanie stared at her, stunned. She'd exchanged a few words with the other woman and found Theresa Manetti to be a very sweet person, but she'd never shared anything remotely personal with her, and certainly not the fact that her fiancé had been killed. Why was the woman saying this to her?

As if reading her mind, Theresa told her, "The director told me about your young man. I am very, very sorry."

Melanie stiffened slightly. "Yes, well, I am, too," she replied, virtually shutting down.

But Theresa wasn't put off so quickly. "I think it's a very good thing, your being here. The best way to work through what you're feeling right now is to keep busy, very, very busy. You have to stay ahead of the pain until you can handle it and it won't just mow you down."

"I am never going to be able to handle it," Melanie told her with finality.

"I think you're underestimating yourself," she told Melanie. "You're already thinking of others. Trying to talk that young mother into taking her son to see a doctor is definitely thinking of others."

Melanie's mouth dropped open. She stared at the older woman. "How did you know?" She'd had that conversation with Brenda before Theresa had come on the scene.

Theresa merely smiled, approximating, she knew, the look that sometimes crossed Maizie's face. She swore that she and Celia were becoming more like Maizie every day. "I have my ways, dear," she told Melanie just before leaving. "I have my ways."

Chapter Two

He was having second thoughts.

Serious second thoughts.

Anyone who was vaguely acquainted with Dr. Mitchell Stewart knew him to be focused, dedicated, exceedingly good at everything he set out to do and definitely not someone who could even remotely be conceived of as being impetuous. The latter meant that having second thoughts was not part of his makeup.

Ever.

However, in this one singular instance, Mitch was beginning to have doubts about the wisdom of what he had agreed to undertake.

It didn't mean that he wasn't up to it because he lacked the medical savvy. What he would be doing amounted to practicing random medicine, something he hadn't really done since his intern days. These days he was an exceptionally skilled general surgeon who garnered the admiration and praise of his colleagues as well as the head of his department and several members of his hospital's board of directors.

Mitch could truthfully say that he had never been challenged by any procedure he'd had to perform. In the arena of the operating world, it was a given that he shined—each and every time. He made sure of it, and was dedicated to continuing to make that an ongoing fact of his life.

But just as he knew his strengths, Mitch was aware of the area where he did *not* shine. While he was deemed to be a poetic virtuoso with a scalpel, when it came to words, to expressing his thoughts and explaining what he was going to do to any layman, he was sadly lacking in the proper skills and he was aware of that.

However, that was not enough for him to attempt to change anything that he did, or even to attempt to learn how to communicate better than he did. He didn't have time for that.

Mitch truly felt that successfully operating on an at-risk patient far outweighed making said patient feel better verbally about what was about to happen. His awareness of his shortcoming was, however, just enough for him to acknowledge that this was an area in which he was sorely lacking.

Hence, the second thoughts.

As he drove to the Bedford Rescue Mission now, Mitch readily admitted to himself that he'd agreed to volunteer his services at the local homeless shelter in a moment of general weakness. His mother had ambushed him unexpectedly, showing up on his doorstep last Sunday to remind him that it was his birthday and that she was taking him out to lunch whether he liked it or not.

She had assumed that as with everything else that didn't involve his operating skills, he had forgotten about his birthday.

He had.

But, in his defense, he'd pointed out to her patiently, he'd stopped thinking of birthdays as something to celebrate around the time he'd turned eighteen. That was the year that his father had died and immediately after that, he'd had to hustle, utilizing every spare moment he had to earn money in order to pay his way through medical school.

Oh, there had been scholarships, but they didn't cover everything at the school he had elected to attend and he was not about to emerge out of medical school with a degree and owing enough money, thanks to student loans, to feed and clothe the people of a small developing nation for a decade. If emerging debt free meant neglecting everything but his work and his studies, so be it.

Somewhere along the line, holidays and birthdays had fallen by the wayside, as well. His life had been stripped down to the bare minimum.

But he couldn't strip away his mother that easily. He loved her a great deal even if he didn't say as much. The trouble was his mother was dogged about certain things, insisting that he at least spend time with her on these few occasions, if not more frequently.

And, once he was finally finished with his studies, with his internship and his residency, it was his mother who was behind his attending social functions that had to do with the hospital where he worked. She had argued that it was advantageous for him to be seen, although for the life of him, he had no idea how that could possibly benefit him. He had no patience with the behind-the-scenes politics that went on at the hospital. As far as he was concerned, gladhanding and smiling would never take the place of being a good surgeon.

In his book, the former didn't matter, the latter was *all* that did.

And that was where his mother had finally gotten him. On the doctor front. She had, quite artfully, pointed out that because of new guidelines and the changing medical field, getting doctors to volunteer their services and their time was becoming more and more of a difficult endeavor.

He never saw it coming.

He'd agreed with her, thinking they were having a theoretical conversation—and then that was when his mother had hit him with specifics. She'd told him about this shelter that took in single women who had nowhere else to turn. Single women with children. She reminded him how, when his father was alive, this was the sort of thing he had done on a regular basis, rendered free medical services to those in need.

Before he was able to comment—or change the subject—his mother had hit him with her request, asking him to be the one to volunteer until another doctor could be found to fill that position at the shelter. In effect, she was asking him to *temporarily* fill in.

Or so she said.

He knew his mother, and the woman was nothing if not clever. But he was going to hold her to her word.

He planned to fill in at the shelter only on a temporary basis. A *very* temporary basis.

Mitch knew his way around surgical instruments like a pro. Managing around people, however, was a completely different story. That had always been a mystery to him.

People, one of the doctors he'd interned with had insisted, wanted good bedside manner, they wanted their hands held while being told that everything was going to turn out all right.

Well, he wasn't any good at that. He didn't hold hands or spend time talking. He healed wounds. In the long run, he felt that his patients were much better served by his choice.

This was just going to be temporary, Mitch silently promised himself, pulling up into the small parking lot before the two-story rectangular building. He'd give this place an hour, maybe ninety minutes at most, then leave. The only thing he wanted to do today was get a feel for whatever might be the physical complaints that the residents of this shelter had and then he'd be on his way home.

It was doable, he told himself. No reason to believe that it wasn't.

Getting out of his serviceable, secondhand Toyota—he'd never been one for ostentatious symbols of success—Mitch took a long look at the building he was about to enter.

It didn't look the way he imagined a homeless shelter would look. There was a fresh coat of paint on the building and an even fresher-looking sign in front of it, proclaiming it to be the Bedford Rescue Mission. A handful of daisies—white and yellow—pushed their way up and clustered around both ends of the sign. Surprisingly, he noted almost as an afterthought, there were no weeds seeking to choke out the daisies.

As he approached the front door, Mitch was vaguely aware of several pairs of eyes watching him from the windows. From the way the blinds were slanted, the watchful eyes belonged to extremely petite people—children most likely around kindergarten age, he estimated.

He sincerely hoped their mothers were around to keep them in line.

Those uncustomary, nagging second thoughts crept out again as he raised his hand to ring the doorbell.

He almost dropped it again without making contact. But then he sighed. He was here, he might as well see just how bad this was. Maybe he'd overthought it.

The moment his finger touched the doorbell, Mitch heard the chimes go off, approximating the first ten notes of a song that he found vaguely familiar, one that teased his brain, then slipped away into the mist the moment the front door was opened.

A young woman with hair the color of ripened wheat stood in the doorway, making no secret of the fact that she was sizing him up. It surprised him when he caught himself wondering what conclusion she'd reached.

"Dr. Stewart," she said by way of a greeting.

A greeting he found to be rather odd. "I know who I am, who are you?" he asked.

For such a good-looking man—and she could easily see all the little girls at the shelter giggling behind their hands over this one—he came across as entirely humorless. Too bad, Melanie thought. She'd take a sense of humor over good looks any day.

A sense of humor, in her eyes, testified to a person's humanity as well as his or her ability to identify with another person. Good looks just meant a person got lucky in the gene pool.

"Melanie McAdams," she told him, identifying herself as she stepped back and opened the door wider for him.

Mitch noticed there was a little girl hanging on to the bottom of the young woman's blouse. The girl had curly blond hair and very animated green eyes. He assumed she was the woman's daughter.

"You run this place, or live here?" he asked her bluntly.

"Neither."

Melanie's answer was short, clipped and definitely not customary for her.

She wasn't sure if she liked this man.

One thing was for certain, though. Theresa was right. He was definitely going to need someone to guide him through the ins and outs of dealing with the residents here. Especially the little residents.

She could tell by the expression on his face that he felt, justifiably or not, that he was a cut above the people who lived here. Obviously not a man who subscribed to the "There but for the grace of God go I" theory of life, Melanie thought.

It jibed with what she'd found out.

Once she'd been told the doctor's name yesterday, she'd done her homework and looked him up on the internet. The list of awards and commendations after his name went on and on, but the few photographs she could find of the doctor—and there were *very* few—showed a man who looked stiff and out of place each and every time. It seemed as if he were wishing himself somewhere else.

She supposed, in his defense, fund raisers—because those were all she'd found—could be seen as draining.

But she had a nagging feeling that the good doctor reacted that way to most people he was around. He probably felt they were all beneath him because, after all, it took a certain amount of intelligence and tenacity to study medicine and pass all those tests.

Or maybe the man was just good at memorizing things, she thought now, looking at him face-to-face. The true test of someone's ability and intelligence was putting their knowledge into action.

Hopefully, the only thing this doctor was going to be putting into action would be his stethoscope and his prescription pad when it came to writing prescriptions for antibiotics.

Once word got out that a doctor was coming to the shelter, suddenly their "sick" population had mushroomed.

Mitch raised a quizzical eyebrow, as if waiting for more information.

"I'm your guide," Melanie told him, explaining her current function.

She thought her word for it was a far more tactful label than telling the doctor that she was going to be his go-between, acting as a buffer between him and the patients he would be seeing because his reputation had preceded him—both his good reputation and the one that was not so good.

"I hope you brought your patience with you," Melanie said cheerfully. "No pun intended," she added quickly, realizing the play on words she'd just unintentionally uttered. "When word spread that you were coming, people couldn't put their names down on the sign-in sheet fast enough."

He looked at her, slightly mystified. "They know who I am?" he questioned.

Mitch didn't see how that was possible. He didn't move in the same circles as anyone who would find herself to be homeless.

He didn't move in circles at all, which was another source of distress to his mother. He preferred to spend his downtime learning new techniques, studying medical journals and observing new methodologies.

"They know that you're a doctor," she clarified. "And some of them haven't been to see one in a very long time," she said tactfully.

So saying, Melanie took hold of his elbow and gently directed him toward the left.

"That way," she said when the doctor spared her a warning look.

She couldn't help wondering if there was some sort of a penalty exacted by him for deigning to touch the man. He didn't look the least bit friendly or approachable.

But then, his competence was what was important here, not how wide his smile was. Smiles didn't cure people. Medicine, competently utilized, did—and that was all that mattered.

But a smile wouldn't have killed the man.

"We've taken the liberty of clearing the dining room for you," she informed him, still doing her best to sound cheerful.

It wasn't for his benefit, it was for April's. The little girl had literally become her shadow, hanging on to her and matching her step for step. She was observing this doctor, looking at him as if he were some sort of rarefied deity who had come to earth to make her older brother well.

"The dining hall?" he repeated as if she'd just told him that he had a complimentary pass to a brothel.

Melanie nodded, wondering what the problem was now. There was no disguising his disdain.

"It's the only room big enough to hold all the people who signed up," she explained.

Not waiting for him to say anything further, Melanie opened the dining room's double doors.

There were women and children seated at the long cafeteria-styled tables. Every seat, every space beyond that, seemed to be filled as a sea of faces all turned in his direction.

Mitch stared at the gathering, then looked at her beside him. "I was planning on staying about an hour," he told her.

"You might want to revise your plans," Melanie tactfully advised. "Some of these people have been sitting here, waiting since last night when they first heard that a doctor was coming. They didn't want to risk being at the end of the line and having you leave before they got to see you."

That was *not* the face of a man within whom compassion had just been stirred. For two cents, she'd tell him off—

More bees with honey than with vinegar, Melanie silently counseled herself.

Putting on her best supplicant expression, she decided to attempt to appeal to the man who seemed rooted to the threshold as he scanned the room.

"Is there any way you could possibly revamp your schedule and give up a little more time today?" Melanie asked him.

Like maybe three more hours?

She knew saying aloud what she was thinking wouldn't go over very well, but then, what had this doctor been thinking? He had to have known this was a homeless shelter which, by definition, meant it went literally begging for help of every kind—and that obviously included medical aid.

Medical aid was not dispensed in the same manner as drive-through fast food was.

"I know that everyone here would be very grateful if you could," Melanie said as tactfully and diplomatically as she could.

Just as she finished, another voice was added to hers.

"Please?"

The high-pitched plea came from the little girl who had been hanging on to the hem of her blouse off and on since she'd opened the front door.

April was currently aiming her 100-watt, brilliant green eyes at him.

In Melanie's estimation, Dr. Mitchell Stewart should have been a goner.

Chapter Three

To Melanie's disappointment—and growing concern—the doctor *wasn't* a goner. He did not melt beneath the pleading look in April's wide eyes.

But at least Dr. Stewart appeared to be wavering just the slightest bit, which was something.

Okay, so the man apparently didn't come with a marshmallow center beneath that tough exterior, but at least his heart wasn't made of hard rock, either, which meant that there was hope. And—except on a very personal level, where she had learned better—when it came to dealing with things at the shelter, Melanie found that she could do a lot of things and go a long way on just a smattering of hope.

Hope was like dough. It could be stretched and plumped with the right kind of preparation, not to mention the right wrist action.

She heard the doctor clear his throat. It wasn't exactly a sympathetic sound, but it wasn't entirely dismissive, either.

And then the next second she heard him say, "I'll see what I can do."

And we have lift off! Melanie thought. The man was conceding—at least a little.

She watched as Dr. Stewart looked around the dining hall, frowning at his surroundings. At first, Melanie thought he was frowning at the occupants in the room, but when he spoke, addressing his words to her, she realized that something else was bothering him.

"Don't you have anyplace more private? I'm not practicing war zone medicine," he informed her. "I don't think these women would appreciate being examined while everyone looks on, as if they were some items brought in for show-and-tell."

"Not exactly diplomatically put, but you do have a point," Melanie agreed.

When he looked at her sharply, she realized that she'd said the first part of that sentence out loud instead of just in her head. She would have to do a better job of censoring herself around this man.

Rather than apologize, she flashed him a quick smile and said, "Stay here. I'll see if I can get Polly to give up her office."

"Polly," he repeated as if he was trying to make a connection. "That would be the woman who runs this place?"

Melanie nodded. "That would be she."

"Why wasn't she out here to meet me?" he asked.

The question was blunt, but she was beginning to

expect that from him. She wondered if his ego had been bruised by the unintentional slight.

Melanie paused for a moment, weighing her options. She could lie to him and say they'd suddenly had an emergency on their hands that required Polly's presence, but she had a feeling that the man valued the truth above diplomacy. She also had the uneasy feeling that he could spot a lie a mile away. That cut down on her viable choices.

"Truthfully," she told him, "I think your reputation scared her."

"My reputation," he repeated slowly. "You mean the fact that I'm an above-average surgeon?"

No failure of ego to thrive here, she silently noted. "Not that reputation," she said out loud. "The other one" was all Melanie told him before she left the dining hall to track down the shelter's director.

Polly French, in her opinion, was one of the nicest people ever to walk the earth. Polly possessed a heart that was as big as she was tall and at six-one that was saying a great deal. But despite the shadow she cast, Polly was also one of the most mild-mannered people ever created. Melanie sincerely doubted if the woman even knew *how* to yell. She was certain that Polly's vocal chords weren't constructed that way.

Taking a chance that the woman was actually in her office, Melanie headed there first. She found that the door was open, but even so, Melanie stopped in front of it and knocked.

Polly, her gray hair neatly pulled back into a tight ponytail at the nape of her neck, looked up. Apprehension immediately entered the brown eyes when she saw who had knocked.

"Is something wrong, Melanie? Didn't the doctor get here yet?" she asked, rising from behind the desk, as if she was better prepared to take bad news standing up.

"He got here and there's nothing wrong," Melanie quickly assured her, then explained the reason she'd sought her out, "but I was wondering if we could borrow your office."

"Of course." Polly, ever accommodating, began to remove things from her desktop. "Isn't there enough room in the dining hall?"

"It's crammed, but so far, everyone can fit in there—but that's just the problem. The doctor thought that privacy was in order during the actual exam," she told the shelter's director. All in all, that seemed rather sensitive of him—something she did find surprising about the man.

"Oh." Caught aback, Polly rolled the thought over in her mind. "Well, that's a good sign," she commented, a small smile curving her mouth. The smile grew as she added, "He cares about their feelings."

"So it would appear," Melanie tentatively agreed, although he certainly hadn't sounded as if that was the case.

Polly picked up on her tone. "But you're reserving judgment," the woman guessed as she closed her laptop and tucked it under her arm.

"I've found it's safer that way," Melanie replied, her tone indicating that she wasn't about to elaborate on the subject in any fashion.

Polly flashed her a sympathetic smile, not unlike the one that Theresa had aimed her way the other day. She accompanied it with the same sentiment Theresa had expressed. "You know that I'm here if you need to talk, Melanie."

"I know you are," Melanie replied, definitely wanting to bring the subject to a close. She appreciated the effort, but she really wanted everyone to stop offering her shoulders and ears and various other body parts to lean on or make use of. Right now, she just wanted to get immersed in work and more work. So much work that she didn't have time to draw two breaths together, much less let herself grieve. "Can I tell the doctor he has his private room?"

"Yes, of course." She looked down at the desktop. "I'll get one of the fresh sheets out of the linen closet. That should help make this look more like an exam room," she said, thinking out loud. Then, just as Melanie began to leave the room, she asked. "Oh, did the doctor bring a nurse with him?"

"Not unless she's very, very small and fits into his pocket," Melanie replied.

"In that case, I'm going to need you to stay very close to the doctor when he's in here with a patient," Polly said.

Melanie looked at the woman uncertainly. "Come again?"

"Legally, even though he is a doctor, he can't perform an in-depth examination on any female patient without another female being present," Polly told her, looking very uncomfortable about her position. "Under normal circumstances, that would be a nurse, of course. However—"

The director definitely seemed agonized over what she was saying. Taking pity on the woman, Melanie stopped her.

"Got it. Okay," she agreed. "Don't worry, I'll stick to him like glue."

Polly headed to the linen closet while Melanie made her way back to the dining hall to inform the doctor that he had his private exam room.

The moment she walked into the hall, April lit up and gravitated to her side as if she were being propelled by a giant magnet.

Melanie barely had time to pat the little girl's head before she found herself looking into the doctor's dark blue, accusing eyes.

"I thought maybe you decided to clock out." There was no missing the touch of sarcasm in the man's voice.

Theresa wasn't kidding when she said the man was lacking in bedside manner—his would have seemed harsh when compared to Ivan the Terrible, she thought.

Out loud she told him, "Things don't happen here in a New York minute. It takes a little time to arrange things. But the director's office is ready for you to use now. So if you're ready to examine your first patient, I'll show you where it is."

He didn't answer her one way or another. Instead, he gave her an order. Orders seemed to come easily to him.

"Lead the way."

For a split second, a comeback hovered on her lips. After all, she wasn't some lackey waiting to be issued marching orders. But then she decided that the man just might get it into his head to walk out on them and while personally she didn't care, she did care about all these women and children at the shelter and they *did* need to see a doctor.

So, for now, she kept any observation to herself, much as it pained her to keep silent.

With that in mind, she turned on her heel and led the way down the hall, preceding the doctor and the woman who was to be his first patient, Jane Caldwell. Like Jimmy, Jane had a hacking cough and Melanie suspected that was possibly how Jimmy had contracted his cough in the first place.

"It's right in here," Melanie told the doctor. Pushing the door open farther, she waited for Dr. Stewart and then his patient to walk in before she followed them inside.

"There's no exam table," Mitch immediately observed, disapproval echoing in his voice.

"No." Melanie indicated the desk. "But Polly thought that you might be able to use the desktop in place of one. It's not exactly what you're used to, but it's flat and it's big," she pointed out.

He found her cheerfulness irritating. "So's your parking lot, but I'm not about to examine this woman on it."

"I'll see what I can come up with for your next visit," Melanie told him.

By the expression she saw pass over the man's face, Melanie had a feeling that the good doctor wasn't about to think that far ahead—or commit to it, either. Hopefully, once he saw how desperately a doctor's services were needed here, the man would change his mind by the end of his visit.

Melanie mentally crossed her fingers.

Still trying to convince the doctor to make do with the conditions facing him, she pointed out, "The director does have a fresh bed sheet spread over the desk. Couldn't you use that for the time being?"

"I guess I'll have to make do," he murmured under his breath, more to himself than to her. Then he said a bit louder, "All right, thanks."

His tone was dismissive.

He turned his attention to the woman who was to be his first patient here. "If you sit down on top of the desk, I can get started," he told Jane.

Mitch had already taken his stethoscope out of his medical bag and he was about to raise it in order to listen to the woman's lungs. A noise behind him made him realize that his so-called "guide" was still in the room, standing before the closed door.

Looking at her over his shoulder, he repeated what had been his parting word, "Thanks."

"You're welcome," Melanie replied, thinking that perhaps the doctor was waiting for some kind of formal acknowledgment of his thanks.

Mitch stifled an exasperated sigh .

"You can go now," he told her.

Melanie smiled patiently in response as she told him, "No, I can't."

He lowered the stethoscope. "What's that supposed to mean?"

Melanie proceeded to take his sentence apart. "Well, *no* is pretty self-explanatory. *I* refers to me and *can't* goes back to the first word, *no*," she told him glibly. "What part of those three words are you having trouble with?"

"The part that involves you." He spelled out his question for her. "Why are you still in the room?"

"Because you don't have a pocket-sized nurse with

you," she answered, following her words with another glib smile.

Did this woman have some sort of brain damage? Why was she here? Why wasn't she committed somewhere? "What?" he demanded.

"You can't examine any female without another female being present. You usually have a nurse present when you conduct your exams in the hospital, right?"

Mitch frowned. He wasn't about to argue with her because she was right, but having to concede to this woman irritated him nonetheless.

Taking a second to collect himself, Mitch barked out his first order. "Make yourself useful, then."

He expected an argument from her. Instead, the woman surprised him by asking, "And how would you like me to do that?"

The first thing that flashed through his mind was *not* something he could repeat and that surprised Mitch even more. So much so that for a second, he was speechless. He was stunned that he'd had that sort of a thought to begin with under these conditions—and that he'd had it about her, well, that stunned him even more.

"Take notes," he said, composing himself.

"Do you want me to use anything in particular in taking these notes?" she asked.

She really was exasperating. "Anything that's handy," he answered curtly, turning his attention back to the patient—or trying to.

Melanie opened the center drawer and took out a yellow legal pad and pen. Stepping back and standing a couple of feet to his left, holding the pad in one hand, she poised the pen over it and announced, "Ready when you are, Doctor."

Mitch spared her one dark glare before he began his first exam.

Like a robot on automatic pilot, Mitch saw one patient after another, spending only as much time with each one as was necessary.

Most of what he encountered over the course of the next three hours fell under the heading of routine. Some patients' complaints, however, turned out to be more complicated, and those called for lab tests before any sort of comprehensive diagnosis could be reached. The latter was necessary before any sort of medication could be dispensed.

Those Melanie marked down as needing more extensive exams.

Three hours later, feeling as if he had just been on a nonstop marathon, Mitch discovered that he had barely seen half the people who had initially lined up to be examined.

This really *was* like war-zone medicine, he couldn't help thinking.

"Do you have to go?" Melanie asked him as he sent another patient on her way. Granted she'd done an awful lot of writing in the past three hours, but she was keenly aware of the patients who were still waiting. The patients who were going to have to accept a rain check.

Mitch hadn't said anything about leaving, although he was ready to pack it in. He looked at the woman beside him in surprise. At this point, he was ready to believe she was half witch.

Maybe *all* witch.

"How did you know?" he asked her.

"Well, you said you were going to give us an hour and you've already gone two hours past that. The math isn't that challenging," she told him matter-of-factly.

Mitch frowned. They were alone in the so-called "exam room" and part of him was dealing with the very real urge of wanting to throttle her. The other part was having other thoughts that seemed to be totally unrelated to the situation—and yet weren't.

"Anyone ever tell you that you have a smart mouth on you?" he asked.

He didn't pull punches, she thought. A lot of people kept treating her with kid gloves and maybe his way was more like what she really needed—to get into a fighting mode.

"It goes with the rest of me," she answered flippantly, then got down to business. What was important here were the children and their mothers, not anything that had to do with her. "When can you come back?" she asked him.

Caught off guard, Mitch paused. "I hadn't thought about that."

In all honesty, the only thing that had been on his mind was getting through this session. As far as he was concerned, he'd fulfilled his obligation. He'd agreed to come here, as his mother had asked him to, and here he was—staying longer than he'd either intended to or wanted to. But apparently, that didn't seem to be enough.

"Maybe you should," Melanie was telling him. And then she added with a smile that appeared outwardly cheerful—but didn't fool him for a minute. "We're available anytime you are."

Mitch sighed. "I'll check my calendar."

"Why don't you do it now?" she suggested, pushing the issue. "This way, I can tell the director and your new fans out there," she nodded toward the door and the people who were beyond that, "when to expect you."

"Definitely a smart mouth," Mitch muttered as he took out his phone and checked the calendar app that was on it. His frown deepened when he found what he was looking for. "I can possibly spare a few hours Friday morning," he told her grudgingly.

She met his frown with nothing short of enthusiasm. "Friday works for us," she assured him. "I'll get the word out."

His tone was nothing if not dour when he said in response, "Why don't we wait and see how things gel?" he suggested, then qualified, "Things have a way of cropping up."

Her eyes met his and there was a defiance in them he found both irritating beyond words—and at the same time, oddly intriguing.

He supposed that maybe his mother had a point. He could stand to get out more. Then people like this annoying woman would hold no interest for him.

"Why don't you write the shelter into your schedule anyway?" she said. "Having a commitment might make you more inclined to honor it."

"Are you lecturing me?" he asked point-blank.

"I'd rather think of it as making a tactful suggestion," she replied.

She could call it whatever she wanted to, Mitch thought. But no matter what label she put on it, they both knew what she meant.

Chapter Four

Melanie looked at her watch. It was the old-fashioned, analog kind which required her brain to figure out the exact time.

Right now, the second hand seemed to be taunting her. As it moved along the dial, hitting each number one at a time, she could almost hear it rhythmically beating out: *I told you so. I told you so.*

A deep sigh escaped her.

It was Friday. The doctor should have been here by now.

She supposed, giving the man the benefit of the doubt, he could have been held up in traffic, but it would have had to have been a monumental traffic jam for Dr. Stewart to be this late. After all, it wasn't like this was Los Angeles. If anything, Bedford was considered a distant suburb of Los Angeles, located in the southern region of the considerably more laid-back Orange County area.

Granted, traffic jams did have a nasty habit of popping up in Orange County, but when they did, they had the decency of doing so between the hours of six and nine in the morning or four and seven in the evening, otherwise whimsically referred to by the term "rush hour," which was a misnomer if ever she heard one.

"Isn't he coming, Melody?" April asked her, the small voice echoing with the same concern that she herself felt. The five-year-old had decided to keep vigil with her today, unofficially appointing herself Dr. Stewart's keeper.

Melanie came away from the window. Staring out into the parking lot wasn't going to make the man appear any faster—if at all.

"I don't know, honey," she answered.

"But he said he would," April said plaintively.

It was obvious that the little girl had taken the doctor's word to be as good as a promise. But then, Melanie reminded herself, according to what she'd said, the little girl still believed in Santa Claus. Apparently the doctor's word fell into the same category as the legendary elf did.

"Yes, he did," Melanie agreed, searching for a way to let the little girl down gently. "Maybe he called Miss Polly to say he was running late."

"How can he do that?" April asked, her face scrunching up as she tried to wrap her little mind around the phrase. "If he's running, how can he be late?" she asked, confused.

"I'm afraid it's something grown-ups do all the

time, sweetie," Melanie said evasively. "Tell you what. You stay here and keep on watching for him," she instructed, turning April back toward the large window facing the parking lot. She felt having her here, standing watch, was better than having April listen in on the conversation she was going to have with the director. "I'll be right back."

"Okay!" April agreed, squaring her small shoulders as she stared out the window, as intent as any soldier standing guard. "He'll be here, I know he will," were the words that followed Melanie out of the room.

"If he's not," Melanie murmured under her breath, "I'll kill him." It would be justifiable payback for breaking April's heart.

Melanie turned the corner just as the director was walking out of her office. A near collision was barely avoided and only because Melanie's reflexes were sharp enough for her to take a quick step back before it was too late.

Her hand flying to her chest, the tall, thin woman dragged in a quick, loud breath.

"I was just coming to look for you," Polly declared breathlessly.

"Well, here I am," Melanie announced, spreading her hands wide like a performer who had executed a particularly clever dance step.

She was stalling and she knew it, Melanie thought, dropping her hands to her sides. Stalling because she didn't want to hear what she knew was coming.

Raising her head, she looked the director in the eye. "He called, didn't he?" she asked. "Dr. Stewart," she added in case her question sounded too ambiguous.

Just because she was thinking of the doctor didn't

mean that Polly was. The woman did handle all facets of the shelter, from taking in donations to finding extra beds when the shelter was already past its quota of homeless occupants. In between was everything else, including making sure there was enough food on hand as well as all the other bare necessities that running the shelter entailed.

The look in Polly's eyes was a mixture of distress and sympathy. "Just now. He said that something had come up and he couldn't make it."

Since it was already almost an hour past the time that Dr. Stewart should have been here, Melanie murmured, "Better late than never, I suppose. So when is he coming?" she asked. She wanted to be able to give April and the others a new date.

Polly shook her head. "He didn't say anything about that."

Melanie looked at her in surprise. The question came out before she could think to stop it. "You didn't ask him?"

"I didn't get a chance," Polly confessed. "I'm afraid he hung up right after saying he was sorry."

"Right," Melanie muttered under her breath. "I just bet he was."

Polly had been in charge of the shelter for a dozen years and had become accustomed to dealing with other people's disappointments as well as her own. She apparently survived by always looking at the positive side.

"We were lucky that he came when he did," she told Melanie.

But Melanie was angry. Angry at the doctor for breaking his promise to the shelter, but most of all, angry that he had in effect broken his promise to April because the little girl had taken him at his word when he'd said he was returning Friday—which was today.

"We'd be luckier if he honored his word and came back," Melanie bit off.

"A volunteer is under no legal obligation to put in any specified amount of time here," Polly pointed out. "Just because he came once doesn't mean that he has to come again."

"No, it doesn't," Melanie agreed. "But most people with a conscience would come back, especially if they said they would." Turning on her heel, she started back down the hall.

"Melanie, where are you going?" Polly called after her nervously.

"Out," Melanie answered, never breaking stride or turning around. "To cool off."

And she knew exactly how to cool off.

She slowed down only long enough to tell April that she was going to go talk to Dr. Stewart.

"Why can't you talk to him here?" April asked, following her to the front door.

There were times when April was just too inquisitive, she thought. "Because he isn't here yet and if I wait for him to get here, I might forget what I want to say to him."

"Maybe you should write it down," April piped up helpfully. "That way you won't forget."

Melanie paused at the front door and kissed the top of her unofficial shadow's head. This was the little girl she was never going to have. The kind of little girl she and Jeremy would have loved to have had as they started a family.

Tears smarted at the corners of her eyes and she blinked hard to keep them at bay. “This way is faster, trust me,” she told April.

With that, she was out the door and heading to her car.

In all fairness, she knew what Polly had said was absolutely true. Mitchell Stewart had no legal obligation to show up at the shelter ever again if he didn’t want to, even though he’d said he would. He’d signed no contract, was paid no stipend.

But how could a man just turn his back on people he knew were waiting for him? Didn’t he have a conscience? Didn’t the idea of a moral obligation mean *anything* to the man?

She gunned her car as she pulled out onto the street.

Maybe it didn’t mean anything to him, but in that case, he had to find out that there *were* consequences for being so damn coldhearted. If nothing else, calling him out and telling him what she thought of him would make her feel better.

As sometimes happened, the traffic gods were on the side of the angels. Melanie made every light that was between the shelter and Bedford Memorial Hospital. Which in turn meant that she got from point A to point B in record time.

After pulling onto the hospital compound, Melanie drove the serpentine route around the main building to the small parking area in the rear reserved strictly for emergency room patients and the people who’d brought them.

Once she threw the car into Park and pulled up the emergency brake, Melanie jumped out of her vehicle and hurried in through the double electronic doors. They hadn't even opened up fully before she zipped through them and into the building.

The lone receptionist at the outpatient desk glanced up when he saw her hurrying toward him. Dressed in blue scrubs and looking as if he desperately needed a nap, the young man asked her, "What are you here for?" His fingers were poised over the keyboard as he waited for an answer to input.

"Dr. Stewart's head," she shot over her shoulder as she hurried past him and over to the door which allowed admittance into the actual ER salon.

Ordinarily locked, it had just opened to allow a heavyset patient to walk out, presumably on his way home. Melanie wiggled by the man and managed to get into the ER just before the doors shut again.

Safe for now, she buttonholed the first hospital employee she saw—an orderly—and said, "I'm looking for Dr. Stewart." When she'd called the hospital on her way over, she'd been told he was still on the premises, working in the ER. "Can you tell me where he is?"

The orderly pointed to the rear of the salon. "I just saw him going to bed 6."

"Thank you."

Melanie lost no time finding just where bed 6 was located.

The curtain around the bed was pulled closed, no doubt for privacy. She was angry at Stewart, not whoever was in bed 6, so she forced herself to be patient and waited outside the curtain until the doctor was finished.

As she stood there, listening, she found that Dr. Stewart was no more talkative with the hospital patients than he was with the women and children he'd examined at the shelter.

It occurred to her that if he was like this all the time, Dr. Stewart had to be one very lonely, unhappy man. Obviously he was living proof that no matter how bad someone felt they had it, there was always someone who had it worse.

In her opinion, Dr. Mitch Stewart was that someone.

Mitch had been at this all morning. Rod Wilson, who had the ER shift right after his, had called in sick. Most likely, Wilson was hung over. The man tended to like to party. But that didn't change the fact that he wasn't coming in and that left the hospital temporarily short one ER doctor. Which was why he'd agreed to take Wilson's place after his own shift was over.

As far as he was concerned, this unexpected event was actually an omen. He wasn't meant to go back to the shelter, this just gave him the excuse he needed.

He'd felt out of his element there anyway, more so than usual. Here at least he was familiar with his surroundings and had professional people at his disposal in case he needed help with one of the patients.

That wasn't the case at the shelter and even though he knew his strengths and abilities, he didn't care for having to wing it on his own. Too many things could go wrong.

Finished—he'd closed up a small laceration on the patient's forearm caused by a wayward shard from a broken wine glass—Mitch told the patient a nurse would be by with written instructions for him regarding the proper care of his sutures.

With that, he pulled back the curtain and walked out.

Or tried to.

What he wound up doing was walking right into the annoying woman from the homeless shelter.

His eyes narrowed as recognition instantly set in. "You."

He said the single word as if it were an accusation.

"Me," she responded glibly.

Since he'd started walking, she fell into place beside him. She wasn't about to let him get away, at least not until she gave him a piece of her mind—or a chance to redeem himself, whichever he chose first.

Mitch scowled at her as he pulled off the disposable gloves from his hands. "You realize that this is bordering on stalking, don't you?"

Her eyes narrowed into slits. "You're not at the shelter."

"Mind like a steel trap," he marveled sarcastically. He paused to drop his gloves into a covered garbage container. "Tell me, what gave you your first clue?"

There were things she wanted to say to him, retorts aimed straight at his black heart, but she had to make sure first that there wasn't the slimmest possibility that he could be convinced to come back with her.

She gave him one last chance. "There's a room full of people waiting for you."

Mitch frowned. "Didn't your director give you the message? I called," he told her.

"After the fact," she pointed out since he had called almost an hour after he should have been at the shelter.

"Better than not at all," Mitch said sharply, wondering why he was even bothering to have this discussion with this annoying woman. He didn't owe her any explanations.

"Better if you came back with me," she countered, going toe-to-toe with him.

Her display of gall completely astounded him.

"Better than what?" he asked. And then his eyes widened. "Are you by any chance actually threatening me?"

She would have loved to, but she was neither bigger than Dr. Stewart was nor did she have anything on the doctor to use as leverage, so she resorted to the only tactic she could.

"I'm appealing to you," she retorted.

"Not really," Mitch shot back.

The moment the words were out of his mouth—and he was glad he'd had the presence of mind to say them—he realized that they actually weren't true. Because, strangely enough, she *did* appeal to him. What made it worse was that he hadn't a clue as to why.

If he'd had a type, which he'd long since not had, it wouldn't have been a mouthy little blonde who didn't know when to stop talking. He liked tall, sleek brunettes with tanned complexions, dark, smoldering eyes and long legs that didn't quit. Women who kept their own counsel rather than making him want to wrap his hands around their throats to stop the endless flow of words coming out of their mouths.

So why the contradiction in his head?

He told himself the double shift had made him more tired than usual. He just wasn't being his usual, reasonable self.

"They need you," Melanie insisted as she continued to follow him down a corridor.

"They need a doctor," he corrected.

His intent was to show her it wasn't personal, that anyone would do and that it didn't have to be him. Furthermore, *wasn't* going to be him because at this point he just wanted to take a shower and go home.

He kept walking. So did she.

"Last I checked, that was you."

He stopped just short of his destination—the locker room. At the last moment, she held herself in check to keep from colliding with him.

"Look, how about if I get you someone else?" he suggested.

"I've always been a great believer in the bird in the hand school of thought," Melanie told him.

This actually might have been amusing if she weren't so damn annoying. "I'm neither a bird, nor am I in your hand," he told her tersely.

"No, but you're here, you're a doctor, and you've already been to the shelter." As if to drive her point home, she said, "The kids saw you."

"They've probably seen a SpongeBob SquarePants movie, too," he said, exasperated. "Would you want him to be their doctor?"

She looked at him, wondering if maybe she was pushing too hard. The next moment, she decided that he was just trying to confuse her and get her to back off.

Taking a breath, she tried another approach. Softening her tone, she said, "Please? They're at the shelter, waiting and right now, they're waiting for you." And then she gave it to him with both barrels. "Somewhere along the line, when you first started studying to be a doctor, didn't you want someone to be waiting for you to come and save the day?"

He laughed shortly at the image she was attempting to promote. "You mean like a superhero?"

"No," she corrected, "like a super-doctor."

Just then, a man in a security uniform approached them. Specifically, Melanie noted, the guard was approaching *her.*

"Is there a problem here?" the security guard asked, looking from her to the doctor. His hand was resting rather dramatically on the hilt of his holstered weapon as he waited for an answer.

All he had to do, Mitch thought, was say yes and this annoying woman would be out of his hair once and for all. But he had to admit—grudgingly so—that there was a germ of truth in what she'd just said. Once, when he was still very young and very idealistic, he'd had great hopes for the profession he was aspiring to. His head—and his heart—had been filled with thoughts of what he could accomplish.

In those days, he'd been inspired by what his father had accomplished before him. Though he'd never said as much, back then, his father had been his idol and he'd wanted to be just like him.

All it had taken was losing a couple of patients to show him how wrong—and foolhardy—he had been. At the end of the day, all he could hope for was the same amount of wins as losses.

"No," he finally said to the guard, "there's nothing wrong. She was just reminding me of an appointment I'd forgotten about."

The guard looked somewhat dubious. "If you're sure everything's all right..."

"I'm sure," Mitch told him.

"Okay, then," the guard murmured. "Have a nice day.

And with that, he withdrew.

Melanie gazed at the man she had come to drag back to the shelter. "Thank you."

"Yeah," he muttered. "I'll probably live to regret that." He started to push open the door behind him. When he saw that his self-appointed conscience was about to come in with him, he said, "Unless you plan to suddenly join the staff, you can't come in here."

Was he going to evade her after all? "Why not?" she asked.

"Because it's the locker room."

"Oh." She suddenly realized he was right. "Sorry."

Was she blushing? It didn't seem possible. These days, everything was so blatant, so out in the open, he doubted if anyone blushed over anything. It was probably just the poor lighting.

Mitch jerked a thumb behind him toward the locker room. "I'm just going to go take a shower and change out of these scrubs."

"Fine," she responded, then, in case there was any doubt, she added, "I'll be out here, waiting."

Mitch made no verbal comment, he merely grunted in response to her affirmation. It never occurred to him to think that she wouldn't be.

Chapter Five

Tucking away the supplies he'd brought with him into his medical bag, Mitch didn't even hear the knock at first. When the sound continued, more insistently this time, he glanced up, bracing himself.

Now what?

He'd already spent forty-five minutes more than he'd anticipated at the shelter and he really didn't want to get roped into anything else that would prevent him from leaving—always a viable possibility whenever that woman, Melanie, was involved. Over the course of the past month, that lesson had been driven home more than once. Even a slow learner would have picked up on that by now and he was far from that.

Anticipation mixed with dread filtered through him when he saw Melanie walking into the alcove that she'd persuaded the director to turn into a permanent exam room—or as permanent as anything could be here in the homeless shelter. Slightly larger than a linen closet, it had room for the necessary examination table and just enough room for him to move around in.

Any sort of lengthy conversation resulting from an exam, however, still took place in the director's office. Polly willingly surrendered her office to him whenever he came to the shelter.

Lately, that was two, sometimes three times a week and never for as short a duration as he initially anticipated.

As he watched Melanie approach him, his attention was drawn to what she was carrying. His eyes narrowed and he nodded at what she'd brought into the room. "What's this?"

"It's a cake," she told him. Then, still leaving it on the tray she'd used to bring it in, she placed the whole thing on the exam table right in front of him. "Well, actually," she amended, "it's a large cupcake."

He had to learn to be more specific when he asked questions, Mitch told himself—at least when it came to things that had to do with Melanie.

"I *know* what it is. I want to know what it's doing on a plate in front of me with a candle in it. A *lit* candle," he underscored.

"Waiting for you to blow out the flame," she told him with a smile that he was finding increasingly difficult to ignore each time he saw it. The reason for *that* he refused to explore.

He made no move to do as she'd just instructed, not until he knew what he was getting himself into. When it came to Melanie, the more information he had before he got further involved, the better. And even then, he wasn't always fully prepared. The woman was just *not* predictable.

"Any particular reason you have this sudden need to set a cupcake on fire?" he asked.

Her smile was patient—and he found it so much more annoying because of that.

"I'm not setting it on fire," Melanie told him. "It's to celebrate—"

"—your one month annie-versay," April piped up excitedly, coming out from behind Melanie.

The next moment she giggled into her hands as if she'd just played some sort of a fine joke on the solemn faced doctor—whom she obviously really liked despite the rather somber expression he usually wore.

Then, in case the significance of what she'd just said had escaped him, April proudly announced, "You've been coming here a whole month!" She made it sound like a feat equal to coming in first in the Kentucky Derby. "Make a wish and blow it out!" she urged excitedly.

He knew there was no way he was getting out of here until he complied with this nonsense, so he put his medical bag down on the floor. Leaning over the exam table, Mitch slanted a glance toward the woman who'd brought in the cupcake—and him, he thought grudgingly—in the first place. Then, none-too-happily, he blew out the candle.

"A month, huh?" he repeated as if the fact was just now registering in his brain. "Funny," he said, looking directly at Melanie, "it seems longer."

"Funny, I was just going to say that it doesn't really feel that long at all," Melanie deliberately countered.

"But then," she allowed, "I wasn't the one who was dragged here, kicking and screaming."

"Who was kicking and screaming?" April wanted to know, a puzzled expression on her small oval face as her eyes grew large.

Melanie ruffled her hair affectionately. "It's just an expression, honey."

April appeared to be only half listening. Her attention, as well as her eyes, was fixed on the large cupcake. After a moment, she shifted both over toward Mitch.

"Aren't you going to eat that?" she asked. "I helped Melody make it."

He didn't want to insult the little girl, but he didn't want to hang around, either. It seemed that the longer he stayed—the longer he stayed.

"Tell you what," Mitch suggested, thinking he had come up with the perfect solution. "Why don't you eat it for me? You like cupcakes, right?"

"Very much," April told him, solemnly nodding her head. And then she pinned him with her large, soulful eyes. "Don't you?"

"Yes, yes I do," he told her, gathering up his medical bag again, his body poised for flight. He deliberately avoided looking in Melanie's direction. "But I'm kind of in a hurry."

April's eyes just grew more soulful. "You're always in a hurry. Don't you wanna stop some time?" she asked.

The logic of children confounded him. He was in over his head.

Mitch finally looked toward the woman who had roped him into doing all this, volunteering his services in a place he must have passed a hundred times in his travels through the city without having noticed even once. She owed him.

"Help me out here," he requested.

Melanie spread her hands wide. "Sorry, I'm kind of curious to hear your answer to that one," she replied.

As always, she ended her statement with a smile, a smile that was beginning to burrow a hole in his gut, working its way through the layers he had applied around himself over the years. Layers that were meant to insulate him from everything and anything so that he could concentrate strictly on doing what he had been educated and trained to do—being an excellent surgeon. To him that meant dedication—and isolation.

Right now, that didn't seem to be enough.

Feeling cornered and outmaneuvered by a five-year-old and her older sidekick, Mitch stifled his exasperation and just sighed in temporary surrender.

"Okay, I'll have some of the cupcake—as long as you have the rest," he said to April. "Deal?"

The sunny little face that came up to his belt buckle lit up even more. "Deal!" April cried.

"I just happen to have a knife, a couple of paper plates and a couple of forks right here," Melanie told her reluctant celebrant, producing said items almost out of thin air.

"Of course you do," Mitch murmured under his breath. He saw April looking at him as if she was trying to understand something. Deciding to get in front of whatever was brewing, he asked, "What?"

"You do that a lot," April told him with a small, disapproving frown.

"Do what?" he asked. He wasn't aware of doing anything out of the ordinary.

"Talk little, like you're whispering to somebody," April answered.

Melanie thought that was a very apt description of the way the doctor mumbled under his breath whenever he disapproved of something. She'd caught him at it a number of times.

"Out of the mouths of babes," Melanie said with a laugh. "Literally."

April surprised her by taking exception to that. "I'm not a baby," she protested.

"You certainly are not," Melanie agreed with feeling, doing her best to keep a straight face.

Cutting the cupcake in half, she split it between the sunny little girl and the dour-faced doctor.

Mitch looked at the two plates, then at her. "Why aren't you having any?" he asked.

She pointed out the obvious. "There's not all that much to go around."

Mitch did the same—or so he believed. "You could have made a bigger cake. Can't be that much more work involved."

"Then I would have had to invite other people here to share it and I don't think you're socialized enough for that," she said bluntly. "At least, I didn't think you'd appreciate me making a fuss over you in front of other people."

The woman was right, he wouldn't have liked that, although he had to admit he was surprised that she actually realized that.

"I didn't know you were that insightful," he commented.

"Lots of things about me you don't know," Melanie responded. She caught a movement out of the corner of her eyes on the exam table. "April, don't you like the cupcake?" she asked.

The little girl had pushed away her plate and moved it so that it was in front of Melanie. There was still a quarter of the cupcake left on it.

The blond head bobbed up and down with feeling. "Very much."

That didn't make any sense to her. "Then why didn't you finish it?"

The small face was utterly guileless as she said, "'Cause I wanted to share it with you."

Melanie had no idea why the little girl's answer caused tears to form in the corners of her eyes, but it took her a second before she could regain control.

Clearing her throat, she told April, "That's very sweet, honey. Tell you what, why don't you take this to Jimmy? I'm sure he'd like to have some, too."

The suggestion met with total approval. "Okay." Scooping up the plate with both hands, April flashed a huge smile at both of them, said, "Happy Annie-versary!" again and took off.

Mitch watched the little girl hurry down the hall with her prize. He also sounded wistful as he commented, "If everyone was like her, this would be a much better world."

Melanie stifled a sigh. "No argument," she responded.

Finished with his share of the cupcake, Mitch pushed the plate aside and laughed shortly. "Well, that's a first."

"And the moment's gone," Melanie declared. Taking the empty plate and putting it on top of the one that had initially held the cupcake along with its candle, she told Mitch, "Well, I won't keep you—"

"Also a first," he couldn't help commenting. "Must be some kind of a record."

Melanie paused to give him a deep, penetrating look, one that silently said she saw right through him. "You make it sound like you don't want to be here."

Didn't exactly take a rocket scientist to figure that one out, Mitch thought. Out loud, he pointed out, "Not exactly my first choice for extracurricular work," he told her flippantly.

Her eyes met his. "Bluster all you want, Doctor Mitch, but we both know that if you didn't want to be here, you *wouldn't* be here. Maybe you've noticed that you're not exactly handcuffed to a radiator."

"Bluster?" he echoed, taking offense at the minor insult rather than the larger picture she'd just painted. "I don't bluster."

To which she merely smiled. "Remind me to bring a tape recorder with me and run it the next time you're here. I think you just might need to actually listen to yourself speak—or grunt as the case may be. It just might change your mind about that denial."

The woman was beginning to sound as if she made her living as a lawyer. And then it occurred to him that he *didn't* know all that much about her—not that he had wanted to in the first place. But now that he was stuck coming back here, he figured he might as well know as much about his enemy as possible. One never knew when information like that might come in handy. Considering who he was up against, he might just need it for counter-blackmail somewhere down the line.

"What is it that you do when you're not bending steel in your bare hands and championing the underdog?" he asked.

Melanie froze for a moment and then tried to behave as if nothing had happened. But he had detected the slight change and wondered about it.

"What do you mean?"

He really doubted that she needed it spelled out for her, but he obliged, wondering at the same time why she was stalling. "Well, everyone here, except for the director, is volunteering their time away from their regular job. I was just wondering what your regular job was?"

"Diva at the Metropolitan Opera House," she told him brightly.

"I thought as much." And then Mitch grew serious. "No, really, what are you?"

"Cornered right now," she told him crisply. Plates and utensils in hand, she headed to the door. "And I've got work to do, so happy one month anniversary and if you'll excuse me—"

With that, she suddenly turned away and left him standing in the room, staring after her. Wondering more questions about the woman than he was really comfortable about wondering.

Mitch wasn't the type to ask questions that weren't directly related to a patient's condition. He didn't bother getting involved in a patient's private life, didn't entangle himself in the deeper layers that could be unearthed once a few probing questions were actually asked.

So no one was more surprised than he was when he found himself seeking out the shelter's director rather than just going out to his car in the parking lot and taking off.

It wasn't as if time hung heavily on his hands. He had more than enough to do to fill up every spare moment of the day *and* night.

But there he was, knocking at the director's door, silently calling himself an idiot and just maybe certifiably crazy.

"Yes?" the woman's voice inquired from within the office.

All thoughts of making a quick getaway and pretending this slip had never happened instantly faded when the door opened and the director looked at him with a welcoming, inquisitive smile.

He might as well see this through, Mitch thought. "You have a minute?" he asked the woman.

"For you, Doctor, always," Polly responded cheerfully. She gestured for him to come in and take a seat before her desk. Crossing back to her side, she sat down herself. "Is something wrong?" she asked with concern once he was seated.

"No, nothing's wrong," he answered.

Yeah, something's wrong. Melanie's rubbing off on me, making me ask questions I shouldn't be asking, shouldn't even want to know the answers to. Just being around her is messing with my head and I don't like it.

Mitch forced a smile he didn't feel to his lips. "I just had question. But if you don't have any time—"

he began, rising again. All he wanted was to make a quick retreat and pretend this never happened—because it shouldn't have.

"I have time," she assured him.

So much for a quick retreat.

"Please, sit. Stay," Polly encouraged, waiting for him to do both. Folding her hands before her on her desk, the thin woman leaned forward slightly, giving him every indication that he had her complete and undivided attention. "Now, please, tell me. What's your question, Doctor?"

He felt like an idiot. A self-conscious, awkward idiot.

What did he care what Melanie did for a living? When he got right down to it, it was really none of his business *what* Melanie did for a living or even *if* she did anything for a living except come here, occupy herself with the women and children who were staying here—and of course, also appointing herself as his unofficial conscience, pricking at it whenever, in her judgment, he wasn't keeping on the true path as she saw it.

Her real calling, now that he thought about it, was to be a royal pain in his posterior—and she did that with aplomb.

The silence stretched out. Rather than take it as an omen and say that perhaps they could talk another time, the director seemed to take her cue from it and head in an entirely different direction with it.

"Please, Dr. Stewart, whatever you say here will stay here, I assure you." Polly lowered her voice, as if that would get her point across more effectively. "You've been a complete godsend to these women and children and anything I can do or say, even in the slightest way, to show our utmost appreciation, well, all I can tell you is that you'd be doing me a favor rather than putting me out."

The director wasn't going to let up, he could tell. It seemed to be a common malady among the female population in this facility.

With an inward sigh, Mitch asked his question. "I was just wondering if Ms. McAdams has a job outside of the volunteer work she does here."

"She came to us as an elementary school teacher," Polly said proudly. Her smile was warm as she added, "That's why she's so good with the children here. It's her background."

Volunteering here had taught him to listen more closely than he was normally accustomed to. It made him catch things he would have previously ignored or, more to the point, overlooked.

"You said she 'came to you' as a teacher. Isn't she one now?"

"Melanie took a leave of absence after..." Polly's voice trailed off. She gave no indication that she was eager to pick up the thread she'd intentionally dropped.

Which just served to arouse his curiosity, something he would have sworn just a month ago that he'd learned to eradicate from his life. Obviously he hadn't erased it; he'd merely painted over it and it was apparently alive and well, just waiting to wake up.

Something else he could hold against Melanie.

"After?" Mitch asked. "After what?"

Polly sighed. "Well, I suppose it's really not a secret. Melanie will probably tell you herself once she feels ready to address the subject. She only told me because I needed something for the record," Polly explained.

"Go on," he urged, trying to sound patient—which he wasn't.

Why did women have this annoying habit of drawing things out like it was dough and pausing at the most inappropriate times?

"Melanie's fiancé, Jeremy, was killed while in the service overseas. It happened just four days before he was scheduled to fly back to the States for their wedding. It hit her very hard," she confided. "Melanie didn't feel that she had the right frame of mind to teach impressionable young children. Her contact with them here at the shelter is informal and that's better for her right now. And, of course, the children adore her and selfishly, I don't know what I would do without her." Polly paused, unofficially closing the subject. "Does that answer your question for you?"

"Yes," Mitch told her, rising to his feet. "It does. Thank you for your time."

"And we thank you for yours," Polly called after his departing back.

But, his mind elsewhere, Mitch was already out of earshot.

Chapter Six

"So? Tell me," Charlotte enthusiastically urged her son.

It had been over a month since she'd talked him into volunteering at the homeless shelter that Maizie had told her about. She hadn't heard from Mitch in all that time. After waiting as patiently as she could, she had decided to take matters into her own hands. Step one was inviting him out to lunch at the restaurant that was near Bedford Memorial.

Step two was getting him to actually talk. Step two was harder than step one.

When Mitch made no response to her question, she tried again. Getting information out of her son took skill and patience.

Lots of patience.

"How is it?" Charlotte pressed, doing her best not to sound impatient.

As if hearing her for the first time, Mitch raised his eyes from the sirloin steak he was enjoying and looked at his mother quizzically. He wasn't sure what she was asking.

There was no question that he loved his mother. Charlotte Stewart was and had always been a kind, decent woman who could have easily served as a prototype model for the perfect mother in all those old-fashioned sitcoms that used to litter the airwaves when he was a kid.

That being said, there were times when he just couldn't seem to understand what wavelength his mother was on.

Or maybe he was the one who was on the wrong wavelength. In either case, there were many times that he and his mother couldn't seem to make a proper connection and he felt bad about that. Bad because he knew that she meant well and she truly wanted nothing more for him than his happiness.

The problem was, he wasn't sure just what that was, or these days even what "happiness" meant. At least, not where he was concerned.

Hard to achieve something if you didn't know what it was even if you tripped over it, Mitch thought philosophically.

"It?" he repeated. No enlightenment came with the repetition. Mitch had no idea what she was referring to, but assumed it had to be something in his immediate surroundings. "You mean the steak?" he asked, indicating what he'd ordered for lunch. He hadn't realized how hungry he was until he'd taken his first bite. There was hardly anything left of the meal.

But she hadn't appeared out of the blue and whisked

him off to lunch just to find out how he liked the steak in this restaurant.

Had she?

Mitch continued to look at his mother, waiting for further enlightenment.

"No, dear, I'm talking about your volunteer work at the homeless shelter," she said patiently, then repeated, "How is it?"

She was genuinely curious about his reaction to what he both did and observed at the shelter. Curious, too, on an entirely different level if Mitch had had any sort of a reaction to the young woman Maizie had told her about, thanks to her friend Theresa. So curious that for the past two nights, she'd hardly slept, wondering how things were—or weren't—coming along.

Many years ago, when Mitch had been about five or six years old, she had made herself a vow that she wasn't going to be like all the other mothers. She wasn't going to be the kind of mother whose offspring cringed at the sound of her voice or the sight of her name on his caller ID. She wanted to be a welcomed participant in her son's life, not one he sought to avoid.

That meant, for the most part, not taking on a supervisory position when it came to what went on in Mitch's private life.

But as the years went by, it became clearer and clearer to her that as far as his life went, there really wasn't anything for her to participate *in*. Mitch was all about his work.

And when he wasn't working, he was reading up on the latest studies that were being made in his field.

She realized that she was very lucky to have a son who was intelligent, who had a profession he was absorbed in. She had friends who lamented that their son or daughter partied too much, or spent money as if they had their own printing press stored away in their spare bedroom. Others had adult offspring who acted as if they were still children, focused only on themselves and indiscriminately gratifying all their own whims and extravagances.

She knew she had a hundred reasons to be grateful that Mitchell was the way he was, but human nature being what *it* was, she couldn't help wanting something more—for him rather than for herself—because someday, she would be gone and she wanted him to have someone in his life who meant something to him. Someone he could laugh with and talk with, or simply just *be* with, sharing a room and a comfortable silence with.

Left to his own devices, she knew he'd never reach that goal she had for him. Which was why she'd decided to secretly take matters into her own hands. And now she needed to know how that was going. Needed to know if she had cause for hope—or cause for remorse.

Mitch shrugged carelessly. "Frustrating," he finally admitted, summing up his feelings in a single word. He didn't believe in using three words when one would more than adequately do.

"Why?"

Frustrating wouldn't have been the first word she would have expected to hear as a reaction from Mitch. She looked at him. Getting information out of him was like pulling teeth. Impacted teeth. "What's frustrating about it?"

It seemed almost funny to him that the first thing

he thought of in response to his mother's question was the name of the woman who was supposed to act as his assistant at the shelter—or whatever it was that Melanie saw herself as being.

He refrained from mentioning her because he knew his mother wasn't asking about a person, she was asking about how he felt about the conditions he found there. Even as a doctor's son, he hadn't exactly grown up in the lap of luxury. But even despite his father's untimely and all-too-early death, he had never actually felt the pinch of deprivation. What he saw at the shelter—and what he found himself listening to because sometimes his patients talked even when he hadn't asked them anything—had left a dark, lasting impression on him.

"Frustrating because there are free clinics located throughout the state and yet a lot of these kids at the shelter have never even had the most common immunizations. This isn't a developing nation." He realized he sounded as if he was lecturing and he toned down his voice. "Their mothers should know better."

Charlotte smiled to herself. Maybe Mitch hadn't connected with that woman—yet—but he had at least found something to be passionate about. She could see it in his eyes. That was the first, important step, she couldn't help thinking. At this singular moment in time, he reminded her very much of her late husband. Matthew would have been pleased.

With luck, the rest would follow.

"Sometimes people just fall through the cracks, dear. That's why I urged you to volunteer at the shelter in the first place," she told her son. "If you wind up helping at least one person there for no other reward than just because it's the decent thing to do, then you've done a very good thing and I will have done my part in raising you right."

Finished eating, he retired his knife and fork and studied his mother quietly. Had he missed something? "You make it sound like you're signing off from the job," he observed.

Charlotte was quick to flash her son a reassuring smile. "Not by a long shot, but none of us know how long we have. Your father thought he was going to live forever, and it didn't quite work out that way," she noted sadly. "I wanted you to experience the feeling of making a real difference in someone's life—sooner rather than later," she emphasized. "These women and children at the shelter, they desperately need someone like you making them feel as if they matter."

"Where's this coming from, Mom?"

"From the heart," she answered without a moment's hesitation. "I just wanted to make sure you had one—a heart," she said in case she'd lost him. "You've been too removed, too distant of late."

"I've been busy," he said pointedly.

Just because Bedford had one of the country's lowest crime rates for a city of its size did not mean that all he ever got to see were cuts and bruises. Some of the things that came into the ER definitely challenged him as a doctor as well as a surgeon.

"I know," Charlotte said soothingly. "But I didn't want you to lose the common touch."

"I never had the common touch, Mother," Mitch reminded her. He made sure of that because something like that, the common touch, left him open to grieving over the lives that were lost on his operating table, had him grieving over the lives he couldn't ultimately save.

He was a better doctor by keeping himself in check and removed.

But his mother obviously didn't see it that way. "All right, then it's high time that you developed it."

Charlotte could see that her son didn't look overly happy about the direction the conversation had taken and she didn't want to irritate him to the point that he was rethinking his volunteer work altogether.

She glanced at the watch he'd given her three Christmases ago. The one she never took off except when she showered—it was her small way of keeping him close to her.

"Well," she announced briskly, putting down her own fork beside her empty salad bowl, "I seem to have monopolized you for too long again. Looks like you need to get back to work, dear," she said, tapping the face of her wristwatch.

Moving his chair back, Mitch dug into his pocket for his wallet.

Charlotte placed her hand on his arm, stopping him before he had a chance to pull the wallet out.

"No, this is my treat, dear," she insisted. "I dragged you out of the hospital, the least I can do is pay for the privilege of seeing my only son for lunch."

Mitch sighed. "You don't have to pay for it and it's not a 'privilege,' Mom," he told her, trying to keep his voice down.

He didn't want to draw any undue attention, but his

mother could irritate him in a relatively short amount of time despite all of her good intentions.

Rather than back off, Charlotte affectionately laughed at her son and firmly held her ground. “Don’t argue with me, dear. I gave you life. Certain rights go along with that little parlor trick.”

She gathered her things together, intending on walking as far as the cashier with him. To make sure he wouldn’t attempt to make off with the bill and pay it, she held it in her hand.

“This was fun,” she told Mitch. “Maybe we can do this again soon.”

He was open to that. “Sure.” Mitch paused to kiss the top of his mother’s head. “Just without the interrogation this time.”

Charlotte paused, stopping just short of the cashier’s desk. “What interrogation?” she asked him innocently.

Mitch almost laughed out loud. “You are definitely going to have to work on your delivery, Mom. That was *not* at all convincing.”

She was in too deep to back down now, Charlotte thought. Besides, if she made any admissions, he would be within his rights to ask her more questions. She couldn’t answer any of those without throwing the plan in jeopardy.

So she said the only thing she could. She embraced ignorance. “I have no idea what you mean.”

Mitch merely grinned. If he’d had any doubts before, they were all gone now. His mother was engaged in something, something he would undoubtedly find annoying and which would, more than likely, add a severely complicating factor to his life. “Uh-huh.”

* * *

As he hurried back to the hospital and the remainder of his shift, it occurred to Mitch that there was a lot about his mother and the way she operated that unfortunately reminded him of the woman volunteering on a permanent basis at the shelter. The annoying one with the light blue eyes and the smart mouth that never seemed to stop moving.

Not that his mother and Melanie looked anything like one another, but there was something about his mother's attitude that immediately made him think of Melanie—except that his mother was a lot kinder.

It wasn't that Melanie wasn't kind, he amended silently. Melanie was just somehow *sharper*. He guessed that was the best word to describe her attitude. Not that her mind was sharp but her tongue certainly was.

Parking his vehicle, he got out and then, as his last thoughts played back in his head, he stopped short just before he walked in through the hospital's rear double doors.

What the hell was he doing, thinking about that woman's attitude?

Or thinking about that woman, period?

Judging by the amount of vehicles he'd just passed in the rear parking lot, he had a full four hours ahead of him. That meant that there would be no downtime for him to think about the shelter or the woman who immediately popped up in his head the second his thoughts turned in that direction.

The time to think about the shelter, Mitch told himself, continuing to walk into the hospital, was when he was actually *at* the shelter.

The time to think about Melanie was *never*.

* * *

"Why do you do it?"

The question was directed to Melanie two days and five hours later.

He'd arrived at the shelter five hours ago, intending on staying roughly two hours this time around. He was immediately caught up with one patient after another. It seemed like being engulfed in an endless rushing stream. He quickly found out the reason why.

There were several new residents at the shelter. Among them were two little boys who, along with their mother, had been diagnosed with the most pronounced case of lice Mitch could ever remember not only seeing, but reading about.

Consequently, everyone had to be treated for lice as a preventative measure, even the ones who had no signs of it and loudly protested being subjected to both the exam and the harsh soap necessary to ensure that they would not be unwilling participants in the infestation.

The past five hours had been a nonstop flurry of activity and he'd reached a point where he felt it was never going to let up.

But it did.

And when it finally began to let up, Melanie momentarily vanished from his side. When he didn't see her, Mitch just assumed that she'd gone to take a well deserved break, possibly even a quick nap, something he caught himself longing for.

So he was surprised when she'd returned a few minutes later with a tall travel mug filled with coffee. Melanie pressed the mug into his hands when he had just looked at her quizzically.

After taking a long, life-affirming mouthful and swallowing it, he began to feel a little more human. A second swallow had him looking very thoughtfully at Melanie.

Since the onslaught of children had let up, he'd allowed himself to sit down on the stripped exam table. She had proceeded to join him, sitting down, producing her own smaller mug of light coffee and silently taking a drink.

The question he'd addressed to her came after he felt, thanks to her, more like himself.

Thoughts of his conversation over lunch with his mother had prompted him to ask Melanie the simple question which, he knew, didn't really have a simple answer.

Holding her mug in both hands, she looked at him a little uncertainly. "Excuse me?"

"Why do you do it?" he repeated. "Why do you come here day after day, ministering to these people the way you do?"

He knew it had to be draining—and she certainly wasn't getting paid for this. He wanted to understand what motivated her to keep coming back.

"I guess the simple answer is that someone has to," she replied in an offhand manner.

He wasn't sure if he was buying that. "What's the less simple answer?" Mitch asked. "Do you see this as some kind of penance?"

Her eyebrows drew together in a mystified line. "Penance?" she echoed, completely at a loss as to what he was really asking.

"Yes." The notion stuck in his head and the more he thought about it, the more fitting it seemed to him.

"You know, 'I feel guilty because my life is so much better than theirs is so I need to do something to assuage that guilt I'm feeling.'"

Melanie looked at him as if he'd lost his mind. She wasn't altogether sure that he hadn't.

"I don't feel guilt," she said indignantly. "I feel compassion." Taking a breath, she forced herself to calm down a bit. "Yes, I can pay my rent and I don't worry where my next meal is coming from—at least, not at this point," she interjected, thinking of her ever-shrinking bank account. Eventually, she would have to get back into the work force to resuscitate her earning power. "But I just want to help other people feel that there's always hope, that they shouldn't give up, not on life, not on themselves."

She paused, looking at him. "Are you here because you feel some sort of guilt or need for atonement?" she asked, turning the tables on him. After all, why else would he have phrased his question like that if he wasn't experiencing the same thing himself?

He should have realized that she would try to use what he asked to try to analyze him. "I'm here because it makes my mother happy."

She waved her hand at what he'd just said. He was playing a game of smoke and mirrors, which was fine, except that he wanted true confessions from her while he wanted to maintain his aura of mystery.

"That's just an excuse. You definitely don't strike me as a mama's boy."

"Okay," he said gamely, his curiosity aroused. "You seem like such an expert. Why *am* I here?"

"For the same reason I am," she told him, referring to what she'd already told him was her reason for being here. "The only reason you won't admit it is because you seem to think that saying so damages the image you have of yourself." She shrugged, pausing for more coffee before adding, "Maybe it even makes you seem too human and for some reason, you want to see yourself—and have the world see you—as some kind of cold, distant robot." Her eyes met his. "And you're not."

"What makes you so sure?"

She sat there beside him, drinking her coffee and lightly swinging her legs to and fro like a woman without a care in the world instead of one whom life had beaten down—or tried to.

Humor curved the corners of her mouth as she told him, "I can just tell."

Mitch laughed shortly, shaking his head. "If you say so."

It was meant to be dismissive. He was in no way prepared for the ambush that happened next.

Nor was he prepared for the reaction that occurred in its wake.

Chapter Seven

One moment Mitch was amused by this steamroller's naive presumption that she felt she knew him better than he knew himself, the next he had turned his head in her direction at the same time that she had turned her face up to his.

For a fleeting moment, it made him think of a flower turning toward its source of light.

However he saw it or tried to describe it to himself, the bottom line was that somehow, their faces wound up being less than an inch away from each other.

Close enough for him to breathe in the breath that Melanie had just exhaled.

Close enough for him to share that same breath with her.

Close enough for their lips to almost touch.

And then they did touch.

To Mitch's astonishment, there was no more space. There was just them.

If the fate of the world depended on his memory of how it had happened—whether he was the one to breach that infinitesimal space or if she was—he wouldn't have been able to say.

All he knew was suddenly, there they were, with no gap at all between them. Not even enough to be able to slip in a straight pin.

He was kissing her and she was kissing him.

And after the surprise of that came an even greater surprise: his reaction to that entirely unplanned, unexpected event.

He wanted to keep on kissing her.

Not just keep on kissing her but he wanted to deepen that kiss until there was nothing of any consequence left beyond its heated boundaries.

He wanted to take her breath away because she had taken the very air out of his world, leaving him winded—and wanting more.

Had she slipped something into his coffee to make him feel like this? Or was he just that deprived, that isolated?

For the life of him, he didn't know.

Code Red! Code Red!

His mind fairly shouted the alarm. In hospital-speak it meant that a fire was occurring in the facility—in this case inside of *him*—and it called for emergency measures to be taken immediately in order to ensure survival.

Which meant that if he intended to survive longer than the next couple of minutes, he was going to have to terminate contact.

Now.

Taking hold of Melanie's slim shoulders—the woman felt far more delicate than he knew she was—he pushed her back, away from him while silently and simultaneously mourning the immediate loss of contact.

He could have sworn he still tasted her on his lips. Blueberries. How the hell did he taste blueberries lingering on his lips when she'd been drinking coffee, same as he?

It didn't make sense. None of it made sense.

Especially not his kissing her. He had so much more restraint than that. Or at least he had, until now.

"Thanks for the coffee," he murmured, leaving the travel mug behind on the exam table. Clearing his throat, he told her, "Maybe next time it should have less of a kick."

"Maybe," Melanie heard herself say.

Or maybe she just *thought* she made a reply. The truth of it was, she was utterly stunned and more than a little dazed by what had just happened.

He'd kissed her.

Just like that, out of the blue.

She would have bet a million dollars—if she'd *had* a million dollars—that Mitch would have never even *considered* kissing her, much less doing it. And yet that was exactly what he'd done.

Her mind reeling, she tried to take stock and center herself. What had just happened here? And *why*? Was the world ending? Had something happened when she wasn't paying attention and they all had barely five minutes to live?

What other explanation *was* there? Sure, they'd

made eye contact on a few occasions, but that was a long way from *lip* contact, even if she'd felt something unsettling going on each time she was around him.

Get a grip, Mel, she ordered herself. *Stop making such a big deal about it. It was just a kiss, less than nothing. People do it all the time.*

Well, maybe *people* did it all the time, but *she* didn't. Ever.

She hadn't kissed another man, not since she was back in high school.

Jeremy had *always* been the one, there had never been any doubt in her mind. And now that he was no longer part of this life, well, she wasn't interested in making another connection with the male of the species, not in *that* way at any rate.

Oh yeah? So who was that I saw kissing Dr. Forget-Me-Not just now?

Closing her eyes for a moment, Melanie sighed. She had no answer for the taunting voice in her head. No theory to put forth to satisfy her conscience and this sudden, unannounced wave of guilt that had just washed over her. She wasn't even sure if the ground beneath her feet hadn't disappeared altogether. She felt just that unsteady.

She'd stayed sitting down even after Mitch had left the room.

Damn it, the man kissed you, he didn't perform a lobotomy on you with his tongue. Get a grip and get back to work. Life goes on, remember?

That was just the problem. Life went on. The love of her life had been taken away ten months ago and for some reason, life still went on.

Squaring her shoulders, she slid off the makeshift

exam table, otherwise known in her mind as the scene of the crime, tested the steadiness of her legs and once that was established, left the room.

Whether Melanie liked it or not, there was still a lot of work to do and it wouldn't get done by itself.

She had almost managed to talk herself into a neutral, rational place as she made her way past the dining hall which, when Mitch was here, still served as his unofficial waiting room. That was when she heard Mitch call out to her.

"Melanie, I need you."

Everything inside of her completely froze.

It was the same outside. It was as if her legs, after working fine all these years, had suddenly forgotten how to move and take her from point A to point B.

She had to have heard him wrong.

The Dr. Mitchell Stewart she had come to know these past few weeks would have never uttered those words to anyone, least of all to her.

And would the Mitchell Stewart you think you know so well have singed off your lips like that?

Okay, so maybe she didn't know him as well as she thought she did, but still, he wouldn't have said something like that to her, especially where someone else—*anyone* else—could have heard him say it.

Knowing she couldn't afford to just ignore him and keep on walking, Melanie blinked and turned her head in his direction. She could feel her heart pounding like a jackhammer set on high.

"Excuse me?" she said in a raspy whisper, unable to produce anything louder out of her mouth at the moment no matter how hard she tried.

Was it her imagination, or was Mitch even sterner-looking right now than he had been at any other given time since she'd first met him?

"I've got to examine Mrs. Sanchez and Ms. Ames," he told her matter-of-factly, indicating the two women who were standing behind him. "I need to have another woman present. Regulations," he specified, looking no happier about having to ask her than she was to be asked. "Remember?"

"Oh." Of course, how could she have been so stupid? He wasn't telling her he needed her, he was telling her he *needed* her. "Yes. Of course," she answered in a stilted voice, feeling like an idiot. "Ready when you are, Doctor."

The problem was, Mitch thought as he walked past her to lead the way back to the makeshift exam room—the room where he had taken leave of his senses—he wasn't ready at all.

Volunteering was *definitely* not working out the way he had been led to believe that it would. He needed to rethink a few things the first chance he got, Mitch promised himself.

"You look feverish, Melanie. Are you all right?" Theresa asked, peering at the younger woman's face.

Concerned, the caterer walked away from the long tables where some of the people she'd brought with her were setting up, preparing to feed the shelter's residents the tenderloin stew that she had whipped up in her catering kitchen before coming here.

She paused now in front of Melanie and studied her a little more closely.

"I'm fine," Melanie protested, turning away self-consciously.

Even so, Theresa politely but firmly got in her way. Then, placing one hand on her shoulder to keep the younger woman from leaving, Theresa first touched the back of her hand to Melanie's forehead, then fell back on the universal Mother's Thermometer—she pressed her lips to Melanie's forehead.

"I don't know," Theresa said thoughtfully. "Your forehead seems a little warm to me."

Melanie supposed she should be grateful that the woman hadn't attempted to take her pulse. It was still doing a drumroll more than an hour after the fact. Mitch might very well have healing hands, but at the same time, the man had a lethal mouth.

"I've been running around," Melanie said evasively, doing her best to dismiss the other woman's less than scientific findings.

"Are you sure that's all it is? With everyone being in such close quarters here and all the little ones always coming down with colds, it's all too easy to catch something." She looked at Melanie knowingly. "Especially if you let yourself get run down."

"I'll keep that in mind," Melanie promised, trying her best to politely disentangle herself from the woman and get away before there were any more questions, ones that could trip her up.

And then, the very next minute, that was exactly what happened. "Maybe you should have Dr. Mitch check you out, just to be sure," Theresa suggested.

Melanie reacted before she could think to censor herself.

"No! I mean, no," she said, uttering the word several decibels lower, "the doctor's busy enough as it is seeing sick people. He doesn't have time to waste on someone with imaginary symptoms."

"Symptoms?" Theresa repeated with interest. "You didn't mention symptoms. What sort of symptoms are you experiencing?"

Flustered, Melanie tried to remember what the woman had said to her initially. "What you told me—that I looked flushed."

"I said feverish," Theresa gently corrected, looking not unlike an elementary school teacher catching one of her favorite students in a lie.

"Right. Feverish," Melanie repeated. "I meant feverish."

And she was getting more so by the second, Melanie couldn't help thinking. She was beginning to feel like a trapped hummingbird, desperately searching for an avenue of escape.

And getting nowhere.

Fast.

Taking Melanie's hand in hers, Theresa gently tugged on it as she deliberately moved farther away from the dining area and its ensuing noise.

Once she felt they had secured more privacy, Theresa fixed the younger woman with a compassionate look. "Tell me what's wrong, Melanie."

"Nothing's wrong," Melanie insisted.

She did her best to avoid the other woman's eyes. It was hard enough avoiding the truth without having to do it while making eye contact, as well. Theresa's eyes seemed to bore into her very soul.

And obviously, she discovered a moment later, she wasn't very successful at avoiding making eye contact.

"Melanie, I've raised two children and been around

a lot more in my time. Please believe me that I mean this in the nicest possible way, but you don't lie very well at all. Now please, be honest," Theresa implored. "Why do you suddenly look like a deer caught out in the open on the first day of hunting season?"

Melanie wanted to tell the woman that it was just her imagination. That there was nothing wrong and that she was most certainly *not* lying.

But she *was* lying and furthermore, she knew that she had no gift for it. To insist otherwise to Theresa would be insulting someone she liked as well as painting herself in a very bad light. Which was what she told her.

Or tried to.

"I—we—this is, he—he kissed me," Melanie finally managed to get out. To her ear, her own words sounded almost garbled.

"He?" Theresa asked, praying she wasn't jumping to conclusions. The last time she'd observed him—from a distance—while he was working, the exceptionally handsome doctor with the chiseled features behaved as if he had a heart to match…it was just under lock and key.

But keys could be used to open locks.

"Dr. Mitch." Melanie had to practically force the words out of her mouth.

"Oh, *he*," Theresa said, more pleased than she could remember being in a long, long time. "That he," she added just for good measure. And then she looked at Melanie a little more closely still. The young woman was obviously distressed. Disappointment descended over her like dark, heavy humidity from a hovering rain cloud.

"Was he that bad, dear?" she asked.

Guilt was pricking at her conscience since she was partially responsible for having orchestrated what was beginning to appear to be a disaster.

"No," Melanie replied, her voice sounding even more sorrowful than before, "he was that good."

Theresa's eyebrows knitted together in apparent complete confusion. Putting her arm around Melanie's shoulders, Theresa drew her even farther away from the dining area to an alcove that despite its rather open appearance, was still off to the side and away from general traffic.

"Forgive me for saying this, but at least in my day, when a young man kissed well, it was a thing to celebrate, however quietly, not bemoan," she added knowingly. "You look as if someone had just told you that a flash flood was imminent and then they tied lead weights to your ankles."

She might as well tell the woman the whole story so Theresa could at least understand why she was acting so upset.

"He kisses better than anything I've ever experienced," Melanie reluctantly admitted. "It's just that…" She knew she had to seem stupid to the other woman. "It's just that…"

Her voice trailed off. Melanie just couldn't bring herself to finish her sentence.

So Theresa finished it for her. "It's just that you feel disloyal to your late fiancé because you're feeling this way."

"Yes!" The word rushed out on its own power and once it was out, Melanie was almost relieved. But she wasn't accustomed to being so open about her feelings. "I mean, no."

"Do you?" Theresa gave her a penetrating look.

"No." Melanie sighed. Against her will, she told Theresa the reason behind her reaction. "That part of my life is over. I don't want to feel anything for another man."

Theresa was nothing if not understanding. She knew exactly what Melanie was experiencing—and she knew exactly why that was wrong at this stage of her life.

"Dear, you're young with your whole life ahead of you. You're not dead and Jeremy wouldn't have wanted you to behave as if you were," she argued.

Melanie stared at her, stunned. Not only had the woman hit it exactly on the head, she had also called her fiancé by his name. A name she had never mentioned to Theresa.

"How did you…?"

Theresa's smile effectively swept the pending question under the rug, to be disposed of at a later, more convenient date. Right now she needed to keep Melanie and the good doctor together.

"I have friends with connections," she told Melanie. "I ask questions about people I care about." She smiled at her. "You are a very good person, Melanie. You're selfless and you're always giving of yourself. Tell you what," she proposed, lowering her voice as if the two of them were planning some sort of necessary, secret invasion. "Why don't you do this? Why don't you give yourself permission to be happy? After all the good you've done here, you deserve to get a little happiness in return."

She gave Melanie a quick squeeze to seal the suggestion.

It was getting closer to dinnertime and Theresa knew she had to be getting back to oversee things. Her crew, as well as the regular volunteers here, were perfectly capable of handling things on their own, but she liked to think that she helped facilitate things a little.

"Trust me. I'm older. I'm right about this," the woman added with a wink. "And by the way, I intend to follow up on this, so get back to me," she instructed Melanie.

Melanie had no doubts that Theresa meant what she said about following up. Which was why the butterflies began dive-bombing with a vengeance in the pit of her stomach.

Chapter Eight

Thanks to several new people who had come to the shelter since his last visit, the rest of Mitch's afternoon was, for the most part, one new patient after another. The time was completely taken up with exams. So much so that despite the fact that he was working beside Melanie, no words were exchanged between them other than the necessary ones involving the patients.

It seemed like an endless shuffle of people with a few of the established patients mixed in. No sooner did one patient exit the tiny makeshift exam room than another entered, leaving absolutely no time for idle chatter, much less an awkwardly tendered apology on his part.

Mitch still wasn't sure if he had initiated what had happened between them, but if he'd learned one thing from listening to others talk, it was always the man's fault. It was far easier to accept blame than to contest it.

And easier still if he bowed out from the shelter altogether, he couldn't help thinking as he went home that evening. Under ordinary circumstances, he would have withdrawn his participation in the volunteer program without any qualms. But something had changed his perspective in the past few weeks. He'd always been a conscientious doctor in general. After coming here sometimes several times a week, he had, almost without actually realizing it, developed a sense of responsibility toward these people.

As a general surgeon, he rarely saw patients more than three, sometimes four times. Pre- and post-op, and of course, the day of the surgery. Once in a rare while, there were two post-op visits. Terminating his association with the shelter would leave the residents at the shelter in a bad way, at least temporarily. He knew he wouldn't feel right about it unless he found someone to take his place. So that had to become his next order of business.

It might be the next order of business but that didn't mean that it was going to be easy for him. He didn't interact with the other physicians at his hospital in that kind of manner. While he was always up for consultations and was ready with a second opinion if asked, Mitch didn't really socialize. He no longer attended hospital fund raisers and he didn't attend any smaller, more private parties. He didn't go out after a shift for a friendly drink. He didn't even go out for lunch with any of them, preferring to eat alone while he caught up on whatever else might need his attention at the time. He was accustomed to multitasking, not maintaining interpersonal relationships.

So how would he go about finding out if anyone would be willing to take his place at the shelter? Mitch wondered. And yet, if he wanted to ease himself out of the arrangement he'd made with the shelter, that was exactly what he was going to have to do.

He still hadn't come up with a solution by his next visit to the shelter. Abhorring awkward encounters, he decided to grab the bull by its proverbial horns and sought Melanie out before getting started with the scheduled exams for the afternoon.

But Melanie didn't seem to be around. It figured, he thought, getting his lab coat out of the closet. At the hospital, he tended to wear suits when consulting with patients and scrubs when operating on them. Here, the director had told him, the sight of a lab coat inspired a feeling of well-being. Though he believed it silly, he went along with it anyway.

"We need to talk," Melanie said, seemingly materializing out of thin air as she came up behind him.

Startled, he swung around. Damn, but she moved quietly. He didn't like being caught off guard. The next moment, he managed to collect himself.

Mitch crisply told her, "No, we don't." He'd just passed several women who'd said they needed to see him about one matter or another, and this convinced him that this wasn't the time or place to discuss his momentary lapse of judgment.

"Yes, we do," Melanie insisted.

She had spent the past two days agonizing over this moment. Despite her conversation with Theresa, she'd decided that she needed to nip this—whatever "this" turned out to be—in the bud. She didn't want that kiss, fantastic though it was, to lead to anything else between them—or to have him think that she expected it to lead to something else. She wanted it to be perfectly clear that she didn't *want* it leading to something else.

Ever.

"Look, if this is about the other day in the exam room—"

"It is," she interjected.

"Then there's no need to talk about it," he told her firmly.

Just as firmly, she said, "I disagree."

"Why doesn't that surprise me?" he asked, more of himself than of her. Thoughts about being chivalrous and accepting the blame evaporated. He just wanted her to agree to stop talking about it until another, more suitable time. "Look—"

She was sure that he was probably accustomed to charming his way through everything. He was handsome, he was successful in his field and undoubtedly used to winning, but she was not about to have him believing that there was a casual fling in the offing. There *was* no fling about to be flung, casual or otherwise.

"No, *you* look," she retorted forcefully. "I want to go on working here—I *need* to go on working here," she emphasized with feeling. "And the shelter definitely needs you to continue volunteering your time here. That's not going to work out if we're feeling self-conscious around one another—and *that's* not going to go away until we clear the air about expectations."

"Melanie," he began, trying to get in a word edgewise to let her know that he didn't have any expectations and if she did, well then he was very sorry about that but he in no way wanted her to believe that he was about to come through in that department, no matter *what* her expectations were.

But Melanie continued as if he hadn't made any attempt to curtail the conversation, hadn't said anything at all.

"There can't be any expectations," she informed him quietly.

The rebuttal he was forming in his mind came to an abrupt, skidding halt. Mitch stared at her, stunned. "What?"

"No expectations," she repeated. "I'm sorry if it seemed as if I was open to something happening between us, but I'm not and I don't want you worrying that this was going to blow up somewhere along the line because there isn't going to be anything to blow up. If I gave you the impression that there was going to be anything like that, that there was something between us, I'm really very sorry."

Listening to her, Mitch was both relieved—and just a little puzzled. Melanie was saying exactly what he had hoped for—that the moment of indulgence carried no consequences with it. He should have been pleased and immensely thankful.

And yet…

And yet he couldn't help being puzzled as to what would have prompted her to say something like that. Was there something about him that she found off-putting? Yet, ultimately this was what he wanted—

so why did he find it so disturbing that she was, in essence, rejecting him?

He was pushing himself too hard. This was what happened when he overextended himself. He started making no sense at all.

"It's fine," he told her in a tone that said just the opposite.

It prompted her concern. Guilt, Melanie had discovered, was never very far away these days. She'd hurt his feelings or his ego, she wasn't sure which. Possibly both and she hadn't wanted to do either. She took another stab at an explanation and trying to make things right.

"It was a moment of weakness and I'm not sure why it happened, all I know is that I don't want anything like that in my life anymore." This was coming out all wrong. "I mean—"

"Anymore?"

That had been an unfortunate slip of the tongue, Melanie silently upbraided herself. At this point, she felt that the more she talked, the worse it was going to get.

"Never mind," Melanie said with finality, hoping to bury the subject altogether. "You have a lot of patients to see."

So now she was telling him his job? "I am aware of that," he retorted coolly.

"Good, then we're on the same page."

Not hardly, Mitch thought as he finally put on the white lab coat he'd gotten out of the closet what seemed like eons ago.

He had no time to wonder about what Melanie had said because the moment he slipped on his lab coat, there was a quick knock on the door frame and his first patient came in.

By now, he was familiar with all their faces, if not their names. But this patient was even more familiar than the others. The first patient of his afternoon was April O'Neill.

Seeing her, Mitch caught himself smiling almost automatically. There was something almost infectious about the little girl's wide, guileless smile and her entire manner was comprised of exuberance, despite the circumstances that she and her mother and brother found themselves in.

Hers was the face of eternal hope.

"Where's your mother?" Mitch asked. Ordinarily, mothers accompanied their children when they were brought in for an exam.

"She's busy with Jimmy," April told him matter-of-factly, as if this was just the way things were. She was the healthy one and her brother was not, which meant that he required more of their mother's time.

April willingly occupied herself at the shelter. She was a pint-size goodwill ambassador, wheedling information out of everyone and becoming part of the main fabric of the shelter in an extraordinarily short amount of time.

"Okay, well, you know the drill," Mitch told her, patting the top of the exam table. "Get up on the table and tell me where it hurts."

He was surprised when his small patient giggled in response, then watched as she scampered onto the exam table. He knew better than to help her up. April was exceedingly independent and proud of it.

This afternoon her progress was hampered because

she was holding a folder in her hand. Mitch assumed that the folder probably contained a note from the girl's mother, explaining the symptoms that had sent April to him in the first place.

"Okay," Mitch said, putting his stethoscope around his neck, "what brings you here?"

"My feet," April answered, looking up at him a little uncertainly because he had to ask. To emphasize her point, she wiggled them.

"No, I think the doctor wants to know why you came to see him this morning," Melanie explained.

"Oh." As understanding washed over her, April nodded her head vigorously. "Okay." Taking a deep breath, she went into her explanation. "I came to see him because I have something to give him. And you," she quickly added, looking at Melanie. Indicating the folder, April proudly declared, "This."

Then, unable to contain herself, April opened the folder before Melanie could reach for it.

Inside the folder were two pieces of eight-by-ten beige construction paper. Both had colorful drawings on them vividly immortalized with a number of different crayons. Below each of the drawings was a swarm of *X*s and *O*s. Beneath *that* someone had obviously helped April print her name in big block letters that seemed to lean into one another. The five letters were all inside of a huge red heart.

April's eyes danced as she held out her handiwork to both of them.

"Do you like it?" she asked eagerly, although from her tone of voice it was easy to see that she thought the answer was a foregone conclusion.

"Oh, very much," Melanie told her enthusiastically.

Holding it between both hands, Melanie held the drawing out as if she was appraising it.

"And you'll keep it forever?" April asked.

"And ever and ever," Melanie assured her with feeling.

April turned her huge bright green eyes on Mitch. "How about you?" she asked hopefully. "Do you like your card, Dr. Mitch?"

"It's very nice," Mitch replied. In his opinion, there was nothing special about it, but the little girl had made an effort and he'd been raised to believe that efforts were to be praised and rewarded if they were to yield something greater in turn. "But what's the card for?"

April cocked her head and looked at him as if she thought he was teasing her.

"Why, it's for Valentine's Day, silly. Today is Valentine's Day and I drew you Valentine cards 'cause you're both my Valentines. Mama thinks it's silly to give out cards, but I think everyone should have a Valentine card. We got some big paper from Mrs. Miller today at school. She told us to make a card for someone who we thought wasn't gonna get one. I asked her if I could make two so then she gave me two pieces of paper," April concluded, running out of breath at the end of her narrative.

She punctuated her story with a huge, sunny smile. But her smile quickly faded away when she look at Melanie. There were tears in Melanie's eyes.

"Don't you like your card?" April asked her, disappointed.

Melanie pressed her lips together, not trusting her

voice for a moment. Instead, because April was looking at her intently, she nodded her head.

"Very much," she finally ventured in a soft voice that was almost a whisper.

"But your eyes are leaking again," April pointed out. "Just like the last time."

"Those are happy tears, remember?" Melanie managed to get out. "Because the card you drew for me is so beautiful."

"Oh. Okay." April brightened, accepting the excuse. Her cards delivered, the little girl wiggled down off the table. "Well, that's all. I'm not really sick," she confided as an afterthought. "I just wanted to come and give you those cards I made for you 'cause it's Valentine's Day."

With that, the little girl grabbed her folder and darted out of the room.

Melanie turned toward the wall, as if desperately trying to collect herself before the next patient walked into the room.

Debating for a moment, Mitch made up his mind and closed the door before anyone could enter. He thought it best to give Melanie a moment before she had to get back to work.

As he eased the door closed, he told himself he wasn't going to say anything, that whatever was going on with Melanie was her own business and in her place, he wouldn't have appreciated being on the receiving end of any questions, however well intentioned they might have been.

Despite this new self-awareness, Mitch heard himself asking her a question. His need to know had gotten the better of him.

"Why are your eyes 'leaking'?" he asked.

Hearing the six-foot-two, stern-faced doctor using April's term for crying caused her to smile. At least just enough to help her push back the dreadful wave of sorrow that had suddenly threatened to swallow her up whole.

"Because it's Valentine's Day."

"Do you always cry on Valentine's Day?" he asked.

He kept his voice mild, thinking that might just coax a response out of her. If he asked point-blank in his usual brusque manner, he knew she'd just close up and make it impossible for him to find out anything.

But maybe having this conversation would bring her around enough to be able to at least face working for the rest of the day.

"Is this something like when Charlie Brown stands by his mailbox and sighs because his dog gets a ton of Valentine cards while he doesn't get any?" he asked when she didn't answer him.

Brushing aside her tears with the heel of her hand, Melanie turned around and looked at the man before her in amazement.

"You've actually read a comic strip?"

"I have," he corrected. "As a kid." It had been years since he'd even glanced at a comic strip. Maybe he should make a point of finding a newspaper and catching up a bit, just for old time's sake, he thought whimsically. Out loud he said matter-of-factly, "Some things stick in your head."

"I guess," Melanie allowed. And then, because he was trying to be helpful—at least for him—she decided that maybe she owed him a little bit more of an explanation than she'd given him. "I completely forgot today was Valentine's Day."

That was no big deal. Certainly not something to cry over. "You're not alone," he assured her.

But Melanie shook her head. "No, you don't understand."

"So you keep telling me," he remarked with a patient sigh.

Melanie drew in a long breath and decided she might as well get the whole thing out rather than harbor it like some deep, dark secret. Secrets usually wound up festering. Besides, it wasn't as if she was ashamed of what she had done or of Jeremy.

"I got engaged on Valentine's Day."

The name of her fiancé escaped him at the moment. He sought for a way to tactfully work his way around that deficit without calling attention to it. "To the man who never came home."

She felt fresh tears threatening to descend. How could she have forgotten that today was Valentine's Day? "Yes, to him."

"Look, if you want to go home, I can have the director find someone else to—"

"No," Melanie said firmly, cutting him off. She knew what he was going to say and she didn't want to hear it. "I don't want to go home. I want to be right here, where I can at least be useful to someone for something. I'll call your next patient in," she said abruptly, striding past him.

He saw no reason to try to stop her. By now he'd learned that he couldn't, even if he tried.

Chapter Nine

"You're good with them."

Mitch made the observation half grudgingly in the exam room several days after April had presented them with her hand-drawn Valentine cards. It was the tail end of the day and as usual, a swarm of children had been herded through the makeshift exam room.

But, unlike usual, the swarm of children had abruptly stopped.

He'd made the remark grudgingly because he *didn't* want to find anything more to admire about Melanie. Things would be a whole lot better for him if he could simply just not notice her at all. But that was like trying not to notice a clear summer day, or a crisp warm breeze on a spring morning.

The truth was he couldn't *help* noticing her and the way the children here not just reacted to her but gravitated to her, as well. It was as if she were this beguiling, all-encompassing magnet and the children were metal filings who instantly were attracted to her the moment they found themselves with her.

He had a set way of doing things, a way of expecting certain results after certain things were done. She, on the other hand, appeared to be as flexible as a licorice whip—physically, if he was any judge, watching her—as well as emotionally.

He had no doubts that if Melanie weren't here, acting as his go-between with the children each time he came to the shelter to minister to them, he would have had a great deal more trouble dealing with his small patients. For the most part, they were lively and exuberant, but they still seemed to *want* to behave for her, which completely amazed him.

Melanie casually shrugged off the doctor's observation. "Most kids want to behave. They just need to be guided a little."

"I think it's more than that," he countered. "I think they want to please you."

And she, he'd noticed, always knew just how to respond to make them laugh and feel good. He didn't have that gift and, until just recently, hadn't even felt the lack of it. But working beside this woman, he'd become acutely aware of the fact that the connections he made with his patients were sorely insufficient. It bothered him that it bothered him—and yet, it did.

"Did you have a lot of brothers and sisters growing up?" he asked.

The way he saw it, that would have been a reason why Melanie could get along so well with children. He, on the other hand, had been an only child and had kept to himself for the most part, preferring his own company to that of the kids in the neighborhood. Consequently, his people skills—much less his ability to communicate with children—had never been honed.

"No, actually," she told him. "I didn't have any. But I remember what it was like."

"What *what* was like?" he asked, feeling as if he'd lost her.

"Being a kid," she explained. "I remember what it was like." It was right there, a vivid part of her, everything she'd ever experienced as a child. "How scary things seemed. I can relate to all that. Most of the time, there was just my mother and me," she told Mitch. "My dad was in the navy and we moved around a lot. Every time I turned around, I was the new kid on the block." She laughed quietly. It hadn't been easy. "That involved a lot of insecurity and a lot of adjusting on my part. I wound up getting a very broad education."

"You were an only child?" he asked.

It gave them something in common, and at the same time, they couldn't have been more different, Mitch thought. She was the very definition of open and outgoing and he could easily be an island unto himself.

Well, maybe not easily, he amended, looking at Melanie, but he still could be.

Melanie nodded. "There were years I would have killed for a brother or sister. Especially an older brother to look out for me when we lived in this one place that I swear was populated with nothing but these sharp-tongued 'mean girls.'" A rueful look passed over her face. "Eventually, I realized that siblings—older *or* younger—weren't coming."

She stiffened just a little, as if bracing herself against the memory of what she was about to say. "Then my dad met someone else and it was just my mom and me." And then she brightened a little. "That's when we settled down in Bedford and for the first time, my life actually became stable. I knew where I'd be from one month to the next. I got to go to the same high school for the whole four years—I felt like I'd died and gone to heaven," she enthused. "And for a while, I guess I had."

He watched as she got a faraway look in her eyes and for a moment, she seemed not even to be in the same room anymore.

"But then things changed," she went on to say matter-of-factly, her voice distant and emotionless. "My mom died, and then—" Melanie blinked, as if she was suddenly hearing herself. "How did I get started talking about this?"

Something akin to what he supposed passed for compassion stirred inside of him. "I remarked that you were good with kids and you took it from there."

Melanie cleared her throat as she shrugged dismissively. "Sorry, I didn't mean to bore you."

"You didn't," he told her.

And that made her feel even more self-conscious, as if she was somehow exposed and unable to hide anything. Although Melanie had no problem talking, she didn't usually talk about herself. Doing that made her feel vulnerable and there was nothing she hated more than that feeling.

Peering out into the dining area, she saw a few of the residents—the ones who weren't lucky enough to find some sort of part-time employment in the local shops in the area—milling around. But none of the women appeared to be waiting their turn with the doctor.

That was a first, she couldn't help thinking.

"Looks like you ran out of patients," she observed, turning around to face him again. "I guess that means you're free to go."

Mitch laughed shortly. "I suppose I am." He paused for a moment, silently debating the wisdom of the question hovering on his tongue. And then it stopped hovering and became a reality. "Do you want to go grab a cup of coffee somewhere?"

"There's coffee in the dining area," she pointed out, wondering how he had forgotten about that.

"I mean a *real* cup of coffee," Mitch emphasized.

"You mean one that costs too much?" She assumed that was probably his criteria—if it didn't cost a sinful amount, the product he was getting couldn't be any good.

The man was still a snob, she thought, but at least he seemed to be coming around.

"I mean one that doesn't taste like someone dipped a brown crayon in hot water for approximately three minutes."

"I'd take offense at that remark," she told him with a straight face—and then she smiled. "But I guess it is pretty weak at that," she admitted.

He was still processing the first part of her statement. "You make the coffee?" he asked. He hadn't meant to insult her, he just didn't associate making coffee as part of what she did at the shelter.

"Some of the time," Melanie admitted. "Coffee's

not much of a priority around here. There's more of an emphasis on milk and wholesome food—and a doctor's care," she added on for good measure. "You're the first doctor some of these women have had contact with since—well, forever, I guess." She looked at him for a moment, as if finally allowing herself to see him. "Frankly, I'm surprised you stuck around."

"That makes two of us," Mitch murmured under his breath.

His admission had her regarding him a little more closely. "Does that mean you might stop coming to the shelter soon?" she asked. It was always best to be braced than to stick her head in the sand. That had become her new motto.

As Mitch watched her, she squared her shoulders and seemed to shut down right in front of his eyes.

"If I did stop coming here, would that matter to you?" he wanted to know. He told himself he was just making conversation—but he actually wanted to know and the fact that he did bothered him. It shouldn't have mattered to him one way or another—but it did.

Melanie shifted the emphasis away from her. It was how she'd learned to survive.

"It would matter to the residents here—especially to the children like April. She's gotten very attached to you, Doctor. Children value a routine. They get used to it, depend on it. You take that routine away from them, you risk making their worlds collapse."

He didn't buy that. Was she trying to guilt him into staying because *she* didn't want him to stop coming—or was she just spinning a theory? He couldn't tell.

"As someone whose father was in the navy, you

know that changes are a part of life. It can happen at any time, any age," he pointed out.

She thought of how she had felt when she'd learned about Jeremy. How her whole world had completely shattered.

"Yes," she said quietly. "I know." And then she forced herself to rally. She didn't want him asking her any questions. "If you do decide that you've had enough of volunteering, I'd appreciate you letting me know before it becomes general knowledge. I'd like to be able to prepare the kids."

"I'm sure that it wouldn't really be that a big a deal for them," he told her dismissively.

Her eyes met his for a moment and he couldn't really begin to guess what she was thinking. "You'd be surprised," she told him quietly.

"Maybe," he allowed. And then he heard himself say something that left him wide open to a whole array of things that he had told himself he was trying to avoid. "When do you leave here?"

She didn't understand the question. "I'm sorry?"

I don't know about you, but I know I might be.

Still, Mitch knew he had to follow this thought through to the end. "In the evening, do you leave at a set time or whenever you want to, or...?" He allowed his voice to trail off, leaving her space to jump in any time.

"Probably more like 'or,'" she told him. When he looked at her questioningly, she elaborated. "There's no real set time. I usually leave when things settle down and the mothers who have jobs come back in time to eat with their kids, help them with their homework if the kids are old enough to attend one of the local schools. In a nutshell, I go home when I'm not needed."

"Oh." He looked at her. Mitch was beginning to think that she really was an amazing woman. "Then you pretty much stay here all the time."

His subtle response tickled her and she laughed. "Is that a compliment?"

"Did sound like one, didn't it?" Mitch seemed to marvel right along with her, turning his comment around to absorb it.

She was still examining his words from all angles, as if they were a rare Christmas gift. "I think that's the first compliment you've given me."

He didn't doubt it. He wasn't the type to be lavish with his praise. It was both his strength and his shortcoming, he thought.

"Probably."

"Any particular reason you're trying to pin me down to a schedule?" she asked him.

He might as well have it all out in the open, Mitch thought. "I guess I'm trying to ask you out to dinner."

"What happened to coffee?"

"Dinner's better," he told her.

Her mind was on expediency. "We could eat here in the dining hall."

"Or we could eat somewhere less crowded, where everyone wasn't watching our every move and counting the number of times we actually spoke to one another."

She would have loved to have gotten an updated tally on that, she thought. Melanie grinned for the first time that day.

"I guess you might have a point."

"I *always* have a point," he told her with total conviction. Then, realizing that he sounded rather stiff and formal, he did his best to lighten up a little. "So, when *are* you free?"

She glanced at her watch. It was a little past four. Barring an emergency, things would be winding down for the day very soon. Half an hour, tops. She could be ready to leave in half an hour.

Tell him no. You don't want to set yourself up, Mel. Been there, done that, remember? Make the right choice. Say no.

She took a deep breath, very aware of the miniwar going on inside her. "I'll have to get back to you about that," she told him.

"Sure," he told. "That's fine. Whenever."

Maybe this was for the best. He didn't want to start something that he might wind up regretting. Relationships were draining—or so he'd heard.

He knew his mother would have loved to have a daughter-in-law, grandchildren—the whole nine yards. But that wasn't his dream. He just wanted to continue doing what he'd been doing—being a doctor who made a difference.

Any other words they might have wanted to exchange on the subject were quickly tabled when they heard someone shouting in a loud, angry voice that threatened to haunt some of the younger children's nightmares for several months or more.

"I said, *Where is she?* I know she's here so *tell me* if you know what's good for you!"

By the sound of it, the man's fury seemed to increase with every word.

Before he had a chance to ask Melanie if she had

any idea what was going on, she'd taken off for the front of the shelter, where the voice was coming from.

He was right behind her and got to the main entrance at the same time that she did. The man doing the shouting was there, screaming and berating the shelter's director. To her credit, Polly appeared steadfast and unfazed, despite the man's considerable height and girth.

In his mid to late forties, the angry man was muscular and formidable looking. He also seemed as if he was the type who could beat anyone to a pulp who had the nerve to get in his way. At the moment, he was towering menacingly over the director.

Polly was standing her ground but it was anyone's guess for how long.

"If you're going to behave this way, I'm afraid you're going to have to leave. You're scaring the children," Polly told the man just as Melanie and he entered.

"Oh, like I give a damn about them," he snorted. Going toe-to-toe with Polly, he went on to rant, "I'll leave. Sure, I'll leave—*as soon as I find that whore and my kid!*" He started to push Polly aside.

"You get away from her!" Melanie shouted at him, rushing to get between the man and Polly.

Mitch snapped to attention, realizing that Melanie was going to try to shield the director from the man's ham-like fists.

Was she out of her mind?

Grabbing Melanie by the arm, he pulled her back and then rather than getting in front of her, he put himself in front of the angry man.

"Looks like it's unanimous," Mitch told him in a

calm voice that belied what was going on inside of him. "The ladies would like you to leave."

"Like I give a damn what the hell they want," the man spat. "What about you, tough guy? You want me to leave, too?" the man sneered at Mitch.

"Please, leave. We don't want any trouble," Polly was pleading, but neither man was listening. Like two lions, they sized one another up.

"I think it would be a good idea, yes," Mitch told the other man, never taking his eyes off him.

"Oh, you do, do you?" the man jeered. "Well, the hell with what you think and the hell with you!" he raged. Pulling back his right forearm, he fisted his hand and was about to throw a punch that threatened to bring the verbal exchange between them to a quick, painful end.

And it might have, if he had been able to follow through with that punch and connect with his intended target.

But to his stunned surprise, the man he obviously looked upon as an easy knockout turned out to be faster than he was.

Faster, more accurate and, as it turned out, had a one-two punch that was far more lethal than he'd counted on.

The first punch landed in the man's solar plexus, the second went straight to his jaw. The lumbering hulk was facedown on the floor in a matter of seconds without having landed so much as a single punch.

Taking no chances, Mitch kept a wary eye on the unconscious, would-be assailant. "Call 911," he told Polly, raising his voice to be heard above a chorus of childish cheers.

The children seemed to have materialized out of nowhere, descending upon the tight circle of angry men like invading locusts, just in time to have witnessed Mitch reduce the irrational assailant to a lump of inert—for now—flesh. The children, drawn by the shouting, had seen the rather quiet doctor who gave them pain-free shots behave like a hero and save Miss Polly—and maybe them, as well—because despite their tender ages, they had all seen that sort of craziness in their short lifetimes and they knew enough to get as far away from the unconscious man as possible.

"Already doing it."

The response came from Melanie, who had her cell phone out and against her ear. Covering the other ear, she turned away the second she heard her call being answered on the other end.

To everyone's relief, the police arrived quickly. The assailant, who turned out to be the ex-boyfriend of one of the shelter's new residents, was still out cold and thus offered no resistance when he was handcuffed and carried off to the patrol car.

Statements were taken down quickly. Since the assailant had taken the first swing—as well as having threatened Polly—he was brought down to the precinct to be booked for assault and disorderly conduct among other charges.

Melanie had held her breath throughout most of the ordeal. She waited until the arresting officers had left with their semiconscious prisoner and Polly had voiced her thanks, which Mitch, in typical fashion, had brushed aside.

Melanie also waited until the children—excited

by the act of heroism they had witnessed—had been herded off, as well.

Eventually, after enough time had passed and the activity had wound down, it was just the two of them standing alone in the foyer.

Aware of the fact that she had remained standing at his side during the entire time, Mitch looked at her now and read between the lines—or tried to.

"Well, say it," he urged. "Get it off your chest. You're obviously waiting to say something to me."

He had a feeling that Melanie was probably one of those women who hated physical fighting for any reason.

"Your knuckles are bruised," Melanie finally told him.

He looked at her, stunned. "That's it?" he asked in disbelief.

"No." She took him by the hand—gently—and began to lead him back to the exam room. "You need someone to take care of that for you. I've watched you work long enough to be the one to do that for you."

"I just have to wash my hands," he said, dismissing her concern.

The way he saw it, the condition of his knuckles didn't need any sort of attention or special treatment to be dispensed. Just some clean soap and water, and maybe a little time.

"No, you need to have that wound disinfected. I wouldn't doubt that that man has rabies. At any rate, you can never be too careful." She stopped to give him what amounted to a stern look. "Physician, heal thyself," she instructed firmly.

"I don't need anyone hovering over me. I can 'heal' myself," he insisted.

Melanie slanted a silencing glare in his direction. "Maybe, but I can do it better."

With that, she continued to lead him back to the exam room, steering him and taking charge as if he were a willful child who needed to be cared for.

Chapter Ten

Mitch was beginning to realize that the only way he was going to be able to leave the shelter with a minimum of difficulty was if he just gave in and allowed Melanie to see to the abrasions and bruises on his knuckles. So he allowed her to lead him into the very same room where he normally treated the shelter's residents.

"Take a seat," Melanie said, indicating the exam table.

He slid onto it. "I know the drill."

As she took out the necessary items, Melanie flashed a smile at him in response. "Good."

He sat there, watching her work, and Mitch had to admit that he was surprised at her efficiency. Obviously the woman had been paying more attention than he thought she had these past few weeks.

Melanie moved quickly and competently, disinfecting the two cuts across his knuckles. One of them went a lot deeper than he'd realized. The sharp sting surprised him and he'd almost winced, but managed to catch himself at the last moment.

Once she'd gotten the cuts cleaned, she liberally applied a salve to both areas and then covered them with two flexible bandages. Both had cartoon squirrels on them.

"Sorry about that," she apologized as she secured each one at a time. "We seem to be out of regular bandages."

The corners of his mouth curved ever so slightly in amusement as he regarded the end results. "Not bad," he pronounced.

"I told you I've been paying attention," she reminded him. After putting the items back into the first aid kit, Melanie closed the lid and set the kit back into the cabinet where it belonged. Locking it, she turned toward him and said, "Okay."

"Okay?" Mitch repeated the word, puzzled. He had no idea what she had just agreed to. He would have guessed that she was telling him that he could go home, but the inflection in her voice didn't match that scenario. "Okay what?"

She shifted so that she was standing right in front of him as she gazed up into his eyes. For just a split second, the very vivid memory of his single transgression rose up like a hot wave, drenching him before it receded again.

"Okay," she told him, "I'll have dinner with you, Mitch."

Well, that had certainly come out of the blue, he thought. "When?"

"Now," she told him. "I just wanted to finish taking care of your hand." She regarded her handiwork for a moment. "I didn't know you were a southpaw." She'd seen him work, and he always used his right hand. But when he'd turned out that rude man's lights, he'd done it by using his left hand.

"I'm not. But the coach in high school got me to switch when I injured my right hand. Said that if I practiced using both hands, that gave me twice the staying power in the ring and that my opponents would never know what was coming." He shrugged at the distant memory. "At the time, it made sense to me. I enjoyed the release that boxing afforded me, so I went along with anything the coach said."

The man was just full of surprises, Melanie thought. "You *boxed* in high school?"

"Yes." He saw the expression of disbelief on her face. "Why do you look so surprised?"

She'd always maintained that people weren't two dimensional, that they were complicated. It was just that Mitch had seemed so aloof, she didn't see him as having any sort of physical contact with other students.

"I guess I shouldn't be, considering how much you like dealing with people," she told him with a laugh. Punching out someone's lights seemed to make sense in that context. Once she finished putting everything away, she turned around and declared, "There, all done."

"Will I live, 'Doctor'?"

Her eyes crinkled ever so slightly at the corners as she said, "I'm happy to say yes."

"Happy?" he questioned.

Melanie raised her eyes to his. The doctor's stock had gone up immeasurably in her estimation when he had come to Polly's rescue like that, without any prompting from anyone. Especially doing it the way he had.

If anything, she would have expected Mitch to attempt to talk the man down, at the very least talk him out of his rage. She was familiar enough with the type to know that words would be wasted in that instance, but she hadn't thought Mitch would be aware of that.

The bull of a man could have easily hurt Polly and anyone else who got in his way. Looking back, this was clearly a case of actions speaking louder than words and she was very, very impressed that Mitch had gotten the situation under control with a minimum of fuss.

She was also relieved that he had only sustained a couple of cuts on his hand. It could have gone a great deal worse.

Melanie smiled at the bemused expression on his face now.

"Yes, happy. It would be terrible if after saving Polly like that—not to mention that man's poor ex-girlfriend and his child—you'd succumb to some microbe that can't be seen by the naked eye."

He didn't bother pointing out that a microbe, by definition, couldn't be seen by the naked eye. He just accepted her display of concern.

"Wouldn't want that."

Something else occurred to her. "Just out of curiosity, are you up on your shots?"

"Why?" he asked, intrigued. "What did you have in mind?"

But she wasn't bantering right now. "Your tetanus shot," she specified in all seriousness.

Mitch shrugged. Things like that were a regular part of his life, but as to when, well that was another story. "I think so."

"You *think* so?" she questioned, surprised that he was so vague about it. "You're a doctor, aren't you supposed to know?"

"I'm a doctor, that makes me too busy to know," he pointed out. Her concern had been almost sweet, but now she was carrying this too far. "I'm sure it's in my records somewhere."

"Somewhere?" She wasn't about to let up. This could have serious implications if his booster was out of date. One hand on her hip, she got in his way just in case he got it into his head that he was fed up and just wanted to take off. "Find out where."

He should have gotten really annoyed by now and couldn't figure out why he hadn't. "You don't let up, do you?"

Melanie moved her head from side to side, never taking her eyes off his. "Uh-uh."

"Okay, I remember," he said glibly. "I've had my shots."

She eyed him suspiciously. "Not good enough. I don't believe you."

"Not my problem," he told her. But when he started for the door, Melanie moved right along with him, blocking his path every step of the way. Mitch stopped moving. "You really *are* serious about this." He was stunned that she could be so adamant about something that would seem so minor to most people.

"Totally." She was dogged about him remaining

well and didn't see that as something to be ashamed of. "Call your doctor, or the hospital since they have to have your medical records," she realized, "and just verify that you had a booster shot within the past ten years. You did a brave thing out there. I'm not going to let it all end badly because you're just too stubborn to check a simple fact."

The woman could definitely be a pain, he thought, though he still wondered why his indignation over this minidrama failed to take root.

With a sigh, he took out his cell phone and called the personnel director at Bedford Memorial. Fifteen minutes and two recorded menu choices later, he finally had a date to give the tenacious, blond-haired bulldog before him.

"Satisfied?" he asked after having rattled off the date.

Her intense expression faded. "Yes. I'm just being cautious," she told him, putting away the booster serum she'd taken out—just in case.

"That's one description for it," he murmured, still trying to summon a little righteous indignation. But the truth was, no one had ever expressed this much concern over his well-being except for his mother. It did make him see Melanie in a totally different light than his initial perception of her.

Finally free to leave, he surprised her by remaining where he was.

"You're not leaving," she noted, getting her own things together for a second time.

"We're having dinner together, remember? Before this little tetanus shot confrontation of yours, you said 'okay,' that you'd have dinner with me," he reminded her.

She'd thought that since she'd refused to back off about the infection, she'd gotten him too annoyed to want to go out for a meal with her.

"You still want to do that?" she questioned in surprise.

"I wouldn't be asking if I didn't," he pointed out. "Any place in particular you'd like to go?" he asked as he escorted her out of the exam room. He locked the door behind him.

"Some place where they serve food would be nice," she deadpanned.

He watched her warily, waiting for some sort of coda to follow, some condition she wanted him to fulfill, like a damsel asking a knight to slay a dragon for her before he came over to the castle.

"Uh-huh. And...?" he asked, waiting for a shoe to drop.

"And nothing," she answered cheerfully. That seemed to be enough to her. "I'm easy."

Mitch stared at her, and then he laughed shortly. "Not hardly. But you go right on telling yourself that and maybe someday that'll almost be true."

With that, he finally got her out the front door and heading in the direction of his car.

"So, how long did you box?" she asked him half an hour later over a plate of Yankee pot roast, mashed potatoes and green beans.

He didn't even have to pause and try to remember. "Not long."

"Afraid someone was going to ruin your pretty

face?" she asked, amused. Since all his features appeared to be perfect, she assumed his high school boxing venture was over before it ever got started.

"Afraid someone was going to ruin my pretty hands," he corrected. "I was still in high school when I decided I was going to be a surgeon." Or rather, when his father had made that decision for him, he recalled. "And that meant not risking breaking anything useful, like my fingers, or my wrist, or anything else in that vicinity."

When his father had found out that he was on the boxing team, he'd read him the riot act and made him quit that very afternoon. He remembered entertaining the idea of just rebelling, then, ever logical, he decided that his father was right and quit the team on his own.

"Makes sense," Melanie agreed. She could feel his eyes on her, as if he were trying to make up his mind about something. She made it easy for him and asked, "What?"

"What was that crack about my 'pretty face'?" he asked.

Her grin was utterly guileless in its delight. "I overheard some of the little girls talking. Seems that more than a few of them have a crush on you. The consensus is that you're even, and I quote, 'cuter than Ricky Harris.' That assessment, by the way, was followed by a chorus of squeals."

Mitch frowned as he tried to place the name. It meant nothing to him. "Who's Ricky Harris?"

Melanie feigned surprise. "You don't know?" And then she took pity on him and told him. "Ricky Harris is the preteen giant heartthrob of the moment. He has a couple of songs out right now and is the current big deal—until the next one comes along," she added, leaving the fact that it was a cutthroat business unsaid but completely understood.

The fact that she actually knew these miscellaneous details boggled his mind. "How do you keep up on all this?" he asked.

"I keep up on the kids and this is important to them, so I make it a point to keep up on who the current teen prince is."

Everything he had witnessed ever since he'd started volunteering at the shelter painted her to be good at what she was doing—in every aspect.

"Makes sense," he commented, then, before he could think his question through, he asked, "Why is it that you don't have any kids of your own?"

The light seemed to leave her face then. It took her another moment to pull herself together enough to answer his unintentionally hurtful question.

"Things just didn't arrange themselves that way," she told him quietly.

He heard the pain in every syllable. "Look, I'm sorry. I'm an idiot. I should have remembered," he could have kicked himself for that. "Or I shouldn't have asked at all. Or—"

He appeared genuinely miserable over upsetting her this way and that in itself helped her rally back to being her usual self, or at least the "self" she allowed the others to see. Otherwise, she was certain that all she would be doing all day was crying.

Melanie placed her hand on his and pressed it lightly. She was silently asking him to stop berating himself.

"It's okay," she told him. "You didn't mean anything by it. It was an honest mistake. And I do love kids." A very fond smile curved her lips. "Had things gone a different route, I might have one day wound up giving the old woman in a shoe a run for her money."

Mitch looked at her blankly, and then shook his head. "I'm sorry," he told her honestly, "I don't get the reference."

"The nursery rhyme," she prompted. "You never heard that nursery rhyme?" she asked in disbelief.

"I never heard *any* nursery rhyme," he told her. "My father believed that everything that was part of my upbringing should be goal oriented and my 'goal' was to be a doctor, a surgeon."

"Was that his idea, or yours?"

He thought of lying, but then he didn't see that there was anything to be gained by that. It didn't even buy him time because he wasn't in the market for it.

"His," he told her honestly.

That explained a lot, she thought. Still, that didn't begin to explain the gap in his knowledge. "Doctors know nursery rhymes."

Mitch shook his head. "Not in my father's world they don't."

Melanie thought of something else, something that her own childhood had been very rich in. She couldn't begin to imagine childhood without it.

"What about cartoons?" she asked.

"What about them?"

"Did you watch any?" she asked patiently.

He thought back for a moment. Some of his fondest memories were rooted in what she was asking about. "My mother snuck me out a few times when my father was away, attending conferences—he was always the main speaker when he attended," he added. "Don't get me wrong, I was proud to be his son. He was an excellent surgeon."

That alone didn't qualify to make the man a nominee for Father of the Year, Melanie couldn't help thinking. "Just not a warm and fuzzy father," she guessed.

"No," he admitted. To say otherwise would have been lying. "But he just wanted me to reach my full potential," he told her.

"Reading a few nursery rhymes wouldn't have prevented you from attaining that," she pointed out.

Mitch laughed, shaking his head. "I don't think he saw it quite that way. To him, watching cartoons or playing games was all pointless downtime."

Everyone needed to have a way to unwind, to be something outside the student, or the lawyer or the engineer.

"He must have been thrilled when he found out that you were on the boxing team," she guessed.

Mitch laughed drily before he could prevent it. "Who do you think pointed out how many different ways I could break my hand not to mention that I could sustain some kind of brain damage from a blow to the head—which," he said, going back to her initial question, "would do a lot more damage than ruining my 'pretty face.'"

Melanie was quick to offer him a sympathetic smile. "We have a lot more in common than I thought," she commented.

He hadn't been aware that they were discussing their pasts. "What do you mean?"

She spelled it out for him without trying to sound

preachy. "Sounds like you had a rough childhood in your own way, too."

"I wouldn't exactly call it 'rough.' If anything I'd call it…isolated," he finally said, settling on a word.

"That's okay," she told him. "I'd call it rough for you." As she picked up her soda to take the last sip, she glanced at her watch. The time on it surprised her. "How did it get to be so late? You probably feel like I talked your ears off," she guessed ruefully.

Still looking at her, Mitch touched each of his ears one at a time.

"Nope, they're both still there," he informed her as if he'd just taken inventory of an actual shipment. "Better luck next time."

"Next time?" she repeated, confused. And maybe just a little bit nervous as well.

"Yes, I thought that since we're still both breathing and no mortal wounds have been delivered—"

He didn't get a chance to finish his sentence, or even to ask her out for a formal date. Anything he had to say on any subject was temporarily tabled as his cell phone began to ring.

The odd thing about that was hers did, as well. She had hers out first.

"It's the shelter," she told him, looking down at her phone's caller ID.

The caller ID on his cell phone was the same as hers. The shelter was calling both of them.

Chapter Eleven

Mitch had never believed in coincidences. Something was definitely wrong here.

Pressing Accept on his phone, Mitch said, "Dr. Stewart," at the same time that Melanie took her call and identified herself to her caller.

"Dr. Stewart, there's just been a horrific accident. I know this is a huge imposition, but are you anywhere close by and able to return to the shelter?"

The question throbbed with emotion. He barely recognized the shelter director's voice. He'd never heard her sound this beside herself or upset. Ordinarily, the woman seemed unflappable.

His first thought was that the man who had threatened to storm the homeless shelter earlier searching for his missing ex-wife and child had managed to make bail and was back.

Rather than speculate, Mitch asked. “Miss French, what happened?”

The director didn’t seem to hear him. Instead, she was disjointedly rattling things off, giving him a summary of peripheral events rather than the main action.

“There’s an ambulance on its way, but I know everyone here would feel a lot better if you could just please come back.” She was literally begging now.

Mitch had a feeling that he wasn’t going to have the blanks filled in by talking to the director. He would have to come back to the shelter and see what was going on for himself.

But what really made up his mind for him was the stricken expression on Melanie’s face.

“On my way,” he promised, closing his phone.

Melanie was doing the same. She forgot where she had put the phone the moment she had tucked it away. Her call had come from Theresa, who, it turned out, had decided to linger a while longer at the shelter tonight. The woman had just been on her way to her catering van when she saw the whole accident unfold.

It was the classic case of a speeding vehicle versus pedestrians.

Mitch immediately noticed that Melanie appeared very unsteady on her feet. He grabbed hold of her arm in case she passed out. He didn’t want her possibly hitting her head. He didn’t need another patient right now.

Taking out his wallet, he left two fifty-dollar bills on the table. He knew roughly what the meals had cost and he made sure that what he left behind more than covered the costs plus a generous tip. He absolutely didn’t want to waste any time waiting for his credit card to be processed and returned for his signature. From the breathless way the director had begged him to come, he had a feeling that minutes might very well be of tantamount importance.

He looked at Melanie now as he ushered her out of the restaurant. The woman hadn't said a word since they had both terminated their calls, nor had she answered his question about the incident.

Had she gone into shock?

"Melanie?"

He stopped just short of where he'd parked his vehicle. Still holding on to her, this time with his hands bracketing both sides of her shoulders, he peered into her face.

"Are you all right?" he asked.

The sound of his voice managed to penetrate the deep fog around her brain. Coming to, she remembered the last thing he'd asked her. He wanted to know about the accident.

"A car hit them," she cried. "They were crossing the street, coming back from the playground and a hit-and-run driver plowed right into them and just kept going." Tears fell as she told him.

"Into who, Melanie?" he asked, repeating, "Into who?"

"April and her family," she answered in a stunned, stilted voice that didn't even sound real to her own ears. The very words tasted bitter.

"Let's go" was all she heard Mitch say.

The next moment, he was pushing her into the passenger seat of his car and closed the door. Rounding the hood, he threw himself into the driver's seat.

"Buckle up!" he ordered in a gruff voice, trying

his best to snap her out of this downward spiral she seemed to be slipping into. “C’mon, Melanie. Snap out of it. If it *is* them, that little girl is going to need you,” he shouted at her.

This wasn’t real. None of it seemed real. “What if…what if she’s…dead?”

The word felt like a lead brick on her throat, threatening to choke her just the way it had when she’d stood there, listening to the kind-faced chaplain telling her life was over because Jeremy’s life had been cut short.

“She’s not dead,” Mitch bit off angrily, revving up his engine. “Do you hear me? She’s *not* dead.”

Melanie looked at him as if seeing him for the first time since she’d taken the call. “You can’t know that,” she cried, fighting panic.

He made no answer because she was right. He couldn’t know that.

He’d gotten even less information from the shelter’s director than Melanie had gotten from whoever had called her, but for whatever reason—and he had no real answer—he just wasn’t going to allow his mind to go there. And he wasn’t going to allow her mind to go there, either—not unless it was absolutely unavoidable.

“We’re not going to make any conclusions until all the information is in,” he told her. “Anything less than that and you’re not going to be any good to anyone—least of all yourself. Now, if the ambulance hasn’t gotten there, I’m going to need you to help, not to fall apart. Do you understand?” he asked, his voice sharp. It was almost a demand.

“I understand,” she answered, trying her very best

not to allow any horrific extraneous thoughts to enter her mind.

She needed to steel herself off for whatever lay ahead.

They got back to the shelter in record time. Mitch ran two lights, something he had never done before in his entire life, not even when he was young. But an urgency had seized him and he couldn't shake the feeling that every single moment counted.

Feeling like a spinning top, he tried to look everywhere at once. The last thing he needed was to be involved in a collision himself.

His heart pounding, he came to a screeching halt in the same parking lot he'd left just a little while earlier. Pausing only to grab his medical bag from the backseat, he ran into the shelter. Melanie was right beside him.

Out of the corner of his eye, Mitch noted that the ambulance he had expected to already be here hadn't arrived yet. Where the hell was it?

Haunted faces clustered around him as he and Melanie raced into the building.

"Where are they?" he demanded.

One of the residents who worked at the shelter as a janitor pointed to the rear of the building. "Out back," he cried. "They're still in the street."

A confluence of voices, all speaking over one another, tried to tell him what was happening. For now, he tuned them all out.

"Blankets!" Melanie cried, yelling the order to no one in particular. "Bring out blankets!" It was all she could think to do. There was a chill in the air and the family needed to be kept warm.

She'd only felt this utterly helpless once before in her life and she fought against the feeling, afraid that it would overwhelm her.

She ran out in front of Mitch, fearful of what she was going to see, just as fearful of hanging back and not getting there in time.

The three bodies looked mangled and broken as they lay on the cracked asphalt, frozen in a grotesque, bloody dance.

Scanning the trio, Mitch tried to decide where he would do the most good. None of them appeared to be breathing.

"Where the hell is the ambulance?" Mitch demanded angrily, straining to hear the sounds of a siren.

There were none.

Dropping to his knees beside the closest body, he quickly assessed April's brother, Jimmy, then Brenda, her mother, and finally, with an increasingly heavier heart, April herself.

The expression on his face grew grimmer with each passing moment.

Melanie felt as if her heart was strangling.

"Mitch?" she cried, distraught and silently begging him for some sort of reassurance.

But he just shook his head. "The mother's gone," he told her.

Checking over the little boy again, he looked up, frustrated beyond words. This wasn't right, this wasn't right, he couldn't help thinking. He felt as if someone had just hollowed out his insides with a dull knife. He thought he was immune to this, that he'd managed to distance himself from feeling anything when he lost a patient, but damn these people and damn Melanie, they had cut through the insulating wall he'd built up around himself.

Grief threatened to undo him.

"I can't get a heartbeat," he told Melanie, each word felt as if he was carving it letter by letter into his own flesh. He began giving the little girl CPR, but it was no use. He wasn't getting a response.

Melanie dropped to her knees beside the little girl, tears flowing fast and furiously, almost blinding her. "April?"

It wasn't a question, it was a plea.

He shook his head. "I'm not getting anything," he told her, feeling sick to his stomach.

All around them, other residents had come out of the shelter and gathered to watch the doctor unsuccessfully try to bring back these three people.

Melanie heard the ambulance siren in the distance. The sound almost echoed in her head.

It all felt surreal.

The next moment, anger exploded in her chest. She wasn't going to accept it! She wasn't going to accept Mitch's pronouncement!

She'd had to accept the death sentence the chaplain had given her over ten months ago, but she absolutely refused to accept this. She didn't care if Mitch was a doctor, she wasn't going accept what he'd just told her.

It wasn't true!

"No! April, c'mon, baby, fight this." Clutching the child to her, she lowered her face to the little girl's ear. "You have to fight this for your mama and for

Jimmy. You have to live for them, do you hear me?" Melanie sobbed. "You have to live!"

"Melanie," Mitch began, attempting to get her to release April's inert body and draw her away from the child. It broke his heart twice over to watch Melanie's grief. "She's gone."

"No, she's not!" Melanie cried fiercely, anger flashing in her eyes. "She's not! I'm not going to let her go, do you hear me? I'm not!" Melanie cried passionately. Turning toward April, she told her, "I'm not letting you go! You come back to me, you hear?"

Mitch gently but firmly drew Melanie to her feet, wanting to put distance between her and the deceased family. At a complete loss how to help her bear up to this tragedy, he looked to Theresa for help.

"I'm so sorry, Melanie," Theresa began compassionately as she tried to put her arms around the younger woman. "You need to let go now, dear. You need to—"

"Mama?"

Melanie swung around. She could just barely make out the weak little voice, the sound wedged between the tears and protestations of sorrow that were echoing around the horrifying scene.

"Mama," April whimpered, "I hurt. I hurt."

Barely audible sobs mixed in with the tiny voice. Tears of pain were rolling down the small, dirty cheeks. April's eyes were shut, but a part of her was definitely alive, definitely present if not fully conscious.

"Mitch!" Melanie all but shrieked.

Stunned, Mitch fell back to his knees, quickly checking April's vital signs as the sound of the approaching siren grew louder and louder.

"She's alive," Mitch cried in disbelief.

He looked up at Melanie, unable to explain what had just happened. A minute ago, there had been no heartbeat, no sound of breathing, no signs of life whatsoever.

And now, April was definitely back among the living.

She was trying to say something, her small heart fluttering wildly like the wings of a hovering hummingbird.

He'd been a doctor for several years now and in all that time he had never witnessed a miracle before. As a general rule, he didn't believe in them.

And yet, he had no other name for it. How else could he explain that one moment, the little girl was gone, the next she was alive again?

Back up on his feet, he took Melanie's hand and drew her to him. He moved out of the way as the ambulance attendants entered, pushing a gurney before them. The EMS who was apparently in charge, Eric, according to the name stitched on his badge, looked at Mitch. It was apparent by his expression that he and his team had only been notified of one victim, not three.

"I'll send for two more ambulances," the EMS told Mitch.

"No need," Mitch informed him grimly. "There's only one survivor." He nodded toward April. "The little girl's alive, the other two are gone."

The driver stepped aside for a moment and grabbed his dispatch radio placing another necessary call.

As quickly and succinctly as possible, Mitch told the head EMS attendant what had happened and gave him all the vital signs he'd noted.

Eric nodded. "Okay, we'll take her to County General."

"No," Mitch said, cutting in. He had no operating privileges at County General and he intended to be in the operating salon with April. "Take her to Bedford Memorial. It's closer."

"I know it's closer," Eric acknowledged. "But Doc, we're contracted with County. We're supposed to take accident victims to County General, especially if they're from the shelter."

The other attendant, who doubled as the driver, nodded, as if to back up what Eric had just said.

Mitch took out his wallet, extracted one of his business cards and handed it over to the head EMS attendant.

"I don't have time to argue and neither does she. I'm associated with Bedford Memorial and she's my patient. Take her there," he ordered. "If anyone gives you any trouble, refer them to me," he said.

The attendant looked down at the card, then slipped it into the breast pocket of his uniform. "You got it, Doc."

Mitch exchanged glances with Melanie as the attendants gently lifted April, transferring her from the ground onto the gurney. As they secured her small body, the little girl was sobbing in pain, calling for her mother.

"Are you up to driving?" Mitch asked, still regarding Melanie.

She was having trouble getting her emotions under control. This had been a wild roller-coaster ride and it wasn't over yet.

"Yes," she managed to get out. "Why?"

"I'm going with April," he began. He wanted Melanie to follow the ambulance either in his vehicle or her own.

Melanie was right beside the gurney as the attendants snapped the legs into position, raising the gurney off the ground.

"I want to come in the ambulance, too," she protested. "April needs me," she added.

The attendant settled the problem for them. "Not enough room for all of you. It's going to be a tight squeeze with the doc here."

She knew Mitch's presence beside April was far more necessary than her own. Still, she felt numb and beside herself as she nodded.

"All right," she agreed. "I'll follow you to the hospital with your car."

Theresa put her hand on Melanie's shoulder. "I'll be right behind you," she promised. It was clear that she didn't want Melanie to be alone in the waiting area.

The sound of approaching sirens was heard again. Disoriented, Melanie looked at the director. But it was Mitch who answered her unspoken question.

"That would be the medical examiner," he told her grimly, having noted the driver making a call earlier.

Just then, April, who had faded on them, regained consciousness. Her eyes fluttered open this time.

"Mama?" she cried, looking at Mitch. It was obvious that she was unable to focus.

Mitch didn't want to tell the little girl what had happened, didn't want to risk what that might do to her fragile condition if she knew that both her mother and her brother were dead.

Instead, he lightly touched April's hand, leaned over the child and told her, "April, it's Dr. Mitch. We're taking you to the hospital. We're going to make you all better."

"Okay," she said, her voice so weak that he had to lean in closer, directly over her lips in order to hear her.

"Doc," the driver politely prodded him, "we've got to get going."

"My thoughts exactly," Mitch said, nodding.

He walked directly behind the gurney as the two EMS attendants steered it over toward the ambulance. Mitch stepped back as the two attendants loaded April's gurney onto the back.

The moment the gurney was secured within the ambulance, Mitch quickly climbed in after it.

"Mama?" she whispered, the forlorn note ripping into his heart.

He wrapped his fingers around April's small hand. "Hold on to my hand, April. Everything's going to be all right."

"Okay," she whispered in a trusting voice that threatened to bring tears to his eyes.

He looked up and his eyes met Melanie's just as the attendant closed the doors.

Within ten seconds, the ambulance was leaving the parking lot.

And the medical examiner's black van was pulling in.

Chapter Twelve

Waiting was utter hell.

Every second that dragged by was etched in pure agony.

The longer the operation took, the more Melanie felt as if she was going to leap out of her skin. She needed to have someone come out of the operating room—and soon—to give her an update.

True to her word, Theresa had remained with her, doing what she could to attempt to distract her, at least to some degree.

But mainly what the older woman was trying to do was build upon the sliver of hope Melanie had been clinging to.

The surgical waiting area was fairly empty this late in the evening. Only those whose relatives or friends had been brought in through the emergency room to undergo unscheduled surgery due to some sort of accident—one woman had brought in her sister with a ruptured appendix, another man had run into his family room from the patio only to discover that the plate glass sliding door was *not* open—were in the room, sitting on less than comfortable orange upholstered plastic chairs.

Everyone was waiting for some news coming from the operating rooms.

Tension was thick within the waiting area, but Melanie hardly took notice of the other people, and while Theresa politely engaged with them in the sparse conversation when it was aimed in their direction, Melanie couldn't gather her thoughts together enough to carry on any semblance of dialogue.

"What's taking them so long?" she asked Theresa, finally putting her agitation into words. "Shouldn't they be finished operating on April by now?"

"You want fast, or do you want good, dear?" Theresa asked her sympathetically.

Melanie sighed. Theresa was right. Some things couldn't be rushed. But that didn't mean she had to be happy about it.

"Good," she answered, never taking her eyes off the swinging double doors. "I want good." Three hours ago, April had been wheeled through those doors with Mitch and two nurses in attendance.

That was the last time that she'd heard anything.

When Theresa rose to her feet, she looked at the older woman quizzically. "Are you going home?"

The infinitesimal part of her that wasn't preoccupied with what was happening behind the operating salon's doors felt a twinge of guilt at having the other woman stay with her in the hospital like this.

After all, Theresa did have a family and a life to get back to. She didn't.

"No, I'm just going to see if I can find out any information about April." With that, Theresa went to the ER admission clerk's desk.

The desk was located too far away for Melanie to catch any of the exchange between the two women. Melanie found herself holding her breath until Theresa walked back to her.

Taking the seat next to Melanie again, she told her, "They're still operating on April."

"Why's it taking so long?" Melanie asked. April was small for her age. The doctors in the operating room had had enough time to rebuild her from scratch, Melanie thought irrationally.

Why wasn't Mitch coming out to tell her that everything was all right?

Maybe he can't, the voice in her head taunted her. Fear gripped her heart.

"There was more internal damage than they initially thought," Theresa explained. She patted Melanie's hand. "But April's still hanging in there. You do the same, dear," she told Melanie, putting her arm around the younger woman's shoulders.

It was another two hours before Mitch finally came out of the operating room and into the waiting area. Melanie instantly shot up to her feet, eager and afraid at the same time.

Mitch looked exhausted and drained as he untied the upper portion of his surgical mask. It hung limply around his neck like a symbol of the fight he'd just fought.

"She's in recovery," he told Melanie and Theresa. The latter took hold of Melanie's hand, as if to infuse her with strength as they listened to Mitch's update. "Her condition is critical, but stable."

The words seemed to just bounce off her head, without penetrating.

"What does that mean?" Melanie cried.

"That means she's hanging in there and with any luck, she'll be upgraded to serious but stable." He offered Melanie a weak smile. "Why don't you have Mrs. Manetti take you home, Melanie? There's nothing you can do here tonight."

He was wrong there. "I can keep vigil," Melanie told him stubbornly. "When April wakes up, she's going to need to see a familiar face."

"I'll be by to look in on her," Mitch assured her. One of the ER doctors had called in sick so, since he was already here, he had volunteered to take the shift. Melanie looked as if she'd been to hell and back and he wanted her to get her rest before she collapsed out here.

"But you can't stay in her room with her. I can," she told him.

He looked at Theresa. "Can you please talk some sense into her?" he requested.

To his surprise, Theresa didn't side with him. "Sorry, Doctor, but she's making perfect sense to me. If I were in her place, I'd be doing the same thing." Turning toward Melanie, she said, "I can stay a little longer with you if you like."

"No, that's okay, really. You've done more than enough," Melanie assured her. "Please go home."

Turning toward Mitch, she asked, "Do they have a room assigned to April yet?"

"You'll have to check with the admission's clerk for that," he told her. And then he paused just before going back to the locker room. "I still think you should go home, too. April's not going to regain consciousness until at least sometime tomorrow."

"That's okay. You thought she was dead and she wasn't. Maybe she'll come around sooner than you think as well." She pressed her lips together, doing her best to keep tears of relief from falling. "Anything's possible."

"Yeah," he said, looking over his shoulder toward the operating room. It had been an uphill battle in there, but he'd won. For now. "Anything is."

"Here."

The deep male voice penetrated the misty layer that had settled in and encompassed Melanie's brain.

It took Melanie a couple of seconds to realize that as uncomfortable as it was—and it felt as if she was sitting in a gravel pit on top of unrefined rocks—she had somehow managed to fall asleep in the chair in Melanie's room.

Hours earlier she had followed the orderlies bringing April and her hospital bed up in the service elevator after the little girl had finally been released from the recovery area. She couldn't remember exactly what time that was, only that the moon was still up.

The sun was lighting up the hospital room now.

From then until now, she'd sat in the chair, just watching April. As in every room, there was a television set mounted on the wall opposite April's bed.

But Melanie just couldn't get herself to turn it on. Her mind felt too scattered to pay any attention to some episodic adventure unfolding within the confines of forty-two minutes, sans commercials.

Melanie didn't want any distractions getting in her way. She wanted her full focus to be on April so that when the little girl came to, she would be aware of it, not just notice it as an afterthought during a mindless commercial.

She had no idea when she had fallen asleep. All she knew was that her body hated her for it now because every single part of it felt stiff and achy, as if she'd just gone through a mammoth marathon involving all the sports meant to make her sweat.

Blinking, Melanie focused on the owner of the voice and what "here" referred to.

Belatedly, she realized that it was Mitch and he was holding out a paper cup with coffee in it.

"I figured you might need this right about now," he told her, still holding the cup in front of her. "You take lots of cream in your coffee, don't you?" he asked her.

She took the cup from him and just held it for a second, allowing the subdued heat to penetrate her palms. The warmth spread out to her limbs from there.

Mitch was wearing the same thing he'd worn earlier, before he'd changed into his scrubs. Hadn't he gone home, either?

"How did you know?" she asked, nodding at the container of coffee.

In her experience, most men, when they got coffee for a woman they weren't involved with, usually got her the same kind of coffee they drank. Mitch's coffee was as black as an abyss. Hers was a caramel cream color.

"Just a hunch." He looked over toward April. "I take it she hasn't woken up yet."

"No, she hasn't." She looked at him with a new measure of respect for his abilities. "Can you tell that just by looking at her?"

"No," he corrected, "I can tell that because there are no reports of a wild-eyed blonde running into the hallway, yelling for a doctor."

She took a sip, letting the coffee wind its way through her system. Somewhat fortified, she felt able to confront him with another question. "Is that what I am, a wild-eyed blonde?"

He thought of taking the description he'd used back, or paving over it somehow, but he had a feeling she valued honesty. So he was honest.

"Well, for a while there at the crosswalk, that was a pretty apt description of you." He checked the monitors that were attached to the tiny body, gathering all of April's basic vital statistics and measuring against the last ones. He added something to her IV solution before turning back to Melanie. "I told you she was going to sleep through the night," he reminded her.

Melanie shrugged. "I just wanted to be here for her in case she woke up. The last thing she saw was her mother and brother being hit by that vehicle. That had to be pretty scary for a five-year-old."

"Not too great for an adult, either," he commented. For just the briefest second, there was a chink in his armor.

Melanie raised her eyes to his, curious. "Is that from experience?" she asked.

He thought of just shrugging off her question, saying that he was just talking in general, but maybe saying so, denying it ever happened would have been disrespectful of the one close friend he'd had.

"Yeah."

Now he had really aroused her curiosity. "Want to talk about it?"

"No." His voice was flat, allowing no room for persuasion.

"Okay."

Her response, given so readily, surprised Mitch. It seemed somehow out of character for Melanie. "Just like that?"

"You deserve your privacy. Everyone does," she told him. "When you're ready to talk about it—*if* you're ready to talk about it—you will. And if you want me to be the one you talk to, I'm not that hard to find."

He paused for a moment, making notations into April's chart. The notations in turn would be transcribed to the hospital's software system by April's nurse, but he didn't have time to do the necessary typing right now. He hadn't really ever gotten comfortable with the system.

When he returned the chart to the metal hook at the foot of the bed, he just began to talk. "He was my best friend in medical school—my *only* friend in medical school," he underscored. "It was winter break and we had a couple of drinks at the local pub before splitting up and going our separate ways. He was heading back home to Iowa until after the first of the year. He never even made it to his car."

"What happened?" she asked in a hushed voice,

watching his face closely so as not to overstep. She was acutely aware of how sensitive feelings in this case could be.

"A drunk driver peeling out of the parking lot hit him. Apparently never even knew it, or so he claimed when the police caught up with him. My friend—Jake, Jake Garner," he said, realizing that he had omitted Jake's name from the narrative, "died on the way to the hospital," he concluded quietly.

Her eyes filled with tears for the friend he had lost. "Mitch, I'm so sorry," she told him, her voice scarcely above a whisper. Without realizing it, she'd put her hand on his forearm in a gesture of shared sympathy.

"Yeah, me, too." He shrugged, as if to push the memory of that night back. "It was a long time ago."

"But not long enough to stop hurting," she pointed out. "It never is." Taking a breath, she changed the subject—for both their sakes. "Have they found the driver who did this to April and her family?"

He shook his head. "Not as far as I know," he answered. "Sometimes, these people get away with it."

Melanie felt anger building up inside of her. "It doesn't seem fair."

"No, it doesn't," he agreed. And then he looked at her. She seemed tired. As tired as he felt. "So, can I talk you into going home now?" he asked.

Melanie shook her head, her mouth curving slightly. "April hasn't woken up yet."

"She might not wake up for days," Mitch pointed out patiently.

Chances were that she would, but he was also aware that there were statistics about trauma patients slipping into comas that lasted for months, sometimes even for years. And then there were the ones who never woke up. He refrained from mentioning them, or even thinking about them himself.

"You have a cafeteria here, I'll find someone to bring me something," she told him.

He shook his head as an exasperated sigh escaped his lips. "You have got to be the most stubborn woman I have ever met."

To which she responded, "Some people think that's my greatest asset."

"Some people like Brussels sprouts, but I don't," he informed her pointedly.

Feeling better just talking to him, Melanie played along.

"Really? Because I have a great recipe for Brussels sprouts," she told him. When he grimaced, she went on to describe it. "It involves bread crumbs and melted margarine. You take the Brussels sprouts—"

"I don't like Brussels sprouts."

Both Mitch and Melanie swung around to look at the small occupant in the hospital bed a few feet away. April's eyes were still closed, but she had made a face, the kind children made when confronted with a vegetable they just can't abide, no matter how healthy it was supposed to be for them.

Melanie instantly gravitated to the side of April's bed. "Did you say something, April?" she asked, barely containing her excitement.

There was no response to her question.

"You heard her, right?" she asked Mitch, looking at him. "I wasn't just imagining that, was I?"

Before he could reassure her that he had heard

April weakly proclaim her dislike of Brussels sprouts, April spoke again.

Each word was a struggle for her. “Mama says… I don’t…hafta…eat them if… I don’t…wanna.”

Melanie took the little girl’s hand, holding on to it tightly as if anything less might cause April to break away and slip back into unconsciousness.

“April, honey, open your eyes. Open your eyes and look at me,” Melanie pleaded. “Please, baby.”

Disoriented, the little girl struggled to raise her eyelids.

As he watched her, it was obvious to Mitch that April had lapsed into that sleep-awake state where she was having a great deal of difficulty opening her eyes because they each felt as if they weighed a ton.

“Open your eyes, April,” he said, coaxing her as he buffered her other side. “You can do it. I know that they feel heavy but you can open them if you really try hard enough.”

For her part, Melanie squeezed the little girl’s hand, as if silently adding her voice to Mitch’s. She didn’t want to confuse April with too many voices coming at her at once, but it was very hard for her to keep quiet.

And then, finally, the small eyelids opened and April looked around. Seeing Melanie and the doctor, she smiled weakly at them.

The next moment, she asked Melanie the question the latter had been dreading.

“Where’s Mama?”

Chapter Thirteen

This was why she'd insisted on staying in April's room, keeping vigil over her. Specifically to field this very question.

Now that it was here, Melanie felt her stomach tightening in a hard, unmanageable knot. She was at a loss as to how to answer April, how to put what was undoubtedly the most horrible news the little girl would ever hear into words.

How did she go about telling a five-year-old that her mother was gone, that she was never coming back because she had died?

The inside of Melanie's mouth had gone bone-dry, but she knew she had to tell April, had to find a way to tell her the truth, but to soften it in some way. Right now, she was all that April had.

Melanie lightly skimmed her fingers along the little girl's forehead. "Did your mama ever tell you about heaven, April?"

April tried to nod, but the motion seemed to hurt too much.

"Yes," she whispered. Her cadence was slow and labored. A sadness seeped into her voice as she continued, as if she somehow sensed what was waiting for her at the end of the conversation. "She said it was a pretty place. That's where Daddy is. Heaven."

Tears gathered in Melanie's eyes as she broke the news. "Well honey, your mama and Jimmy went to be with your daddy." It was getting really difficult to talk. The very words felt unwieldy, as if they were getting stuck in her throat.

A tear slid down April's cheek. "Without me?"

Oh Lord, Melanie thought, April sounded so lost, so crushed.

"It wasn't your time to go yet, honey." That sounded so terrible and so stilted. She raised her eyes helplessly to Mitch. What had made her think that she'd be any good at this?

Before Mitch could find anything reassuring to say, April asked in a small, lost voice, "What's going to happen to me?"

"We're going to take care of you, honey. Make sure you get all better," Melanie promised her. "Dr. Mitch saved your life."

"Why couldn't he save Mama's?" April cried.

"Because she had already gone to heaven before he got there," Melanie said, sparing Mitch from having to answer the little girl.

Rather than say anything, Mitch took the little girl's hand in his and squeezed it, silently conveying a great many things that couldn't be put into words. Telling her that she was safe.

"And when Dr. Mitch says you can go home," Melanie told her, "you can come home with me."

Mitch glanced at her sharply, but Melanie focused her attention on the frightened, battered little girl in the hospital bed. She was trying her best to reassure her and give her a feeling of being safe.

"Okay," April whispered. The next moment, her green eyes had shut and she'd fallen asleep.

Mitch frowned. "And just how are you going to manage to pull *that* off?" he asked.

Melanie shrugged, moving away from the bed. "I'll find a way."

He stared at her in disbelief. "You're serious." It was more of a stunned statement than a question.

Melanie never wavered. "Very."

Taking her by the arm, he drew her aside, not wanting anything he had to say to possibly be overheard by the little girl. Mitch shook his head.

"You can't just walk off with a kid anytime you feel like it," he pointed out.

"I'm not planning on 'walking off with her,'" Melanie protested heatedly. "I'm going to apply to be her foster mother. And then, when the time's right, I'm going to adopt her."

For a moment, he was at a loss for words. He had no idea where to begin to take apart this fantasy Melanie had constructed in her head.

"You're letting your emotions run away with you," he accused.

She wasn't about to argue that part with him. "Maybe. But the more I think about it, the more it just feels right." She could see he totally disagreed with her. She didn't need his permission, but getting his backing would help her. "Look, the social services system is overloaded right now and April is going to need to be taken care of until she makes a full recovery."

Melanie could get him exasperated faster than anyone he'd ever dealt with. "Yes, I know that, but that still doesn't change the fact that—"

She cut him off, needing to get him on her side. "If no one notifies Social Services, they won't know about her situation. Let me take care of her for a while," she implored him. "One step at a time, Mitch. First, she needs to get well."

Mitch dragged a hand through his hair. What she was proposing was insane, even though he knew why she was doing it.

"This is crazy, you know that, don't you?"

"It can be done," she insisted.

"All right, just how do you intend to provide for her?" he asked. April moaned. Afraid that his voice might be waking her up, he lowered it. "You're at the shelter everyday."

She'd already worked that out while sitting here, waiting for April to regain consciousness. "I can get my old job back. The principal at the school left the door open for me, told me I could come back anytime I wanted to. April gives me a reason to come back." She caught hold of his wrist, as if to anchor him in place until she could convince him to see things her way. "Please, Mitch. This little girl just lost everything. She and I have made a connection. Let me help her."

She was relentless, he'd give her that, Mitch thought with a weary sigh. Still, he gave talking her out of it one more try.

"Melanie, you've got a good heart," he began, "nobody's disputing that. But there are rules we're supposed to follow."

Melanie pressed her lips together, debating telling him something—and making him an accessory after the fact. After a moment, she decided to risk it, praying that he wouldn't give her away and that he would take her side.

"While I was sitting here, one of the hospital administrators came in with some paperwork for April that needed to be filled out. I put myself down as her next of kin."

He stared at her, stunned. "You did what?"

"I said I was her late mother's cousin." It was a vague enough connection, she thought. "All you have to do is not saying anything."

"So what you're telling me now isn't just a spur of the moment thing," he concluded.

His expression was dark. She had no idea if she'd just made a mistake. Would he give her away? "Like I said, I've had a while to think about it," she told him.

Mitch blew out a ragged breath as he glanced back at April for a moment, then back at Melanie. He could see that there was no talking her out of what she intended to do. If he tried to stand in her way, she'd probably find a way around it.

And, at bottom was the fact that she was right. Once in the system, April would be lost in it. He'd heard enough secondhand horror stories about the way children were treated to know he didn't want that happening to anyone, least of all a little girl whose crayon drawing resided on his refrigerator.

Looking at Melanie, he shook his head. “Like I said, you are the stubbornest woman I’ve ever met.”

And then he looked back at April. “Looks like the sedative I gave her earlier has kicked in.”

“You gave her a sedative?” Melanie questioned.

He nodded. “When I first came in. She needs to sleep in order to heal. I’m surprised she woke up just now. Looks like you and she are cut out of the same cloth,” he commented. “She’s going to be asleep until at least the morning. I’m going home,” he told Melanie. “Why don’t I drop you off at your place? No offense, but you look like hell.”

She laughed softly. “You do know how to flatter a girl.”

“Yes, I do,” he said. “But this isn’t one of those times. Now, if you want me to back up your story, you’re going to have to do as I say.”

Her eyes narrowed as she looked at him uncertainly. “Are you blackmailing me?”

Mitch never hesitated in his response. “As a matter of fact, yes I am.”

For a moment, he didn’t know whether or not to expect an argument from her. And then he saw her smile. “Then I guess I don’t have a choice.”

“No, you don’t,” he agreed.

Melanie hesitated as she paused for a moment longer to look at April. “I don’t want her waking up and finding herself alone.”

That was no problem. “I can have a nurse posted here with her. Anything else?”

She shook her head, suddenly incredibly weary.

Yesterday's events were finally catching up to her. "No, you seem to have covered all the bases."

"Good. Then let's go."

Mitch stopped at the nurse's station long enough to request that a nurse remain with April, saying he was worried that her fever might spike. If it did, he left instructions to be called immediately, regardless of the time.

That done, he took Melanie's arm and directed her toward the elevator. Pressing the down button, he asked in a low voice, "Satisfied?"

"Satisfied," she replied.

"I'm not biting off more than I can chew, you know," Melanie said in her own defense, breaking the silence in the car fifteen minutes after they had left the hospital parking lot.

They were almost at her door. She had debated saying nothing and just thanking him for the ride once he pulled up at the curb, but since Mitch *was* going along with her request to, in effect, become April's guardian, she felt as if she did owe him some sort of assurance about what she was doing.

Lost in his own thoughts about April and the woman he was, by virtue of his silence, agreeing to lie for, he didn't hear what Melanie had just said.

"What?"

"I know that's what you're thinking," she told him. "That I'm biting off more than I can chew, but I'm not," she said emphatically. "I've always wanted to have children."

"There is a more traditional route to that end, you know," he pointed out.

She knew he meant getting married. "I wanted to, but it didn't work out," she said, her tone indicating that she wanted to leave it at that.

He knew Melanie was referring to her late fiancé and out of deference to her, he didn't pursue the matter. It was none of his business anyway, he reminded himself. If she wanted to take on the responsibility of taking care of the little girl, maybe it was for the best for both of them. He'd done his part. He'd put April back together. Melanie could supply the love that was needed.

But as he pulled up at the curb before Melanie's house, he saw that she was trembling.

Turning off the engine, he shifted to look at her. "Are you all right?"

"It's just been a hard eighteen hours," she replied. "And I'm tired." The last thing she wanted was for him to think she was falling apart. It was bad enough that she felt as if she was. She'd get this under control, she promised herself. To her surprise, Mitch got out of the car, came around to her side and opened her door. She looked down at the hand he held out for her. "I can get out on my own power."

"Maybe," he allowed. "But I'm still walking you to your house."

This whole thing with April being at the brink of death and then being revived had brought back memories. Memories that made her feel vulnerable. She didn't think that having him walk her to her home was a particularly good idea.

She needed to put distance between them now, while she still could.

"You don't have to. Really. I'll be all right."

He leaned into the vehicle, his hand still out. "Humor me."

She could see that he wasn't about to be talked out of it. All she needed to do was keep it together a little while longer, Melanie told herself, and then she'd be home free.

Resigned, Melanie got out of his car and then walked ahead of him to her front door. Turning around to face him, she gestured at it.

"Well, here it is, the door."

"Unlock it," he told her.

He was really making this hard for her. "You said you want to walk me to my door and you did. Chivalrous obligation met."

"No, I said that I was walking you to your house. That means I want you to open the door and go inside," he told her sternly. "I don't want to hear a story on the local morning news about the heart-of-gold volunteer who passed out in front of her front door."

"What are you talking about?" she demanded.

He pointed out the obvious. "You're still trembling."

Melanie shrugged indifferently. "I'm cold," she lied.

Mitch frowned. He wasn't buying her excuse. "Then you're coming down with something because it's really pretty warm tonight."

This wasn't getting her anywhere and she could feel herself weakening. Could feel herself growing more and more in need of the feel of strong arms around her, holding back the darkness.

"Fine, I'll unlock the door." Inserting the key into the lock, she turned it, then opened the door.

Turning around in her front foyer, Melanie started to ask him if he was satisfied. But the words never materialized. Instead, just as she was afraid of, the full impact of the past few emotional hours hit her.

The thought of what could have been April's fate if they hadn't arrived at the accident when they did and if Mitch hadn't been the skilled surgeon that he was hit her full force and she began to cry.

As a rule, Mitch avoided being around a woman's tears. They made him uncomfortable and he had no idea how to even begin to offer any sort of words of comfort or condolences.

But the past several hours had definitely left their mark on him. He had fought death and won—and he wouldn't have if not for Melanie and her refusal to give up.

Moreover, because of Melanie and her almost militant cheerfulness, the past several weeks had left an impression on him, as well. She'd softened him, filing down his hard edges. So rather than mumble some inane words of comfort that he neither felt nor believed, or offer Melanie the handkerchief he had stuffed into his pocket, Mitch found himself crossing the threshold, closing the door with his elbow and taking her into his arms.

He held her close to him as she cried, moving his hands along her back soothingly.

And somewhere in those first couple of minutes, something came completely loose within him, as well.

"It's going to be all right," he told her. "The worst part is over. She's lost her mother and her brother, but she has you and you'll help her heal. We both will," he added quietly.

Melanie raised her head from his chest, tears staining both her cheeks. Mitch had said the one thing that made her feel less alone. Rather than abating her tears, he'd just made them flow more freely. But now they were tears of relief mingled with joy. "You really think so?"

Why hadn't he realized how beautiful she was before? "I do," he told her softly.

"You're the one who really saved her."

He knew he would have given up when he'd thought April was dead. Melanie was as responsible for April being alive today as he was.

"And you made her realize she's not alone. It's a joint effort," he concluded.

"You really believe that?" she asked in a whisper.

"I do."

And then, because he couldn't seem to help himself, he lowered his head and kissed her.

He only meant to brush his lips against hers, to comfort Melanie more than anything else—or so he told himself. But kissing her reminded him just how attracted he really was to her.

He realized now that all along, he'd tried to bury it, to deny it and to talk himself out of it every time he felt things stirring within him—like when he'd kissed her in the exam room.

And all the while, he'd tried to keep her at arm's length. But the tragedy that had befallen April's family and then the battle to save her life had unleashed all his tightly wound emotions. He'd forgotten what it was like to actually *feel* something, what it was like to immerse himself in another person and to allow his emotions to flower.

So, for just a moment, he went with the moment, telling himself he was in complete control—until he realized that he wasn't. Because if he had been in complete control, he could have stopped himself, walked away from what was happening with a few well-placed words and made his way back to his car.

And driven away like the very devil was after him.

But any plans for a quick getaway evaporated in the heat of his desire. The more he kissed Melanie, the more he *needed* to kiss her until the matter was entirely out of his system. He found himself caught up in a sea he couldn't begin to navigate.

It all came racing back to her.

She'd forgotten what it was like. Forgotten what it felt like to be a woman with a woman's needs. Forgotten how it felt to be wanted.

His kiss had brought it all back to her.

She had no illusions. This wasn't something with "forever" attached to it. This was a onetime deal because he had saved April's life and she just desperately needed to make human contact again. To shed all her concerns, her fears and all the dark, shadowy things that haunted her days and her nights, consciously or otherwise.

Just for tonight, she wanted to make love and to be made love to. Tomorrow she would go back to her austere world, knowing there was nothing else waiting for her. Not in this venue, not ever.

But that didn't matter because tomorrow there would be a little girl waiting who needed her. Someone to whom she mattered. Someone who depended on her—and that was more than enough.

But tonight, well tonight she needed something else, something more.

She needed to revisit the ability to have fiery passions explode within her, to just be a woman alone with a man.

So when Mitch's lips touched hers, at first softly, then with more heat, more passion, she kissed him back. And then she kissed him again and again, each kiss more demanding than the last, until she lost all track of just who was seducing whom.

All she knew was that for the duration of the evening, it felt wonderful and she was grateful to Mitch for everything.

For being able to feel normal and real again.

Inhibitions and clothing came off and with each layer, something wondrous took a firmer hold. She shuddered with pleasure as he ran his hands along her body, and she kissed him with passion as a frenzy seemed to take hold of her.

Maybe she'd known all along that this was waiting for her. Maybe that was why she'd backtracked on several occasions, afraid of getting closer to him, afraid of where it might lead because there was always a price to pay for feeling like this and she didn't want to ever be in that position again.

But even so, she couldn't deny what her body already knew. That she was very attracted to this man, not just physically, but emotionally, as well. She saw that he tried to keep a distance between himself and everyone he ministered to—and yet he had gotten involved nonetheless. He had stepped out of his comfort zone for her, for April and for the people at the shelter.

That was a kindness she found even sexier than his handsome face and athletic body. He was a package deal and for the evening, he was hers and she was his.

Chapter Fourteen

It seemed clichéd and almost absurd to Mitch. He knew he would have been skeptical if someone had been relaying all this to him as something *they* were going through.

But he had never felt this way before.

Moreover, he had never believed it was *possible* to feel like this, like something inside of him had suddenly lit up and was close to, Lord help him, singing.

Certainly he could have sworn that there was *music* humming through his veins.

Music as well as an overwhelming need to not just unite with this woman, but to just *be* with her without anything physical happening at all.

He had never felt that way before, never thought that people, that *he,* could feel like this before. But rays of light and something akin to sunshine seemed to be shining all through him. Whatever it was—and he was fairly convinced that it was *her*—he didn't want it to stop, to change or go away even though it meant, most likely, saving himself in the end.

Cradling her against him, he kissed Melanie over and over again, finding himself desiring more with each kiss rather than drawing closer to the point of satiating himself.

His excitement heightening each time he kissed not just her lips but every single part of her soft, yielding and heating body. With each pulsating moment, he felt more and more as if he had crossed some sort of a line, going from a place he was vaguely familiar with to a place he hadn't believed existed. A place that seemed to welcome him with both arms.

A place he never wanted to leave ever again.

He knew he had to be going crazy.

He didn't care.

Finally, close to the brink, he moved his primed and more than ready body over hers. His eyes locking with hers, Mitch took the final step and united them.

His entire body pleaded for instant release but he went about it slowly.

Gently.

Bringing the union to an ever faster growing, more intense rhythm.

And as it increased, he could feel her response, could hear her breathing becoming more rapid, more ragged. The very sound of that brought his own excitement to an even higher level.

Joined together in the most intimate of dances two people could undertake, the tempo seemed to increase of its own accord until they reached the peak together—he could tell by the way she grasped onto his shoulders, arched her body into his and moaned his name that she was climaxing at the exact same moment as he was.

Enraptured by the moment, he found to his surprise that he was more taken with her reaction than just his alone. That was different and once he would have thought that there was something wrong, but he had never felt anything so right in his life as this eternal moment he was sharing with her.

And then it was over, fading into the very air around him.

Spiraling downward, he held on to her, shifting his position so that she was resting her face against his chest.

Words still failed him, but words weren't necessary here. Not when the touch of his hand along her hair conveyed the very intensity of what he was experiencing this second with her.

So they lay there, separated from time and the rest of the world for this very short, very precious interlude. And he held her and just absorbed the goodness of the moment and of the woman who was in his arms, lying against his heart.

Melanie had lost track of time.

Raising her head, she looked at Mitch, almost afraid of what she would see.

But there was no smug expression, no look of distance in his eyes the way there had been when she had first met him. There was a look she had never seen before and she was afraid to put a name to it because she knew what she was hoping for. Something that she had already accepted as not possible.

Not from him—and, besides, she had told herself that above all else, she didn't want it. Didn't want it because she didn't trust it. She knew all the pitfalls that were waiting for her if she did truly become involved with a man. The exhilaration of love—my Lord, was she actually even *thinking* in those terms?—had a very dark downside to it.

It was bitter, burning and she wanted no part of it.

And yet, what was the point of life without it?

"Well, that was unplanned," Mitch murmured as he ran his hand along her silky hair in a movement that was not quite possessive and yet definitely not indifferent.

"I didn't mean for that to happen," Melanie said defensively.

At least, she hadn't meant for it to happen in the absolute sense, she thought.

All of this was a result of an incredible moment of weakness on her part and in no way had she *ever* expected him to respond with this amount of intensity.

And she certainly hadn't expected him to have rocked her world the way he had.

She supposed that at best she had hoped for a few minutes of diversion that would in turn help her stop hurting and caring and just respond on a basic, automatic level.

In no way had she expected something of this magnitude to affect her.

"Well, I did." It was as if he had stepped out of his own body and was watching all this at a respectful distance. Supervising events rather than actually being involved in them.

And yet, what else could he possibly call it? He

was involved. He, who almost took *pride* in being removed, was involved.

Mitch raised her chin with the crook of his forefinger until their eyes met. "Are you sorry?" he asked.

His eyes seemed to look straight into her soul. She couldn't lie, not when he was looking at her like that. "No."

"Then stop talking," he told her.

His hand along the white column of her throat, he tilted her head back and captured her mouth with his just for a moment.

Or so he had thought.

But just as before, a moment stretched out into two which multiplied into four. And that just continued at a breathtaking pace as he found himself wanting her all over again, even more than the first time.

Mitch was completely stunned by the event and completely captivated by the woman he had initially taken into his arms a small eternity ago.

The second time turned out to be as wondrous as the first. He knew what to expect and yet was still stunned by what he was feeling.

Once was a complete surprise.

To feel that twice bordered on a miracle as far as he was concerned. And he knew he wasn't feeling this because he was overworked or overwhelmed by the intensity of what had happened with April.

Granted, he was tired, but he was still far from wiped out—which would have been his go-to excuse for feeling like this.

So what, really, was going on here? If he were

being honest with himself, Mitch knew that he was almost leery of finding out.

It was enough that it had happened and that he was lying there, in the dark, with her in his arms.

Just then, his phone went off.

Both of them jackknifed up in bed in unison to the jarring sound.

"April?" Melanie asked, fear lacing itself around her voice.

Guilt instantly raised its head. What kind of a person was she, to seek refuge in a physical coupling, not once but *twice* while that poor child was lying in a hospital bed, very possibly still closer to death than not.

Mitch reached for his cell phone. "I do still have a day job," he reminded her. He glanced down at the caller ID. "And I think it's calling me. Dr. Stewart," he said, his voice formal as he swiped his phone and answered it.

She could feel the distance coming between them as Mitch listened quietly to whoever was on the other end of the line.

Not only did the man have a day job, she silently upbraided herself, but in all likelihood, he probably had a full life, as well. Just because he had never mentioned it to her didn't mean he didn't have one. He hadn't mentioned a great many things to her.

She knew very little about the man. For all she knew, he was involved with someone already.

No. If he were, she'd know. She was certain that she'd know. He would have allowed something to slip, allowed a telltale piece of information about his personal life to surface.

This was a man who had no personal life. She would have sworn to it.

After all, she couldn't be *that* bad a judge of character, could she?

Melanie watched as he terminated the call. "You have to go," she said. It wasn't a question.

"Van versus truck," he recounted simply.

Her stomach churned just thinking about the incident. "Anyone left alive?"

He nodded. "So far, according to the hospital, all four drivers and passengers."

She slid to the edge of the bed, ready to throw her clothes on at a moment's notice and follow. All he had to do was say the word.

"Can I do anything to help?" she asked.

"Not unless you're a nurse," he answered matter-of-factly as he hurried into his clothes.

"I can pray," she replied simply.

Then, out of the corner of his eye, he saw Melanie getting her clothes together, then quickly getting dressed, as well.

"You need clothes to pray?" he asked, mildly curious as to what she was really up to.

"No, but I need clothes to get back into the hospital," she answered, pulling her hair out of the collar of her pullover. "They frown upon naked people unless they happen to be lying on one of their operating tables."

Mitch stopped putting his shoes on for a moment. "I said there's nothing you can do," he reminded her.

"Not for the people you're going to be operating on who were involved in that awful accident, but I can go back to the hospital in case April wakes up earlier than we thought she would."

"I left a nurse with her, remember? And you need your rest," he told her seriously. "Doctor's orders."

Something warm and precious moved within her and she smiled up at him. "You're not my doctor," she told him sweetly, and then added, "Besides, I rested."

Mitch raised a dubious eyebrow. "When?" he asked. "Seems to me that wasn't exactly the most rest-provoking endeavor we were engaged in just a little while ago."

"Maybe not restful," she allowed, slipping the remainder of her clothing on, "but definitely energizing which, on some levels, is even better," she concluded with a satisfied smile.

Ready, Mitch paused for a moment to study her. He was definitely getting to know sides of her that hadn't been evident initially, but this was something that had been there right from the start.

"What was it you said you were before you took your leave of absence?" he asked her.

She might have mentioned it in passing, but she had never been specific about it. "A second-grade teacher. Why?"

"You sure you weren't really a lawyer?" he asked, pretending to scrutinize her closely. "Because you use words like a weapon and you're stubborn, all useful skills for a top-grade lawyer."

"And a teacher," she told him. "You would be surprised how devious some of those innocent-looking second graders can be."

"Maybe not so surprised," he qualified, pausing to give her a fleeting kiss. It was all he could trust himself to do at the moment. Anything even slightly deeper and he'd be sorely tempted to linger with her a little while longer. Time in his chosen profession was always of the essence.

"Okay," she announced as he headed for the door and she fell into step beside him, "if I can get you to swing by the shelter, I can pick up my car." Opening the front door, Mitch looked at her blankly for a moment, not following her. "When this all started, you took me out to dinner from the shelter in your car."

She'd followed the ambulance in his car and had remained at the hospital with April until he'd driven her home in his car. She hadn't seen her own vehicle in all that time.

"As far as I know, my car is still parked there." Melanie saw him glancing at his watch and realized that time, as it had been with April, was of tantamount importance. "Or I can always call a cab to bring me to the shelter."

He waved away her offer. "No, it's just a little out of the way," Mitch told her, doing a quick calculation. "As long as you're ready."

"So completely ready," she declared, grabbing her purse.

"Okay," he responded.

The thing was he really didn't know if he was. Ready for her, that was. She was taking him to a brand-new place, one he liked but one that also made him wary.

It could be a matter of something being too good to be true. And yet, all he could think about was getting back here, back to her. Back to making love with her.

What the hell was going on here?

He didn't know, couldn't explain. All he could do, with luck, was ride the wave.

Getting from the shelter to the hospital proved a little trickier for Melanie than getting from point A to point B. That was strictly because point A came with a large amount of people who had questions for her.

The moment she was spotted in the shelter's parking lot, about to get into her vehicle, she was seen by several of the children who were playing in the designated playground area. The latter consisted of little more than a couple of swings and an old-fashioned sandbox, but the area was well populated and the moment the children saw Melanie, they came running out to shower her with questions. Everyone wanted to know how April was doing.

Their raised voices and the volley of nonstop questions attracted some of the mothers residing at the shelter and soon Melanie found herself answering questions coming from adults instead of children.

She was aware that the director had come to the hospital to look in on April herself—she'd seen the woman in April's room—but as for the other women, though concerned, they were relying on the reports of others to satisfy their questions.

Melanie didn't want to seem rude, so consequently it took her a bit of time before she could get away. The upshot was that it took Melanie far longer to get to the hospital than she was happy about.

Coming into the little girl's room, she found that April was sound asleep. Whether she was still asleep from when she had initially left her or had woken up and then fallen back to sleep, Melanie had no way of knowing—but she intended to find out.

The nurse that Mitch had left in the room was not there, which really concerned her.

Going to the nurse's station on that floor, Melanie was about to ask after the nurse's whereabouts. At that moment, her cell phone vibrated.

Taking it out, she experienced an eerie moment of uneasiness, as if in anticipation of something major. Melanie glanced down to see that the call was coming from within the hospital. Which was odd.

"Hello?" she asked uncertainly.

"Hello, Ms. McAdams?" a rather young female voice asked.

Melanie had no idea why her stomach instantly tightened the way it did. "Yes?"

"This is Jennifer Donnelly," the caller told her, identifying herself. "The nurse involved in this matter said I should give you a call. I'm from Social Services and this is about April O'Neill. You're familiar with that name?"

Melanie could feel her heart all but constricting within her chest. This was what she'd supposedly been waiting for. But rather than having a case of nerves, the way she'd anticipated, she could feel her temper surging in her chest.

"Yes," she replied evenly. "Of course I know April O'Neill—"

"We were informed that her mother was killed two days ago by a hit-and-run driver. With no father in the picture, she automatically becomes our responsibility. However, the nurse insisted that before we begin any paperwork to take custody, I call you. To be honest, I'm not exactly sure why."

Melanie's hand tightened on her cell phone. "Well, that's really very simple, Ms. Donnelly," she heard herself saying. "She told you that because I'm April O'Neill's next of kin."

Good luck in pulling this off, Melanie thought to herself.

Chapter Fifteen

There was a momentary silence on the other end of the cell phone.

Melanie knew she'd hit the woman with something she hadn't been expecting, even though, if the social worker had looked at the hospital forms that she had filled out for April, Donnelly would have realized that April was not the orphan that she was perceived to be.

"Well, that certainly is a reason to call you," Donnelly agreed, the woman's voice sounding a bit too chipper to her for her peace of mind. "When can we get together?"

Melanie would have loved to have had a few hours to get her act together. Certainly she could have used at least that much time to make herself look presentable instead of probably something a self-respecting cat might hesitate to drag in.

But apparently she wasn't about to have that luxury. Melanie had this very uneasy feeling that if she put this so-called meeting off she would wind up regretting it.

"Now is fine."

It was obviously the right answer because it met with Donnelly's approval.

"All right. Now it is," the woman told Melanie. "We can meet in the chapel. I'm told it's empty at the moment. I can be there in ten minutes."

"So can I," Melanie said, her stomach sinking to new depths.

Melanie arrived at the chapel before the other woman. Her nerves barely had time to settle down before Jennifer Donnelly entered the small, welcoming nondenominational chapel.

The social worker looked to be a little older than she was, Melanie observed. She also looked as if she was the epitome of efficiency, to the possible exclusion of actual sympathy. That worried Melanie.

But she wasn't about to walk out of this chapel until she was granted some sort of custody of April no matter how long it took, that much she knew.

Indicating a pew, Donnelly sat down after she took a seat. The cool, dark eyes made no secret that the social worker was sizing her up.

Her voice was distant, reserved when she finally spoke. "I just want you to understand that I am doing this out of a sense of decency since there is no requirement for anyone in the department to notify perfect strangers as to our intentions regarding a child who comes to our attention. As soon as April is back on her feet, Social Services will be taking custody of her since she has no next of kin as far as we can see," Donnelly informed her with finality, underscoring the last six words.

"You can't do that," Melanie cried.

The more agitated Melanie sounded, the more reserved the other woman became. "And why not?"

"Because she and I have built up a rapport since she first got to the shelter." Her mind scrambling, Melanie remembered the form she'd filled out when April was admitted and what she'd told the woman to bring this meeting about. Why was Donnelly "conveniently" forgetting about that? "And like I told you, I'm April's next of kin."

The social worker's small mouth twisted into a sneer. "Oh, really? Well, we have no record of you." It was clear by her tone that she expected there to be some sort of record since in this day and age, there was a great deal of information available in cyberspace to back up a claim one way or another.

Desperate, Melanie was making it up as she went along. "This only came up recently. Her mother—Brenda—and I lost track of one another for a long time. She was my cousin. Her mother, I mean."

"I see." It was obvious by her expression that Donnelly didn't believe any of it.

The way she was tapping a file in her hand, Melanie had a feeling that the woman had already done some extensive research into April's background. Or as extensive as was possible, given the situation, Melanie thought, mentally crossing her fingers.

Was there something in that file about her, as well? That she worked at the shelter and nothing more? Melanie anxiously searched her brain for something to work with. She couldn't allow April to be taken into the system or she would never see the little girl again. She couldn't bear losing April, losing someone else. That just couldn't happen to her twice. She wouldn't let it.

"So, which is it?" Donnelly asked sarcastically. "You've built up this rapport with April or you're her long-lost cousin, twice removed?"

Melanie raised her chin. Chapel or not, she wasn't about to take this quietly. "I don't think I like your tone."

Donnelly's eyes narrowed with contempt. "Doesn't matter what you like, Ms. McAdams. I represent the best interests of the child."

The hell she did. "So, taking her from the only environment she is familiar with and has learned to trust and throwing her in with a bunch of strangers where she'll be frightened is in her best interests?" Melanie demanded heatedly.

Donnelly drew herself up indignantly. "Ms. McAdams, you have no idea how many people out there pose as one thing and are something else entirely. All they want to do is get their hands on an innocent child and, best-case scenario, they want to use that child for a meal ticket in order to get extra money." The woman paused for half a second. "Worst case, well, I don't even want to get into that."

"My point entirely," Melanie stressed. "My first, my *only* concern, is April."

The expression on the social worker's face said she highly doubted that. "Then let the professionals do their job."

At a loss, Melanie tried another approach to attempt to gain custody of the little girl. "So, you have a home waiting for her right now?"

Annoyance furrowed the almost perfect brow. "No, but—"

"Well, I do," Melanie said, cutting in. "A good, clean, loving home."

The look Donnelly gave her could have easily cut a lesser woman dead in her tracks. "I was about to say that not yet, but by the time April is released from the hospital, arrangements will be made."

Yeah, she'd bet. She'd heard enough horror stories from some of the single mothers at the shelter about the battles they had to wage in order to regain custody of their own children. Some of them were still fighting the court.

"No disrespect as to your 'arrangements,'" Melanie told the woman, "but April won't know any of these people you're thinking of placing her with."

Thin shoulders shrugged indifferently. "An unfortunate situation, I admit, but—"

"She knows me," Melanie insisted. "She feels *safe* with me." Melanie continued, praying some of this was sinking into the woman's hard heart. "I stayed in her hospital room from the time they found her in the street until she woke up. Run any background check on me you want," she challenged. "I have a spotless record and I love her."

Donnelly pressed impatient lips together. It was clear she didn't like wasting time this way. Her next words indicated that some checking into her background had already been done, most likely because of what she'd filled in on the hospital forms. The woman came prepared, Melanie thought in despair.

"You have no source of income, Ms. McAdams. How do you intend to help pay for this child—or are you banking on Social Services to take care of that little detail for you?" she asked contemptuously. "For that matter, if we granted you temporary foster-care custody, how would we even *know* that the money intended for April would go to April?"

It was obvious from the way she spoke that Donnelly was all too familiar with that aspect of cheating within the system.

The woman was talking down to her. Melanie struggled to hold on to her temper as she tried to clear up the numerous misunderstandings. "Number one, I am on a leave of absence—"

"According to our records," Donnelly said, cutting her off, "you quit."

"Your records don't go deep enough," Melanie countered. "I tried to quit, but my principal wouldn't let me. She talked me into taking a leave of absence instead and told me my job would be waiting for me when I was ready to come back."

"Your quitting only proves how unstable you are," Donnelly pointed out with almost relish. "April needs a stable environment—"

She should have known this wouldn't have been the end of it. The social worker wouldn't be satisfied until she wound up cutting her up into little pieces.

"My fiancé was killed overseas by a suicide bomber four days before he was scheduled to come home to me for our *wedding*. Tell me, Ms. Donnelly, how would *you* have held up under that?" Melanie challenged angrily. "And I didn't just run off, I came to the homeless shelter to volunteer full-time so that I could feel that at least I was being useful to someone."

The woman was momentarily at a loss as to how to answer. Then, taking a breath, to Melanie's surprise Donnelly said in a somewhat kinder tone, "Be that as it may, there is still the matter of your financial situation—"

Melanie cut her off. "Look, I don't want to be April's foster mother and have you people paying me for taking care of her. I want to take her in so I can adopt her," she emphasized. Why couldn't the woman get that through her head?

Donnelly closed her eyes, as if searching for patience. "Yes, because you're this long-lost relative—"

"Because I love her," Melanie stressed, banking down her anger.

"And if we did this extensive background check you said you wanted and found that you're not related to April's mother at all?" Donnelly challenged. The look on her face said what she knew the outcome of that check would be.

Melanie rose to her feet, ready to just walk out before she really lost her temper and exploded.

"Aren't you listening?" Melanie cried. "I want to *adopt* her. Most people who adopt children aren't related to them. Most of the time, they haven't even had time to develop a relationship with the child before they adopt them. April and I have—"

"—bonded, yes, so you said," Donnelly said in a singsong voice. "Still—"

"Is there a problem here?"

Melanie could have sobbed when she heard Mitch's voice coming from behind her. She swung around immediately and had to struggle not to throw her arms around his neck out of pure relief.

Finally someone to back her up.

She had no idea what he could say that she hadn't, but the very fact that he was a surgeon here at the hospital and not just *any* surgeon, but one with a rather well-known reputation, meant that this woman from hell had to listen to him.

Didn't she?

Donnelly rose to her feet instantly. "No problem here, Doctor," the woman said crisply, but with an obvious respect that had been missing from her voice when she spoke to Melanie. "Ms. McAdams here is taking exception to the Department of Social Services taking custody of one of the patients here."

Mitch's somber expression was almost intimidating, Melanie thought and for once, she was extremely glad of that.

"April O'Neill, yes I know," he replied.

Donnelly's dark, probing eyes took complete measure of the man in front of her before she spoke. "Then you are familiar with the little girl?"

"I should be," Mitch informed the woman. "I operated on her. Prior to that, I treated her and Jimmy, her late brother, at the Bedford Rescue Mission."

"I see. Very kind of you—" Donnelly began, about to use the throwaway line as a transition to get to the heart of her subject. It was obvious that she felt flattery was the way to get on his good side.

The social worker had a thing or two to learn about the man, Melanie thought.

"Kindness had nothing to do with it, Ms. Donnelly." The nurse who had alerted him about the social worker meeting with Melanie at the chapel had given him the woman's name. "Especially in the beginning." He glanced at Melanie. "That, I think you should know, was all Ms. McAdams's doing. I'd initially volunteered for what I thought would be a single visit to the shelter. It was Ms. McAdams who came to the hospital, found me and literally *dragged* me back over to the shelter to impress upon me just how necessary it was for a physician to make regular visits there so that the women and children residing at the shelter could receive proper care and proper follow-up care."

At the time Melanie's presumption had irritated the hell out of him, but now that he looked back at it, that had been the beginning of his own transformation.

"We have programs—" the woman began rather indignantly, apparently taking what he was saying as an attack on her department's services.

Unable to hold her tongue any longer, Melanie interjected, "Which their pride keeps them from utilizing."

"Oh, and bringing a doctor to them is different?" Donnelly asked sarcastically, directing the question at her.

"Yes, it is," Melanie retorted. "If he's right there, they can't very well avoid him. And more importantly, Dr. Stewart doesn't make them feel like they're charity cases. That's often the problem when they go to some authorized clinic on the other side of town to see doctors who would rather be somewhere else, getting paid what they felt they were actually worth. It makes them feel as if they're worthless inconveniences instead of normal human beings who just happen to have fallen on hard times—sometimes through no fault of their own," Melanie pointed out with feeling.

"A volunteer who comes to *them* wants to see them and the whole atmosphere between doctor and patient is different. The patients *trust* the doctor which in turn helps him treat them effectively," Melanie concluded.

Donnelly blew out a skeptical breath. "And this is your story," the woman asked Mitch.

Mitch never wavered. Instead, he met her gaze head on. "Quite honestly, it wasn't before, but it is now. Ms. McAdams has made me remember the real reason why I became a doctor in the first place."

He'd spent enough time waltzing around with this irritating woman, Mitch thought. He got down to the crux of the reason he'd come to the chapel. To back Melanie up any way he could.

"Now, I understand that there is a problem about her taking custody of April once the little girl is released from the hospital—which won't be for at least several days if not longer," he emphasized. "She sustained a number of serious internal injuries. Frankly," he interjected because he saw this as being of tantamount importance in this custody case that was erupting, "we thought we lost her. She stopped breathing at the scene of the accident. It was Ms. McAdams who refused to give up on her even when April's heart stopped beating. She continued holding on to April, pleading with her to come back to us. I had almost managed to get Ms. McAdams to let go of her when April opened her eyes."

Donnelly's skepticism mushroomed. "Ah, so perhaps I should add Miracle Worker to Ms. McAdams's résumé," she said, her voice dripping with sarcasm.

Mitch's expression never changed. Remaining stony, it was almost unnerving. Melanie could see Donnelly eyeing him nervously.

"I think that most of us would agree that faith, no matter how clichéd it sounds, works in mysterious ways," Mitch said. "I know it was an eye-opener for me. Now, I can give you a written recommendation for Ms. McAdams in order to make this custody thing happen. I can also get you a statement, if necessary, from the chief administrator of this hospital." When Donnelly made no response, he went on to say, "I also know several heads of—"

Donnelly held up a hand as if in mute surrender. "Not necessary," the social worker told him. "Your statement is more than sufficient, Doctor." She glanced at Melanie, obvious less than happy about the fact that she had to concede the battle to her. As a parting shot, Donnelly said, "It might help matters if Ms. McAdams was married, but—"

"That is in the offing, as well," Mitch told her in a quiet, serious voice, cutting her off.

It took considerable concentrated effort on Melanie's part to keep her jaw from dropping. She had to remind herself that Mitch was saying a great many things right now just to make the woman back off and go away and for that she would be eternally grateful.

Jennifer Donnelly was a bulldog when she needed to be, but she also knew when she was outgunned and defeated. And she was now.

"I'll get to the paperwork right away." Donnelly put her hand out to Melanie. It wasn't a heartfelt gesture, but it was as genuine as she could manage. "Congratulations, Ms. McAdams. A lot of paperwork has to be finalized but it looks like you have yourself a little girl." The smile that followed the statement could be called nothing short of spasmodic.

"Thank you," Melanie answered with relief and enthusiasm. "I'll take excellent care of her. This *is* for her best interests."

Donnelly couldn't resist one final sniff. "So I am told," she said, looking directly at Mitch. "I'll be back with the papers in the morning."

"I'll be here," Melanie assured her. The moment the woman had left the chapel, she turned to Mitch. "Do you actually *know* all those people you just offered to get letters from?"

There was no change in his expression. "I do."

Okay, maybe he did, but that still didn't touch the important issue. "But they wouldn't go as far as give me a statement of recommendation—"

"They would," he told her without fanfare. "They don't like bureaucracy any better than I do. And if their letters failed to do the trick, I could always sic my mother on that woman. *That* would definitely do it. My mother is one gutsy little lady." A smile curved the corners of his mouth as he looked at Melanie. "Kind of like someone else I know," he told her.

"Thank you," Melanie said, suddenly choking up. Tears were coming at an unstoppable rate, sliding down her cheeks and threatening to go on indefinitely.

Sitting back down in the pew, Mitch took her into his arms and held her until she could regain control of herself.

"No," he told her quietly when her tears finally subsided, "Thank *you*. I meant what I said. If it wasn't for you, I wouldn't have been volunteering at the shelter, which means I wouldn't have been there in time to save April—and even then, if not for you, April would have been lost. You opened my eyes to a great many things," he told her.

Melanie wiped her eyes and did what she could to pull herself together. She glanced in the direction that the social worker had taken.

"She'll be back, you know," she said. "In the morning, like she said."

"I know," he told her. "I never doubted it for a moment. Her kind always is. But I'll be here to back you up, just like I said. In writing, in spirit, in any way you need. If she wants letters of recommendation, she'll get them." And then he had a question for her. "You know for a fact that you have that job waiting for you at your old school?"

Melanie nodded. "Absolutely. The principal still calls me on occasion to check in and see how I'm doing. I spoke to her about a week and a half ago, told her I was slowly getting there."

Taking it in, Mitch nodded. "Good, although not entirely necessary," he went on to tell her. When she looked at him quizzically, he explained, "The factor here as far as Social Services is concerned is money—"

Melanie thought she knew what he was about to say. "No," she told him firmly.

His brow furrowed. "No?"

Melanie backtracked, knowing she'd jumped the gun but fairly confident she hadn't guessed wrong. "If you're about to tell me you'll lend me whatever money you think they want in my bank account, the answer's no. I won't take any money from you."

Mitch's expression was unreadable as he murmured, "I see."

"You've done too much for me already," Melanie insisted. "You saved April—twice," she emphasized. "Once right after the accident and just now." As far as she was concerned, that was twice he'd brought the little girl back to her. "I can never repay you for either time, but that doesn't mean I'm not going to really try." She went on to explain her reasoning. "Borrowing money from you would only make the debt that much more huge," she told him.

"Are you finished?" Mitch asked mildly when she finally paused for breath and stopped talking for a moment.

Melanie inclined her head. "Yes."

He looked into her eyes, as if expecting to find his answer there. "You're sure?"

"Yes." Impatience rimmed itself around the single word.

"Okay, because I wasn't going to offer to lend you money—" Mitch started to tell her. He didn't get any further.

"I won't *take* any from you, either," she said with feeling, guessing that he was going to just make it a matter of semantics.

He gave her what she thought was a reproving look, the kind a teacher would give a particularly trying student after being tested yet again. "I thought you said you were finished."

"Okay. Yes, *now* I'm finished," she told him. Melanie saw him looking at her as if he was waiting for her to add a PS to her statement. "Totally," she added by way of a closing. Since he was still waiting for a better sign, she crossed her heart to seal the deal.

"Satisfied?" she asked.

His nod was her answer. "All right. I wasn't going to offer to lend—or *give*—you money," Mitch told her, his tone quiet, subdued. "What I was going to do was ask you to marry me."

Melanie was utterly and completely stunned, not to mention speechless.

Chapter Sixteen

"Not right now," Mitch quickly qualified when Melanie said nothing. He didn't want her to think that he was in any way rushing her. "I mean, I'm asking you now, but I'm not asking you to marry me now."

He saw confusion slipping over her features. He found himself *really* wishing he had better communication skills.

"Not coming out very well, I know, but then, I never exactly pictured myself being in this position, either. Asking someone to marry me," he specified. "I was fine just the way I was. Or, at least I *thought* I was fine just the way I was," Mitch added. "What I'm asking you to do is *think* about marrying me. Doesn't have to be today, next week or even next month. I just want you to *think* about the idea.

"I won't lie to you, I've been trying to talk myself

out of this ever since I first experienced this strange, overwhelming feeling. I thought it was my imagination, or just the result of being on overload, a byproduct of the marathon stressful situation I found myself under—double shifts, volunteer work," he went on to explain. "But the more I tried to tell myself this, this *excuse*, the more I realized that I was just rationalizing, and doing a damn bad job of it."

He smiled at her, wondering how he'd gotten so lucky without even trying. "I realized that I was actually *feeling* what some people spend their whole lives chasing after and never feeling. I love you," he told her in case there was some confusion about what he meant. "And now, I need to know how you feel." He summoned his courage and put it all on the line. For perhaps the first time in his life, he was scared, scared he wouldn't hear what he desperately needed to hear. "I need to know if you love me."

Melanie pressed her lips together, struggling to keep her tears back. Crying would only add to the stress here. "I don't want to love you."

Mitch nodded, but that wasn't what he had asked. "I get that." He understood, or thought he did, the depth of her fear, the sheer terror of being afraid of having her heart ripped out again because someone she loved was taken from her. Which made her love all the more precious if she could just risk it. Risk it for him. "But do you?"

"Yes," she admitted quietly, looking down at the floor. She tried to turn away, but he gently placed his hands on her shoulders and forced Melanie to look up at him.

He looked into her eyes, confident that he would

see the truth no matter what she actually tried to say, or tell him.

"You love me." It was half a question, half a hopeful statement.

She closed her eyes and sighed, as if saying the words out loud were hurtful to her, as well as setting her up for an entire ocean of pain down the line.

"Yes."

"Open your eyes and look at me, Melanie. Please," he added when she was slow to comply. Melanie opened her eyes. They looked right into his. "Now say it."

"Yes."

He needed to hear the entire sentence. Desperate to be convinced, he needed it all. "Yes what?"

"Yes, I love you." The words were accompanied by fresh tears. The admission was actually painful. "Satisfied?"

"It's not a matter of being satisfied, Melanie. It's a matter of needing to know if I'm forcing you into something or if you really mean it on your own." What he saw in her eyes at that moment gave him his answer. "You do."

"Yes," she told him in a choked whisper, "and I'm scared to death."

Oh damn, her tears were going to be his undoing. "I don't want you to cry—"

Melanie struggled to smile through the tears. "Sorry, comes with the territory, can't have one without the other."

"Duly noted," he told her, taking her back into his arms. Then, very gently, he raised her chin until she was looking up at him and then he kissed her. Softly, as if her lips were rose petals and if he pressed too hard, they were liable to be crushed and drift down to the floor.

"I can't make you promises that are beyond my power to keep," Mitch told her honestly. "I can't tell you that I'm going to live forever, although I certainly am going to try," he added with a fond smile. "What I *can* promise is that for as long as I *do* live, I will love you and do everything in my power for you to never even have one moment's regret for loving me."

That much *was* in his power to promise her.

"Can't ask for more than that," she replied in a voice so low that it was almost a whisper.

And then, taking another breath, she knew there was something that they *hadn't* really talked about yet. Not as far as it related to the situation he had just painted for the two of them.

"You do realize that I come as a set," Melanie said, broaching the subject carefully.

Having said it out loud, she knew and readily accepted the fact that she loved this man who had come so unexpectedly into her life. But she didn't have just herself to think of anymore.

Mitch tilted his head a little, as if trying to absorb what she had just alluded to.

"I *am* going to adopt April," she told him.

Why did she feel she had to tell him this, he wondered. "I know. I just made it easier for you, remember?"

"That's not going to change your mind?" she asked. "Taking on a wife *and* a child?" she stressed to make sure he got the full impact of his proposal. "That's a ready-made family and there're going to be a lot of adjustments needing to be made—on everyone's part."

"I'm aware of that," then added tongue-in-cheek although he kept a straight face, "I took psychology as part of my doctor training."

"That's a pretty brave move for a man who is 'just fine' being alone."

He knew he should have put that part better, Mitch thought, but it was too late to go back and begin again. "Let's just say I was in a cave all this time and now that I've 'stepped out into the light,' I want it all—the light, the warmth, the whole nine yards. Make that twelve yards."

"Twelve?" She didn't understand the reference.

He grinned and she found him appealingly boyish-looking when he did that. "I was always an over-achiever," Mitch told her.

She felt like laughing and crying at the same time. It took everything Melanie had not to throw her arms around his neck.

"We need to run this by April," she told him. "I know she loves you, but I want her to be prepared for all the changes that are going to be coming."

"Understood." How could one woman be so warm and loving and yet so incredibly organized, he couldn't help wondering in complete admiration. "I really doubt she's going to have any objections, not the way she hung on to you," he reminded her.

"And your mother," Melanie suddenly said, thinking out loud.

Mitch looked at her, puzzled. What was she talking about?

"April didn't hang on to my mother," he told her.

Melanie shook her head. Her tongue was getting all tangled. "No, I mean you're going to want to run this by your mother, aren't you? I mean, she doesn't even know I exist." The more she talked, the more nervous she grew at the idea of facing this hurdle. "This is some bombshell you're going to be dropping on her. A lot of mothers are kind of possessive when it comes to their sons," she told him.

She'd seen it time and again at the shelter. More than a few single mothers there *were* single mothers because of this exact problem. The men they were with had mothers who squelched the entire union between their son and the women they had created families with.

Mitch laughed. "My mother is going to be even more on board with this than April. There'll probably be fireworks."

"Fireworks?" Melanie repeated nervously.

Was he saying that his mother was going to read him the riot act over this? Or blow up when he told her? The last thing she wanted was to come between Mitch and *anyone*, least of all his mother.

"As in the kind they use on the Fourth of July to celebrate," he elaborated. "Skywriting will probably be involved, as well."

Melanie could only stare at him. What was he talking about? "Skywriting?"

"As in, My Prayers Have Been Answered. He's Finally Getting Married!" Laughing, Mitch kissed her fleetingly, but nonetheless with feeling. "Trust me, she wasn't the type to nag, but my mother has been waiting a very long time for this. All of her friends' children have already made them grandmothers."

Now that it was behind him, he could laugh as he recalled certain scenarios. "She got very creative with dropping hints indirectly." His mother, he thought, was going to *love* Melanie. "Now I guess the only thing left is to decide when."

"When we'll get married?" she asked, guessing at the rest of his sentence.

That was getting ahead of the game. "No, when you'll answer me."

Melanie's eyebrows narrowed as she tried to understand what he was saying. "I'm not sure I follow—"

"You haven't given me your answer and I promised not to pressure you, so after we go see April to tell her that she'll be coming home with us—with you for the time being," Mitch corrected himself, "when she's discharged from the hospital, then the next order of business will be—"

"Yes," she interjected almost breathlessly. It felt good to say the word, she couldn't help thinking. Everything felt right about this.

Stopping abruptly in his narrative, Mitch looked at her. "Excuse me?"

Melanie smiled broadly and repeated. "Yes."

He was afraid to allow himself to believe this could be so easy. There was something he was overlooking. "Yes, what?"

"Yes," she told him, enunciating each word slowly, "I'll marry you."

"I said I didn't want to pressure you," he reminded her. Even so, the sound of her acceptance caused his heart rate to accelerate.

"I know. And I said yes. You're not pressuring me, Mitch," she assured him. "If anything, *I've* been pressuring me. Pressuring me *not* to set myself up so that I would ever possibly be in that awful position to feel that kind of pain again. But ultimately that means not feeling at all and you know, not feeling is just as bad as feeling too much."

He smiled at her. "Tell me about it," he thought, remembering how he'd been such a short while ago.

"Besides, I'm already in that position," she admitted. "I love April to pieces and the thought of that little girl being forced to live somewhere else just because some autonomous department felt it was for 'her own good,' the thought of her being frightened and lonely and possibly who knows what, well, that was already ripping out my heart—so what's a little more added fear in that mix?" she asked.

"What indeed," Mitch agreed, giving in and kissing her again. This time, it took more of an effort to get himself to stop than it had just previously. "We'd better get out of here," he told her, rising in the pew and taking her hand. "Otherwise, if we stick around here any longer like this, I might just forget I have a reputation to maintain."

Melanie looked at him in surprise, although she would have been lying if she'd said that what he'd just admitted shocked her. Part of her was feeling the same thing, even though she pointed out the obvious deterrent. "We're in a chapel."

"We're alone," he countered which, right now, seemed more to the point to him than *where* they were.

Drawing her out into the hall, he said, "C'mon, let's go see April and give her the good news."

But then a slight bit of hesitation came over him.

It was a feeling he was definitely unfamiliar with—as unfamiliar as what he experienced each and every time he was around Melanie these days, or even just *thought* of Melanie these days.

"She will see that as good news, won't she?" he asked Melanie. "I don't mean her being with you, but her getting me in the bargain as her dad."

Rather than try to convince him, Melanie simply took his hand and said, "Let's ask her."

"Best news ever!" the little girl declared less than ten minutes later.

They'd found her in her room, awake and struggling not just to sit up, but to get out of bed. Apparently she hadn't really been asleep when Jennifer Donnelly had made her intentions clear to the nurse who was there watching over her—the nurse who then called Mitch to alert him as to what was going on.

Afraid that she would be taken away at any moment, April was trying to get up and get dressed so she could make good her escape before the social worker came back to her room.

"No, honey, no," Melanie had assured her once April had blurted out why she was trying to get away. Very gently she'd pressed April back into her hospital bed. "No one is taking you anywhere, especially since you're not well enough to leave the hospital for a few days yet."

"But then that lady with the big voice is going to come get me and I don't wanna go with her," April had cried, big tears sliding down her small face. "I want to be with you." She'd looked at Melanie as she'd said it. Melanie had felt her heart twisting in her chest for what April had been going through.

"No, she won't. Dr. Mitch saw to that," Melanie had told her. "He won't let her take you." She'd taken April's hand in hers before continuing. "April, how would you like to come live with me and be my little girl?"

"I could do that?" April had asked, her eyes wide with surprise.

"Most definitely. I'd like to adopt you so that nobody can ever take you away from me again." She looked down into the little girl's open face, thinking how much she loved her. It didn't seem possible to love someone so much so quickly, and yet she did. Twice over, she thought, glancing toward Mitch. She had looked back at April and asked, "Would that be okay with you?"

"Yes!" April had cried, looking happy enough to burst.

"There's more," Melanie had went on, choosing her words carefully. "Dr. Mitch asked me to marry him."

"What did you say?" April had asked, looking not at her but at Mitch.

"I said yes," Melanie told her.

Instead of looking happy, April's face had become pensive. It had been obvious that she was trying to sort some things out. "So that means you *won't* adopt me?" she'd asked, confused.

"No, that means I—we both want to ask you how you feel about something," Melanie began.

Impatient, Mitch cut in. "How would you feel about me becoming your dad?" he asked April, unable to stay silent and remain in the background any longer, not when something was this important.

And that was when the little girl had cried, "Best news ever! I mean, I wish Mama and Jimmy were here," she added quickly, "but if they can't be, I'm sure glad that you are. We're gonna be a family?" she asked excitedly, looking from Melanie to Mitch and then back again, unable to contain her enthusiasm.

"Yes, we are," Mitch told her. Everything felt right he thought. For the first time, everything felt as if it had fallen into place just where it belonged.

"Does this mean you'll hug and kiss, too?" April asked out of the blue. "Mama said that when Daddy was alive, he used to hug and kiss her all the time. She said that was what she missed about him the most. That was why I used to hug and kiss her a lot, so she wouldn't miss Daddy so much. But if Dr. Mitch is gonna be my daddy," she went on in that innocently wise way that some children had, "that means he can hug and kiss you, right? I like hugging and kissing," she told them, her voice growing smaller, "but I'm tired right now so if you need a hug," she said to Melanie, then turned toward Mitch, "can you do it for me?"

"I think I can manage that, yes," Mitch told April, doing his best not to laugh. "As a matter of fact, I can give you a little demonstration right now."

"Okay," April told him.

It was the last word she said before her eyelids, already heavy, closed and she fell asleep.

Mitch didn't notice.

He was too busy fulfilling his new daughter's request and hugging Melanie. He threw the kissing in for good measure.

There were no complaints from Melanie.

Epilogue

"Well, ladies, one more for our plus column," Theresa Manetti whispered to her friends as she slid into the last pew of the Bedford Rescue Mission's chapel, taking a seat beside Maizie and Celia Parnell.

Theresa had just finished checking—again—on the meal she had prepared and was catering for Mitch and Melanie's wedding reception. She joined Maizie, who had just gotten into the pew a couple of minutes ahead of her, having given a final hearty congratulations to the groom's mother, an utterly thrilled, and grateful, Charlotte Stewart.

The wedding, at both the bride *and* the groom's insistence, was taking place here, at the Bedford Rescue Mission where they had first met and become, with the recently finalized addition of April, a family.

It was difficult to say who among the guests, and this included Polly, the shelter's director, was the most thrilled about the union: the guests, the director, the groom's mother, their newly adopted daughter, or the two main participants of the ceremony. From all indications, it appeared to be a multi-way tie.

Celia leaned in toward her friends, keeping her voice extra low so that only they heard her. "That worries me," she confided.

The other two exchanged glances before looking in unison at their friend. Although thought to be the more thoughtful and somber of the trio, Celia wasn't exactly anyone's idea of a pessimist.

"How so?" Maizie asked.

Celia was not happy about the reason she offered. "Well, so far, we're batting a thousand, agreed?"

"That's what it's called when there's a hundred percent success, yes, dear," Maizie confirmed indulgently.

And, as amazing as it might seem to the outside observer, every single one of the couples they had stealthily brought together using dozens of pretexts had not only hit it off, but had gotten married and were *still* happily married.

Celia hesitated, searching for the right words. "Well, don't you think that's kind of like, tempting fate?"

"Tempting fate to do what, exactly?" Theresa wanted to know. She was still unclear about their friend's reasoning.

"Tempting fate to have our efforts fall short and fail," Celia finally said, looking less than happy about putting her feelings into actual words.

Maizie looked totally unfazed by Celia's theory. "I don't know, I'd rather say that it puts the odds in our favor."

"Yes, but—" Celia began.

But Maizie waved the woman beside her into silence—at least for now.

The opening strains of the wedding march had begun to swell through the mission's chapel and as the rear entrance doors parted, April, fully recovered and dressed in a frilly pink dress Melanie had let her pick out herself, was doing her version of a two-step, proudly strewing pink rose petals from the open basket that was slung over her small forearm.

There was a huge pink bow on the basket and a smaller one jauntily tied in her hair.

A moment later Melanie entered on the arm of Theresa's son. The latter had offered to give the bride away since own her father was deceased.

"What a beautiful bride," Celia sighed.

"Each one of them looks more beautiful than the last," Theresa whispered as tears began to slide through her lashes.

"As it should be," Maizie murmured to her friends. "As it should be."

"Shhh," Celia warned, not wanting their voices to carry and distract the bride as she walked by.

There seemed to be little danger of that. Melanie only had eyes for the man standing tall and proud at the front of the altar. The man for whom her heart had broken all of her rules.

Dr. Mitchell Stewart, her second chance at love and happily-ever-after.

Blowing a kiss to April, who was watching her intently from the sidelines now, Melanie took her place beside Mitch, a place from which she planned to face the rest of her life.

* * * * *

The Vineyards of Calanetti

Saying 'I do' under the Tuscan sun…

Deep in the Tuscan countryside nestles the picturesque village of Monte Calanetti. Famed for its world-renowned vineyards, the village is also home to the crumbling but beautiful Palazzo di Comparino. It's been empty for months, but rumours of a new owner are spreading like wildfire… and that's before the village is chosen as the setting for the royal wedding of the year!

It's going to be a roller coaster of a year, but will wedding bells ring out in Monte Calanetti for anyone else?

Find out in this fabulously heart-warming, uplifting and thrillingly romantic new eight-book continuity from Mills & Boon Romance!

A Bride for the Italian Boss by Susan Meier

Return of the Italian Tycoon by Jennifer Faye

Reunited by a Baby Secret by Michelle Douglas

Soldier, Hero… Husband? by Cara Colter

His Lost-and-Found Bride by Scarlet Wilson

The Best Man and the Wedding Planner
by Teresa Carpenter

His Princess of Convenience by Rebecca Winters

Saved by the CEO by Barbara Wallace

All eight books are available now!

SAVED BY THE CEO

BY

BARBARA WALLACE

First Published in Great Britain 2016
By Mills & Boon, an imprint of HarperCollins*Publishers*
1 London Bridge Street, London, SE1 9GF

Special thanks and acknowledgement are given to Barbara Wallace for her contribution to The Vineyards of Calanetti series.

ISBN: 978-0-263-91960-8

23-0216

Our policy is to use papers that are natural, renewable and recyclable products and made from wood grown in sustainable forests.The logging and manufacturing processes conform to the legal environmental regulations of the country of origin.

Printed and bound in Spain
by CPI, Barcelona

Barbara Wallace can't remember when she wasn't dreaming up love stories in her head, so writing romances for Mills & Boon is a dream come true. Happily married to her own Prince Charming, she lives in New England with a house full of empty-nest animals. Occasionally her son comes home, as well.

To stay up-to-date on Barbara's news and releases, sign up for her newsletter at www.barbarawallace.com.

To my fellow Calanetti creators for making this project so fun to work on. And to Carol, Val, Darlene and Michelle, who always make me feel like a rock star. Thanks.

CHAPTER ONE

"I THINK I'M in love."

Louisa Harrison bit off a piece of *cornetto*, moaning as the sweet cake-like pastry melted like butter on her tongue. Crumbs dotted her chin. She caught them with her finger, not wanting to waste a drop. "Seriously, Dani, how do you not weigh a thousand pounds living with this man?" If she were married to a chef as wonderful as Rafe Mancini, she'd be the size of her palazzo, the grounds and the vineyards combined.

Her best friend laughed. "Trust me, it's not easy. Fortunately, running around the restaurant all day keeps me in shape. Especially now. Ever since the royal wedding, we've been slammed with requests for reservations. Everyone wants to eat at the restaurant that fed Prince Antonio and his bride."

"As well they should." Danielle's husband, Rafe, entered the restaurant dining room brandishing a coffeepot. "You make it sound as though Mancini's is some ordinary royal wedding caterer."

"I'm not sure there is such a thing as an *ordinary* royal wedding caterer," Dani replied, kissing him on the cheek, "but you're right, Mancini's is anything but ordinary. Once people taste Rafe's food, they are desperate to come back."

"Only they can't for at least eight weeks. My beautiful bride is right—we are booked solid through the harvest festival."

"That's fantastic," Louisa replied helping herself to a cup of coffee. Rafe Mancini not only created wonderful food, he made the best American coffee in Tuscany.

That was Dani's doing. She'd insisted Rafe add a few New World touches to his traditionally Italian menu to placate US tourists. One of many small changes she'd implemented over the past few months. It hadn't taken long for her friend to establish herself as an equal partner both in the relationship and the business. But then, Louisa had heard there were men in this world who actually liked when their wives had minds of their own. Not to mention lives.

She just hadn't married one.

"Mancini's isn't the only place that's doing well," Dani continued. "Business has been up all around the village. Donatella told me sales at the boutique are up over 40 percent from last year."

Louisa wasn't surprised. Over the past nine months, Monte Calanetti had gone from sleepy Tuscan village to must-see tourist destination. Not only had they been selected to host Halencia's royal wedding—considered the wedding of the year in most circles—but art experts had recently discovered an unknown fresco masterpiece hidden in the local chapel. Now it felt as if every person in Italy, tourist or resident, made a point of driving through the town. That they arrived to discover a picture-perfect village *and* an Italian *Good Food* rated restaurant owned by one of Europe's premier chefs only enhanced the town's allure.

"Quite a change from when you and I arrived here, huh?" she noted. It'd been an early spring day when the two of them had met on the bus from Florence. Two expatriates, each on her own quest to the Tuscan Valley. For Dani, the tiny village represented a last adventure before deciding on her future. Louisa, on the other hand, had taken one look at the terracotta roofs rising from the valley and decided luck had granted her the perfect place to escape her past. A place where she could heal.

"I knew as soon as I stepped off the bus that Monte

Calanetti was special," Dani said. "There's something magical about this town. You can feel it."

More like her friend felt the attraction between her and the man she eventually married; there'd been sparks from the second Dani and Rafe had laid eyes on each other. Louisa kept the thought to herself. "The royal wedding planner certainly thought so," she said instead.

"Unfortunately, we can't ride the wedding momentum forever. Once harvest season ends, people will be more interested in the ski resorts." Rafe said.

"People will still seek out Mancini's," Louisa said.

"Some, yes, but certainly not the numbers we've been enjoying. And they certainly won't spend time visiting other businesses."

True. So much of Monte Calanetti's appeal revolved around being able to stroll its cobblestone streets during the warm weather. It would be hard to make a wish in the plaza fountain if the water was frozen. There was a part of Louisa that wouldn't mind the crowds thinning. She missed the early days when she could walk the streets without worrying that some American tourist would recognize her. Another part, however—the practical part—knew the village needed more than a seasonal income. Prior to the wedding, several of the smaller businesses had been on shaky ground.

A third part reminded her she needed income, too. Till now she'd been surviving on the money the royal family had paid her to use her property, and that was almost gone.

"It won't matter if Mancini's is the best restaurant in the world, if it's surrounded by empty buildings," Rafe was saying. "We need something that will encourage people to spend time here year-round."

Funny he should say that. Louisa sipped her coffee thoughtfully. The practical part of her had also been kicking around an idea lately. It was only a germ at the moment, but it might help the cause. "It would be nice to see the village continue to prosper," she had to admit. Even though she, like Dani, was a relative newcomer, she'd already come to consider the place home, and nobody wanted to see their home suffer economically.

"What do you have in mind?" she asked him. He obviously had something up his sleeve or he wouldn't have put on this breakfast.

Pushing up his sleeves, the chef rested his forearms against the edge of the table and leaned close. "I was thinking we could start some kind of committee."

"Like a chamber of commerce?" Did they even have those in Italy? They must.

"Nothing so formal. I'm picturing local business leaders brainstorming ideas like the harvest festival that we can put on to attract traffic."

"And since the palazzo is such a big part of the village…" Dani started.

"You'd like me to be on the committee." That made sense, especially if she carried through with her own idea. "Count me in… What?"

Her friend and her husband had suddenly become very interested in their breakfast plates. "There's one problem," Dani said.

"Problem?" Louisa's fingers gripped her fork. "What kind of problem?" As if she didn't know what the problem would be. Question was, how had they found out?

"I want Nico Amatucci on the committee, as well," Rafe answered bluntly.

Oh. Her fear vanished in a rush, replaced by a completely different type of tension. One that started low in her stomach and moved in waves through her. "Why would that be a problem?"

"Well," Dani said, "we know the two of you haven't always gotten along…"

Memories of wine-tinged kisses flashed to life. "That's in the past," she replied. "We worked together on cleaning up the plaza, remember?"

"I know, but..."

"But what?"

The couple exchanged a look. "At the wedding, you two looked like you'd had a falling-out."

Louisa would have called it a momentary loss of her senses. "It's no big deal." And it wasn't. Beneath the table, her fingers tapped out a rhythm on her thigh. In comparison to what she thought they were going to say, her "falling-out" with Nico amounted to nothing.

She barely remembered, she thought, tongue running over her lower lip.

"Working together won't be awkward, then?" Rafe asked.

"Don't be silly—Nico and I are adults. I'm sure we can handle sitting on a committee together."

"What committee?"

As if waiting for his cue, Nico Amatucci strolled into the dining room. If he were someone else, Louisa would accuse him of waiting to make a dramatic entrance, but in his case dramatic entrances came naturally.

"Sorry I'm late," he said. "We've been working around the clock since the wedding. It appears people can't get enough of Amatucci Red." The last part was said looking straight at her. As Louisa met his gaze, she forced herself to keep as cool an expression as possible and prayed he couldn't see how fast her heart was racing. This was the first time she'd seen him since the wedding. The vintner looked as gorgeous as ever.

He'd come straight from the fields. The ring of dampness around his collar signaled hours of hard work, as did the dirt streaking his jeans and T-shirt. Louisa spied a couple smudges on his neck, too, left behind after wiping the sweat from his skin. She'd say this about the man: he worked as hard as his employees. Something he, as the owner of one of Tuscany's finest boutique wineries, didn't have to do. Probably did it to make up for the fact he was arrogant and presumptuous.

A frown marred his Romanesque features as he pointed to the coffeepot. "American?"

"That a problem?" Rafe asked.

"No." His sigh was long and exaggerated.

Rafe rolled his eyes. "There's no need to be dramatic. If you want espresso, just say so."

"Make it a double," Nico called after him with a grin. "I've been up since sunrise."

Despite there being three empty seats on the other side of the table, he chose to sit in the one his friend had just vacated, which positioned him directly next to Louisa. "I trust I didn't keep you waiting too long," he said to her. His crooked smile made the comment sound more like a dirty secret. But then, that's what Nico Amatucci did. He used his charm to lure people into bending to his will. When they didn't bend to his authority, that is. His sensual mouth and sparkling dark eyes could worm their way past a person's defenses, trapping them in his spell before they knew what was happening.

He reached for a *cornetto*, his shoulder brushing against Louisa's as he moved. The hours of hard work had left him smelling of fresh-tilled dirt and exertion. It was a primal, masculine scent, and though Louisa tried her best not to react, her own basic instincts betrayed her and she shivered anyway. To cover, she ignored his question and took a long sip of coffee.

Nico countered by taking a bite of pastry. "Has everyone recovered from the wedding?" he asked, licking the crumbs off his thumb. Louisa narrowed her eyes. She swore he was purposely trying to make the action erotic.

Especially when he added, "I know I'm still feeling the aftereffects. Are you?"

Again, he looked straight at her. Louisa lifted her chin. "Not at all," she replied with a crispness that made her proud.

Apparently it wasn't crisp enough, since he reacted with little more than an arched brow. "Are you sure?"

Dani jumped to her feet. "I'm going to go see if Rafe needs help. Marcello rearranged the pantry yesterday, and you know how he gets when he can't find things."

Who did she think she was fooling? Rafe wouldn't allow anyone to rearrange his pantry without supervision.

"Subtle," Nico remarked when Dani was out of earshot. "One would think she was trying to give us time alone."

"One would think," Louisa muttered in return. "Though I don't know why."

"Perhaps she thinks we need to talk."

"Well, she would be wrong. We don't need to talk about anything."

"I see. Is that why you're avoiding me, *bella mia*?"

His beauty indeed. *I'm not your anything*, she wanted to snap. She didn't belong to anyone. Not anymore. And especially not to someone like him. Bad enough she let herself fall under his spell at the wedding. "Who says I've been avoiding anyone? Maybe I've been busy. You're not the only one who's had a lot to do since the wedding."

"My apologies. You're right." His chair made a scratching noise on the floor as he angled it so they were facing one another. Taking the last *cornetto* from the center of the table, he tore the pastry in two and divided the pieces between their plates. "So tell me, what have you been up to that has kept you so busy?"

Louisa glared at the fluffy delicacy in front of her. "Things," she replied.

"Things?" His chuckle was smooth like syrup. "That's a very broad category."

"I'm a very broad person."

"Ah, *bella mia.* 'Broad' is definitely not what I would call you." His hand moved forward. Thinking he was about to brush the bangs from her eyes, Louisa jerked back, only to turn red when he picked up his half of the pastry. "I wanted to talk about what happened at the wedding."

"I told you, there's nothing to talk about. We made a mistake, that's all. Why don't we forget it ever happened?"

Sounds from the kitchen drifted into the restaurant as Nico chewed his pastry. Louisa listened, trying to determine how far away she was from rescue. There was an uneasy familiarity to the way they sat with Nico's leg close but not touching hers.

Slowly his eyes lifted to meet hers. "What if I don't want to forget?"

"One double espresso as ordered!" Rafe announced. The chef returned to the dining room carrying a gold-rimmed demitasse. Behind him trailed Dani, who shot Nico a look. From their mutually taut expressions, Louisa wondered if there hadn't been a disagreement over interrupting the conversation. She offered a silent thank-you to whichever one of them had won.

First thing Dani did when she sat down was to try to catch Louisa's eye, but Louisa continued to stare at the tablecloth and prayed that the floor might swallow her up. She hated scrutiny. Hated the feel of people's eyes upon her. Trying to look inside her. Thinking they could read her thoughts. Her fingers crept to her neckline to tug the suddenly too-tight collar.

"Will there be anything else, your highness?" Thank God for Rafe. Again. He set the cup on the table with a flourish, forcing Nico's attention back to the business at hand.

The vintner's bronze fingers wrapped around the handle. "This will do for now," he replied.

"You do know that when I said 'your highness,' I meant it sarcastically, right?"

"Yes, but you wait on me all the same." Nevertheless, Nico saluted his friend with the cup before taking a sip. "So," he said after he swallowed, "you said something about a committee?"

"You *were* listening," Rafe replied. "Yes, I want to create a committee for developing tourism."

"Monte Calanetti already has a person in charge of tourism." Nico explained. "Vincenzo Alberti."

"Tell me you're joking. Everyone knows Vincenzo did nothing and that the only reason we hosted the wedding was because your brother was in town to write the proposal. It could have just as easily gone to some place in Umbria."

"True. Vincenzo is rather useless."

"What I'm talking about is something independent and more grassroots. I'm certain if the local businesspeople put their heads together, we can come up with a host of ideas to increase tourism. Not to mention run them better."

"I certainly won't complain about increased business, especially during the dormant months," Nico said. Leaning back, he hooked an arm over the back of his chair. "Who else do you have in mind besides the four of us? I assume it is the four of us, since we're all sitting here."

The two men began tossing names back and forth, some of whom Louisa recognized, some she didn't. She wasn't surprised when, as the conversation progressed, the dynamic between the friends shifted with Nico slowly taking the reins. That was something else Nico Amatucci did. No matter how commanding others might be—and Rafe certainly qualified as commanding—Nico was always the one in charge.

Her ex-husband had been the exact same way. Minus

the rugged sensuality that is. Steven had been painstakingly glossy, his looks created from the pages of fashion magazines whereas Nico was more earthy. The kind of man who got his hands dirty from actually working with them, not from helping himself.

She remembered the roughness of Nico's calloused hands as his thumbs had fanned her cheeks…

And how effortlessly he'd managed to dance her into a secluded corner without her realizing. In charge till the end, just like Steven.

"We need to make it clear to everyone involved that we don't want to be too commercial," she heard him say. "It's one thing to increase tourism, it's another to lose the very thing that makes Monte Calanetti special."

Rafe agreed. "Absolutely. Ideally, we want events or attractions that highlight our traditions and Old World charm. That's what the tourists want. Maybe there's something we can do around the *Madonna and Child* painting in the chapel. Something historical."

"I read the other day that Santo Majorca is building a spa around its underground springs. Too bad we can't unearth a spring here."

"Wouldn't that be nice?"

"Ow!" Louisa jumped as pain shot up from her shin. Damn it, but Dani wore pointy shoes. That kick would leave a bruise.

The two men turned to look at her. "Everything all right?" Nico asked.

"Fine," she said, rubbing her leg. Beneath her index finger she could feel a small divot. There was definitely going to be a bruise.

Across the table, her friend didn't even have the decency to look apologetic. She was too busy gesturing with her eyebrows for Louisa to say something. Louisa replied with a shake of her head.

Why not? Dani mouthed.

Because of a zillion reasons. The concept was still too vague and unformed, for one. She wasn't ready for people to start poking holes in her idea. Or take it over, she thought, sliding a look in Nico's direction. She wasn't sure she was ready period.

"Did I miss something?" Nico asked.

Of course he would say something. Those sharp brown eyes didn't miss a thing, not that either she or Dani were being very subtle.

"Louisa's been working on a terrific idea," Dani said.

"Really?" He turned to face her. "What is it? If it's something that will help, by all means tell us."

"It's still at the very beginning stages. I haven't worked out all the details yet."

"But the general idea is brilliant. She wants to turn the palazzo into a hotel."

Some of Nico's enthusiasm faded in favor of concern. "What kind of hotel? You're not planning to alter the property, are you?"

"Nothing drastic, I assure you," she said as she shot a narrow-eyed look in Dani's direction. Why couldn't she have found an unenthusiastic best friend? "I was thinking of something more like a high-end boutique hotel."

"Isn't that a great idea?" Dani piped in, clearly unfazed by Louisa's glare. "People love to stay in historic buildings. Remember that couple last month who told us they were staying at Palazzo St. Rosa? They couldn't stop raving about the place."

"She's right, they couldn't," Rafe said. "No matter how hard I tried to make them."

"They showed us the photos, and the place can't hold a candle to Louisa's."

"That's because Palazzo di Comparino is special." Intended as both a compliment and a warning, Nico's comment made Louisa bristle. It'd been nine months since she'd moved in and he still acted as though the palazzo was his responsibility. And Dani wondered why she didn't want to talk about her plans.

"Special, yes," she replied, "but it's also very large and expensive for one person to keep up." Especially if said person had no other source of income. "Opening it to the public is one way to cover some of the expenses." As well as help her stay independent. Being in charge, having total control of her life again, seemed almost too good to be true.

Maybe she could finally put the past behind her.

No sooner did the thought form than her old friend insecurity came rushing in to take its place. "Of course, the building needs a lot more upgrading before I can do much of anything, and I still have to secure financing. Who knows how long it'll take before anything happens."

"Well, I agree with Dani—I like the idea. A high-end hotel is exactly what Monte Calanetti needs," Rafe said as he warmed both her and Dani's coffee. "If you need anything, let us know. Nico and I will be glad to help. Isn't that right, Nico?"

"Absolutely." The vineyard owner slid his empty cup across the table for a refill, which Rafe immediately provided, remembering Nico preferred espresso. There was a roguish gleam in his eyes as he smiled. "As the two of us have proven, we make a good team, do we not?"

A good team. In a flash, Louisa's mind traveled back in time…

The Royal Wedding

"Ask and you shall receive. Your cake, *signorina*." Nico's exaggerated bow as he handed her a slice of cake made Louisa laugh. The wedding had brought out the lightheartedness in everyone, even her. It felt good, laughing. She'd faked happiness for so long that she was afraid she'd forgotten how to truly enjoy herself.

"Grazie," she replied with her best regal nod before noticing he'd returned with only one plate. "No slice for you? Don't tell me there isn't enough." She saw the cake; it was large enough to feed all of Italy.

"Ah, but it's more fun to share, don't you think?" From his breast pocket, he produced two forks. "To commemorate our successful partnership. We make a good team, do we not?"

"Surprisingly, yes." If anyone had told her that one day she and the vineyard owner would be civil to one another, let alone work together, she would have told them they were crazy. But the two of them had organized the massive village cleanup in preparation for today's wedding. As a result, the palazzo and the plaza had never looked lovelier—a pretty big achievement considering the village had started out picture-perfect.

And now, here they were enjoying each other's company at the wedding reception, as well. Things between them had definitely thawed since Louisa's first day in town when he'd demanded to see her ownership papers. Or maybe she was the one who was starting to thaw?

It certainly felt as though something inside her was shifting.

She focused her attention to the cake Nico was sliding toward her.

"If we're toasting, shouldn't we be raising a glass?" she asked, taking one of the forks.

"We've been raising our glasses all day. I thought we could use a change of pace." He moved his chair so that they were sitting side by side, close enough that his elbow nudged hers. Cutting off a bite of cake, he raised it in the air like a glass. "To teamwork."

"To teamwork."

Louisa moved to cut her own piece of cake, intending to salute him back, only to have him press the cake to her lips before she could. "The lady should always have the first bite," he said, his low voice.

A warm tightness moved through her as the fork slid between her teeth. Chocolate and raspberry melted on her tongue.

"Good?" he asked.

"Amazing." She ran a tongue over her lower lip, chasing the hint of frosting that had been left behind. "Try some."

With what could only be called a wicked smile, he did, and when the fork disappeared into his mouth, the tightness in her stomach intensified. A hint of chocolate remained on her lips. Though tempted to lick the taste away, she reached for her napkin instead. After that display, running her tongue over her lips seemed too much like answering in kind and the summer air already felt thick and stifling.

While she'd never let him know it, Nico was quite possibly the most handsome man here, even more handsome than the crown prince. Months of working outdoors had left him with a permanent tan that gave everything else about him—his smile, his eyes, his crisp white shirt—a kind of brilliance the other men couldn't match.

Why on earth was he sitting here eating cake with her? Giving voice to her thoughts, she said, "I have to admit, I was surprised when you suggested we attend together." Handsome, rich…she assumed he had a black book of supermodels at the ready for occasions like this.

"Made sense, did it not? We're both here because our businesses are involved in the celebration.

"Why?" he asked with another grin. "Is there someone you would rather be sitting with?"

"Well, the best man is sort of attractive."

"The best man is only interested in the wedding planner. Face it, *bella mia*," he said, stretching an arm across the back of her chair. "I am the best offer you have."

Another laugh bubbled its way from her chest. She must have had too much wine because his arrogance was sounding damn sexy at the moment.

The room grew quiet. "*Signore e signori*, his Royal Highness Prince Antonio and his bride invite you to join them in this, their final dance of the evening."

"Wow," she said, "last dance already? Time goes by fast."

"Looks like my company was good after all."

Louisa cut another bite off the cake. "Don't get too carried away."

"Come on, admit it." He nudged her shoulder. "You had a good time."

"Yeah, I did." And for the first time in years, she meant it. This had been her first black-tie event since the divorce, and she'd feared the memories of her old life would prove too much to deal with, but Nico had proved a wonderfully entertaining companion. She was actually sorry to see the evening end.

"We need to dance," Nico said, setting down his fork in a way that made it sound more like a command. "One doesn't refuse an invitation from a future king."

Apparently not. All around the room, couples were making their way to the dance floor to join Antonio and his bride, Christina. A few feet away Dani and Rafe were already wrapped in each other's arms, as were Nico's brother, Angelo, and his fiancée. Even Nico's extremely pregnant sister, Marianna, was swaying to the music.

She looked back at the hand Nico was holding out. Such strong capable hands, she thought, the tightness giving way to an internal shiver. "I haven't danced in a long time," she warned. "Your feet might want to be prepared."

"Consider them forewarned."

She needn't have worried. As soon as Nico's arm entwined her waist, she forgot all about being rusty. Their bodies moved together like two synchronized pieces of a whole.

Nico's eyes swept the length of her. "I've been meaning to tell you how beautiful you look. You outshine the princess."

"Careful, talking like that could be considered treason in Halencia." She tried to brush off the compliment with a smile. Flattery had lost its meaning to her a long time ago. Looking good had been part of the requirements when she was married. Looking good, behaving properly, doing what she was told…all part of the job.

"I'll take the risk," he said as he pulled her close. Louisa's eyes locked with his as they moved across the floor. They were darker than she'd ever seen them, the pupils giant pools of black. While Steven always expected her to look beautiful, he never looked at her with such blatant appreciation. The glint in Nico's eyes made her feel like a bite of wedding cake, waiting to be sampled. The thought should have frightened her. Instead, hot shivers danced along her spine.

God, but it'd been a long time since she'd felt like a woman instead of a possession.

The orchestra faded away, drowned out by the sound of their breathing and the rasp of his jacket as it brushed her sequined bodice with every rise and fall of his chest.

She wasn't sure who leaned in first. Once his mouth closed over hers, who had made the first move didn't matter, not when his lips were moving against hers as if he were trying to kiss his way inside. She kissed him back just as hungrily, too many passionless years making her desperate. They kissed hard and deep, only stopping when the need to breathe became too much.

Blinking, Louisa slowly remembered where they were. "I—"

"Shh..." He pressed a kiss to the corner of her mouth. "It's okay, *bella mia*."

Bella mia. My lovely. *Mine*. Louisa stiffened.

"Don't worry," he said, misreading the reaction for embarrassment. "No one can see us."

Turning, she saw that they were in a secluded corner, just outside the ballroom door. While she'd been lost in his spell, Nico had steered them safely away from prying eyes.

How thoughtful and practiced of him. But then, men like Nico didn't do anything spontaneously, did they? They were always in control. Like hunters stalking prey, only instead of bullets they used smiles and seduction. Their victims were trapped in their gilded cages before they ever knew what was happening.

Except Louisa did know. And she was never ever going to be trapped again.

Pushing just enough so as to not make a scene, she stepped out of his embrace. "The bride and groom will be leaving shortly. I better make sure everything is set for their departure." She left him standing in the corner without turning back...

"Louisa?"

Yanked from the memory by the sound of Dani's voice, she saw the three of them staring at her. "You okay?" her friend asked.

"I'm fine," she lied. Part of her was still back on the dance floor, lost in a pair of dark eyes. "You were saying?"

"I was saying that as far as financing your hotel is concerned, I would consider investing..."

"No." She didn't mean for the word to come out so strongly, but Nico was looking straight at her while he spoke and the memory of how those eyes distracted her was so fresh…

Just as well, though. Better to be blunt than let him think he had a chance. As an investor or anything else.

Monte Calanetti was her chance at a new life. No way was she going to let someone sweep in and mess things up.

Not this time.

CHAPTER TWO

NICO SQUINTED AND double-checked the line on the refractometer. "Twenty-two point four."

"Is that on schedule?"

"Close." Pulling the battered leather journal from his back pocket, he flipped through the pages until he found last year's data. "One hundredth of a point off," he reported before turning the page and making note of today's measurement. Even better than he expected. He'd been afraid the easy summer had accelerated the ripening process. So far, however, the sugar levels were holding close to previous years, which boded well for this year's vintage.

"When will you harvest?"

He turned to the young man at his elbow. Mario, a viticulture student from the university was hanging on his every word. "Depends upon the weather and the variety, but for Amatucci Red, I like the Brix level to be between twenty-five and twenty-six. A hair shy of precocious, as it were," he added with a chuckle.

Mario nodded as he took notes. Nico would never admit it out loud but he enjoyed being seen as a master. It made him feel as though he'd achieved what Carlos had hoped for him. "Precocious?" he asked. "I've never heard that winemaking term before."

"That's because it's not really a winemaking term, just something Carlos Bertonelli used to say. 'Grapes are like children. You want to raise them to be sweet, but not so sweet they overwhelm you.' In other words…"

"A hair shy of precocious."

"Exactly." Tossing a grape into the air, he caught the

plump berry in his mouth. "Carlos was full of sayings like that," he said crushing the skin between his teeth. The juice was tart on his tongue; a ways to go before precociousness. "His version of Old World wisdom."

"Signor Bertonelli is the man who used to own these vineyards, right? The ones surrounding the palazzo?"

"*Si.* He was my mentor. Taught me everything I know about winemaking." Nico's heart ached a little every time he thought of the old man, which was often.

"Is that why you're still maintaining the vineyards? Out of respect for him?"

"Out of respect, and partly because Monte Calanetti wouldn't exist without these vineyards. I don't want to see part of our tradition disappear."

There was more to the story, naturally—the truth was always complicated—but Mario didn't need to know how Carlos had kept him grounded when life got crazy. With his even, unflappable demeanor and vat full of wisdom, the old man had been mentor, grandfather and safety net all rolled into one.

When he was a little boy, Nico wondered if the stork hadn't delivered him to the wrong house. That he should have been dropped in the Bertonelli fields instead of his own family's. Truth was, Carlos had been so much more than a mere mentor. Not a day went by that Nico didn't miss the man.

If he were alive, perhaps he could help Nico understand his grandniece better. Looking over the vines to the palazzo, he spied Louisa's platinum-blond hair reflecting the sun as she watched them from the terrace. He nodded hello only to have her move out of view. Still avoiding him. She'd been doing so since the wedding.

Never had he met a woman who was so difficult to read. Cold one moment, warm and tender the next. He'd thought they'd turned a corner at the wedding. A very satisfying corner at that. He smiled, remembering the press of her mouth against his. So soft, so receptive. Then suddenly—poof!—everything changed, and they were back to those frigid early days when she barely gave him the time of day.

"Signor Amatucci?"

Mario was staring at him, obviously waiting for a response of some kind. "Nico," he corrected. "Not *Signor*."

"Sorry. Nico. I was wondering what you wanted to do next."

Figure out what's going on in my blonde American's head. He doubted that's what Mario meant, though. "I want to gather a few soil samples from the southern fields," he said. "Why don't you head back to the winery and begin testing the grapes we've collected?" It was standard practice to double-check the field readings using the equipment at the lab. Unlike his mentor, Nico liked to have solid data to corroborate his taste buds.

"Are you sure?" Being on the field must truly be making him nostalgic, because the way the kid straightened with the prospect of responsibility brought back memories of the first time Carlos had given him a task to complete on his own. Had he looked that earnest? "I suggested it, didn't I?"

"Yes. Of course. I'll leave the results on your desk."

"Along with your recommendations. I'm eager to hear your suggestions."

The kid nodded again, wide-eyed and serious. "Absolutely."

Of course, Nico would repeat the tests himself later on—the crops were far too valuable to trust to a university student—but there was no need to say anything. Better for Mario's confidence if he believed he was operating without a safety net.

He started packing his test gear back in his canvas

satchel. The faded bag had been with him since his days with Carlos, and looked older than that. "If you have any problems, talk to Vitale. I'll be back later this morning."

"How are you getting back? Do you want me to come back for you?"

"No need. I'll hop the wall. There's a low spot," he added when the student frowned. "The Amatuccis and the Bertonellis have been cutting back and forth through these properties for years." At least this Amatucci had. His brother and sister had found other ways to escape.

Once Mario's taillights disappeared in the dust, Nico shouldered his bag and headed south. Above him, the sun lit a cloudless blue sky. The air was ripe with fruit and olives, and if the breeze hit just right, you could catch the faint undertone of lavender. Another perfect day, he thought, wiping the sweat from his forehead.

He was by himself, walking the terraced hill. Back when he was a little boy, these fields had been filled with workers. He remembered the first time he ventured through the archway that divided the properties, a stressed-out, scared boy looking for a place where doors didn't slam and voices were calm. Stepping into the fields of Comparino had been like finding paradise. There was a tranquility in the steady tick-tick-tick of the sprinkler, the low hum of the insects. And it never changed. Oh, there were storms and blights. Natural disasters that caused temporary disruption, but no matter what, Nico knew that come summer, the sounds would be there. Grapes would grow and wine would get made the same as it had for hundreds of years. How he loved the predictability; so unlike the world on his side of the arch, where he never knew from one day to the next whether his parents were together or apart.

Such is the price of grand passion, Carlos said once,

after one of his parents' explosive breakups. *It's either sun or storm. No in between.*

Nico wouldn't know. His passion didn't run that deep.

The vines in the south garden had grown thick and tangled with neglect. Left unmolested, insects had nibbled holes in the leaves. Ignoring the bee buzzing near his ear, Nico knelt in the shade. Using his utility knife, he churned the hardened topcoat, unearthing the moist soil beneath. Then he carefully shoveled several inches of the rich black dirt into collection jars. He was wiping the residue on his jeans when a flash of white caught the corner of his eye. He smiled. Part of the reason he'd picked this morning to test the soil was because the southern fields abutted the verandah. This time of morning, Louisa would be having breakfast outside, the way she always did, and while she might be avoiding him, she wouldn't be able to resist spying on what he was doing. Pretending to study the overgrown rose bush marking the end of the row, he kept his back to her. "Careful, *bella mia*," he said, breaking into English, "people might think you are interested in what I am doing."

"I'm always interested in what people do on my property," came the deliciously haughty reply.

Slowly, he turned around. Louisa stood at the railing, a mug cradled between her palms. Despite the early hour, she was fully dressed in jeans and a soft flowing shirt. She hadn't done her hair yet, though. Instead of being pulled tight in her signature severe hairstyle, the strands hung long and loose around her shoulders. If she knew that was how Nico preferred she wear it, she'd no doubt tie it back tighter than ever.

"Do you plan to scrutinize your hotel guests with the same intensity?"

The mention of the hotel was ignored. "I was out here

having breakfast. You're the one who crossed into my field of vision."

Apparently they were also going to ignore the fact she'd been watching him earlier. At least she'd answered him. Did that mean they were back on speaking terms?

Only one way to find out. "Breakfast, you say. I don't suppose there is enough coffee for two?" When she didn't immediately answer, he grabbed the terrace balustrades to haul himself up and over the wall.

"I thought you despised American coffee."

"It's growing on me. Like a lot of American things," he added with a smile.

He nodded his head toward the bistro table that held the rest of her meal, including a tall thermal carafe. "Should I drink from the container?"

"Please don't. I'll get you a cup."

She didn't ask him to leave. Did that mean she was thawing again?

"You know that you are going to have to learn how to make a proper espresso if you plan to open a hotel," he said, following her inside.

"I didn't realize you were also an expert on hotel management."

"No, just an expert on being Italian."

As they passed through the glass doors into the room that had been the *piano nobile*, he instinctively paused. "I'll wait here." When Louisa frowned over her shoulder, he lifted his dusty work boot. If Carlos had been alive, he would have walked across the floor without a second thought, but Louisa seemed more the clean and orderly type. The last thing he wanted was to ruin their fragile accord by tracking dirt across the clean terracotta tiles. The gesture must have been appreciated because she nodded rather than arguing the point. "I'll be right back."

The palazzo looked good. Louisa had accomplished

a lot over the past few months. The dated furniture had been replaced by comfortable modern pieces but the Old World elegance remained. The intricate coffered ceiling and carved archways gleamed they were so clean. Hard to believe it was the same property. Carlos had never seemed to care about his living conditions, especially after his wife died. And then, of course, there were the years it had sat unclaimed. If Nico hadn't kept an eye on the property, Carlos's legacy would have fallen into even greater shambles.

Louisa never did say why she'd ignored the property for so long. He asked her once, but she told him it was none of his business. And now, after years of neglecting her inheritance, she was breaking her back attempting to return the palazzo to its former glory.

His American was definitely a confusing and complicated woman.

"If you want pastry, you'll have to go home," Louisa said when she returned. "Today is market day."

"Coffee is fine. Thank you." It didn't escape him that she held the cup at arm's length, keeping a healthy distance. Things might be warmer between them, but not completely thawed.

"I'd offer milk, but I know you prefer it black."

"I'm flattered you remember."

"Hard to forget black coffee." She brushed past him, leaving behind a soft memory of Chanel.

"May I ask what you were doing digging in the dirt?"

"Taking soil samples."

"Why?"

For a chance to talk with you. "To determine what needs to be done to make the dirt suitable for new vines." Depending upon the soil levels, he planned to recultivate the field, with canaiolo or cabernet sauvignon, if he was feeling untraditional. "Since it will take a few years before the plants yield a usable harvest, I want to replant sooner rather than later."

"Is that so?" She tossed him a cryptic look before turning to the hills. "Funny. I don't remember selling you the property."

She had to be joking. She was going to claim sovereignty now? "That's funny, because I don't remember you complaining about my maintaining it on your behalf."

"On my behalf and to your benefit. Or are you going to tell me you didn't double your vineyard without paying a penny?"

"No," he replied with a shrug. "Why deny the truth?" He had benefited from using Carlos's land. Carlos would have wanted as much. "You chose to stay away, and I saw no sense in letting good land go to waste."

"I didn't choose, I…" Whatever she was going to say was swept aside by a deep breath. "Regardless, that doesn't give you the right to do what you want. No matter how good you are at it," she muttered into her cup.

"Good at vineyard management or doing what I want?" Her side eye gave him his answer. "Fine. You're the owner. If you don't want to recultivate, what would you like to do with your neglected vineyards?"

"I'll let you know," she said, jutting her chin for maximum haughtiness.

They both knew he would replant; she was being stubborn for stubbornness' sake. He wondered if she knew how attractive she looked when she was being argumentative. Maybe that was why he enjoyed pushing her buttons. Like a person with a stick poking at a hornet's nest and getting off on the risk, provoking her to annoyance had excitement curling low in his stomach. And damn if it wasn't easy to push her buttons. Seemed as though all he had to do was breathe and her eyes were flashing.

Those eyes were flashing brightly at the moment. Reminding him of how she'd looked right after they kissed.

Ah. Clarity dawned.

"This isn't really about recultivating, is it?" he asked, stepping closer. "This is about what happened at the wedding."

She whipped around to face him. "I told you I didn't want to talk about that."

And yet the moment hung over them begging to be mentioned. "Come now, *bella mia*, don't tell me you expect us to pretend it never happened?"

How could they possibly ignore such an amazing kiss? Surely he wasn't the only one who lay awake at night remembering how perfectly their bodies fit together. The way her breath quickened when he'd stepped closer, told him he wasn't.

"Don't call me *bella mia*, and I'm not asking you to pretend about anything. It's simply not worth talking about. We drank a little too much wine and let the romantic atmosphere get to us, that's all."

"Really?" He leaned in, angling his head near the curve of her neck. "That's all it was? A drunken mistake? I'm not sure I believe you." Especially when her skin flushed from his proximity.

"Why not?"

"Because..." Nico let his gaze take the path his fingers wanted to take. "For one thing, I wasn't drunk."

This time it was Louisa who closed the distance between them, her eyes ablaze from the confrontation. "Maybe you weren't, but that doesn't mean I wasn't. Much as your ego would like to think otherwise."

Oh, how his little hornet's nest enjoyed poking him as much as he enjoyed poking her. "Trust me, *bella mia*," he said, "my ego doesn't need stroking. Go ahead and call it a drunken mistake if you have to. Same way you can tell yourself that you wouldn't enjoy a repeat performance."

Louisa's lips parted with a gasp, like he knew they would. With a smile curling his own, Nico dipped his head to claim them.

Just as their mouths were about to touch, she turned her face. "Okay, fine, I admit it was a great kiss, but it can't happen again."

"Why not?" Again, he didn't understand. Two people obviously attracted to one another; why shouldn't they explore the possibilities?

"For a lot of reasons. To start with, I'm not looking to get involved in a serious relationship."

All the better. "Neither am I." *Serious* came with certain expectations, and as history had proven, he lacked the depth to meet them.

"And—" she dodged his outstretched hand "—we're neighbors, plus we'll be working on that committee Rafe is creating. We'll be around each other all the time."

"Perhaps I'm misunderstanding, but doesn't that make things easier?"

"It will make things awkward."

"Only as awkward as we let it be," he replied.

Her sandals slapped softly against the floor as she returned to her breakfast table, a position, Nico noted, that put a barrier of glass and wrought iron between them.

Of course, she already knew that, or else her hands wouldn't be gripping the chair back so tightly. Nico knew the cues; she was working up to another reason. "Look, right now I can't be involved with anyone seriously or casually. I need to concentrate on taking care of myself. Do you understand?"

"Si." Better than she realized. The last woman who'd said those words to him had been suffering from a broken

heart. Was that Louisa's secret? Had she come to Monte Calanetti because some bastard had let her down?

If that was the case, then far be it for him to add to her injury. One woman was enough to have hurt in a lifetime. There were other women in Monte Calanetti whose company he could keep, even if they weren't as enigmatically fascinating. "Consider the kiss forgotten," he told her.

Louisa's back relaxed as she exhaled. "Thank you," she replied. It felt good to clear the air between them. She'd been acting like a complete brat the past couple of days, stuck between wanting to stand up for herself and being afraid of succumbing to the attraction. She'd treated Nico like the enemy rather than the neighbor she'd come to know and respect. But now that they were on the same page…

Maybe she could finally stop thinking of how much he reminded her of Steven. Her ex-husband's kisses had made her head spin, too, she recalled. The first time she'd been kissed by a man who knew what he was doing.

Feeling Nico's dark eyes studying her, she added in a low voice, "I appreciate your understanding."

"I am nothing if not agreeable."

The joke broke the spell and Louisa laughed. They both knew he could be as stubborn as she could. "Yes, I've seen how agreeable you can be." He'd been particularly "agreeable" earlier this year when his sister, Marianna, had announced her unplanned pregnancy. Louisa had had to talk him out of staking the baby's father in the garden.

"I brought a smile back to your face, did I not?" His smile was crooked and way too sexy.

"I'm glad you said something," he added in a more serious voice. "I did not like that our friendship had turned awkward again."

He was being kind. "I was being a bit irrational, wasn't I?" *Bitchy* would have been a better word.

"A bit. But I may have egged you on."

She laughed. "You think?"

"A bit. How about if we both promise to be on our best behavior?"

"Sounds like a plan."

"Good." To her surprise, there wasn't an ounce of seduction in his smile. If anything he looked genuinely happy. Damn if that didn't make her stomach flutter.

"But," he continued, changing topics, "you should do something about these fields. It is a waste of good cropland."

Not to mention bad business. Guests weren't going to pay to stay at a nonworking vineyard.

Shoot. She was going to have to let him replant, wasn't she? "As soon as I finalize the plans for the hotel, I'll make some decisions." He might be getting his way, but he would get it on her schedule.

"How are your plans going?"

"They're coming along." Only last night she'd put the finishing touches on a preliminary marketing plan.

"Glad to hear it. You know—" he set down his cup, the contents of which, Louisa noticed, were untouched "—my offer still stands. If you need investors…"

Louisa tensed before remembering she'd promised to behave better. It wasn't his fault his offer set her teeth on edge. "I won't need investors," she told him. "I've got a meeting with the bank this afternoon to discuss opening a line of credit. If plans go as I hope, I might be able to open on a limited basis this winter."

"That soon?"

"I did say limited. Waiting until the palazzo is fully renovated could take years, and I want to move fast enough that I can capitalize on the royal wedding." She sounded defensive, the way she used to whenever Steven questioned her. *But he's not Steven, and you don't need any-*

one's permission anymore. "I figured I'd concentrate on upgrading the infrastructure, plumbing, electrical, that stuff, and make sure the front half of the palazzo is in perfect working order, before expanding into the back."

"Sounds smart."

"I think so." She did *not* feel a frisson of pleasure at the compliment. "Now I just have to hope the bank comes through with financing quickly." And that the loan officers would take the palazzo for collateral without looking too far beyond the fact she was Carlos Bertonelli's grandniece. Her post-divorce financials were sketchy at best. And heaven help her if the bank looked into her former life. She'd never get financing.

"Who are you meeting with?" Nico asked.

"Dominic Merloni."

"I know him. He's a smart businessman. When I get to my office, I'll call—"

"No. Thank you."

"I don't mind. I'd do the same for any friend."

"Did you do it for Rafe when he opened the restaurant? That's what I thought," she said before he could answer. Rafe would have had his head if he'd interfered.

So would she. "Look, I appreciate your wanting to help, but it's very important to me that I do this 100 percent on my own."

"I understand," he said. Except that he didn't. Louisa could tell from how his brows knit together. He was studying her, looking for the reasons behind her need for independence. Louisa said nothing. She'd already revealed more about her past than he needed to know.

"But," he added, "I hope, if you need a reference, you won't hesitate to give Dominic my name. I'm told I have influence in this town. With some people, that is."

Louisa couldn't help but return his smile. "With some people."

They chatted for a few more minutes, mostly about superficial things. Rafe's committee, plans for the harvest festival. A series of nice safe topics that would prove they'd put the awkwardness of the kiss behind them. Nico had just started describing the traditional grape-stomping ceremony when his cell phone rang.

"Mario, the student who is working for us this summer," he explained when he hung up. "He's finished with the task I assigned him and wondering if I'm coming back before lunch."

"Is it that late?" Louisa looked to her bare wrist. They'd let time get away from them. Her bank appointment was in the early afternoon.

"Only for people who had breakfast before sunrise," Nico replied. "The rest of the world is safe."

"Good to know, seeing as how I just finished breakfast."

"And my second."

"Such as it was." She nodded to his untouched coffee. "Guess you're not as fond of American coffee as you claimed."

"I must have confused it with something else American, then. Good luck with Dominic." With a parting wink, he jumped over the walk.

He was lucky he didn't break his leg leaping off terraces like that, Louisa thought as she watched him disappear into the vines. She decidedly didn't think about how graceful he looked when he moved. Or about how firm and muscular his arms looked while supporting his weight.

She always did have a weakness for men with nice biceps, she thought with a shiver.

Too bad Nico Amatucci was every mistake she'd vowed not to repeat. She'd had her fill of charismatic, dominating men, thank you very much.

She checked her bare wrist a second time. Her Rolex

was long gone—sold to pay off bills—but the habit remained. Didn't matter—Nico's comment about lunch told her the morning was getting on. If she wanted to be prepared for her meeting, she'd best get her act together.

Gathering her plate and the coffee cups, she headed into the palazzo, where the latest draft of her business plan lay spread on the coffee table. Nico must not have noticed, because he wouldn't have been able to resist commenting if he had.

Pausing, Louisa scanned the numbers on the balance sheet with a smile. A solid, thorough plan, but then she'd always been good with numbers. Sadly, she'd forgotten how much she enjoyed working with them. Once upon a time, she'd had a promising career in finance. Until Steven had talked her into staying home shortly after their marriage, that is. Cajoled, really. For appearance's sake, he'd said. People were already gossiping about how the CEO was dating his extremely young employee. Made sense not to add fuel to the fire. "Besides," he'd told her, "as my wife, you have far more important things to focus on."

Like making sure she looked and behaved perfectly at all times. She should have seen the signs then, but she'd been too in love to notice. Lost in her personal fairy tale. The little nobody Cinderella swept off her feet by the silver-haired billionaire Prince Charming.

It wasn't until the feds took him away that she wondered if he hadn't been afraid she'd figure out what he was up to.

Oh well, that was in the past now.

It had taken her a while to settle in at the palazzo, but over the past few months, she'd developed a very comfortable routine. First came breakfast on the terrace, where she would practice her Italian by reading the local papers. The language immersion tape she'd bought in Boston had turned out to be useless—fluent in two weeks, ha!—but nine months in, she was getting pretty comfortable. After breakfast, she would go online to catch up on the American news and check her email. Usually her inbox didn't contain more than a handful of messages, a far cry from the days when she would get note after note. Now her messages were mostly from Dani, who liked to forward jokes and pictures of baby animals. On the plus side, she didn't have to worry about whether the message was some kind of ruse arranged by Steven to catch her in a lie.

At first she didn't look twice at the internet alert, the helpful online tracker she'd created to stay on top of the news. Another reference to the wedding, she assumed. Every day brought two or three mentions. It wasn't until she was about to log off that she realized the alert was one she'd set up before leaving Boston. The words *Louisa Clark* leaped from the screen in boldface type.

Her heart stopped. A year. A whole year without mention. Why now?

She slid her fingers to the mouse. *Please be a coincidence*, she prayed.

And she clicked open the link.

CHAPTER THREE

SCAM KING'S EX HOSTS ROYAL WEDDING
Is Luscious Louisa Looking for a New Partner?

> After nine months under the radar, Louisa Clark, the blonde bombshell who seduced and ultimately brought down bogus financier Steven Clark has reappeared. This time in Europe under the name Louisa Harrison…

A BIG FAT PHOTO of her smiling at the royal couple ran under the headline.

The article went on to list her as the owner of Palazzo di Comparino and suggested that hosting the wedding had been her way of snagging a new billionaire husband. Because, after all, that was how she'd landed Steven, right? She was the young femme fatale employee who'd seduced her older boss, only to sell him out when the feds began closing in. Never mind that the narrative didn't remotely resemble the truth. That she was the one who had been seduced and betrayed. Just as long as the story sold papers.

Louisa tried to breathe, but an invisible hand had found its way to her throat and was choking the air out of her. The site even used that god-awful nickname. *Stupid headline writers and their need for memorable alliteration.* No way would this be the only article. Not in the internet era when every gossip blog and newspaper fed off every other.

Sure enough. A few shaky keystrokes later, the search results scrolled down her screen. Some of the stories focused on rehashing the case. Others, though, created all-new speculation. One politician in Florence was even demanding an investigation into the al fresco discovered in the palazzo chapel last summer, claiming it could be part of an elaborate art fraud scheme. Every page turned up more. Headline after headline: Ponzi Scheme Seductress Turns Sights on Tuscany *and* Italy: Lock Up Your Euros! and Royal Scandal! Is Halencia's Financial Future at Stake?

Oh God, Christina and Antonio. She'd turned their fairy-tale wedding into a mockery. They must hate her. Everyone must hate her. Dani. Rafe. *Nico.* They loved Monte Calanetti; all they wanted was for their village to thrive, and she was tainting the town with scandal. How could she ever show her face in town again?

The phone rang. Louisa jumped. *Don't answer it. It could be a reporter.* Old habits, buried but not forgotten, kicked right in.

Not a reporter, thank goodness. The bank. The name appeared under the number on her call screen. One guess as to why they were calling. Forcing air into her lungs, she answered.

"Signorina Harrison?" an unfamiliar female voice asked.

"Y-yes." Louisa fought to keep her voice from shaking, and lost.

"I'm calling for Signor Merloni. He's asked me to tell you he can't meet with you today. Something has suddenly come up."

"Right. Of course." What a surprise. A lump formed in her throat. Only pride—or maybe it was masochism—made her hang on the line and go through the motions. "Did…did Signor Merloni give you a new date?"

"No, he did not," the woman replied. "I'm afraid his calendar is full for the next several weeks. He's going to have to call you when a time becomes available."

And so the ostracism started. Louisa knew the drill. Signor Merloni wouldn't call back. No one would.

They never did.

Phone dropping from her fingers, Louisa stumbled toward the terrace doors, toward the fresh air and rolling hills she'd come to see as home, only to stop short. Paparazzi could be lurking anywhere, their telephoto lenses poised to snag the next exclusive shot of Luscious Louisa. They could be hiding this moment among the grapevines.

So much for going outside. Backing away, she sank into the cushions when her calves collided with the sofa. What now? She couldn't call anyone. She couldn't go outside.

It was just like before. She was a prisoner in her own home.

Damn you, Steven. Even in prison, he was still controlling her life.

The Brix level matched the portable reading exactly. Nico wasn't surprised. When it came to grapes, he was seldom wrong. *Of course not. Making wine is the only thing you really care about.*

The voice in his head, which sounded suspiciously like his former fiancée's, was wrong. Making wine wasn't the *only* thing he cared about; there was his family, too. And tradition, although tradition involved winemaking so perhaps they were one and the same. Still, while he found great satisfaction in bottling the perfect vintage, if Amatucci Vineyards collapsed tomorrow, he wouldn't collapse in despair. That was his parents' domain. If he couldn't make wine anymore, he would cope, the same way he'd coped when Floriana had walked out on him, or whenever he'd come home to discover his parents had broken up—again. Dispassion, when you thought about it, was a blessing. Heaven knew it had saved him from going mad when growing up.

If the trade-off for sanity meant living a life alone, then so be it.

Why was he even thinking about this? Louisa's comment about needing time for herself, that's why. Someone had hurt Louisa badly enough that she'd fled to Italy. Her pain was too close to the mistakes he'd made with Floriana. Poor, sweet Floriana. He'd tried so hard to want her properly, but his tepid heart wouldn't—couldn't.

Was the man who'd broken Louisa's heart trying to be something he wasn't, too? Hard to believe a man would throw her over for any other reason.

"Mario, could you turn down the volume?" he hollered. He could hear the television from in here.

Leaving the beakers he'd been measuring on his lab table, he left his office and walked into the main processing area where Mario and his production manager, Vitale, stood watching the portable television they had dragged from the break room.

"Last time I checked, football didn't need to be played at top volume," he said. With the equipment being readied for harvest, it didn't take much for the noise to reverberate through the empty plant. He motioned for Giuseppe to hand him the remote control. "I didn't know there was a match today."

"Not football, *signor*, the news," Mario replied.

"You brought the television in here to watch the *news*?" That would be a first. Football reigned supreme.

"Si," Giuseppe replied. "Vitale's wife called to say they were talking about Monte Calanetti."

Again? Nico would have thought they were done discussing the royal wedding by now. "Must be a slow news…" He stopped as Louisa's face suddenly appeared on the screen. It wasn't a recent photo, she was far more dressed up than usual, and it showed her with a man Nico didn't recognize. A very handsome man, he noticed, irritably.

The caption beneath read Luscious Louisa—Back Again?

Luscious Louisa?

"Isn't that the woman who owns the palazzo?" Vitale looked over at him.

Nico didn't answer, but the news reader droned on. "…key witness in prosecuting her husband, Steven Clark, for investment fraud and money laundering. Clark is currently serving seventy-five years…"

He remembered reading about the case. Clark's pyramid scheme had been a huge scandal. Several European businessmen had lost millions investing with him. And Louisa had been his wife and testified against him?

No wonder she'd run to Italy.

Another picture was on the screen; one from the royal wedding. Nico gritted his teeth as a thousand different emotions ran through him. The presenter was talking about Louisa as if she were some kind of siren who'd led Clark to his doom. Had they met the woman? Alluring, yes, but dishonest? Corrupt?

His ringtone cut into his thoughts. Keeping his eyes on the television, he pulled his phone from his back pocket.

"Have you seen the news?" Dani asked when he answered.

"Watching it right now," he replied. On-screen, the presenter had moved on to a different headline.

"The story's on every channel. It's all anyone in the restaurant can talk about."

It's untrue, he corrected silently. The ferocity of his certainty surprised him. He had not one shred of evidence to support his belief, and yet he knew in his bones that Louisa wasn't guilty of anything. One merely had to look in her eyes to know that whatever the press said, they didn't have the entire story.

"Did you know?" he asked Dani. Rafe's wife was Louisa's closest friend. If Louisa had told anyone of her past...

"No. She never talks about her life before she got here," Dani answered. "Hell, she barely talks about herself."

Nico's gut unclenched. Silly, but he'd felt strangely hurt at the idea of Louisa sharing her secrets with someone else.

"There are reporters all over town," Dani continued. "One even came in here asking questions. I've been trying to call her since the story broke to see if she's okay, but she's not answering her phone."

"Probably avoiding the press."

"I'm worried, though. She's so private, and to have her life story plastered all over the place..."

Terrifying. "Say no more," he replied. "I'll head right over."

Louisa had lost track of the time. Curled in the corner of her sofa, away from the windows, she hugged her knees and tried to make her brain focus on figuring out the next step. Obviously, she couldn't stay in Monte Calanetti. Not without tainting the village with her notoriety. And going back to Boston...well, that was out of the question. What would she do? Go to her mother's house and listen to "I told you so" all day long?

Louisa hugged herself tighter. Ever since seeing the media alert, there'd been a huge weight on her chest, and no matter how hard she tried to take a deep breath, she couldn't get enough air. It was as though the walls were closing in, the room getting smaller and smaller. She didn't want to leave. She liked her life here. The palazzo, the village...they were just starting to feel like home.

She should have known it wouldn't last. Steven's shadow was destined to follow her everywhere. For the rest of her life, she would be punished for falling in love with the wrong man.

"...you're doing?" A giant crash followed the question. The sound of tinkling glass forced Louisa to her feet. Running to the terrace door, she peered around the corner of the door frame in time to see Nico dragging a stranger across the terrace toward the wall. The crash she'd heard was her breakfast table, which now lay on its side, the top shattered.

"Hey, what do you think you're doing?" she heard the stranger gasp. "This is my exclusive."

"Exclusive this," Nico growled. Holding the man's collar in one hand, he yanked the expensive camera the man carried from around his neck and hurled it over the wall.

"Bastard! You're going to pay for that."

"Be glad it was only your camera." Nico yanked the man to his feet only to shove him against the railing. "Now get out. And if I ever see your face in the village again, you'll find out exactly what else I'm capable of breaking, understand?" He shoved the man a second time, with a force that made Louisa, still hidden behind the door frame, jump. Whatever the reporter said must have satisfied him, and Nico released his grip on the man's shirt. Louisa stepped back as the man started toward the stairs.

"Where are you going?" Nico asked, his hand slapping down on the man's shoulder. "Leave the way you came in."

"Are you kidding? That's a five-foot drop."

"Then I suggest you brace yourself when you land." The two men stared at one another for several seconds. When it became obvious Nico wasn't backing down, the reporter hooked a leg over the railing.

"I'm calling my lawyer. You're going to pay for that camera."

"Call whoever you'd like. I'll be glad to explain how I'm calling the police to report you for trespassing on private property. Now are you leaving, or shall I throw you over that railing?"

The reporter did what he was told, disappearing over the rail. Slowly Louisa stepped into the light. Nico's shoulders were rising and falling in agitated breaths, making her almost afraid to speak. "Is he gone?" she asked in a soft voice.

"Is he the first one?" he asked, voice rough.

He turned, and the dark fury Louisa saw on his face had her swallowing hard to keep the nerves from taking over her throat. She nodded. "I think so."

"He was climbing over the wall when I got here. Probably saw your terrace door was open and thought he could catch you up close and off guard."

"In Boston, they preferred using telephoto lenses."

"You're not in Boston anymore."

"I know." She should have realized how ruthless the press would be. After all, this was Italy; they'd invented the word *paparazzi*.

"At least you won't have to worry about this one trespassing again. That is, if he's smart."

"Thanks."

"Can't promise there won't be more, though," he said brushing past her. "You'd best be prepared."

More. He was right, there would be others. It was all she could do not to collapse in a heap where she stood. Those months of hiding in Boston had nearly destroyed her. She wasn't up to another go-round. The stranger on her terrace was proof enough of that. If Nico hadn't shown up when he did…

Why had he shown up? Returning to her living room, where she found her neighbor searching through the bookshelf cabinets. "What are you doing?"

"Carlos kept a stash of fernet tucked in back of one of these cabinets. Do you still have it?"

"Two doors to the left." She hadn't gotten around to finding a better location. "I meant why are you here?"

"Dani called me. She saw the news on television."

"Let me guess, she's horrified to find out who she's been friends with and wants me to stay away so I won't drag the restaurant into it." Seeing the same darkness on Nico's face that she'd seen a few moments ago, it would seem her neighbor felt the same way.

"What? No. She and Rafe are trying to figure out what's going on. A reporter came to the restaurant asking questions." He paused while he pulled a dust-covered bottle from the cabinet. "She said she tried calling you a half dozen times."

That explained some of the phone calls then. "I wasn't answering the phone."

"Obviously. They asked if I would come over and make sure you were okay. Good thing, too, considering you were about to have an unwanted visitor."

He filled his glass and drank the contents in one swallow. "This is the point in our conversation where you suggest that I'm an unwanted visitor."

"What can I say? I'm off my game today." She sank into her corner and watched as Nico drank a second glass. When he finished, he sat the empty glass on a shelf and turned around. He wore a much calmer expression now. Back in control once again.

"Why didn't you say anything about your former husband?" he asked.

And say what? *My ex is Steven Clark. You know, the guy who ran the billion-dollar investment scam. I'm the wife who turned him in. Maybe you've read about me? They call me Luscious Louisa?* She plucked at the piping on one of the throw pillows. "The idea was to make a fresh start where no one knew anything about me," she replied."

"You know how unrealistic that is in this day and age?"

"I managed it for nine months, didn't I?" She offered up what she hoped passed for a smile. Nine wonderful months. Almost to the point where she'd stopped looking over her shoulder.

When he didn't smile back, she changed the subject. "You said a reporter came into the restaurant?"

"This morning. That's how Dani knew to turn on the television."

She could just imagine the questions he'd asked, too. "Tell them I'm sorry. Things will die down once they realize I'm not in Monte Calanetti anymore."

Nico's features darkened again. "What are you talking about?"

"I'm catching the bus to Florence tonight."

"You're running away?"

He made it sound like a bad thing. "I certainly can't stay. Not anymore."

"But the palazzo... What about all your plans for restoring the property and turning it into a hotel? Surely, you're not planning to abandon Palazzo di Comparino *again*?"

His voice grew harsh on the last word, causing Louisa to cringe. His feelings regarding the palazzo were no secret; to him, the fact she allowed the property to sit unclaimed for so long was as big a crime as anything Steven had done. Of course, she had good reason for the delay, but he didn't know that.

"Have you seen what they are writing about me?" she asked him. The stories would only get worse. "That guy you threw off my terrace is probably down in the village right now trying to dig up dirt. And what he can't find, he'll make up. Whatever he can do to sell papers."

"So?"

"So, I'm doing Monte Calanetti a favor by leaving. The town is on an economic high. I don't want to do anything to take that away." Unable to stand the way his eyes were bearing down on her, Louisa pushed herself to her feet and walked toward the rear corner of the room, as far from the windows—and Nico—as possible. A tapestry hung on the wall there, and she focused on the intricate weave of brown thread. "Better I leave the palazzo empty than stay and let the town become branded as the home of Luscious Louisa," she said.

"How noble of you, running away without saying goodbye to your friends. I mean, that's what you were going to do, no? Leave without saying goodbye?"

"Like people would care." Rejection hurt enough when it was people you didn't like. The idea of walking down the street and seeing disdain in the eyes of people she cared about made her sick to her stomach. "Trust me, everyone will be more than happy to see me gone."

"Happy? Did you say we would be happy?" There was the sound of footsteps, and suddenly a hand was on her shoulder, yanking her around and bringing her face-to-face with a pair of flashing brown eyes. So angry; so ready to correct her.

It was instinctive. The corner of her vision caught his hand starting to rise, and she couldn't help it.

She flinched.

Madonna mia, did she think he was going to strike her? As he raked his fingers through his hair—completing the motion he'd started before Louisa recoiled—Nico felt his hand shaking. What scared him was that he did want to hit something. Not Louisa. Never Louisa. But something. The wall. That miserable paparazzo's face. So much for the liquor calming his nerves. The swell of anger that he'd been fighting since seeing the news was pushing hard against his self-control. Mixing with another emotion, one he couldn't identify but that squeezed his chest like a steel band, the feelings threatened to turn him into someone he didn't recognize.

How could she just leave Monte Calanetti? For nine months they'd treated her as one of their own, made her part of their family, and she didn't think they cared? Did she truly think so little of them?

He felt betrayed. "If you think so little of us that you believe we would let a few gossip articles sway our opinion, then perhaps you should go somewhere else," he said. "After all these months, you should now have realized that people in Monte Calanetti are smarter than that."

"That include Dominic Merloni?"

The banker? What did he have to do with anything?

"He canceled our meeting as soon as the news broke. He won't be the only person to cut me off. Just the first."

"Dominic Merloni is an arrogant bastard who thinks everyone in the village should worship him because he once played football for Genoa."

"That's not what you said about him this morning."

"This morning I was being polite." But if she was going to be irrational, then there was no need to keep up the pretense. "I'm talking about the people who matter. Like Dani, your supposed *best friend*. You think she is so petty?"

"Of course not," she replied. "But Dani loves everybody."

"Yes, she does, but you were going to leave her without saying goodbye anyway."

"I already told you, I'm—"

"Yes, yes, doing the village a favor. Let us start organizing the benediction. Saint Louisa the martyr. Abandoning Palazzo di Comparino for the good of the people."

Louisa stood with her arms wrapped around her as though they were the only thing holding her up. As far from the woman he'd come to know as could be. Where was the haughty American who challenged him on every turn? The hornet who threatened every time he poked her nest? "I don't know why you care so much," she muttered.

Nico didn't know either, beyond the emotions that continued squeezing his chest. He shouldn't care at all. He should accept the change in circumstance as another one of life's upheavals and move on.

He couldn't, though. All he could think about was how the more he watched her retreat into herself, the more he wanted to grab her by the shoulders and shake the fight back into her. He wanted to…to…

He stalked back to the bookshelf. Grabbing a clean glass from the bar, he poured two more glasses of fernet and walked back to her. "Here," he said, holding one of the glasses out. "Drink. Maybe you'll start thinking more clearly." Maybe he would, too.

"I don't need to think clearly," she replied. Nonetheless, she took the drink. "I need to leave town."

"And go where?"

"I don't know. Africa. New Zealand. Someplace where they can't find me. I'll figure something out. I just know I have to leave.

"No, damn it!" he said, slamming the bottle on the shelf. "You can't!"

The air between them crackled with tension. Nico looked at Louisa cradling her glass with trembling hands and grew ashamed. Since when did he yell and slam objects?

Taking a deep breath, he began again, this time making sure his voice remained low and level. "Leaving town is the worst thing you can do."

"How can you say that?"

Again, Nico wasn't entirely sure. Several answers came to mind, but none of them felt completely whole or honest. The true, complete answer remained stuck in the shadows, unformed.

"Because the town needs you," he said, grabbing the first reason that made sense. "You've become an important part of our community. Whether you believe in them or not—" she turned away at his pointed dig "—the people here believe in you."

"Besides," he added in a voice that was even lower than before, "if you run away, the press win. People will believe what's written—the stories will start to sound true. Is that what you want? To give Luscious Louisa life?"

"No."

"Then stay, and show the world you've got nothing to hide. That what the press is saying is nothing more than gossip."

He let his reasoning wash over her. For several minutes, she said nothing, all her concentration focused on an invisible spot inside her drink. When she finally spoke, the words were barely a whisper. "What if you're wrong?"

"I'm not." It hurt to hear the doubt in her voice. Damn her ex for killing her trust. "Whatever happens, you already have three people on your side."

"But last time…" She shook her head.

"Last time there was a trial, no? This time it is only gossip. In a few days the press will have moved on to a new scandal and forgotten all about Luscious Louisa. Then you go back to your life. Surely, you can handle a few days of whispers, can't you?"

"You have no idea how many whispers I've handled in my lifetime," she replied, looking up at last.

Finally, there was a spark. A bit of the fire he'd come to expect. "Good. Then, it's settled. You're staying here, where you belong."

Louisa had opened her mouth to reply but stopped abruptly. He heard the sound of rustling outside on the terrace. She'd heard it, too, because the fingers holding her glass grew white with tension.

For the third time in less than an hour Nico could feel his temper rise. At this rate he would need an entire case of fernet to keep him from murdering the entire Italian media corps.

"Wait here," he mouthed, then held an index finger to his lips. Moving as softly as possible, he headed toward the terrace door, which they'd accidentally left propped open, and peered around the corner. There was another rustle, followed by a flutter before a lark flew past his face. Nico started at the sudden movement, his cheeks turning hot. "Just a bird," he said unnecessarily.

"This time," Louisa replied.

She was right. This time. Sooner or later the paparazzi would get their shot. "Maybe you should stay with Dani and Rafe," he said.

"I thought you didn't want me running away."

"I don't, but I also want you safe." He didn't say it, but it wasn't only the paparazzi he was worried about. There were also those unhinged few who would want to see if Luscious Linda was as sexy as the gossip pages implied. Until the story died down, trespassers were a real threat.

"I don't know..."

Surely they were past her insecurity at this point, weren't they? "What's the problem? As long as you are staying with them, you won't have to worry about the paparazzi. Rafe will make sure no one bothers you." Nico would make sure he did.

"Rafe and Dani have a business to run. I'm not going to ask them to waste their time babysitting me."

"No one is babysitting anyone."

"Aren't they? If they have to spend their time protecting me from all the paparazzi in town then it's babysitting," Louisa replied. "I'm better off grabbing the bus." She took a sip of her drink and grimaced. "What is this stuff?"

"Fernet-Branca."

"I hate peppermint," she replied, and set the glass on the coffee table.

"It is an acquired taste." Her change of topic wasn't going to work. She could complain about the drink all she wanted, he wasn't going to let her leave Monte Calanetti.

Tossing back his own drink, he slapped the glass down before the liquor even started cooling his insides. "If you don't want to stay with Rafe and Dani," he said, "then you'll just have to stay with me."

"Excuse me?"

If the situation weren't so serious, he'd laugh at the shock on her face. It was the perfect solution, though. "You will be able to avoid the paparazzi in the village, plus you'll be close enough to keep an eye on the palazzo. Can you think of a better location?"

"Hell. When it freezes over."

This time he did laugh. Here was the feisty Louisa he was used to.

"I'm serious," she said. "If I don't want Rafe and Dani playing babysitter, I sure as hell don't want you doing it.

She was being stubborn again. It wouldn't work any more than trying to change the subject had. "Fine. If it makes you feel better, you can work while you are staying with me."

"Work?"

"Yes. I told you, since the wedding, we've been inundated with orders for Amatucci Red. I can barely keep up as it is, and with the harvest and the festival coming up, I'm going to need as much help as I can get. Unless you don't think you can handle filing invoices and processing orders."

"You—you'd trust me to do that?"

"Why wouldn't I?"

"What about Luscious Louisa?"

God, how it hurt to see her looking so vulnerable. Tears

rimming her eyes and her lower lip trembling. Silently, he damned Steven Clark for dragging her down with him.

He might have promised to keep his distance, but at this moment, he couldn't stop himself from closing the space between them. He brushed his thumb across her quivering lip.

"Like I told you before, anyone who has spent time with you knows you're not the icy seductress the press makes you out to be."

"Thank you." A tear slipped out the corner of her eye and he fanned it away with his hand. So vulnerable and so beautiful. It shocked him how badly he suddenly needed to keep her safe. But then, this afternoon had been full of shocking reactions he'd never experienced before.

There was one reaction he recognized, though. The stirring in his jeans as he breathed in her scent. He brushed the hair from her face, the strands reminding him of corn silk. Promise be damned. He wanted to kiss her. Quickly, he stepped away before he could take action. Now was not the time to push his luck. "Go pack a bag," he told her. "We'll leave before the paparazzi realize you're gone."

You made the right decision, Louisa reminded herself on the way upstairs. Hiding out *was* better than running away, and Amatucci Vineyards did make the ideal hiding place. Plus she would be earning her keep. It wasn't as though she was going to become Nico's kept woman. She'd insist on the entire arrangement being professional and platonic.

Why, then, was her stomach in knots? Maybe, she thought as her eyes fell on the suitcase in the corner, because she'd gone from leaving town to working for Nico in less than an hour without knowing how she made the journey.

Or maybe it was because saying yes had become a whole lot easier once Nico had brushed her cheek.

CHAPTER FOUR

LUSCIOUS LOUISA'S LATEST CONQUEST?

"TOO BAD THEY couldn't find a proper synonym. *Conquest* spoils the alliteration." Nico said, turning the newspaper over.

Louisa didn't share his sense of humor. The headline screamed across the front page along with a photograph of her and Nico cropped from one of the official wedding shots. Apparently the photographer Nico kicked off her balcony had done some research following the altercation. The article described how the "enraged" vintner had come to her rescue and implied the two of them had been an item for weeks. Or, as the article put it, she'd managed to charm the richest man in town.

This was exactly what she didn't need after a restless night. There was still a large part of her dying to grab the first bus to Florence. Screaming loudly, in fact. She couldn't stop thinking how easily she had agreed to Nico's idea. Sure, he had a point about staying and proving the press wrong, but to put herself in his care like this? It reminded her of how things had begun with Steven. He'd liked to swoop in and take care of everything when they were dating, too. *Only you're not dating Nico*, she reminded herself, staring down at her breakfast pastry.

And unlike with Steven, this time she had age and hindsight in her favor. She may have agreed to stay here, but she would keep her bags packed. That way if the situation changed and the walls started closing in, she could be out of here in a flash.

Meanwhile, her breakfast partner was enjoying his pastry as though he didn't have a care in the world.

"I don't know how you can be so cavalier," she said watching him chew his pastry. Anyone would think he liked being dragged through the tabloid mud.

Nico shrugged. "How am I supposed to act?"

Indignant, perhaps? Angry? Some *show* of emotion. He'd practically exploded when he discovered the paparazzo yesterday, and that had nothing to do with him. These headlines were personal. "The article makes you sound like a lovesick fool."

"Which anyone who knows me will immediately recognize as a complete fabrication. I'm not and have never been the lovesick type."

A fact that should comfort her, seeing as how she was now sleeping under his roof. It didn't, though. Instead, she felt a dull ache in the pit of her stomach.

"So what was yesterday? An anomaly?"

He looked away. "Yesterday I caught a man breaking into your home. I was upset for your safety. This," he said as he waved his cup over the tabloid "is entirely different."

"How? It's still an invasion of privacy. And the things they wrote about us..." As though Nico were some kind of fly trapped in her web. She shivered. "Surely you care what people think."

"I already told you, anyone who knows me will recognize it for the garbage it is."

"Why is that?" Not that she wasn't glad, but she wanted to know why he was so certain.

A strange shadow appeared behind his eyes, turning them darker than usual. "Like I said, I'm not the lovesick kind," he replied. "Now, the fact they referred to me as the 'royal vintner'? That is something I hope people *will* believe. You cannot buy better publicity."

"Glad you're happy." One of them should be.

She took a look around the surroundings that were to be her home away from home for the next few days. Worn out and uncomfortable last night, she'd insisted on being shown straight to her room. Nico's rust-and-green kitchen was warm but dated, like the kitchen of a man who didn't spend too many meals at home. Did that mean he didn't entertain much either? Would people notice he had company?

A sudden, horrifying thought struck her. Now that Nico had been identified, the press would start stalking him, too. For all they knew, a telephoto lens could be trained on them right now. Reflexively, she looked over her shoulder at the kitchen window.

"Relax," Nico told her. "I drew the curtains when we got home last night. No one can see you."

Sure, they couldn't see her now. But eventually… "This was a mistake. I'm better off just going to Florence."

"No one is going anywhere except to the winery." Nico's hand reached across the table and grabbed her wrist, preventing her from standing. "Trust me, everything is going to be fine. In a few days, another scandal will erupt and the press will forget all about you."

Louisa looked down at the bronzed hand gently encircling her arm. His thumb brushing her pulse point, the tiny movement as soothing as a caress. That his slightest touch could calm her was disturbing in itself.

Slipping free, Louisa reached for the newspaper and flipped it back over. The picture on the front page showed the two of them with their heads together in quiet conversation. Arm slung casually over the back of her chair, he was leaning forward as she spoke in his ear, her hand resting lightly on his forearm. She remembered the moment. The orchestra had started playing, and she'd moved closer so she could comment on the song selection. Thanks to the angle, they looked more like a couple who had eyes only for each other.

A second photo greeted her when she turned the page. The two of them dancing. No need to mess with the angle this time. Their gazes were locked; their bodies pressed together like lovers'. Must have been taken only moments before Nico had kissed her.

What if there was a photo of them kissing? Louisa's stomach dropped. The blogosphere would have a field day. Her horror must have shown on her face, because when she looked up, Nico was watching her. "If they had a photo, they would have used it," he said, reading her mind.

He was right, Louisa thought, letting out her breath. "The one they used is bad enough. Did we really look like that?" Like they couldn't get close enough.

"Considering what followed, I would have to say yes."

That's what she was afraid of. Louisa dropped her head on her arms with a groan. "It's only a couple of photographs," he said, patting the back of her head. "We'll survive."

He didn't understand. Any photograph was one photograph too many. "Believe it or not," she said, lifting her head, "there was a time when I liked having my picture taken." She remembered her first public date with Steven and how the local press surrounded them. She'd felt like someone had dropped her on a Hollywood red carpet. "I thought being featured in the paper was the coolest thing ever."

Letting out a long breath, she balanced her chin on the back of her hand. "After Steven was arrested, reporters started camping out in cars across the street. They'd call my name each time I left the house, and I would hear the cameras snapping. Click-click-click-click. It never stopped. After a while I stopped going out unless it was to go to court. I had my food delivered. I kept the curtains drawn.

I swear Steven had more freedom in prison." Out of the corner of her eye, she caught Nico's gaze slide toward his windows and the green linen drapes blocking the view.

"Did you know, I couldn't even take out my garbage, because they would go through the contents?" she asked. "I had to let it pile up in the basement until after the trial was over." If she concentrated, she could smell the stench. The horrible sour smell that drifted up the stairs every time she opened the basement door. "I actually dreamt once that the bags overflowed and buried me alive."

"Bella mia..." He reached for her hand.

Louisa pulled back with a shake of her head. No more comforting touches. "I wasn't trying to make you feel sorry for me." Honestly, she didn't know why she'd told him at all. The memory had simply popped out and it had been the first time she shared the secret with anyone. She supposed it was because the situation was repeating itself again now.

"Well, I promise no garbage here."

How was it he knew the way to make her smile no matter how aggravated or sad she got? "Well, if there is," she said, "you're responsible for taking it out."

"Agreed." Nico smiled, and the warmth in his eyes was as reassuring as any embrace. For that moment, anyway, Louisa felt as if everything would be okay.

Seeing Louisa smile cheered him. It was strange how important seeing her smile was becoming to him. Nico tried to imagine what it must have been like for her during the trial, trapped inside her home while the wolves with their cameras gathered around in wait.

It made him doubly glad that he had lied about the photographs not bothering him. He would never tell Louisa, but seeing the pictures actually bothered him a great deal, although not for the reason she thought. It was his expression in the photographs, a dazed, trancelike appearance that upset him the most. He'd been photographed by the press dozens of times, but never could he remember seeing a shot where he could be seen looking so intently at his partner. Then again, he couldn't remember ever sharing a dance as memorable as the one he shared with Louisa either. Looking at the photograph had brought every detail back into focus, from the softness of her silk gown to the floral scent of her hairspray as she curled into his neck.

Unfortunately, Louisa's reaction was far different. Even though he expected her to get upset, he was surprised at the disappointment her response left in his stomach. Clearly, being the one who usually kept the emotional distance, Nico wasn't used to a woman's disinterest.

Sensing her attention about to return to the headlines, Nico gathered the newspaper and folded it in two. "No more gossip," he said, slapping the paper on the countertop. "We move on to better topics. You need to finish your breakfast. Today is a workday. If you're serious about earning your keep, then we need to get to the winery."

"Are you always this bossy with your houseguests?" she asked, the smile staying in place.

"Only the Americans," Nico countered. What would she say if she discovered she was the first woman to be one of his houseguests? Not even Floriana had been given such an honor. Since his parents had moved away, Nico had preferred the house to remain a place of peace and tranquility, something it had never been when he was a child.

And didn't Louisa, with her damp hair and bare feet, look as if she belonged to the place. The novelty of having company, he decided. Other women would look equally at home, if he ever bothered to invite them.

But would other women engender such a strong desire to protect them? Last night, he'd literally found himself patrolling the house, and again first thing this morning.

Frankly, he was surprised he hadn't stood guard outside Louisa's bedroom door to keep her safe.

Keep her safe or keep her from leaving? The dread that gripped him when she mentioned going to Florence was no less today than it had been yesterday. He wished he understood why her leaving Monte Calanetti disturbed him so much.

He looked past her shoulder to the back door and the thin dark line scored in the wood just to the left of the doorknob. A reminder of the time his mother had thrown a carving knife at his father's disappearing back. "Did you sleep well?" he heard himself ask.

"Okay," she said. "It's never easy sleeping the first night in a new place and all."

"Perhaps, after a full day's work, tonight will be better." For both of them. Wiping his mouth, he tossed the napkin onto his empty plate and stood up. "Speaking of… we have a busy day. Get your shoes on and I'll show you what you'll be doing for me."

Beyond the vineyards themselves, Amatucci Vineyards had two primary sections. There was a medieval stone villa that housed the store and wine-tasting rooms as well as a modern production facility. It was to the second building that Nico and Louisa headed, cutting through the rear garden and vines. Something else Louisa had been too stressed out to appreciate yesterday. Unlike the villa, which was stately and ripe with family heirlooms, Nico's garden was a breathtaking display of natural beauty. The vines draping the pergola beams had minds of their own, their branches dipping and weaving into a unique overhead tapestry. Likewise, urns had been placed around the terracotta terrace, their roses and olive plants spiraling up cedar trellises with stunning wildness.

"I like to be reminded of how rugged the hills can be,"

Nico said when she complimented him. *Rugged* was a good word and fit him perfectly, she thought, dodging a low-hanging branch. Nico was earthy and independent. Civilized, but not completely.

"Most of the employees are in the field at this time of day," Nico told her as he unlocked the facility door. "I'll set you up in one of the back offices so you'll have maximum privacy. I also sent an email to the staff last night reminding them that I expect professionalism and discretion at all times, and that I won't tolerate gossip."

"Sounds like you've thought of everything." *Swooping in to take control...* A tightness found its way into her stomach, which she immediately pushed aside. *Not the same thing*, she silently snapped. *Stop comparing.*

The door opened into a small receiving room dominated by filing cabinets and a cluttered metal desk at which a lanky young man too big for his chair sat reading. Behind him a glass window looked out over a warehouse-sized room full of gleaming stainless-steel processing machines.

He practically jumped to his feet when he heard Nico shut the door. "*Signor!* I was just—just—" Seeing Louisa, he stopped midsentence and simply stared. This morning's newspaper lay open on the desk, the photo of her and Nico on display.

"Good morning, Mario. I'd like you to meet Louisa Harrison from Palazzo di Comparino. She's offered to help us fulfill shipping orders so we can get ready for harvest."

"Hello."

"Mario is studying viticulture at the university. He wants to learn how to become a great vintner."

Mario was doing his best to look anywhere but at her. Still, if Nico could breeze in here and act as though there wasn't a suggestive photo of them lying a foot away, then so could she. Mustering up some fake confidence, she flashed the young man a smile. "Pleasure to meet you, Mario," she said holding out her hand.

"Um, yes. Likewise," Mario muttered. Still avoiding her gaze, he hurriedly shook her hand before picking up a stack of paperwork. "I'd better finish getting these field readings recorded into the system," he said. Clasping the papers to his chest, he rushed out of the office.

"Told you people would have problems with me," she said once the young man disappeared.

Nico's mouth was a thin tight line. "I will talk to him. Let him know that kind of behavior is unacceptable."

"Don't. It's not his fault."

"But of course it is. I won't have my employees treating you poorly. He needs to know that."

"Please." She grabbed his hand as he headed toward the door. "I don't want to make a scene." Mario's behavior was nothing compared to what she'd endured in Boston. What she didn't want was to feel as though she was under an even bigger spotlight. "Just show me where I'm supposed to sit and let me get to work."

"You're going to stay, then? I don't have to talk you out of leaving?"

"For now." She was here. She might as well try to tough it out for a little while. After all, there was always the chance Mario was just shy or something, right?

The way Nico's face brightened helped, too, as did his softly spoken "I'm glad."

"But, before I bring you to your office," he added, "I want to show you the facility. You should know your way around the building if I'm not here and you need to find something."

The office exited into the main plant. Standing on the landing just outside the office door, Louisa was shocked to see the facilities empty.

"Where is everybody?" she asked.

"I always close right before harvest. Gives the employees time with their families and lets me make sure the equipment is in working order. Enjoy the silence while you can. Come next week this building will be so loud you won't be able to hear yourself think."

"I bet." She didn't have a clue what any of the machines did, but simply given the sheer number of machines she'd expect a lot of noise. "It all looks so modern," she remarked. "Not quite how I expected wine to be made."

"No doubt you pictured a dark cavern full of oak casks where a group of Italian gypsy women crush the grapes by foot?"

"Nothing that dramatic."

"Are you sure? That's what the tourists believe. Why do you think my store is in the oldest building on the property? To continue the myth."

Meanwhile, their Old World wine was being produced in the finest of twenty-first-century stainless-steel and concrete surroundings. "So no grape stomping at all, then?" Louisa asked as she followed him down the stairs and onto the plant floor.

"Only at the harvest festival."

Ahead, they caught the flash of a pale blue work shirt near one of the machines. "Vitale," Nico called out. "Is that you?"

A silver head appeared. "Yes, *signor.* I was replacing the timer belt." Just like Mario had, the man avoided looking in her direction. "You were right, *signor*," he said. "It had worn thin. We shouldn't have any more problems."

"Good. Good. Vitale, I'd like you to meet Louisa." Once again, Nico forced an introduction, and again Louisa was acknowledged with a nervous smile and a nod before Nico offered Vitale an excuse to leave.

"Give them time," Nico told her when she started to comment. "They'll warm up to you."

Sure they will, she thought with a sigh. “People are going to believe what they want to believe, Nico.” Sometimes even when the truth was right in front of them—the way she had with Steven. “And in this case, the headlines have had way too big a head start.”

“Headlines be damned. Once they get to know you, they’ll realize what is written in the papers is garbage. In a few weeks no one in Monte Calanetti will even care about Luscious Louisa.”

“From your lips…”

While they were talking, he’d moved closer, narrowing the space between them until he stood no more than a foot away. Close enough she could see the dark hair peering out from the open collar of his shirt and smell the spicy citrus of his aftershave. “Louisa,” he said, his gentle voice sounding as though he were stating the simplest of truths. “It doesn’t take a rocket scientist to see the truth about a person.”

“Don’t be so sure. There’s an entire town back in Massachusetts that could prove you wrong.”

Nico chuckled. Despite the gap between them, his fingers had somehow found their way into her hair and were combing the strands away from her face. “You’re being dramatic, *bella mia*. I’m sure your true friends knew better.”

“They might have, if I’d had any.”

“What are you talking about?”

“Nothing.” Distracted by his touch, she’d opened a door she hadn’t meant to open. “Like you said, I’m being dramatic.”

He didn’t believe her, but Louisa didn’t care. She’d revealed enough secrets for one day.

“I’m tired,” she said instead. “It’s making me say silly things.”

“You should get some rest, then.”

Easier said than done. True *rest* had eluded her for years. The last time she'd relaxed—truly relaxed—had been when? The first few months of her marriage? Such a long time ago.

Dear Lord, but she was tired of being on guard, and Nico's touch felt so wonderfully comforting. With a soothing brush of his hand, her resistance slipped a little further. It felt so good having someone on her side. Nico's shoulder was right there. Broad, capable, strong. Would it be so bad if she leaned on him for just a little bit? She was so very tired of being alone.

With a soft sigh escaping her lips, she curled into him.

"It's all right," she heard Nico whisper as his arms wrapped around her. "I'm here. I'll take care of everything."

This was a first for Nico. Taking a woman in his arms without any intention of making love to her. But as he drew her close, her sweet floral scent wrapping itself around him, his only thought was of reassurance. He knew why, of course. Louisa's cool and distant mask had slipped, and the vulnerability he saw deepened the queer sense of protectiveness she'd awakened in him. Every time, the depth of what he was feeling shocked him. What was it about this blonde American that made him want to fly to America and strangle every reporter in the country personally for causing her such pain?

At least he could make sure the European press didn't copy their American colleagues, even if he had to physically throw every paparazzo in Italy off his property. Cradling her head against his shoulder, he whispered. "It's all right. I'll take care of everything."

Instantly, she stiffened. "No," she said pulling out of his embrace. "Don't."

Nico opened his mouth to argue, expecting to see the

same indignant expression he'd seen at the wedding, the last time she reacted this way. The color had drained from her face, turning her so pale her skin nearly matched the white blond of her hair. Her eyes were pale, too, as though she were struggling to keep fear from invading their depths.

If he didn't know better, he'd say she seen a ghost.

What had he done? Or had something else happened in Boston, something more than the paparazzi trapping her in her home?

She blinked and the expression disappeared. Back was the Louisa he knew best. Distant and guarded. "It was wrong of me to lean on you like that," she said. "I lost myself for a second. It won't happen again."

"There's nothing wrong with turning to a friend when you're upset." He wondered if the word *friend* sounded as wrong to her ears as it did his. Surely holding a friend didn't feel as good as holding Louisa did. There was an amazing rightness in the way her body connected with his.

"I know, but…" She looked past him, to the window that looked into the front office. Inside, Vitale and Mario could be seen talking. "You've already done enough, letting me hide here."

That wasn't what she was going to say. She was worried what others would think.

"You are not hiding; you are working. Believe me, it is you who will be doing me the favor."

"Do you invite all your employees to stay at your house?"

"Only the beautiful ones," he teased. When she didn't share the joke, he turned serious. "No one will know that you're staying at my house."

"You don't think they'll figure it out?"

"Only if we tell them," he replied. "I've never had much taste for airing personal business in public."

Finally, she smiled. “Nico Amatucci, the model of discretion.”

“Something like that.”

“Just in case, now that I am working here, I think it’s important that you treat me the same as any other employee. Especially considering today’s headlines. No sense feeding the gossip.”

“You’re right.” A voice in his head, though, told him gossip was only part of her reason. There was something more to her distance. And not the need to spend time alone, as she’d claimed the other day. It was as if she feared the attraction simmering between them. He supposed he couldn’t blame her; the desire was stronger than anything he’d experienced before, as well.

“A regular employee,” he said, echoing her words. Now was not the time to push for more. “I’ll leave the hugs to your female friends. Speaking of, have you spoken to Dani?”

Louisa shook her head. “Not yet.”

“Why not?” *Of course.* The way she looked away said everything. She was embarrassed. In spite of his lecture yesterday, she still worried her friends thought less of her.

If I had friends. Her comment from earlier came rushing back, and his insides tensed with anger on her behalf.

“You should call her,” he said. “She’s worried.”

“I will. After I’ve settled in.”

“Good.” If she didn’t, he would tell Dani and the others to come visit. She needed to know she had friends on her side, that the people of Monte Calanetti cared what happened to her.

As much as he did.

They spent the rest of the morning touring the winery. Nico explained the entire winemaking process from when the lifts brought freshly picked fruit to the loading dock to the fermentation stage, when the wine aged in oak barrels, just as it had for hundreds of years.

Occasionally, they passed an employee who would murmur a quick hello and rush away. While Louisa pretended not to mind the chilly reception, the words *if I had friends* repeated in his head. All he could picture was her barricaded in her house, surrounded by garbage she was too afraid to take outside while the world stared at her in judgment. He refused to let that happen again, not while she was under his protection.

By the time they finished and she was settled in the rear office with a stack of orders that needed fulfilling, his anger was at the boiling point. He marched back into the processing room and straight toward Mario and Vitale. "You will be friendly and polite to Louisa," he growled. "Is that clear?"

Both men nodded rapidly. He never raised his voice unless trying to yell over the machinery. "Good. You let the rest of the company know, as well. If I hear of anyone showing her disrespect, they will answer to me personally."

The people of Monte Calanetti would warm up to Louisa, even if he had to make them.

CHAPTER FIVE

"I DON'T BELIEVE IT. You really *are* working here."

Louisa froze in her chair at the sight of Marianna, Nico's sister, standing in the doorway wearing a decidedly vexed expression. "When Dani told me, I thought she was joking," she said.

Dani worked fast. Louisa had only called her best friend a few hours ago. Clearly the youngest Amatucci had rushed right over the second she got the news.

"It's only a temporary arrangement," she said. She managed to keep the defensiveness out of her voice, Barely. "I'm helping with order fulfillment."

The brunette waved away the answer as she stepped into the room. Being in her third trimester, her pregnant belly entered a full step before her. "He better not be making you work for a free dinner the way he used to make me. I don't care how wonderful a chef Rafe is, he's not as good as euros in your pocket."

She wanted Louisa to get paid? That was her concern? Louisa didn't know what to say. "You mean you don't mind my being here?"

"Why should I?" She eased herself into a nearby chair with a sigh. "Oh," she said seeing Louisa's expression. "You mean because the press said you two were dating."

"Among other things."

Again, the woman waved her off. "Who believes anything the newspapers say? Are those wine orders?" She motioned to a spreadsheet of names and addresses on the desk.

"Yesterday's telephone orders." Louisa grabbed the

change of topic with more gratitude than she thought possible. "I haven't printed out the internet orders yet."

"Wow, Nico wasn't kidding when he said the business was doing well."

No, he wasn't. Wine vendors, restaurants, tourists—everyone was eager to stock Amatucci Red. "No surprise," Nico had remarked, winking in her direction. "Once they have a taste, they want more."

Louisa had poured herself a glass before bed last night, and it was as delicious as she remembered. *When it had been a lingering flavor in Nico's kiss*, she recalled with a shiver. Between the wine and yesterday's embrace, it was no wonder she'd dreamt of him all night.

Once they have a taste, they want more.

"At this rate he won't have much stock left for the harvest festival," Marianna said, dragging Louisa back to the conversation at hand. "Unless he bottles more."

"I don't think the next vintage is ready." As Nico explained yesterday, the liquid needed to ferment at least five years before it was considered ready for bottling. "He said something about relabeling the remaining stock as Amatucci reserve."

"Relabeling and jacking up the price to reflect the reduced supply," Marianna mused aloud. "An old winemaker's trick, although few pull it off as well as my brother does. There's a reason he's won the country's Winemaker of the Year two years in a row."

"He has?"

"You didn't know?"

"No." She'd had no idea. "I knew the winery was successful." The sheer scope of his operations said as much. "But I didn't know how much so."

"Much as we tease him, my big brother has done very well with our family business. He's considered one of Italy's brightest wine stars."

"Careful, Marianna. Keep saying things like that and I'll believe you mean them." The subject of their conversation strolled in wearing a cocky grin. As Louisa had come to expect over the past couple of days, he already bore the evidence of hard work in the sun. The sight of his glistening biceps made her stomach flutter.

He nodded in her direction. "Although I hope you're suitably impressed."

"I am," she replied. "Very." Smug as the man was, the only awards he'd ever mentioned were the medals various vintages had won over the years, and those he attributed to the grapes, not to himself.

Now that she thought about it though, he didn't need to trumpet his accomplishments. His self-confidence said everything. "I was telling your sister that you planned to relabel the Amatucci Red," she said.

"Nothing wine lovers love more than to think they are getting something unique. And in this case they are."

He smiled again, straight at her this time, and Louisa found herself squeezing the arm of her chair. Who knew legs could give out while you were sitting? When he turned on the charm, it was all a person could do to keep her insides from turning to jelly. What her ex-husband could have done with magnetism like Nico's... *With a little charm, a man can sell anything*, Steven used to say.

Only Nico didn't just sell, he *made* wine. Good wine that he worked hard to produce. He came by his success honestly. That was what she found impressive.

Across the way, his baby sister offered a disdainful sniff. "Don't compliment him too much, Louisa. His head is big enough as it is."

"Not as big as your belly," Nico replied. "Are you supposed to be out in that condition?"

"You're as bad as my husband. I'm pregnant, not an

invalid. I'm also bored stiff. Ryan is in Melbourne until tomorrow."

"So you came here looking for entertainment."

"Isn't that what big brothers are for?" the brunette asked, winking in Louisa's direction.

Louisa felt herself smile in return. Marianna's openness had her flummoxed. She was so certain she would be furious at her for involving Nico in her scandals. Yet here she was, joking as if none of the stories had ever happened.

"If you're going to stay, you're going to have to work," Nico told his sister.

"You want me to pick grapes?"

"No, we—" waving his arm, he indicated himself and Louisa "—can pick your brain. That is the reason I am here," he said. "We need to decide what the winery is going to do for the festival."

"You haven't decided yet?" Eyes wide, Marianna pushed herself straight. "Little last-minute, don't you think?"

"In case you haven't noticed, I've been busy. We still have time." He sounded confident, but Marianna rolled her eyes nonetheless.

"What kind of contribution are you talking about?" Louisa asked. More important, what did Nico expect from her?

"All the major businesses in Monte Calanetti are expected to build a float for the festival parade," Nico explained. "Something that celebrates the harvest or Tuscan heritage."

"Decorated with native foliage," Marianna added. "Grapes, olives, flowers."

"Wow." Louisa hadn't realized the festival was so elaborate. In her mind, she'd pictured a street fair similar to the St. Anthony's Feast in Boston's North End. "Sounds like a lot of fun."

"It is," Marianna told her. "Everyone works together to

decorate and all the businesses compete to see who can outdo the others. The winner gets to display the harvest festival trophy. Amatucci Vineyards came in second last year. We created a miniature version of the plaza, complete with a working fountain." Pulling out her phone, the woman tapped a few buttons before turning the screen toward Louisa. "See?"

The photo showed Nico standing in front of the fountain, hands upon his hips. His smile dripping with pride. He looked like a superhero.

"Impressive," she murmured. Bet whoever took home the trophy didn't look nearly as good.

Marianna assumed Louisa meant the float. "Well, we started planning early. It's nearly impossible to assemble a prize-winning contribution at the last minute."

"Nearly, but not completely impossible," Nico retorted. "All we need is a good idea."

"Don't forget time," Marianna added.

Her brother waved her off, the same wave, Louisa noticed, his sister had used when dismissing the newspaper articles. "We will keep the design simple. It's not about being complicated, it's about being memorable. Like an Amatucci vintage."

His sister rolled her eyes again as Louisa stifled a snort. She was beginning to think some of his audacious behavior was on purpose. To see what kind of reaction he could elicit.

As far as the parade float went, however, he might have a point. She tried to remember the New Year's parades she used to watch on television as a kid. Most of the floats were a blur of colors. "Is there a theme?" she asked.

"Oh, there's always a theme," Nico replied. "But no one pays attention."

"No one meaning Ni—"

All of a sudden, Marianna gasped and clutched her

stomach. Louisa and Nico were on their feet in a flash. The brunette held up a hand. "No need to panic. The baby kicked extra hard, is all. Going to be a little football player, I think. Uncle Nico is going to have to practice his footwork." Her face radiating maternal tranquility, she rubbed her swollen stomach. "Are you ready to play coach, Uncle Nico?"

Louisa's heart squeezed a little as the image of Nico and a miniature version of himself chasing a soccer ball popped into her head.

"I'm not sure I'd be the best coach," Nico replied. It was an uncharacteristically humble comment.

"I suppose you'd be happier if he or she wants to pick grapes."

"I—I just think we shouldn't be making plans for the child's future yet. It's too early. You don't want to court bad luck."

Funny, Louisa wouldn't have pegged Nico as the superstitious type. She supposed it came from being a farmer. No counting on the harvest until it happens or something like that.

Marianna acknowledged his reluctance with a frown. "Fine," she said. "We'll wait until he or she is born before making plans.

"Although I still think she's going to be a football player," she said under her breath.

They brainstormed ideas for a while, until a problem in the wine cellar drew Nico away. Louisa and Marianna continued for a little while longer, but it was obvious the pregnant woman was beginning to tire, despite her protests.

"Story of my life," Marianna said with a yawn. "I can't do anything for more than a half hour before needing a nap."

"Might as well enjoy it while you can," Louisa told her. "Who knows when you'll get this much sleep again?"

The brunette nodded as if she'd delivered some great wisdom. "So true. I'll call you tomorrow and we can talk more about the project."

The two women walked to the front door. As usual, the few employees in the production area watched as they passed by. Marianna waved to each one with a smile while Louisa tucked her hair behind her ear and tried to act nonchalant. The past hour, watching Nico and his sister tease each other back and forth, had been the most relaxed she'd felt in forty-eight hours. She hated the idea that as soon as Marianna left, the atmosphere would go back to being tense and awkward.

They'd reached the door to the front office when Marianna suddenly turned serious. "May I ask you a question?" she asked.

Louisa's stomach tensed. Things had been going so well. What would change Marianna's mood so abruptly? It didn't help to see the other woman looking over her shoulder for potential eavesdroppers. "Of course," she said. "Anything."

"Is it me, or was Nico strangely disinterested when we were talking about the baby?"

Now that she mentioned it, Nico's reaction had been odd, especially considering how invested he had been when Marianna had first announced her pregnancy. Of course, at the time Marianna and her husband had been estranged and he had been worried about his sister's future. "You heard him; he doesn't want to court bad luck," she said.

"I know, but he's never been superstitious before," Marianna replied with a frown. "If anything, I'd expect him to tell me superstition was a bunch of nonsense. He used to hate it whenever our mother saw one of her omens."

"Your mother saw omens?"

"Oh, all the time. Usually after a fight with my father telling her they should make up."

Interesting. "Well, this is the first baby in the Amatucci family. Maybe it's making him tap into his roots."

"Maybe. He does like tradition."

"Plus, he's probably distracted. He has been super busy, between harvest and helping the town get ready for the festival." *And finding time to help her.*

"That is true. He does seem more distracted than usual these days." Marianna's frown quickly turned into a smile that was disarmingly similar to her brother's. "At least some of those distractions are good distractions, no?"

She didn't think that Louisa and he... The brunette's eyes sparkled, causing Louisa's stomach to tumble. "You said you didn't believe the papers."

"Oh, I don't believe the stuff about Luscious Louisa, but you and Nico... I saw that photo of the two of you dancing." She nudged Louisa's shoulder. *"Molto romantico."*

"It was just the camera angle," Louisa said, shaking her head. "The two of us are just friends."

"Friends, eh? Did he really throw a photographer off your balcony?"

Louisa sighed. "Yes, but again, it's not what you think. He was helping me out. You know your brother. If there's a situation that needs handling, he automatically takes charge."

"Hmm. I do know my brother," Marianna said with an odd smile.

"What does that mean?"

"Nothing. You are completely right. My brother does like to take charge. And in this case, I couldn't be happier."

Meaning she still thought they were involved. Louisa would have to have Nico set his sister straight. Still, it was nice to know her friend didn't think Louisa was out to seduce Nico for his money. Her trust meant a lot.

"You really don't care about what they said about me...

about what happened in Boston? What they implied I was doing here in town?"

"Don't be silly. You're not responsible for what your ex-husband did. And you're the last person I'd call a temptress. I mean, look at what you're wearing..." She gestured at Louisa's jeans and green cotton sweater. "I'm dressed more seductively."

"It's the stiletto heels. They make everything seductive." Louisa tried to punctuate the remark with a laugh, but tears sprang to her eyes anyway. Marianna would never know how much her faith meant. Unable to form the words, she threw her arms around the pregnant woman's neck.

"Don't you know you're not supposed to get teary around a pregnant woman? My hormones won't be able to take it and I'll start crying, too." The young woman squeezed her tight, then released her with a watery grin. "I'll call you tomorrow."

Wiping her own eyes, Louisa nodded. "Do you mind if I don't walk you any farther? There might be reporters hiding across the street."

"Of course, I understand. And Louisa?" The brunette reached out to squeeze Louisa's hand. "I'm glad you and my brother are such good friends. He doesn't have that many."

Not many friends? "You're kidding right? We are talking about the same Nico Amatucci, aren't we?" The man with charisma to spare.

"Those are acquaintances, not real friends. He doesn't open himself up to many people. That makes you special."

Special. Right. Marianna's hormones were definitely out of whack.

A sound caught her attention. Looking across the room, she spied Nico talking to an employee by the wine cellar doorway. Almost as if he knew she was thinking about him, he stopped what he was doing to look in her direction. He smiled and, for a moment, Louisa swore the entire winery tipped on its axis. *That makes you special...*

Apparently, Marianna wasn't the only one out of whack.

Louisa was upstairs asleep when Nico got home. He'd planned it that way. Following their embrace the day before, he decided it made sense for them to keep as much distance as possible, so he made a point of working as late as possible, along with heading into the fields before sunrise. The idea was for the long hours to make him too tired to remember the way her body had fit against his, allowing him to sleep without disturbance.

He didn't count on Marianna stopping by and stirring up other disturbing thoughts.

His sister was having a baby, he thought as he poured a glass of Chianti. Despite knowing this for months, it hadn't truly dawned on him until she'd called him Uncle Nico that she was starting a family of her own. Both she and his brother, Angelo, were moving forward with their lives, while here he was in the ancestral home maintaining the past. He, who was so determined never to repeat the madness of his parents.

Settling back on the sofa, he stared in the dim light at the dark square of the unlit fireplace. In his head, he could hear the sound of his parents laughing and clinking glasses. When they were happy, they laughed a lot, but when they stopped laughing… At least his father stayed in nice hotels when Mama threw him out.

All highs and lows, Carlos used to say. *No in betweens.* He never understood how that worked. How people could go from hot to cold to hot again in the blink of an eye. He once told Floriana that it was one thing to have passion in the bedroom, but it was quite another to have passion rule your life. Right before Floriana left, she told him that he had no passion, period.

She'd made a strong argument. He'd barely blinked when she'd said it.

He wondered what she would have said if she'd seen him throw that photographer off the balcony? Probably that she didn't recognize him. Again, she would have a point; Nico barely recognized himself the past couple of days, he was behaving so out of character.

Maybe Louisa really was a siren like the tabloids said. The thought made him chuckle into his glass.

"Nico? Is that you?"

The object of his thoughts appeared at the top of the stairs, a backlit silhouette. It took about two seconds for Nico to become aroused. Another thing that was out of character for him was how he couldn't seem to stop wanting her. Usually, when a woman said she wasn't interested, he moved on. No sense knocking on a door that wouldn't open. With Louisa, however, he didn't want to just knock, he wanted to kick the door in.

"Sorry to wake you," he said. "I was just having a glass of wine before bed."

"Long day?"

"Harvest takes a lot of preparation. Did Mario get you home all right?" He'd ordered his intern to escort her in case there were photographers lying in wait.

"He did. I hope you don't mind, but I got hungry and made some dinner. Puttanesca. There are leftovers in the fridge."

The notion of her at home in his kitchen caused a curious end-over-end sensation in the center of his chest. "Thank you."

"No problem. Good night," she said. Her silhouette hesitated. "Will I see you at breakfast?"

He thought of how good she looked drinking espresso across from him, and the sensation repeated itself. "Afraid not. I have to be in the fields early."

"Oh. Okay. I'll see you at the winery then."

Any disappointment he heard in her voice was pure imagination. As he finished his Chianti, he made a note to take the newspapers with him again when he left tomorrow. The "Royal Wedding Scandal," as they were calling it now, continued to dominate the tabloids, and he wanted to protect Louisa from the exposure.

Is that the argument you're using? Not that you don't want her leaving town? The very thought of her getting on the bus made his heart seize.

Out of character indeed.

The newspapers were missing again. For the second day in a row, Louisa came down for breakfast to discover both Nico and the papers gone from the house.

Who did he think he was, censoring her reading material?

She tracked him down in the fields and asked him that exact question.

"Keep your voice down, *bella mia*," he replied. "Unless you want people to know about our living arrangement." He nodded down the row where a pair of farm hands were watching them with curiosity. "And to answer your question, I wasn't aware I was 'censoring' anything."

"Then where are the newspapers?"

"I took them with me to read over coffee."

"Read about the Royal Wedding Scandal, you mean."

"Where did you hear about that?" The mask of indifference he'd been wearing slipped, proving his deception. Louisa glared at him. "Princess Christina called me this morning to ask how I was doing. She wanted me to know she and Prince Antonio didn't care what people were saying."

"See? Didn't I tell you that your friends would stand by you?"

Yes, he had, and Christina's phone call had meant more to her than she could say. That wasn't the point at the moment, however. "Don't try to change the topic. This is about you keeping information from me."

Nico sighed. "I was trying to protect you from useless gossip."

"Useless or not, you don't have the right to decide what I read and what I don't read." She rubbed her arms. Despite the sun beating down, her skin had turned to gooseflesh. She felt as though she'd had this conversation before with Steven. Only then the argument had been in her head because she'd not dared to speak her mind. Today was the first time she'd said the words aloud.

"I'm sorry. You were so upset by the headlines the other morning, I wanted to save you further distress." While talking, he pulled a grape off the vine and crushed it between his fingers. "I hate seeing you sad," he added, staring at his stained fingers.

The sweetness behind his answer dispelled a little of her anger. Only a little, however. "That's not your call to make, Nico. It's not your job to protect me from the headlines."

"No, just the paparazzi," he replied.

Louisa winced. He had her there. She was using him for protection, making her indignation over the newspapers sound more than a little hypocritical. "Do you want me to move back to the palazzo?"

"Do you want to move back?"

She toed the dirt with her sandal. Short answer? No. She liked having him nearby. Which meant maybe she should move back. "I don't know."

"Oh." He grabbed his satchel, which sat on the ground by his feet, and headed down the row.

She followed him. Thankfully the workers had moved

to another row, leaving them in privacy. "That's all you're going to say?"

"You're not a prisoner, Louisa. You can do whatever you want."

Though cool, she could still hear the hint of hurt in his voice. Problem was, what she wanted scared her. She wanted the security she felt when she was wrapped in Nico's arms. *Which is exactly the opposite of why you came to Italy in the first place. What happened to standing on your own two feet for a change?*

"So what did the headlines say anyway?" she asked.

"You mean you didn't go online and look?"

"No." Her cheeks burned. Going online would have been the easy solution, but she'd been too busy being indignant to turn on the computer. "I came looking for you instead."

"Well, you didn't miss much," Nico replied.

"Apparently I did, or you wouldn't have taken the papers." And he wouldn't be studying the Sangiovese leaves so intently. The winemaker had two very distinct stares, she'd come to realize. His intense "never missed a beat" stare that made her skin tingle, and his "I'm not telling you the whole story so I'm going to look at something else" stare. "Tell me."

"No doubt Christina told you about the royal wedding part. Halencia's government is afraid you might try to entice the royal family into making dubious investments."

"She told me." That wasn't the whole story, though. Not based on how Nico continued to stare at the vines. He took a deep breath. "They also interviewed my former fiancée."

CHAPTER SIX

"OH." IT WAS not the answer Louisa expected. She had suspected the papers would continue plumbing their erstwhile romance, but, in her self-involved haze, she hadn't thought about them digging into Nico's past. Dozens of questions came to mind, but the only words she could manage to say out loud were "I didn't realize you'd been engaged."

He shrugged. "It was a long time ago."

But not so long ago the memory didn't bother him. "Did she say something bad?" Was that why he continued to avoid her eyes?

"Actually she was surprisingly diplomatic. But then, Floriana was—is—a very good person."

If she was so good, why then why was she an ex? Louisa tried to picture the kind of woman Nico would propose to. Someone beautiful, no doubt. And smart. She would have to be smart to keep up with him. More questions came to mind, like what had kept them from the altar? From the shadows filling his expression, the decision hadn't been his, at least not completely.

Her annoyance from before all but forgotten, she reached out to touch his arm. "I'm sorry if it dredged up a lot of bad memories."

At last, he shifted his gaze, turning from the grapes to where her fingers rested on his forearm. As always happened, when his eyes fell on her, the attention made her body tingle. "Not everyone is made to get married."

True or not, his answer, with its lonely, resigned tone, hurt her to hear. Louisa found it hard to think of Nico as ever being lonely—the concepts *Nico* and *alone* seemed like polar opposites. But lines had suddenly appeared around his mouth and eyes as he spoke, lines that could only be etched from sadness.

"Sometimes we just pick the wrong person the first time around, is all," she said, thinking of her own mistake.

"Sometimes. I should check the Brix content on these vines." Pulling away from her touch, he reached for his satchel.

He didn't want to talk about it. Fine. If anyone understood the need to bury past mistakes, she did, and if changing topics took the sadness away from his eyes, all the better.

Nico wasn't the only one who hated to see another person sad.

"Are they ready for harvest?" she asked.

"You tell me." Picking a grape, he pressed it to her lips. Louisa could taste the sweetness the moment she bit down. Once she moved past the feel of his fingers on her lips, that is. "Mmm, delicious."

"If the sugar content matches up, I'll tell the foreman to have his team start working this field tomorrow. By the time we finish, the other fields, yours, should be ready."

"You mean they aren't all ready at the same time?" She stole another grape. The fruit was still sweet, but it didn't make her lips respond like the one he fed her had.

"Grapes on the northern side of the vineyard always ripen sooner. They're on a slope angled to get the most sun throughout the day. Carlos used to call Northern grapes *favorito della Natura* because they got the most sunshine."

"Nature's favorites?"

"He had names for all the fields. The ones in the southern field he called *scontroso*—grumpy—because they were often slow to ripen."

"Wouldn't you be grumpy, too, if the other field was the favorite?"

"That's what I used to tell him."

Louisa smiled, imagining the two men walking the rows, nicknaming the plants. "Carlos sounds like a character."

"He was a very wise man. A born winemaker."

Whose fields would be ruined, but for Nico's care. Guilt kicked at her conscience. If only she could have claimed her inheritance sooner. "I had no idea any of the Bertonellis ever existed," she said. "My mother never talked about my father's family." Never talked about her father, period, actually. Geoffrey Harrison was a smooth-talking liar best left unmentioned.

"Don't feel bad. I never knew he had relatives in America."

"Tight family bonds, huh?" she said. The sarcasm came out more bitter than she meant.

"Trust me, family bonds aren't always so wonderful. They can get in the way, too. Like baby sisters deciding you need to entertain them when they are pregnant and bored."

Who did he think he was kidding? He'd loved Marianna's visit yesterday and they both knew it.

"I would have killed for a brother or sister," she said. "Most of my life, it was just my mom and me. We used to joke it was us against the world."

"Must be upsetting for her to see her daughter being lambasted in the press. Have you talked to her?"

"No. She…um…" It was her turn to study the grape vines. How did she explain that she'd screwed up the one good relationship in her life? She'd love to blame Steven again, but this time she had only herself to blame. "I don't want to bother her."

Just as she recognized his evasion tactics, Nico recognized hers. "You don't think your mother's aware of what's going on?" he asked.

"I'm sure she is, but..." But Louisa was too embarrassed to call and talk about it. "The two of us were estranged for a while. I don't want to spoil things by bringing up bad news right as we're getting on better footing."

This wasn't the direction she planned for their conversation to take. Seemed as though whenever the two of them talked lately, she found herself sharing some facet of her past she'd sworn to keep secret. Frightening, how easily she exposed herself to him, more frightening than her desire to lean on his shoulder, and yet at the same time, the words tumbled out without pause.

Perhaps it was because Nico accepted what she said without pushing for more. Like now, he simply nodded and, hands in his back pockets, began sauntering down the row. Made her feel, in spite of how easily the information came out, that she was in control of the information she chose to share.

Mimicking his posture, Louisa headed after him, and the two of them walked in silence for several feet.

"Carlos taught me to appreciate the art of winemaking," he said after a moment, returning to their earlier conversation. Again, Louisa silently thanked him for not pushing. "He never let me forget that ours is a centuries-old craft, and as such we have an obligation to make the best wine possible."

"And your father? He was a vintner, too, was he not?" Strange that Nico's allegiance would be to his neighbor and not the man who raised him. "Did Carlos teach him, as well?"

"My father made wine, but not like Carlos. He was, shall we say, too distracted by other things."

Distracted how? Dying to know, Louisa had to bite her tongue to keep from asking. After all, she owed Nico the same courtesy he showed her when it came to privacy.

He answered anyway. "My mother, for one thing.

Women who weren't my mother, for another. Don't worry," he added before she could offer sympathy. "Mama gives as good as she gets."

"They're still together?" She didn't know why that surprised her, but it did.

"They have what you would call a fiery relationship," Nico replied. "They've separated and reunited more times than I can count, swearing to God every time that they cannot live without each other, and they can't, for about a year or so. Then the plates begin to fly again." The early-morning sun caught his eyes as he cocked his head. Even when sad, he was beautiful. "You could practically hear the clock ticking between breakups."

"I'm sorry."

"Why are you apologizing? You didn't do anything."

No, but she felt as though she needed to say *something*. She knew that feeling of heavy expectancy all too well, the horrible sense of foreboding as you waited—and waited—for some undefined disaster to strike. "Is that how you ended up at the palazzo?"

"The palazzo vineyards were my escape. No chaos, no drama. Just peace and quiet." He took a long, deep breath, making Louisa wonder if he wasn't trying to internalize those very same qualities now. "At first I just went and watched the workers. Then one day Carlos came by—I think the workers told him about me—and he understood.

"My parents' reputations were well-known," he added with a smile. "Anyway, after that, he said if I was going to spend time in the vineyards, I was going to learn about them."

"You're very lucky," Louisa said. How often had she wished she had an ally like Carlos, only to end up hating herself because her isolation was no one's fault but her own?

"I know."

It dawned on her that Carlos Bertonelli had rescued them both, albeit in different ways. Shame rolled through her as she thought about how long it had taken her to claim her inheritance. She'd nearly let her sanctuary fall to pieces because she'd foolishly let herself be convinced there was no escaping her marriage.

"I'm sorry I never got to meet him," she said.

"Me, too." His lips curled into a smile. "He would have liked you a lot, you know," he told her. "The old man always had a soft spot for beautiful women. Right up to the end."

Louisa blushed at the compliment. "He must have loved Marianna, then."

"Of course he did. After his wife died, he would ask her to play the role of harvest queen. He used to tell people it was easier than choosing someone different each year, but everyone knew it was because he had a soft spot for her."

"There's a festival queen?"

"No one told you?"

"No." Although she could certainly picture the beautiful Marianna being selected as queen no matter her age.

"Oh yes, it's a tradition for the local nobility to lead the festivities." Nico told her. "If the nobleman wasn't married, then he would select a maiden from the village to act as his queen for the day. Although in those cases, I suspect there were a few other duties involved, as well." He grinned. "You seriously did not know?"

Louisa shook her head. The thing about Monte Calanetti's traditions running so deep was that everyone assumed they were common knowledge. "It's not something that normally comes up in conversation," she said. "Who took over as the festival king after Carlos died?" The sunburn on Nico's cheeks grew a little darker. "Why am I not surprised?" She could only imagine the crowd clamoring to play his queen.

"Someone had to," he said. "Of course, now that you're here I will gladly abdicate the title."

She laughed. "Oh sure. People would love to see me lead the harvest parade. I can see the headlines now—Luscious Louisa Reigns from on High."

Why wasn't Nico laughing? Granted, it wasn't the funniest joke but he could at least smile at her attempt to make light of her problems. "Actually…" he began.

"You're joking." He was joking, right? "You're suggesting I play the role of harvest queen?"

"It's not a suggestion," he replied.

"Good."

"It's what's expected."

"Excuse me?" Did he say *expected*? The word ran down her back. She didn't do *expected* anymore.

"It's tradition," Nico continued. "As owner of Palazzo di Comparino, *you* are the local nobility. Therefore, people will expect you to take Carlos's place."

"No, they won't." Nico was the town nobility, she was merely notoriety.

"Yes, they will," he quickly retorted. "It's tradition."

Again with tradition. As if that justified everything. Who cared if it was tradition or not? Had he forgotten about the paparazzi, the whole reason she was hiding out at the vineyard? "I'm trying to avoid having my picture taken, remember? Not encourage the papers by parading down the middle of the street."

"You won't be encouraging anything. The festival isn't for another week. By that time, the scandal will have gone away," he said.

Says you. "Scandals never go away," she shot back. They were like weeds, going dormant only to crop up during another season. "People have long memories. Just because the headlines fade, doesn't mean they will have forgotten who I am. The people here aren't going to want to expose Monte Calanetti to ridicule."

An aggravated growl vibrated deep in Nico's throat. *"Madonna mia,"* he said, gesturing toward the heavens, "I thought we were past this. You have got to have faith in the people you live with."

"Oh sure, because the world has been so supportive up until now." She couldn't go through another round of sneers and whispers. She *wouldn't*.

"Monte Calanetti is not Boston."

"Maybe, maybe not," she said. That didn't matter. "What's the big deal anyway? So I don't lead the parade. Traditions can change, you know. There's no law that says everything needs to stay exactly the same."

"I know," he spat.

Then why were they even having this foolish argument? He knew she wanted to stay under the radar. "Look, it's not just the risk of gossip," she told him. Why she was bothering to add to her argument, she didn't know, but she was. "Even if you're right, and people don't care about the headlines, I'm not living that kind of life again."

"What do you mean, 'that kind of life'?"

"The whole socialite thing. I played that role long enough when I was with Steven." She was done with plastic smiles and faking happiness. With being told when and where and how.

He frowned. "So you don't care that when Carlos passed on the palazzo, he passed along the responsibilities that came with it?"

"No, I don't." She'd come to Italy to live *her* life and no one was going to make her do anything different.

"I see," Nico said, nodding. "Now I understand."

"Do you?"

"*Si.* Comparino is merely a piece of property to you. No wonder you ignored its existence for so long."

Ignored? *Ignored?* Oh, did he just say the wrong thing. Louisa's vision flashed red. "Don't you dare," she snarled. "I didn't ignore anything. From the moment I opened the lawyer's letter, I wanted to be here." He had no idea how badly. How many nights she'd lain awake wishing she could board a plane and escape.

"Of course you did. Your desire to be here was obvious from all those months you left the place to ruin."

"I was testifying against my husband!"

Her shout sounded across the vineyard. If the field workers didn't know her business before, they certainly knew it now. Let them. By this point, the damn trial was public knowledge anyway. What was another mention? Taking a deep breath, she added in a lower voice. "I couldn't leave the country for an entire year."

The explanation might have been enough for some, but not Nico. Crossing his arms, he positioned himself in front of her, his broad shoulders blocking the path. "You ignored us for over *two* years, Louisa, not one," he reminded her. "Or did the authorities refuse to let you leave the country before the arrest, as well?"

Not the authorities. Damn it all. How had she ever let the conversation turn in this direction? To the one secret she hoped to never have to say aloud.

"It's complicated," she replied. It would be too much to ask for Nico to continue accepting her terse answers at face value. Not this time. He was angry; he would want answers.

Sure enough, his eyes burned dark and intense as he stood, arms folded, waiting for her to continue. Louisa's skin burned from the intensity. She thought about lying, but she'd never been very good at it. Pretending, masking her emotions, sure, but out-and-out lies? Not so much. Looking back, it was a wonder she'd managed to keep Comparino a secret at all.

"I didn't have a choice—I had to stay in Boston. If Steven had known I had property in my name—property of my own—he would have..." Angry tears threatened. She looked down so he wouldn't see them.

"He would have what?" Nico asked.

"Taken it," she replied, choking on the words. "He would have taken the palazzo the same way he took everything else I had."

At last, the ugly truth was out in the open and Nico would never look at her the same way again. How could he? She was a stupid, gullible fool who let a master manipulator ruin her life. Shame rose like bile, sour and thick in her mouth. She didn't dare raise her eyes to look into his face. She couldn't bear to see pity where there'd once been admiration. There was only one thing she could do.

Spinning around, she took off down the path.

What the—? Nico stared at Louisa's retreating figure before sprinting after her. "Louisa, hold up!"

"Leave me alone," she said. "I have to get to the winery." She sounded as though—was she crying?

It didn't take long for him to close the distance between them. When he did, he touched her shoulder hoping to slow her pace, only to have her tear free of his grip so fiercely you'd think he was physically restraining her. She turned and snarled, "I said leave me alone."

She was crying. Tears streaked her cheeks. Their tracks might as well have been scratches on his skin, they hurt that much to see. This was about more than her thief of a husband stealing property. "What did that bastard do to you?"

"Nothing. It doesn't matter. Forget I said anything."

She tried to surge ahead again but he had height to his advantage. It was nothing for him to step ahead and block her path. Not unexpectedly, she shoved at his shoulder trying to make him move. "I said forget it."

"I can't," he said, standing firm. Not after seeing those tears. "Talk to me."

"Why? So you can laugh at what a stupid idiot I am?"

Idiot? Nico shook his head. "I could never think that of you."

"Then you're a bigger fool than I am," she said, jaw trembling. "And I'm…I'm…"

Her face started to crumble. "I'm a damn big one."

CHAPTER SEVEN

LOUISA BURIED HER face in her hands. Nico stood frozen by the sight of her shaking shoulders, wanting to comfort her but afraid his touch might make her run again. Eventually his need to hold her won out, and he wrapped her in his arms. She sagged into him, fists twisting into his shirt. His poor sweet Louisa. Steven Clark should be glad he was in prison because otherwise Nico would… Heaven knows what he would do. He pressed his lips to the top of her head and let her cry.

After a while, the shaking eased. "I'm sorry," she said, lifting her head. "I didn't mean to lose it like that. It's just sometimes I think, no matter how hard I try, Steven will always be there, taunting me. That I'll never completely escape him."

Suddenly all her comments about needing to be on her own took on new meaning. She was running from more than scandal and a failed marriage, wasn't she? He could kick himself for not realizing it sooner. He risked another brush of his lips against her hair before asking, "Did he hurt you badly?"

"You mean physically?" She shook her head. "He never laid a hand on me."

Thank God. Not all abuse was physical, however. Emotional abuse was insidious and painful in its own way. His parents played mind games all the time, driving one another to madness out of revenge or jealousy. "But he hurt you all the same, didn't he?"

"Yeah, he did," she said, giving a long sigh. Backing out of his embrace, she stumbled just far enough to be out of reach, wiping her tears as she walked. "It's my fault, really. The signs were all there from the very beginning, but I chose to ignore them. Love makes you stupid."

"He was also an accomplished liar," he reminded her, his nerves bristling when she mentioned the word *love*. From everything he'd heard of the man so far, Steven Clark didn't deserve Louisa's affection, and he certainly didn't deserve her self-recrimination.

If his underlying message made it through, it wasn't evident in Louisa's answering sigh. "He certainly was. But he was also incredibly charming and romantic, and I was twenty-one years old."

"Barely an adult."

"True, but I was certain I knew everything."

"What twenty-one-year-old isn't?" he replied.

His attempt to lighten the moment failed. Tired of standing, and suspecting getting the entire story would take some time, Nico motioned for her to follow him a few feet ahead, to a small gap between plants. He sat down beneath the branches, the dirt cool and damp through his jeans, and patted the space beside him. Louisa hesitated for a moment before joining him.

"How did you meet him?" he asked when she finally settled herself. He told himself he was asking because he wanted to understand what happened, and not because of the burning sensation the man's name caused in his chest.

"At work. My first job out of college. I was so psyched when I got the job, too," she said, in a voice that still held lingering pride. "Clark Investments was the hottest business in the city at the time. Steven was a rock star in Boston financial circles."

A rock star with twenty years on his starry-eyed employee, Nico thought, gritting his teeth. "You must have been very good to get the job."

"I was."

There was such gratitude in her smile, as if it had been a long time since someone had acknowledged her abilities. Nico laid the blame at the feet of her ex-husband. "Anyway, I met Steven a couple months after I started—on the elevator of all places—and all I could think was *Steven Clark is talking to me.* Later, he told me he was so impressed he had to ask me out."

That, thought Nico, might have been the most honest thing Steven Clark had ever said. What man with two eyes wouldn't be impressed by her?

"I felt like Cinderella. Here I was, a girl from a single-parent family in a blue-collar town while Steven was sophisticated and had experienced things I'd never dreamed of doing. Things like skiing in the Alps and diving with sharks." She scooped a handful of dirt and let it sift through her fingers. "I should have known then, the stories were too outrageous to be true, but like I said, love—"

"Makes you blind," he finished for her. Why that phrase bothered him so much, he didn't know. Of course she'd loved the man; he was her husband.

"He flew us to Chicago once because I said I liked deep dish pizza. Who wouldn't fall for a gesture like that?" she asked. "I thought I'd met Prince Charming.

"My friends didn't think so. They said he made them feel uncomfortable. Steven said it was because they were jealous."

"Perhaps they were."

"My mother, too?" she asked. "She didn't like him at all. Called him a slicker version of my father and said she didn't trust him."

That was why they were estranged. Nico could guess what happened. Her mother didn't approve, and Steven took advantage of the disagreement to push them further apart.

"We had this awful fight," she told him. "I accused

her of not wanting me to be happy, that because she was alone and miserable, she wanted me to be alone and miserable, too. When I told Steven, he said, 'that's all right. I'm all the family you need now.'" The fresh tears in her eyes had Nico moving to take her in his arms again. She shook him off, getting to her feet instead. "I didn't talk to her for almost five years. She could have died and I wouldn't have known."

"That's not true." She was letting her guilty conscience color her thinking.

"Isn't it?" she replied, turning around. "Who would tell me? I cut myself off from everyone I used to know. Because they didn't fit with my new life."

And Nico could guess who had put that thought in her head. A chill ran through him as he slowly began to understand what she meant by Steven taking everything from her.

She'd turned away from him again, her face turned to the foliage. Nico could see her fingering the edge of one of the leaves. Her hands were shaking.

"You tell yourself you're too smart to fall for someone's lies," she said. "You read stories of women trapped in bad relationships and you can't understand how they can be so foolish. That is, until it happens to you."

"Louisa, don't..."

"Don't what? Blame myself? Tell the embarrassing truth?"

Don't tell me at all. Rising to his feet, Nico walked behind her and curled his hands atop her shoulders to steady her. There was no need for her to go on; he'd heard enough.

Unfortunately for both of them, Louisa had unsealed a bottle that insisted on being emptied because she immediately shook her head. "I think maybe I need to tell someone," she whispered. "Maybe if I say the words aloud..."

Nico could hear her breath rattle with nerves as she

took a deep lungful of air before she began to speak. "When it first started, I barely noticed. When you're in love you're supposed to want to spend every minute with each other, right?"

"Yes," Nico replied. His hands were still on her shoulders, and it was all he could do not to pull her tight against him.

"And then, after we were married, when Steven suggested I stop working to avoid gossip, well that made sense, too. It was expected I would be with him at corporate dinner parties and charitable functions. Could hardly do that if I was working full-time."

Lots of women managed both, thought Nico. Louisa could have, as well. But that would have meant having a life of her own, and it sounded as though having an independent wife was the last thing Steven Clark wanted.

He honestly could strangle the man. Here was one of the things that made Louisa such a treasure. Challenging her was exciting. If Nico had a woman like her in his life, he'd do everything in his power to aid in her success, not pin her down like some butterfly under glass. Steven Clark was an idiot as well as a thief.

"When did you realize…?"

"That I was trapped?"

"Yes." Actually, he hadn't known what he'd meant to ask, but her question was close enough.

"I skipped a charity planning committee to do some last-minute Christmas shopping. One of the other members told Steven, and he lost it. Demanded to know where I'd been all day and with whom." She pulled the leaf she'd been playing with from its branch, sending a rustling noise rippling down the row. "To this day I'm not sure what frightened me more. His demand or the fact there were people reporting my actions to him."

Neither aspect sounded very comfortable. "You stayed, however." Because she loved him.

"Where was I supposed to go? None of the assets were in my name. I'd alienated everyone I used to know, and Steven didn't have friends so much as business associates. I couldn't trust those people to help me, not when Steven was handling their money. I couldn't go anywhere. I couldn't talk to anyone. I was stuck."

The proverbial bird in a gilded cage, Nico thought sadly.

"Surely your mother or your friends..."

"And have to listen to them tell me how right they'd all been? I couldn't." Nico wanted to smile despite the sad situation. That was his American. Stubborn to the end, even when it hurt her.

"Discovering I'd inherited the palazzo was torture. Here I had this safe haven waiting for me, and I couldn't get to it. Even if by some miracle I did find a way to evade Steven's radar, with his money and connections, he would have eventually tracked me down."

The leaf she'd been holding fluttered to the ground as she sighed. "In the end it was easier to go along to get along."

"You mean accept the abuse," Nico said.

"I told you, it wasn't abuse."

They both knew she was lying. Steven might not have hit her or yelled insults, but he'd abused her in his own despicable way. He'd stolen her innocence and her freedom and so much more. Nico could feel the anger spreading through him. If it was possible to kill a man by thoughts alone, Steven Clark would be dead a thousand times over.

Arms hugging her body, Louisa turned to look at him with cavernous eyes, the white-blond curtain of her hair casting her cheeks with shadows.

"The day I stumbled across those financial reports was the best day of my life, because I knew I could finally walk away," she said.

Only walking away hadn't been as easy as she made it sound.

The truth wasn't as simple as she described. Walking away was never easy. The details didn't matter. Her story explained a lot, however. Why she balked every time he offered to help, for example. It definitely explained why she feared her friends would cut her off.

"Do you still love him?" It was none of his business, and yet he could not stop thinking about her words before. Love makes you blind.

"No. Not even in the slightest."

If he shouldn't have asked the question, then he should definitely not have felt relief at her answer. He did, though. To save her heart from further pain, that was all.

"I'm sorry," he said.

"I told you before, I don't want your pity."

Her voice was rough from crying, the raw sound making him hate Steven Clark all the more. "I don't pity you," he told her truthfully. He didn't. He *admired* her. Did he know what kind of strength it took to pull herself free from the hell she had become trapped in? Not only pull herself free, but to begin again?

"What I meant was that I am sorry I accused you of abandoning the palazzo," he said.

"Oh." The tiniest of blushes tinged her cheekbones as she looked down at her feet. "Thank you," she said. "And I'm sorry I lost my temper."

"Then we are even." Funny, but he'd forgotten why she'd lost her temper in the first place.

By silent agreement, they started walking toward the production facilities. They'd been in the field most of the morning, Nico realized, or so said the sun beating on the back of his neck. His employees would be looking for him. Wasn't like him to ignore the winery for so long. Add another uncharacteristic behavior to the growing list.

Even though Louisa's confession answered a lot of questions, Nico found his mind more jumbled than before. Mostly with vague unformed ideas he couldn't articulate. Finally, because he felt the need to say *something* while they walked, he said in a quiet voice. "I'm glad you made it to Italy."

The sentiment didn't come close to capturing any of the thoughts swirling in his head, what he wanted to say, but it was enough to make Louisa smile.

"Are you really?" she asked.

She sounded so disbelieving.

"Yes, really," he replied. More than he'd realized until this moment. The town wouldn't be the same without her. The palazzo and Monte Calanetti needed her. He…

The thought lingered just out of reach.

He knew he was taking a risk, but he closed the distance between them anyway, reaching up with his hands to cradle her face. "I can't imagine Monte Calanetti without you."

Her trembling lower lip begged for reassurance or was it that he begged to reassure her? To kiss her and let her know just how glad he was to have her in Monte Calanetti.

Cool fingers encircled his wrists, holding him. Stopping him. She was backing away yet again. "Thank you," she said, slipping free.

This time when she began to walk, Nico purposely lagged behind.

CHAPTER EIGHT

"MAY I BORROW you for a moment?"

Louisa was in the middle of attaching mailing labels to boxes when Nico appeared in her doorway. As soon as she looked in his direction, her stomach somersaulted. She blamed it on the fact that he'd startled her.

Along with the fact he looked as handsome as sin in his faded work clothes. How did the man do it? Look so perfect after being out in the fields for hours. None of the other workers wore hard labor as well. Of course there was always the chance he was supervising more than actually working, but standing around didn't seem his style. More likely Mother Nature wanted to make sure Nico looked a cut above all the rest.

Mother Nature did her job well.

Nico arched his eyebrow, and she realized he was waiting for a response. What had he asked? Right. To borrow her. "Sure," she replied. "What do you need?"

"Follow me to the lab."

Louisa did what he asked, her heart pounding in her chest. She couldn't blame being startled this time. Your palms didn't sweat when you were startled.

It'd been two days since their conversation in the vineyard, or rather since Louisa had bared her soul regarding her marriage. They hadn't talked since. Nico continued to leave the house before breakfast and didn't return until late. To be honest, Louisa wasn't sure he came home at all. After all, the dinner plate she left last night hadn't been touched. If it wasn't harvest season, she'd worry he was purposely avoiding her.

Oh, who was she kidding? She still worried, just as she was worried how to behave around him now. Strangely enough, however, it wasn't her meltdown—or her confession—that had her feeling awkward. It was the memory of Nico holding her close yet again.

Since arriving in Italy, Louisa could count on three fingers the number of times she'd truly felt safe and secure. All three had been in Nico's arms, and they were as engrained in her memory as any event could be. If she concentrated, she could feel his breath as it had brushed her lips when he'd said he couldn't imagine Monte Calanetti without her. The simplest of words, but they made her feel more special than she'd felt in a long time. With his touch gentle and sure on her cheeks, she'd wanted so badly for him to kiss her.

Still, the last time a man had made her feel special, she'd wound up making the biggest mistake of her life, and while she might be older and wiser, she was also a woman with desires that had been neglected for a long time. The idea of giving herself over to Nico's care left a warm fluttery sensation in the pit of her stomach—a dangerous feeling, to say the least. Thank goodness she managed to keep her head.

Thank goodness, too, that Nico understood. In fact, seeing his relaxed expression, she'd say he'd managed to brush the moment aside without problem.

Louisa was glad for that. Truly.

Nico's "lab" was located at the rear of the building a stone's throw from where the grapes were stored after being picked. Now that harvesting had begun, the rolling door that led to the loading dock was left permanently open so that the forklifts could transport the containers of grapes from the field trucks to the washing area. Louisa breathed deep, taking in as much of the sweet aroma as she could.

"Do you mind if I close the door?" Nico hollered. "It'll be easier to hear each other."

She shook her head. Out here the sound was much louder than by her office, where the machines were still dormant.

There was a click and the decibel level was suddenly reduced by half. "Much better," Nico said.

Better was relative. In addition to being small, the room was stuffed with equipment making the close space tighter still. Standing near the door, Louisa found herself less than a yard away from Nico's desk, and even closer to Nico himself. He smelled like grapes. To her chagrin, the aroma made her stomach flip-flop again.

Trying to look casual, she leaned against the door, arms folded across her midsection. "What is it you needed to talk about?" she asked him.

"Not talk. Taste."

He pointed to the equipment on his worktable. "I need a second opinion regarding this year's blend."

"This year's blend?" She knew that super Tuscans were wines made by combining different varieties of grape, but she assumed that once the formula was created, the blend stayed the same.

"Every harvest is different," Nico replied. "Sometimes only subtly, but enough that the formula should be tweaked. Mario and I have been playing with percentages all day, but we're not quite sure we've achieved the right balance."

"I see." Speaking of the university student, she didn't see him.

Nico must have seen her looking around because he said, "Mario has gone home. He was a little too enthusiastic a taster."

"You mean he got a little tipsy."

"Don't be silly. He needed a break, is all." He'd gotten tipsy. "Anyway, I think I'm close, but I could use a fresh palate."

"Wouldn't you be better off asking someone else? I'm not much of a wine connoisseur." If he wanted to know about finish and undertones, she couldn't help him.

"You don't have to be," he told her. "You just have to know what you like."

Stepping to the worktable, he retrieved two beakers containing purple liquid and a pair of wineglasses. "Fancy bottle," Louisa joked.

"Good things come in odd glass containers," he joked back. He poured the contents from each into its own glass and set them on the edge of his desk. "Tell me which one of those wines you like better."

"That's it?"

"That's it."

Simple enough. Picking up the first glass, she paused. "Am I supposed to smell it before I drink?"

"Only if you want to."

Louisa didn't. Things like that were better left to someone like Nico who actually understood what they were looking for. "And do I spit or swallow?" She vaguely remembered there was supposed to be some kind of protocol.

"Drink like you would a regular glass of wine. If you normally spit…"

She returned his smirk. "Fine. I get the point."

The contents of the first glass tasted amazing. Sweet but not overly so with just enough tang to make it stay on your tongue. Delicious. "Mmm," she said, licking her lips.

She was about to declare the choice easy until she tasted the second glass and found it equally delicious. "You're kidding," she said, setting the glass down. "There's supposed to be a difference?"

"Don't focus on finding the difference. Tell me which one you like better."

She tasted each one again, this time with her eyes closed in order to really focus. Took a couple of sips, but in the end, the first glass won out. "This one," she said, finishing the glass with a satisfied sigh. "Definitely this one."

When she opened her eyes, she found Nico watching her with an unreadable expression. His jaw twitched with tension as if he was holding back a response. "Tha…" He cleared his throat. Nevertheless his voice remained rough. "Thank you."

"I hope I helped."

"Trust me, you helped me a great deal."

"Good." Their gazes stayed locked while they talked. Louisa never knew there could be so many different shades of brown. The entire color wheel could be seen in Nico's irises.

"Would you like some more?" she heard him ask.

Wine. He meant more wine. Louisa blinked, sending everything back into perspective. "Better not," she said. "I'm not as practiced a wine taster as you are. Or are you purposely trying to send me home like Mario?"

Nico slapped a hand against his chest, mimicking horror. "Absolutely not. We're shorthanded tonight as it is."

The float-decorating party. It was Marianna's idea. With so many of the employees working long hours, she didn't think it fair to ask them to help decorate the winery float, as well, so she'd convinced a group of friends to do it instead. Louisa had been the first person she'd recruited.

It would be Louisa's first public appearance since the headlines broke.

"Maybe I will have another glass," she said reaching for the beaker.

Nico's hand immediately closed around her wrist, stopping her. "There is no need to be nervous," he said. "These are your friends."

"I know." What amazed her was how much she meant

it. A week ago she'd have been a crumbling basket of nerves, but not so much now. Partly because the story was winding down.

And partly because the man next to her was scheduled to be there, as well. Her personal protector at the ready, his presence made being brave a lot easier.

After much back and forth, it was decided the vineyard would have to give up on trying to win any awards and instead design as simple a float as possible. Something that could be assembled with minimal manpower in as short a time as possible. Nico was the one who came up with the idea. Some of the parts of last year's float, namely the fountain, were in storage. All they needed was fresh foliage. While it was too late in the day for the fountain to spout water again, they could easily recycle it into a different design. And so it was decided they would recreate the royal wedding. Two of his employees would play Prince Antonio and Princess Christina while others played wedding guests. The couples would waltz around the fountain, pretending to dance beneath the stars. It might not be an entirely accurate representation, but it would do the winery proud.

As she watched Nico and Mario retrieve the fountain later that afternoon, she couldn't help wondering if the idea reminded Nico of the kiss they'd shared. The one she'd told him to forget had ever happened. Which he apparently was having much better luck doing than she was.

Marianna's party attracted a crowd. In addition to Dani and Rafe, who came on their day off, there were several other couples Louisa had met at Marianna's baby shower and other events. There was Isabella Benson, one of the local schoolteachers, and her new husband, Connor, along with wedding planner Lindsay and her husband, Zach Reeves, who'd just returned from their honeymoon. Louisa chuckled to herself, remembering the jokes she and Nico had made at the royal wedding about Lindsay and Zach's obvious adoration for each other. Even Lucia Moretti-Cascini, the art expert who'd worked on the chapel restoration and who was in town visiting her in-laws, was there. Having appointed herself the unofficial design supervisor, she sat on a stack of crates with a sketch pad while swatting away suggestions from her husband, Logan. In fact, the only person missing was the organizer herself.

Not a single person mentioned the tabloid stories or Louisa's history in Boston. The women all greeted her with smiles and hugs, as if nothing had changed. After years of phony smiles and affection, their genuine embraces had her near tears. Only the reassuring solidity of Nico's hand, pressed against the small of her back, kept her from actually crying. "Told you so, *bella mia*," he whispered as he handed her a glass of wine.

In spite of Marianna's absence, the work went smoothly. In no time at all, the old pieces were in place and covered with a plastic skin, ready to be decorated.

Louisa and the other women were put in charge of attaching the foliage while the men assembled the foam cutouts that would make the frame for the palazzo walls.

"This is a first," Dani said as she pressed a grape into place.

"Hot gluing fruit to a chicken-wire nymph. Are we sure this is going to look like marble?"

"Lucia says it will, and she's the art expert," Louisa replied.

"Art expert. There aren't too many museums who deal with produce."

"They used grapes last year," Isabella reassured them, "and it looked wonderful."

"She's right. I saw pictures," Louisa said, remembering the photograph of Nico that Marianna had shown her. "Hopefully we'll do as good a job. I'd hate to embarrass the vineyard."

"I'm sure we won't, and if it does turn out a disaster, Nico can always keep it locked in the garage."

"True." Louisa reached for a grape to glue into place only to pick up her wineglass instead. Something had been nagging her since the party began and she needed Dani's perspective. "Did you know that as palazzo owner, I'm supposed to play the part of festival queen?" she asked as she took a drink.

"Really?"

"Nico told me it's a tradition."

Dani's eyes flashed with enthusiasm. "How exciting. Do you get to ride on the back of a convertible and wave to a crowd like a beauty queen and everything?"

"I have no idea." Although Dani had painted an image she'd rather not contemplate. "I wasn't planning to do it at all."

"Why not, if it's tradition? Sounds like fun." Dani asked. "I always wanted to be the homecoming queen, but the title always went to some tall cheerleader type."

"I was a cheerleader."

Her friend took a sip of wine. "I rest my case."

"Hey, less drinking, more gluing," Isabella said, her dark head poking over the nymph's outstretched arm. "Do not make me come over there and take your wineglasses away."

Chastised, the pair ducked their heads, though Dani managed to sneak one more sip. "Seriously though," she said, reaching for the glue gun. "You should totally do it. You'd make a gorgeous festival queen."

"I'd rather be part of the crowd," Louisa replied. "I've had enough of the spotlight for one lifetime."

"That I can understand." Dani said, putting another grape in place. "I didn't want to bring up a sore subject, but how are you doing? You sound a lot better than you did when I spoke to you on the phone."

"I feel better," Louisa answered.

"You have no idea how worried I was when I saw those headlines. Rafe told me how brutal the paparazzi can be, and I was afraid one of them might try something scary."

"One did try," Louisa said, "but Nico scared him off."

"So I read in the papers. Thank goodness he showed up."

"Thank goodness is right." Not giving it a second thought, Louisa looked to the other side of the truck bed where he was arguing with Rafe over the foam placement. Sensing he was being watched, he looked over his shoulder and grinned.

She dipped her head before he could see how red her cheeks were. "I'm only sorry his help dragged him into the gossip pages, too," she said to Dani, hoping her friend didn't notice the blush either. "He's a good man."

"Rafe wouldn't be his friend if he wasn't," Dani replied. "I don't know if you've noticed, but my husband can be a little hard to please."

"A little?" Rafe Mancini's demanding reputation was legendary. He'd been known to toss vendors into the street for selling him what he considered subpar products.

And yet, the same chef and his wife had accepted Louisa without question. Louisa felt the swell of emotion in her throat again. Swallowing hard, she did her best to make her voice sound lighthearted "Have I told you I'm really glad we met on the bus from Florence?"

"Is this your not so subtle way of thanking me for being your friend?" Dani asked.

"Maybe."

Her fellow American gathered her in a hug. "I'm glad we're friends, too," she said. "Although if you get hot glue in my hair, I will kill you."

"And Lindsay and I will kill you both if you do not get

to work," Isabella scolded. "We are not gluing all these grapes by ourselves."

"Jeez, I'm glad I'm not one of her students," Dani whispered.

"I heard that."

Louisa snorted, almost dropping the grape she was putting into place. The teasing reminded her of old times, when she and her college friends would get together and giggle over cocktails. Steven had hated that.

"You too, Louisa," Lindsay admonished. "Just because you're dating the boss doesn't mean you get to slack off."

Dating—? The newspaper photographs. Just when she thought she'd actually put them behind her. The only saving grace, if there could be one, was that at least these women didn't consider her some kind of financial predator. Like Marianna the other day, they saw it as a potential romance. "Nico and I aren't dating," she told them.

"Are you sure?" Isabella asked. "Those pictures—"

"Were pictures, that's all," she said, cutting her off. "The two of us are just friends."

"Sure, just like Zach and I are friends," Lindsay replied. She and Isabella exchanged smirks.

"Something tells me the lady protests too much," the teacher replied.

Louisa stared at the grape covered plastic in front of her and reminded herself the women were only teasing. Nevertheless, that didn't stop her skin from feeling as if it was on fire. Not because she was embarrassed or ashamed, at least not in the way she expected to be. She was embarrassed because they were right.

She *was* protesting too much.

"I didn't realize you found the gluing of grapes so fascinating, my friend."

Nico did his best to look annoyed at his best friend, but

the heat in his cheeks killed the effort. "Checking to see how much progress they are making, that is all."

"Not as much as there would be if you waited longer than thirty seconds between looks," Rafe replied.

He inclined his head to where the women were laughing and topping up their wineglasses. "It's all right, you know. She's a beautiful woman."

"Who? Your wife?"

"Of course, my wife. But I'm talking about Louisa. I saw the photograph of the two of you in the newspaper. Very romantic."

"We were at a wedding. Everything about weddings looks romantic."

"This was different. You were looking at her like…"

"Like what?"

"I don't know," his friend replied honestly. "I've never seen you look at a woman that way."

Perhaps because he'd never met a woman like Louisa before. "She's different," he said.

"Because she's an American. They have a different kind of energy about them. It's very…captivating."

Captivating was a good word. He felt as though he was under a spell at times, what with the uncharacteristic moods he'd been experiencing. He could feel his friend's eyes on him. "It's not what you think," he said.

"You aren't attracted to her?"

"Of course I am attracted. Have you looked at her?"

"Then it is exactly what I think. And, if that picture is to believed, the feeling is mutual. And yet the two of you…" His friend set down the foam block he was holding to give Nico a serious look. "You are not together. Since when do you not pursue an interested woman?"

"I told you, Louisa is different." Other women hadn't been traumatized by an emotionally abusive Prince Charming. "She's not the kind of woman you toy with."

"So don't toy."

Rafe made it sound so easy. Problem was Nico wasn't sure he could do anything else. "Not everyone is made for commitment like you are, my friend."

A warm hand clapped his shoulder. "What happened with Floriana was a long time ago. People change."

"Sometimes. Sometimes they don't." More often than not, they were like his parents, repeating the same mistakes over and over. With everything she'd been through, Louisa deserved better. "I've already broken the heart of one good woman," he said.

"And haven't you punished yourself enough for it?" His friend squeezed his shoulder. "You can't be afraid to try again."

Nico wasn't afraid, he was trying to be kind. Rafe meant well, but he didn't know everything. There were secrets Nico couldn't share with anyone.

Almost anyone, he amended, eyes looking at Louisa. He'd certainly shared about his parents.

It was a moot point anyway. "You are assuming the decision is 100 percent mine to make," he said. "Louisa is the one who is not interested. It was Louisa's choice to keep our relationship platonic." If she went through with selling the palazzo, they wouldn't even have that.

"That's too bad."

"Yes, it is." Why lie about his disappointment? He watched as Louisa laughed with her friends. She had her hair pulled back, and there was purple staining her fingers. Beautiful. Seeing her relaxed made him happy.

"But," Nico said, "you can't force emotions." If anyone knew that, it was him.

His cell phone rang, saving him from any further rebuttals. "About time," he said as the caller ID popped onto the screen. "It's Ryan," he told Rafe. "You tell my sister she better have a good reason for skipping out on her own party. The rest of us have been here for hours working on this float."

Ryan's reply came back garbled. The building and its terrible service. "Say it again?" he asked.

"I said, would a girl be a good enough excuse?"

"What do you mean 'a girl'?" Nico straightened at Ryan's announcement. "Are you talking about a real girl, as in—?"

"A baby, yes." His brother-in-law gave a breathy laugh. "The most beautiful girl you'll ever see. Seven pounds, nine ounces and as perfect as her mother."

Nico's jaw dropped. He didn't know what to say. "Congratulations!" he finally managed to get out.

No sooner did he speak than Rafe nudged him with an elbow. "Baby?" he asked. Nico nodded, setting off a small cheer in the garage. Immediately, both Dani and Louisa dropped what they were doing to join Rafe by his side. "Boy or girl?" Louisa asked.

"A girl," he whispered back. It was hard to believe his baby sister was a mother herself. "How is Marianna?" he asked Ryan. "Is she all right?"

"She's fantastic. Amazing. When you see what a woman goes through to give birth..." Admiration laced every word Ryan said.

Nico felt a pang of jealousy in the face of such love and devotion. His eyes sought Louisa, who waited for details with folded hands pressed to her lips and eyes turned sapphire with anticipation. Like everyone else, her emotions showed on her face. Everyone but him, that was. His insides were numb as he struggled to process Ryan's news.

The gulf that separated him from others in the world widened. *See?* He wanted to tell Rafe. *People don't always change.*

He certainly hadn't.

CHAPTER NINE

MARIANNA WORE MOTHERHOOD as though it was a designer dress. Sitting on the living room sofa of her villa, wearing pajamas and a terry cloth robe, she'd never looked lovelier. Every time she looked down at the bundle sleeping in the bassinet, her face glowed with contentment. "We named her Rosabella," she said to Louisa, who was sitting next to her. "Rosa for short."

"She's beautiful," Louisa said. As peaceful as an angel, her little lips parted in slumber. It was all Louisa could do not to run her finger along a downy cheek.

"The nurses said not to be fooled by how much she's sleeping," she said. "In a day or two she'll be wanting to nurse all the time."

"Then we'll be wishing she'd sleep," Ryan added. He looked as smitten as his wife.

"What do you mean, *we*? I'm going to be the one doing all the work. You'll probably just roll over and go back to sleep."

"Ah, *amore mio*, you know I'd help nurse if I could. It would let me bond with the baby."

"Then it's a good thing I bought you this," Louisa said, reaching for the pastel pink gift bag she'd set on the floor. She'd almost said "we." Living and working with Nico the past week had her thinking of them as a pair.

"A breast pump!" Marianna announced with what could almost be described as evil glee. "Thank you, Louisa; it's perfect. Looks like you'll be able to bond with the baby after all, *amore mio*."

"Yes, Louisa," Ryan said, much less enthusiastically. "It's exactly what we needed."

They were both exaggerating for effect. From the moment he'd learned of the pregnancy, Ryan had been determined to be as active a father as possible. Louisa had no doubt he would be awake every time no matter who did the actual feeding. She looked over at Nico, to see what he was thinking. The man had barely said a word since their arrival. In fact, he'd been unusually quiet since Ryan had called to announce little Rosa's arrival. Currently, he stood next to the bassinet, staring down at the sleeping baby.

"She's so tiny," he said.

"Not for long," Marianna replied. "She's got her father's appetite. Would you like to hold her, Uncle Nico?"

At his sister's suggestion, Nico paled. "I wouldn't want to wake her…"

"You won't, and if she does wake up, she'll probably fall right back to sleep. The little angel has had a busy couple of days. Haven't you, Rosa?" Adoration beaming from every feature of his face, Ryan ran the back of his finger along his daughter's cheek. "You might as well get used to being hands-on," he said to Nico. "No way is your sister going to let you get out of babysitting."

"Absolutely. With Angelo living in the States and Ryan's family in Australia, you're the only family she has in Monte Calanetti. Now hold her. I want a photo for her baby album."

"Better do what your sister says," Ryan said.

The vintner's face was the picture of anxiety as Ryan placed the swaddled baby in Nico's arms. Looking as if he'd rather be doing anything else, he balanced Rosa's head in the palm of one hand while the other held her bottom.

"She's not a bottle of wine," Marianna admonished.

"Hold her close. And smile. I don't want her first memory of her uncle to be that he's a grouch."

"Forgive me; I've never held a baby before," Nico replied. But he did what he was told.

It made for a beautiful photo. Nico with his bronzed movie-star features, baby Rosa with her pink newborn skin. Something was off, though. Louisa couldn't say exactly what, but something about Nico's eyes didn't fit. For one thing, they lacked the sparkle she'd come to associate with his smiles. They looked darker—sad, even—and distant. Not unlike the way they'd looked the other day when Marianna visited.

Did his sister notice? Probably not, since the new mother was too busy directing the photo session. "Go stand next to Nico," she ordered. "We need one of the three of you."

"Um… You want me in your baby album?" Louisa wasn't sure that was a good idea.

"Of course. Why wouldn't I?" Marianna waved at her to move. "Go."

"Sooner you do it, the sooner she'll be done taking photos," Nico said.

She took her place by Nico's shoulder, and wondered if she would ever get used to being welcome. It didn't dawn on her until after Marianna showed her the pictures on her phone that she was in her most casual clothes and not wearing a stitch of makeup. The woman smiling back at her from the view screen looked like someone she used to know a long time ago, before she ever heard the name Steven Clark. Someone she hadn't seen in a long time. Maybe she'd stick around a little while.

"You make an attractive family," Marianna teased. "Maybe I should sell it to the papers."

"You do, and I'll return my breast pump." That she could have such an exchange without blanching spoke volumes about how well she was recovering from the scandal. She turned her attention back to the phone screen, her gaze moving from her face to Nico's to Rosa's and back to Nico's. There was definitely distance in Nico's smile…

Meanwhile, Ryan had retrieved Rosa, who hadn't woken up, and was tucking her into her bassinet. "I meant to tell you," he said, "the cradle fits the space perfectly."

"I'm glad," Nico replied.

"Nico had the family cradle restored," Marianna explained.

"He did?" She hadn't known, although knowing his respect for tradition, the gesture didn't surprise her.

"It has been in our family for generations," he replied, eyes still on the baby. "Made sense that it be used by the first member of the next generation."

"The piece is almost too beautiful for Rosa to sleep in," Ryan said.

"Come with me; I'll show you."

After casting a protective glance into the bassinet Marianna led her toward the nursery. "You know, I almost took the baby monitor with me," she said as they walked up the stairs. "But I thought that might be overprotective."

"With Ryan sitting five feet away from her, I would say yes," Louisa teased. Her friend's extreme mothering was adorable. Might not be so cute when Rosa was older, but seeing as how Marianna had only been a mother for two days, she couldn't help smiling. The Amatuccis didn't do things halfway, did they?

The room was a baby's paradise. The couple had forgone traditional baby colors in favor of restful lavender, browns and greens. The Tuscan hillside, Louisa realized. Stuffed animals and books already filled the shelves, and there were, not one, but two mobiles, one hanging over what looked to be a small play area in the corner.

On the back wall hung a large landscape of the vineyards with baby animals playing peek-a-boo among the vines. Louisa spied a rabbit and a kitten straight off. "Logan Cascini's wife, Lucia, painted it as a baby gift," Marianna told her. "There are supposed to be eleven different baby animals hiding in the fields. So far Ryan and I can only find eight."

"It's amazing." This was a gift that would amuse a child for years to come. Something Louisa would want for her own child. "Makes my breast pump look lame," she said.

As exquisite as the painting was, however, it paled in comparison to the cradle below it. Ryan hadn't exaggerated. It was gorgeous. It wasn't that the piece was fancy; in fact the design was actually very modest, but you could feel its history. The tiny nicks and dents told the story of all the Amatuccis that had slept safe in its confines. She ran her hand along the sideboard. The restorer had done a great job, polishing the olive wood to a gleaming dark brown without destroying what made it special.

"My great-grandfather built this when my grandfather was born. According to my father, it was because my great-grandmother demanded he not sleep in a drawer. Baby Amatuccis have slept in it ever since."

Louisa tried to picture Nico as a baby with his thick dark curls. Bet he had a smile that could melt your heart.

She wondered why he hadn't told her what he was planning. But then, why would he? No doubt the idea came to him when Marianna had announced her pregnancy. If she recalled, the two of them had hardly been friends at the time. Not like they were now.

Actually she wasn't sure what they were to each other anymore. Did a friend lie in bed listening for the sound of footsteps in the hall, relieved yet disappointed when the steps didn't draw near her door? Did a friend watch her friend while he worked, wondering what it might feel like to run her hands down his muscular arms? Louisa doubted it. Yet she had done both those things the past couple of days.

Then there was the fact she was continuing to stay at the vineyard. The headlines had stopped. There was little reason she shouldn't return to the palazzo and start figuring out what she wanted to do for the future.

So how come the two of them were continuing to cohabitate as though they were a couple?

"...godparents."

She realized Marianna was talking. "I'm sorry," she said. "I was thinking about something else."

"Here I thought I was the one with distractions," the brunette teased. "Please tell me you'll pay better attention to your goddaughter."

"G-goddaughter?" Was Marianna asking what Louisa thought she was asking?

"Ryan and I were hoping you would be Rosabella's godmother."

Godmother? She had to have misunderstood. In Italy, a godparent was expected to play a huge role in a child's life. More like a second parent. And they were asking *her*?

That's why they'd insisted on including her in the photograph. "Are—are you sure?" she asked. "There isn't someone you want more?" Her brother Angelo's wife, for example.

"Ryan and I can't think of anyone we'd want more," the brunette said, reaching over and resting a hand atop hers.

"But the scandal?"

"Who cares about the scandal? The scandal is what makes you so perfect. We want our daughter to grow up knowing that doing the right thing isn't always easy, but that truly strong people find a way to make it through."

Louisa couldn't breathe for the lump in her throat. Marianna and Ryan...they thought her brave? Talk about ironic. She'd felt nothing but fear from the day she discovered Steven's duplicity. "All I did was tell the authorities the truth." And seize an opportunity to escape.

"You did more than tell the truth. You paid a price publicly. It couldn't have been easy being destroyed by the press the way you were. That's the kind of person I want to help guide my daughter. A woman who's strong enough to bounce back."

Had she really, though? Bounced back? There were still so many fears holding her back. She wasn't sure she'd ever completely escape Steven.

Still, the invitation meant more than Marianna would ever realize. Louisa felt the tears pushing at her eyes. Seemed like all she did was tear up lately. "You just want me to give you a better baby gift," she said, sniffing them away.

Marianna's eyes were watery. "So is that a yes?"

"Yes!" Louisa didn't stop to think twice. "I would be honored."

"Perfect. I'm so happy." The brunette clapped her hands together the way a child might when getting a special gift. "This will be perfect. You can teach Rosa how to be strong and gracious, and her godfather will teach her how to be smart and respect tradition. Along with winemaking, that is."

Wine? "Who are you going to ask to be godfather?" she asked. As if she didn't know. There was only one man who fit that description.

Her friend looked at her with surprise. "Nico, of course."

Of course.

"Is that a problem?"

Only in the sense that she and Nico would be bound together for the rest of Rosa's life. Flutters took over her insides.

"No, no problem," she said.

Marianna's reply was preempted by a high-pitched wail coming from downstairs.

"Looks like I didn't need to bring the monitor after all," the new mother said. "Rosa has inherited my lungs."

"Ryan and Marianna are going to have their hands full fending off the boys when Rosa's older, that's for sure," Louisa said as they crossed the plaza a short while later. "I won't be surprised if Ryan decides to ship her off to a convent when she's older just to keep them away."

"Yes," Nico replied. "Because naturally Italy is full of convents where the residents can hide their children."

"It's an expression, Nico."

"I know what it is." He tightened his grip on the shopping bag he was carrying, the plastic handle threatening to snap in two from the pressure. The knot at the base of his neck had been tightening since they'd left Marianna's villa, fed by his companion's continual gushing over baby Rosabella. How beautiful, how sweet, how tiny, how wonderful. Every adjective reminding him of his shortcomings, because he felt *nothing.*

"I'm sure Ryan will deal with the onslaught of suitors when the time comes," he told her.

"I'm sure he will, too." She looked at him with a frown. "What gives? You've been in a bad mood all morning. Is everything all right?"

No. Everything was horrible. How else could it be when the world decided to remind you of unvarnished truths? "I have a lot to do at the winery, is all."

"You sure that's all it is?"

"What else would it be?" he asked, in a casual voice. Thank goodness for his sunglasses. He wasn't sure his eyes looked nearly as impassive as his voice sounded.

"I don't know. I was wondering if it had something to do with baby Rosa."

He stumbled over a cobblestone. "Contrary to what you think, the birth of baby Rosa is not the biggest event taking place in this town."

"No, but it is the biggest thing to happen to your family. I would think you'd be happy for Marianna and Ryan."

"I am happy for them." Granted he hadn't been thrilled when he'd first discovered Marianna was pregnant by a man she barely knew, but since then Ryan had proven himself devoted to both his sister and their child. "I hope Rosa is the first of many children."

"Good, because back at the villa you looked like you didn't want anything to do with the baby."

On the contrary. He turned to look at her. "I wanted plenty."

If Louisa caught the pointedness in his comment, she let it pass. They'd reached the town center. It being only a few days until the festival, tourists crowded the cobblestone square. Camera phones at the ready, they posed in front of the fountain and raised them to snap pictures of brightly decorated balconies. Many carried shopping bags like his. Monte Calanetti's economy was still going strong. Rafe would be happy. A lot of these people were no doubt eating at Mancini's this evening.

As though by mutual agreement, he and Louisa stopped in the square where they'd had their first kiss. He wondered how often she thought of that afternoon. As often as he did? Thinking of their kiss had become practically an obsession.

He wasn't sure if nature was trying to soothe him by pointing out that he could at least feel physical passion, or if she were mocking him by giving him a pointless attraction.

To rub salt into his wounds, he stole a long look at Louisa's profile. The way her hair turned white in the bright sun was something he'd never grow tired of studying.

He loved the way her hair wasn't one color but a collection of platinum and gold strands woven together to create a shade that was uniquely Louisa. It was her hair, no doubt, that had caught Steven Clark's attention on the elevator. Had his fingers itched to comb through the colors the way Nico's did?

Louisa turned in his direction, and he quickly looked away.

"Did your sister tell you she asked me to be Rosabella's godmother?" she asked him.

"She did?" He hadn't known, but he wasn't surprised. Marianna had told him how much she'd come to care about Louisa these past months.

"She said she picked me because I could teach her daughter about being strong. Funny, but I don't think of myself as strong."

Because she didn't give herself enough credit. "You're stronger than you think."

"Maybe," she said, looking away. The knot at the back of Nico's neck returned as he guessed what her next comment would be. "She told me they asked you to be the godfather."

"They did." For some insane reason, they actually wanted him as a backup parent. The question had caught him so off guard he couldn't answer.

"It's not going to be a problem, is it?" Louisa asked. "Being paired with me? I know it's a big deal here, and if you'd rather stand up with someone else…"

"What? No." He hadn't stopped to think that his unenthusiastic answer might sound like an objection to her. "I think you'll be a wonderful godmother. It's me that I'm worried about."

"If you're afraid you're going to drop her…"

"No, I'm not afraid of dropping her."

"Then, what's the matter?"

"It's complicated," he replied. Hoping she'd drop the subject, Nico walked toward the fountain.

Monte Calanetti's famed nymph reclined across her rocks, the clamshell in her hand beckoning to all who wanted to toss a coin. Based on the silver and gold coins shimmering beneath the water, a lot of tourists had tried today. "Have you ever wished on the fountain?" he asked when he felt Louisa standing behind him. A silly question. Everyone in Monte Calanetti had tried at least once to land a coin in the clamshell.

"Sure," she replied. "My coin missed the shell, though."

"Mine always missed, too."

"And I thought you were perfect."

She was joking, but Nico grimaced all the same. He was most definitely not perfect.

So much for changing the subject. "Didn't matter. My wish came true anyway," he replied.

"What did you used to wish for?"

"That I wouldn't be like my parents. In and out of love. Jumping from one drama to another. I would not live on an emotional roller coaster."

Her hand came to rest between his shoulder blades, the warmth from the contact reaching through his linen shirt. "Can't blame you there," she said "Who would?"

No one, or so he'd thought, which was why he'd stood here as a little boy and tossed coin after coin. He could see himself, standing at the fountain's edge, his jaw clenched with determination. "Unfortunately, it worked too well," he said, with a sigh.

"You're confusing me."

Of course he was. Louisa felt things deeply. He saw the warmth in her eyes when she looked at Rosa, the immediate affection. His sister couldn't have picked a better woman to help guide his niece through life. She would love Baby Rosa like her own. Unlike…

Fear gripped his chest. “Everyone sees me as some kind of leader,” he said. “A man they can count on.”

“Because you are. You certainly hold Monte Calanetti together. Not to mention the vineyard, the palazzo.”

“Those are things, businesses. Anyone can manage a business. People, on the other hand...” He took off his sunglasses, wanting her to see how serious he was regarding his question. “What if I let her down?”

“Who?”

“Baby Rosa. What if she can’t count on me? What if I can’t love her enough to be there emotionally when she needs me to?”

“You’re serious? That’s why you kept pulling away when we talked about the baby.” She sank to sit on the fountain wall. “Do you really believe you won’t be able to care about your own niece?”

“Care about, yes, but care enough?” He shook his head. “I’ve already proven I can’t.”

“When? Oh, your fiancée.”

“My fiancée.” Taking a space next to her, he let his shopping bag rest on the ground between his feet. Thankfully the noontime heat had chased many of the tourists to the shade, leaving them momentarily alone.

“Floriana was a wonderful girl. Smart, beautiful, kind. We shared all the same interests. We never ever argued.”

“She sounds perfect.”

“She was,” he said, staring at his hands. “We were perfect for each other.” The answer tasted sour on his tongue. In a way, singing Floriana’s praises to Louisa felt wrong.

“What happened?”

“Simple,” he said. “I broke her heart.”

There had to be more to the story. Something that Nico wasn’t telling her. The man she knew wouldn’t carelessly break a woman’s heart.

Although wasn't that exactly the kind of man she'd thought he was when she'd met him?

Yes, she had, but she knew better now. Knew him better now. "Surely it's not as simple as that," she said.

"Ah, but it is," he replied. "As perfect as Floriana was—as we were for each other—I couldn't love her. Not truly and deeply, the way a person should be loved. That's when I realized I'll never be like my parents or like Angelo or Marianna. I don't have it in me."

"It?"

"Passion. Real, deep emotion.

"It's true," he said when Louisa opened her mouth to argue. "Angelo and Marianna, they are like my parents. They feel things. Highs. Lows. Excitement. They thrive on it, even. But me…I don't want highs and lows. I want calm. I want…"

"Consistency," Louisa supplied. Certainty. To know when he walked through the door that his world hadn't been turned upside down. She had the sudden flash that Nico had been as trapped by his parents' chaos as she had been by Steven's control.

"Consistency is one way of putting it, I suppose. Much better than saying I lack depth."

"Is that what Floriana said? She was wrong."

"Was she?"

"Just because you don't throw plates like your parents doesn't mean you're not capable of passion." It killed her to hear him beat himself up so needlessly. Couldn't he see how impossibly wrong he was about himself? She'd witnessed his passion plenty of times. In the vineyards when he talked about Carlos. When he talked of Monte Calanetti's traditions.

When he'd kissed her. She'd never felt such passion before.

Nico stared at his hands as if they held the argument

he needed. “Then why didn’t I feel anything today?” he asked. “The three of you—Marianna, Ryan, you—you couldn’t stop oohing and aahing at Baby Rosa. Meanwhile, the only thing going through my mind was that she looked…small.”

“What did you expect to think? She’s three days old. It’s not like she’s going to be filled with personality.”

“But everyone else…”

Okay, now she wanted to shake him and make him see sense. For a smart man, he was being incredibly stupid. “Marianna and Ryan are her parents. If she wrinkles her nose they think it’s a sign of genius.”

“And you…”

“I’m a woman. I’m programmed to think babies are adorable. You, on the other hand, are a guy. Until babies actually do something, you don’t see the point.

“Look,” she said. Grasping his face between her hands, she forced him to look her in the eye to make sure he heard what she was saying. “Just because a person seems perfect doesn’t mean they are. Believe me, I know. You’re going to make a wonderful godfather. The very fact you’re worrying about doing a good job shows how much you care.

“Besides,” she added, “I refuse to do this godmother thing without a good partner. Last time I looked, we made a pretty good team.”

The worry faded from around his eyes. Giving her a grateful smile, Nico rested his forehead against hers. His hands came up to cup her face. “Thank you, *bella mia*,” he said, the whisper caressing her lips. Louisa closed her eyes and let the sensation wash over her.

They sat entwined like that for several minutes, neither in a rush to break the moment. As far as she was concerned, she could sit there all afternoon. She didn’t even care if there were paparazzi watching.

CHAPTER TEN

THE NEXT DAY, a cold front invaded the valley and everyone feared the harvest festival would be threatened by rain. "The tourists will still come," Nico had said as they gathered to finish the float. "We've never failed to attract a crowd, rain or shine."

"But sun brings a better crowd," Marianna had been quick to point out, "and this is the one year when we can count on the crowd being especially large."

Turned out Nico's sister needn't have worried. The morning of the festival, Louisa woke to see the sun brightening a cloudless blue sky.

"Luck is on our side," Nico had remarked over coffee before adding, "Perfect day for playing festival queen."

"Nice try," she'd answered, "but no." With the headlines diminishing daily, why court trouble?

Nevertheless, she agreed to accompany him to the parade's staging ground to give their float a proper send-off. While he was in the shower, she snuck over to the palazzo and got out a tiered skirt and peasant blouse from her closet. A peace offering. She might not be queen, but she could dress in the spirit of the occasion.

The thought didn't occur to her until she was ducking through the archway leading to Nico's villa, that if she was comfortable enough crossing the fields alone, she could move back home.

Tomorrow.

For so many years her thoughts had revolved around escaping—escaping Steven, escaping Boston, escaping the paparazzi—and suddenly here she was focused on staying.

Something had shifted between her and Nico that day at the fountain. There was a depth to their friendship she hadn't felt before. An openness brought about by shared fears. Whereas before there had been attraction, she felt pulled by an attraction of a different sort. Didn't make sense, she knew. But there it was.

"Wow," Nico said when stepped back into the kitchen. "Like a proper Tuscan peasant."

Appreciation lit his eyes, turning her insides warm. She hadn't done all that much. "Thank you. I figured when in Rome, or in this case Tuscany..."

"You look just like a proper Tuscan gypsy." And he, a proper Tuscan vintner in his jeans and loose white shirt. Louisa had never seen him look more appealing. He offered his hand. "Shall we?"

The festival itself was to be held in the plaza. Last night Nico and several of his employees had gone into town to set up a quintet of large half barrels around the fountain, and so she assumed that was where they were heading for the parade, as well. To her surprise, however, he turned his truck toward Comparino. "We start at the palazzo," he told her, "and head into town, recreating the route the farmers took back when the *mezzadria* system was in place. That's when the sharecroppers would present the landowners with their share of the harvest. Back then the Bertonellis would have used the grapes to make wine. Today we use a lesser quality crop and put the fruit in the vats for stomping."

"I can't believe people still stomp grapes." Louisa thought the tradition was reserved only for movies and old sitcoms.

"Tourists come from all over the world to see Old World traditions. The least we can do is provide them."

She bet Nico loved every minute of them, too, lover of tradition that he was. In fact, there was a special kind of glow about him this morning. He looked brighter, more alive. His body hummed with energy, too, more so than usual. Standing by his side, she found it impossible not to let it wash over her, as well.

They turned a corner and drove into a field that had become a makeshift parade ground. In addition to the floats, Louisa spied dozens of townspeople dressed in costume. There were women wearing woolen folk dresses and large straw hats and men dressed as peasant farmers. She spotted musicians and what she guessed were dancers, as well.

"Later on, they'll demonstrate the *trescone*," Nico said. "Everyone present is invited to join in."

And here she thought the festival was just an excuse to eat and drink.

"Can I ask you a question?" she asked once Nico had parked the truck. "Why is tradition so important to you?" She suspected she already knew the answer, but wanted to hear it from him.

"I don't know," he replied. "I suppose it is because tradition helps define who we are and what we do. There's a sacred quality to knowing that you're walking in the footsteps of generations that came before you. Time has passed, but the traditions, the core of who we are, doesn't change."

In other words, he loved the consistency. For a man whose entire life had been fraught with chaos, tradition—like Carlos's vineyard—never let him down. No wonder he'd been so adamant that she lead the parade.

And yet, he was willing to let go of tradition to make her feel more comfortable. Once again, he was rushing to her rescue.

Maybe it was time she returned the favor. "I'll do it," she said.

"Do what?"

"I'll lead the parade."

If everything else went wrong today, the way Nico's eyes lit up would be reason enough for her answer. "Are you sure?" he asked her.

"Absolutely." What were a few miles, right? She could do it. "But only if you'll walk with me."

"Are you asking if I'll be your king?"

Dear Lord, the way he said the sentence… Her insides grew warm. "Don't be literal," she said, trying to hide her reaction by making light of the comment. "More like a royal companion who's there to help me when I screw up."

Damn if the way he brushed a tendril of hair off her cheek before speaking didn't turn her inside out. "It would be my pleasure, *bella mia*."

Royal companion wasn't the right term at all. Nico was a king. Smiling brightly and waving to the crowds, he belonged at the front of the parade far more than Louisa did. The town loved him.

Or maybe Monte Calanetti was just full of love today. The streets were lined with revelers who laughed and cheered them along as they wound their way slowly down the cobblestone streets. Behind them, the costumed men carried baskets of grapes while the women tossed bags of sugared nuts they had stored in the pockets of their aprons. If photographers were there, they were hidden by the throngs of tourists who, it was clear, were only interested in enjoying the day.

"Signorina! Signorina!" A little girl wearing a dress the colors of Italy, ran into the street carrying a crown made from ribbons and roses. *"Per voi la Signorina Harrison,"* she said, holding it in her hands. *"Una corona per la regina."*

Louisa beamed her. A crown? For her? *"Grazie,"* she said, placing the flowers on her head. The wreath was too big and slid down to her ears, but Louisa didn't care. She grinned and flicked the ribbons over her shoulder.

There were more children. More flowers presented. Too many for Louisa to carry, so she began giving them to the women behind her, running from the front of the parade to the rear and back again. It became a game between her and the children, to see how fast she could run the gamut before another flower appeared. By the time they reached the fountain, she was laughing and gasping for breath.

"Told you the town wouldn't care," Nico whispered in her ear. She turned to discover his eyes glittered with laughter, too. "This is amazing," she told him.

"You are having fun, then?"

Was he joking? What she was feeling at this moment was so much more than amusement. She felt free. All those years of being the outsider were but bad memories. She'd found a place where she'd belonged. A home.

To think, if Nico hadn't gone to the palazzo the day the headlines broke—if he hadn't insisted she stay—she might still be looking.

What would she have done without him?

"I'm having a wonderful time," she said. She moved to throw her arms around him in a hug only to be thwarted by the enveloping crowd. Having emptied their baskets into three oversize half barrels, the marchers stood clapping rhythmically. "They're waiting for you," Nico told her. "The queen is the first to stomp the grapes."

As though they'd been waiting, two of the men wearing medieval costumes appeared at her elbows and began guiding her forward. "Wait, wait," she said, laughing. "I still have my shoes on."

"Just kick them off," a familiar voice hollered. Looking left, she saw Dani waving from a few feet away. "I'll grab them for you," her friend said.

She made her way to the front barrel that, despite its size, was overflowing with large bunches of purple grapes.

"I'm not doing this without my royal companion," she said, looking over her shoulder.

Evidently the crowd thought this a wonderful idea, because a second later, Nico was pushed into the circle. As he stepped closer, his laugh faded to a mischievous gleam. "Now you've asked for it, *bella mia*."

Grabbing her by the waist, he lifted her in the air and plopped her feetfirst into the barrel.

Louisa shrieked as the grapes squished between her toes. "It's cold!"

"You expected a warm bath?" he asked with a laugh. Stepping into the barrel with her, he took her by the hands. "Be careful, it's slippery."

No kidding. The crushed grapes and skin quickly stuck to the bottom of the container, creating a layer of slickness. Twice already, she would have lost her balance if Nico hadn't been holding her up. Still, as cold and slippery as the grapes were, it was fun marching in place. Particularly with Nico's hands sending warmth up her arms.

A few minutes later, the rest of the crowd joined them, kicking off their shoes and crowding into the vats. Laughter abounded as everyone was eager to take their turn mashing the grapes to a pulp.

"I can't believe this is how people used to make wine," she said to him over the noise. "They must have had incredibly muscular thighs."

"Not really." Nico had leaned in to speak. His breath floated over her collarbone leaving goose bumps. "Italian winemakers have used presses to crush grapes since the middle ages. This is just for the tourists."

"You mean there is no Old World tradition?"

"Not that I know of."

"I'm up to my ankles in pulverized grapes because of a gimmick? You—"

He laughed and she gave his shoulder a shove, only to have her feet slide out from beneath her.

"Careful!" Nico scooped her up into his arms just as she was about to fall bottom first into the mashed fruit. "We wouldn't want you to be trampled," he said, smiling down at her.

No danger of that now. With her arms wrapped around his neck, and his arms holding her tight, Louisa had never felt safer. "I'm not worried," she said. "You'd rescue me."

His smile faded. "Always."

Louisa's breath caught at the seriousness in his voice. Just as it had at the royal wedding, the world receded, leaving only the two of them and the sound of their breathing. Nico's eyes grew heavy lidded, his attention focused on Louisa's mouth. Slowly she ran a tongue over her lower lip, an action for which she was rewarded with the tightening of his hand on her waist. "Louisa…" His voice was rough and raw.

He wanted her. But he was holding back to let her make the first move. That she held the power was all Louisa needed to reach a decision.

She pulled his head down to meet hers…

Dear Lord, how on earth could she have gone so long without kissing him? Nico might have given her the power to decide, but once their mouths joined, he took control, kissing her so deeply Louisa couldn't tell where she ended and he began. She didn't care. She was too swept away by the moment.

It was the cheer rising from the crowd that finally broke the moment. "I think the crowd approves," Nico said, rubbing his nose against hers.

Heat rushed to Louisa's cheeks. Let the crowd cheer,

she decided. She held his gaze and wondered if her eyes looked as blown and glazed over as his.

"Why don't we go someplace more private?" he said. Without giving her a chance to answer, he carried her out of the barrel and through the crowd.

Nico pressed a kiss to the head resting on his shoulder. Louisa and he were in his garden, ensconced on a lounger beneath the pergola. Insects could be heard buzzing in the foliage above, their soft droning working with the wine to make him comfortable and drowsy. An interesting sensation, since only an hour before he'd been consumed with lust. Once alone, the urgency had receded. The best wines were made with patience. So it was with lovemaking, as well. They had all night. Why rush when you could draw out the pleasure?

Besides, strange as it seemed, being close to Louisa like this was pleasure itself.

"What was she like?"

Her question came out of nowhere. "Who?" he asked, fingers playing with the tendrils of her hair.

"Your fiancée."

"Floriana? Why do you ask? Are you jealous?" That she might be gave him a jolt of satisfaction.

"I'm curious. What made her so perfect?"

He thought back. "I told you, she liked the same things I liked, she had the same sense of humor. Plus we wanted the same things out of life."

"Which were?"

"To create wine and live a life free of drama."

"I take it you never threw a reporter off her balcony."

"She didn't own a balcony,"

"You know what I mean."

"Yes, I do." Floriana would never need to take refuge in his winery to avoid scandal. Rational to a fault, she would never have fallen for a man like Steven in the first place. On the other hand, she also never ignited a fire in the pit of his stomach the way Louisa did. Standing in those grapes, with that silly floral crown falling about her ears and her clothes wrinkled and damp from the heat, Louisa had been the most gorgeous thing he'd ever seen.

"She sounds like someone Steven would have liked. Whenever I found an interest Steven didn't like, he would find a way to suck the fun out of it."

"I don't understand." The American colloquialism threw him, although he could wager a guess.

"Well..." She shifted so she could prop herself up on one elbow. "He would either get condescending and make me feel like it was silly, or he'd suggest it wasn't the kind of thing 'Mrs. Steven Clark' should be doing."

The man was a bully. Nico was glad they'd put him in prison. Her ex deserved to be locked up in a cell as lonely and sad as he'd made his wife.

"He didn't deserve you. You know that."

"When we met, I thought I didn't deserve him."

A most foolish notion. If anything Steven Clark must have known from the start that he'd discovered a treasure and that was why he'd insisted on wrapping her up so tightly.

"What's sad is how I was so impressed by something that wasn't real. I mean, all his power and breeding. Turned out he wasn't any better than me."

"You were the better one," Nico said. "To begin with, you weren't a thief."

Louisa smiled. "Thanks, but I meant background-wise. He was just some guy from the Midwest. His fancy family history was as phony as his investment scheme. When I contacted the feds, the whole house of cards came tumbling down. The only truly real thing that survived was the palazzo." She nestled back against the curve of his neck, her hand coming up to play with the edge of his shirt collar.

"Thank God, I never told him about the place or it would be gone, too."

Prison was too good for him. "The bastard is lucky he wasn't the one on your balcony," he muttered.

"Might have been interesting if he was. I think I'd have liked to see you throw him over."

"Satisfying, too," Nico said. Propping himself on an elbow, he smiled down at her face. "What is it about you that incites me to violence?"

"I don't know."

Neither did he, and he'd been looking for the answer for the past few weeks. All he knew was that the idea of Louisa hurting made him see red. He wanted to punish Steven and the others for making her life so hard.

Come to think of it, Louisa made him feel a lot of strong emotions. He didn't just want to kiss her, he wanted to kiss her senseless. And he didn't want to enjoy her company, he wanted to spend every moment he could spare with her.

Where on earth did these feelings come from? He'd never behaved this way around Floriana. Or anyone else for that matter.

Could it be that this—Louisa—was what he'd been missing all these years?

He turned on his side until they lay face-to-face. All it took was one look into her blue eyes and his pulse started racing again. "Thank you," she whispered.

"You don't have to thank me for anything."

"But I do. Did you know," she asked as he freed a stray petal from her hair, "that this past week was the first time in years that I've felt like I truly belonged."

"I'm not surprised. Monte Calanetti loves you."

"No, Monte Calanetti loves you. I'm just lucky to have won approval from its favorite son."

"Oh, you have more than my approval, *bella mia*." She'd awakened a part of him he didn't think existed and now it belonged to her forever.

Suddenly, his desire couldn't wait any longer. Slanting his mouth across hers, he drank in her sweet taste. This—this—was perfection, he realized. All these years he believed his soul was incomplete, it had merely been in hibernation, waiting for his blonde American to move in next door.

"Louisa, Louisa, Louisa," he chanted, his lips raining kisses down her throat. "I've waited for so long."

He paused when he reached the lace neckline blocking the rest of her skin from exploration. The top button strained to be released. All it would take was a flick of his fingers.

His hand hovered. The memory of her pushing him away at the royal wedding forced him to slow down. "Are you sure?"

Looking up, he saw eyes more black than blue, the pupils wide with desire. Out of the corner of his own eye, he saw a shaky hand reaching toward her blouse. She smiled, and a moment later, the button was undone.

It was all the answer Nico needed and he crushed his mouth to hers. Later, as his fingers made short work of the remaining buttons and as Louisa breathed his name, he wondered if maybe it wasn't only Monte Calanetti that was in love…

"You are a lying lie-face. I hope you know that."

What the heck? Louisa blinked at the nightstand clock and decided it was far too early to decipher what Dani meant.

"I just want you to know that I forgive you," her friend continued.

"Forgive me for what?" She brushed the hair from her eyes.

"For telling me nothing was going on between you and Nico, of course. You're not going to keep insisting the two of you are only friends after what we saw yesterday."

Louisa smiled, thinking about what Dani and the others hadn't seen. "No."

"Good. Because unless you let all your friends literally sweep you off your feet, no one would believe you," Dani told her. "By the way, Rafe and I completely understand why the two of you wanted to keep things private for a while. Especially given the circumstances."

"Thank you." No sense explaining how she and Nico weren't together until yesterday. Like Dani said, after the way she'd kissed him in the plaza, no one would believe her anyway.

Nico had swept her off her feet, hadn't he? *In more ways than one.* Her stomach dropped a little at that.

He's not Steven. This was a different kind of affair.

"Louisa, are you there?"

She yawned and pushed herself to a sitting position. "I'm here," she said, pulling the sheet up.

"Good. I was afraid Nico might be distracting you."

"Nico isn't here. He went to see how the harvest was going." *I'll wake you when I get back*, he'd whispered upon kissing her cheek. So much for that fantasy. Maybe she could pretend to be asleep. "Is there a reason you're calling this early," she asked, "or did you just want to call me a liar?"

"I have your sandals. You left them in the plaza, in case you were looking for them." Oh, right. Now that she thought about it, Louisa didn't remember Nico getting his shoes either. Definitely wouldn't be able to sell the idea of friends.

"Thank you," she replied, sheepishly.

"Also now that the festival is over, Rafe wants our economic development committee to start meeting in earnest. Can you ask Nico if he's available next Tuesday morning, since you'll probably see him before any of the rest of us will?"

Wow, the little blonde was really enjoying this wasn't she? Louisa shook her head, despite Dani's not being able to see her. "I'll try to track him down."

As if on cue, no sooner did she speak than the bedroom door opened and Nico strolled in wearing a shirt that should have been tossed several washes ago as it was at least a size too small. The fabric clung to his biceps and flat stomach.

When he saw her sitting up, he gave an exaggerated pout. "Dani," she mouthed. Her breath was too short to talk anyway. That shirt left nothing to the imagination, especially to a woman who knew exactly what lay beneath the cotton.

She watched him putter around the bedroom only half listening while Dani talked on about the meeting. Finally, guessing that a pause meant the conversation had ended, Louisa told Dani she had to go.

"What did Dani want?" Nico asked, when she tossed the phone aside.

"To give me grief for not telling her about our affair."

"But we weren't having an affair until..."

"I know," she replied. "And you didn't think people believed the tabloids."

"People will definitely believe them now," he commented. Hard to call them liars, that was for sure. "Does it bother you?"

He looked so serious, standing there smoothing the

wrinkled duvet. "Don't have much of a choice now, do I?" she replied. "I mean, the time to object would have been before I kissed you, and if I recall…"

She rolled onto her stomach, and hugged his pillow beneath her, grinning to herself at how the movement left her shoulders and back exposed. "As I recall, I wasn't doing all that much objecting at the time."

"That is true. I did not hear an objection," he replied. To her surprise, however, his smile didn't last. "I hope I don't hear one today."

An odd question considering she lay naked in his bed. "What could I possibly object to? That yesterday wasn't perfect enough?"

"This."

Louisa sat up as Nico pulled a rolled-up newspaper from the back of his waistband. The pages had been folded to a gossip column. Near the bottom of the page, she saw a brief mention of her holding court at the harvest festival with her latest millionaire boyfriend. Two lines. No more. Her fifteen minutes of notoriety was fading. A weight lifted from her shoulders.

"Looks like I've been replaced by bigger news." Finally. Heaven help the poor person who took her place, whether they deserved the attention or not.

"So you don't mind the mention?" Nico asked.

Honestly? She'd rather they not mention her at all, but given how bad things had been? "Two lines on page thirteen I can handle."

At last, a true smile broke across Nico's face. "Good. I'm glad. I was concerned…"

"About what? That I would freak out?"

"You did before." He pressed a knee to the edge of the bed, and leaning close, cradled her face in his palm. "I never want anything to hurt you that badly again."

"*Never* is a very big promise," she told him.

"Not where you're concerned. If I have to buy up every newspaper in Italy to keep the paparazzi from hounding you, I will."

A shiver ran down Louisa's spine. He's just trying to make you feel safe and special. Even so, when he said things like that she couldn't help thinking of Steven.

"No need to do anything so drastic. I'll settle for your arms around me."

"Ask and you shall receive, *bella mia*." A twinkle appeared in his eye. "Is a hug all you need?"

Well, when he looked at her like that… She grabbed the neck of his T-shirt and tugged him forward. "Now that you mention it, I might have a few other requests."

Following their lovemaking this morning, he'd wanted nothing more than to burrow with her beneath the sheets and, maybe after some rest, make love again. Unfortunately, Louisa insisted they needed to make an appearance at the winery before the gossip got too out of control.

As he leaned back against the bed watching her dress, he marveled at how light and full his chest felt. Never in his entire life could Nico remember feeling this way. It was as though overnight the entire world had grown brighter: every color more brilliant, every smell and sound more pronounced. And Louisa—beautiful, beautiful Louisa—he couldn't get enough of her. Not sexually, although making love with her was amazing, but of *her*. Her company, her presence, her happiness. It overwhelmed him how much he wanted to keep her close and protect her.

Suddenly, it hit him. He was in love.

For the first time in his life, he, Nico Amatucci, was truly, madly and deeply in love. The knowledge swelled inside him, inflating his heart until he thought it might burst.

To distract himself from the desire to haul her down the hall and back into his bed, he pretended to check the messages on his phone. Comprehension was difficult, what with his beautiful American standing a few feet away clad only in jeans and a bra.

"You should move your clothes into the closet," he said as he watched her taking a shirt from her suitcase. This long under his roof, and she hadn't unpacked? They would need to remedy that.

"Actually," Louisa said, "I was thinking it might be time for me to move back to the palazzo."

What? He sat a little straighter. "So soon?"

"It's hardly soon, Nico. I've been here two and a half weeks. This was only supposed to be until the press died down, remember?"

He remembered. He didn't want her to go. Her decision felt too much like her deciding to leave Monte Calanetti. How could she want to leave when they were only just were discovering their feelings.

It took all his effort to keep his voice light and not spoil the moment with his panic. "I suppose," he said, heaving the most dramatic sigh he could muster, "if you prefer to sleep alone in a cold palazzo than in my warm bed..."

"I never said I *preferred* the cold palazzo." She mocked his exaggerated voice with one of her own. "But I will have to go back eventually."

"I know. Not tonight, though?"

"Well..." He could tell from the sparkle in her eyes that she was only pretending to hesitate. "Okay, not tonight. But soon."

"Soon," he said, with a smile. He was surprised at how strongly he wanted her to stay. This new passionate self was going to take some getting used to.

Returning his attention to his phone, he noticed a message from Rafe. Agenda Items for Next Tuesday, the subject line read.

"Did Dani say any more about what Rafe wanted to talk about at this meeting?" he asked Louisa.

"Just that he wanted to get plans rolling on some type of event to attract visitors now that the harvest is wrapping up." She was buttoning the same silk blouse she'd worn when moving in. "He was thinking maybe something in February," she said. Around Valentine's Day."

"A holiday that will attract couples to his restaurant. Why am I not surprised?"

"Well, it is a romantic time of year. What could be more romantic than candlelit dinners with fine wine?"

"True." No sooner did she say the words than the image of the two of them nestled together in a corner table came to mind. "Very romantic indeed," he murmured.

"You could relabel one of your wines for the occasion. The winery must have something bubbly. A prosecco maybe?"

She was on to something. The winery had a very nice prosecco they produced on a limited basis. He could easily convince the local businesses to incorporate it into any plans they came up with.

Tossing his phone aside, he got up and, giving in partially to his desire, wrapped his arms around her waist. "Beautiful and brilliant," he said, kissing her neck. "You are definitely a prize worth keeping."

"Glad you think so."

Was it his imagination or did she tense slightly before breaking the embrace. She had a smile on her face, so he must have.

"Isn't Valentine's Day when you were hoping to open the palazzo to guests?" Since she obviously wasn't going to leave Monte Calanetti now, she could put her project back into motion.

To his surprise, she answered his question with a very sarcastic laugh. “I’m pretty sure those plans bit the dust when Dominic Merloni canceled our appointment.”

Dominic Merloni. That shortsighted idiot. “He is not the only financier in Italy. There are other banks. Other sources of funding,” he reminded her.

Louisa set down the hairbrush she was using to look at him. “Who’s going to lend Luscious Louisa money? It was naive of me to think I could slide by on my maiden name. Too much of my past financial history is tied to Steven’s.”

“There is still the investor route. I’m sure there are plenty of people who would be interested. I’ve already said I would—”

“No.” Her refusal was sharp and sudden, cutting him off. The reaction must have shown on his face, because her voice immediately softened. “We’ve already had this conversation Nico. I can’t take money from you.”

“Yes, but…” But that was before they became lovers. Surely, the situation had changed. Why not let him help?

“The whole idea of the hotel was to create something of my own,” she said, cutting off his protest. “If I take money from you, then it won’t feel that way. Especially now. The papers claim I’m dating you for your money,” she added, picking up her brush.

“I thought you no longer cared what the papers said.”

“I said I could deal with a small mention. What I don’t want to do is give them more ammunition.”

“So, what are you going to do? Give up on your plan?”

“I’m not ‘giving up’ on anything. The palazzo is going to make a wonderful hotel. Just not as soon as I hoped, is all. In another year or so, maybe, when I’ve had time to build a better financial profile.”

Hearing Louisa put her dream on hold broke his heart. It wasn’t right, her suffering another setback because of that cretin she'd married. Especially when he had the wealth and connections to make things happen.

Maybe… He looked down at his phone. Maybe she wouldn't have to wait too long. Wouldn't hurt to make a few phone calls and see if he could open a few doors, would it?

CHAPTER ELEVEN

MORE THAN A few heads turned when Louisa and Nico entered the winery together. Dozens of pairs of eyes all staring knowingly in her direction.

Suppressing the old, familiar apprehension, Louisa nodded hello to everyone. "Looks like our secret is out," she said. The din of the machinery forced her to holler directly into Nico's ear.

He turned and looked at her with such concern, her heart wobbled. "Will you be all right?" he asked.

"I'll be fine." Even if she wouldn't, there was no way she could tell him that when he was looking at her so tenderly. "If I was worried about discretion, I wouldn't have kissed you in front of the whole village, would I?"

Nico looked about to reply when one of the workers called his name.

"Duty calls," he said. He flicked the hair from her eyes with his index finger. While not a kiss, the gesture was still intimate enough that, if there had been any employees who didn't suspect their affair, there weren't anymore.

Trying her best to look nonchalant, Louisa headed toward the back office. She was nodding hello to the women at the destemmer when she noticed the two men behind them exchanging euros.

"They've been placing bets ever since the picture of you and Signor Amatucci appeared in the paper," Mario said, appearing at her shoulder.

Bets. Her stomach churned a little at the news. "On what?"

"On you and Signor Amatucci. Half the staff believed

the two of you were just friends; the other half was convinced the two of you had been together for months."

"Months? You must have heard wrong." Up until the royal wedding, she and Nico had only crossed paths when necessary, and half the time they'd butted heads.

The young man shrugged. "I only know what people told me."

"Which side were you on?" she asked.

"I don't like to place money on anyone who is writing me a reference."

"A smart man," she replied.

"For what it's worth," Mario continued, following her into the office "the majority were hoping the rumors turned out to be true."

"They were?" Come to think of it, while people stared, nobody seemed particularly acrimonious. There were no cold shoulders like in Boston. In fact, Louisa realized, some of them had amusement in their eyes.

"Public consensus seems to be that it was high time Signor Amatucci had a serious relationship."

"It is, is it?"

"At least among the older female employees."

"I see." She wondered if Nico knew he had a mothering contingent. Probably.

Feeling slightly better, she sat down at her desk. Today's order list wasn't as long as previous days' as most people had purchased their bottles in person at the festival. She counted fewer than two dozen names.

"Those should be the last of the orders," Mario said. "We'll be out of Amatucci Reserve after today."

"Guess that means my job will be finishing soon, as well. No wine, no need to fulfill orders." With the headlines dying down and the wine gone, it was definitely time to go home.

"That's too bad," Mario replied. "You'll be missed."

"I know. What will people have to bet on?"

"I'm serious. I'll admit, when you first arrived some of us were concerned. We didn't know what to expect. But then we got to know you, and we realized what Signor Amatucci said at the staff meeting was true..."

"I'm sorry." Louisa put down the paper she'd picked up. "What staff meeting?"

"Right after you started. *Signor* held a staff meeting and told us the headlines were all exaggerations and that we should make a point of getting to know you."

So that's why Mario and the others had warmed up to her. Because Nico had told them to. "How very kind of him," she replied. Inside, she wanted to wring Nico's neck.

"Well, like *signor* said, once we got to know you, we'd realize we shouldn't believe everything we read. At least I don't believe it."

"Thank you." She did her best to keep her voice calm and kind. The young man was being sincere. Besides, her annoyance wasn't with him, it was with his boss.

"This reminds me..." Palms pressed to the desk top, she pushed herself to her feet, deliberately moving slowly so as to stay calm. "There's something I wanted to ask Nico about today's orders. Do you mind?"

"Not at all. I saw him and Vitale heading toward the wine cellar."

Perfect. They could talk without being overheard.

Cool and dark, the wine cellar Nico had proudly told her about on her first day had changed little from when the Amatuccis first started making wine. The stone walls and floor were the same ones against which his great-grandfather had stacked his wine barrels. At the moment the tradition meant little as she stalked the floor-to-ceiling stacks looking for Nico.

She found him in the farthest room, clipboard in hand.

Soon as he saw her, a smile broke across his face. "Now here is a pleasant coincidence. I was just imagining what it would be like to bring you down here and have my way with you."

"You'll have to keep imagining," she replied, sidestepping his grasp.

Immediately his smile turned into a frown. "Is something wrong?"

"You tell me. Did you really tell your employees they had to be nice to me?"

"Where did you hear that?"

"Mario told me about your staff meeting." Not that it mattered who'd told her. The way he was avoiding looking her in the eyes told her it was true.

The irritation she'd been tamping down, quickly roared to life, making it a herculean effort for her not to snatch the clipboard from his hands and toss it on the ground then and there to make him look at her. She settled for spinning around and slamming the door shut. "I can't believe you did that," she hissed once she had his attention.

"Did what?"

"Forced your employees to be my friends. Who do you think you are?"

"Their boss," he replied, sharply, eyes flashing. "And I did not force anyone. I told them to treat you with respect, something I thought you were sorely in need of at the time. Or don't you remember how upset you were on that first day? When you told me about the trial?"

And broke down in his arms. "I remember," she said. All too well. Like so many times, Nico had been the rock she so desperately needed.

"That doesn't entitle you to go around speaking on my behalf." Hearing the complaint aloud, it sounded a lot less egregious than it had when she came marching down here. Still, she pressed on. There was some merit to her grievance. "I needed to win people over on my own, not because of your influence."

"And you did," Nico replied. She rolled her eyes. "Look, I simply told people to give you a chance. That if they got to know you, they would see that what the newspapers were saying was nothing but a load of garbage."

Exactly what Mario said.

"I assure you, *bella mia*, any goodwill you received you earned on your own." With a duck of his head, he offered a small smile. "You are irresistible, you know."

In spite her annoyance, Louisa's stomach gave a little wobble. He wasn't getting off that easily, though. "Regardless, you should have told me what you were planning. I don't like the idea of everyone talking behind my back."

"They were already talking; I wanted to make sure they talked correctly. Besides, if I had mentioned my plans, you would have told me not to, making your job twice as hard."

He had a point, even if the logic didn't sit completely well with her.

"What else did you tell them?" she asked.

"Nothing. I swear."

She believed him. Knowing she could verify whatever he said, he had no reason not to answer truthfully.

His index finger hooked her chin. "My only intention was to make sure people treated you fairly," he said, thumbing her lower lip. "When you told me how badly your 'friends' treated you in Boston, I… I swore I wouldn't let you suffer like that again. I just wanted to erase the hurt from your eyes."

He gazed at her from beneath lowered lids, the black of his eyes obscured by thick dark lashes. Louisa found herself lost in them anyway. He had the power to distract her with a single touch, no matter how slight. Being with Nico was unlike anything she'd ever experienced. Not with Steven or any other man. It was as if she'd been stuck in darkness her entire life and had finally stepped into the light. Nico made her feel beautiful and smart and special and a thousand other adjectives she couldn't name. The sensation scared her to death.

And yet she couldn't stop herself.

"I hate seeing you sad," he whispered. "All I want is to make sure you are happy. I'm sorry if I overstepped."

"Your heart was in the right place."

"It was." He wanted to help her by encouraging her co-workers to get to know her. A far cry from trying to isolate her, the way Steven had done.

"Then I suppose I can forgive you. This time."

Smiling, Nico leaned in to kiss her. *"Grazie, bella mia."*

Oh, but she was so weak, Louisa thought to herself. One brush of Nico's lips, and she was ready to forgive everything. Forgot everything. He could betray her a thousand times and with one touch, she'd be his again. Heart and soul. The thought would terrify her, if Nico hadn't started kissing the patch of skin right below her jaw, obliterating all coherent thought.

From the way the clipboard just slipped from Nico's grasp, she wasn't the only one about to lose control. "What have you done to me, *bella mia*?" he whispered.

Precisely the question Louisa was asking herself. But then Nico kissed her deep, and she was swept away.

"Absolutely not," Louisa said, shaking her index finger. "I'm not letting you talk me out of it again."

Oh, but the spark in her eyes said he was welcome to try. They were discussing Louisa's moving back to the palazzo. The past two nights, Nico had managed to convince her she should postpone her departure. Not that she needed too much convincing.

Tonight, however, Louisa insisted she was sleeping in her own bed.

"Fine," he told her.

"Really?" Nico chuckled at how high her brows rose. She'd been expecting an argument. After all, as they'd both discovered, the persuasion was half the fun.

"Sure. You may sleep wherever you like. Of course," he said, trailing a finger down the back of her neck, "you won't be sleeping alone."

She made a soft strangled sound in her throat that made him want to kiss her all over. He loved how easily she responded to his suggestion and how she stubbornly fought to keep him from knowing. Her eyes would flutter shut and she would bite her lower lip. Inevitably her reaction would leak out anyway, and then he would be the one fighting to hide how she affected him. Surely, she knew how crazy she made him. He would give her the world on a silver platter if she asked.

So if she wanted to go back to the palazzo, to the palazzo they would go. The only reason he kept persuading her to stay was because he didn't want to spend a night without her.

Frightening how much he needed her. Frightening and exhilarating. Was this how his brother and sister felt when they fell in love? Or his parents? If so, perhaps he finally understood them a little bit better.

Although he would never throw a plate at Louisa. Of that he was certain.

"You never told me what you thought of dinner," he said, slipping an arm around her shoulder. The two of them had played guinea pig for Rafe's fall menu.

"It was delicious," she replied. "I've never had rabbit before. And don't try to change the subject."

"*Bistecca alla fiorentina* is a Tuscan specialty. And I'm not changing the subject. I already agreed to let you win."

"Let me, huh?" She reached up and entwined her fingers with the ones on her shoulder, a move that brought her face into perfect kissing proximity. Nico had no choice but to brush his lips across hers.

"Always,' he murmured.

"Except when you don't. Like the past two nights."

Recalling how they'd spent those two nights, Nico felt a satisfied groan rise in his throat. "I like to think we both won those arguments," he replied.

It was early still; the stars had yet to appear in the sky. Nevertheless, the fountain spotlights were already on. The brightness bounced off the coins scattered in the basin.

Reaching into the water, he picked up the first coin he saw and held it up. "A halfpenny for your thoughts," he said.

She laughed. "I was thinking about how much things have changed since I arrived in Monte Calanetti."

"Good changes, I hope."

"Some very good ones," she replied.

She looked so lovely, with the light framing her face. An angel to rival the nymph of the fountain. All those people tossing money and making wishes. He already had his wish standing before him. A fierce ache spread from the center of Nico's chest, giving birth to emotions that begged to be released. "I love you," he told her, the words bursting out of him in a rush.

Louisa's heart jumped to her throat. Of all the things he could have said, why did he have to say those three words?

"Nico—"

"I know," he rushed on, "it's too soon. It's too fast. Too... Too many things, but then again, it's not." His hand trembled as he stroked her cheek. "I think I have loved you for a very long time. Since long before the wedding."

Louisa wasn't sure if she wanted to run or cry. He was

right; it was too soon. If she said the words back, it would mean accepting the fact she had once again fallen in love without thinking things through.

Even if it was already true.

That he seemed to know what she was thinking made the panic worse. "It's all right," he said, pressing his fingers to her lips. "I understand if you're not ready to say the words back. I just needed to tell you."

She was about to tell him she needed time—a lot more time—when a voice interrupted from behind them. "Nico! I thought that was you."

A wiry man with slick black hair approached them with a smile. "And Signorina Harrison. How lucky that I should run into you. Saves me the trouble of tracking you down by phone."

"Me?" She looked at Nico for help.

"I'm sorry, I should have introduced myself. I'm Dominic Merloni."

"From the bank?" Apparently he'd decided she was worth talking to after all.

If the banker noticed the chill in her voice, he was unfazed. "Yes, I wanted to apologize for canceling our meeting so abruptly the other day. There was a family emergency that took me out of town."

"How terrible," she said, not sure she believed him. "I hope everything's okay now."

"Better than ever, thank you. Anyway, since I didn't know when I would be returning, I told my secretary not to reschedule anything. Now that I'm back, I'm looking forward to sitting down and hearing more about your project. You are still thinking of turning the palazzo into a boutique hotel, are you not?"

"Yes! Definitely."

"Wonderful. Call my office tomorrow and we'll pick a time."

This was unbelievable. Here she'd convinced herself that her plans would need to wait another couple of years.

"Um…" She still didn't want to get her hopes up yet. Signor Merloni might be willing to listen, but that didn't erase her weak credit history. "I think before we meet, you should probably know that I'm recently divorced. My personal credit history is relatively new."

"Oh, I don't think that will be a problem," the banker said. "I'm sure you'll be a solid risk." His gaze darted to Nico as he spoke.

She should have known it was too good to be true.

"Well, it looks like we have occasion to celebrate," the winemaker said as they watched him walk away.

"Really?" she asked, narrowing her eyes. Whatever elation she was feeling had vanished, wiped out when the banker had tipped Nico's hand. "And what exactly do you want to celebrate? The fact that you talked Dominic into meeting with me or the fact you're a controlling jerk?"

As she hurled the words at him, Nico stiffened. "Louisa…"

"Don't try to deny it," she said. "I saw Dominic looking at you. He was about as subtle as an elephant. The guy might as well have come out and said you were backing the loan."

"I'm not backing anything."

He also wasn't denying his involvement. "You did talk with him, though."

"I told him I thought the project had potential."

The Amatucci seal of approval. Which, as everyone in Monte Calanetti knew, was as good as a guarantee. Louisa could tear her hair out. No, correction. She could tear Nico's hair out. Every curly strand.

"I can't believe you," she said, shaking her head.

"I don't understand. What did I do that's so terrible?"

What did he do? "You went behind my back, that's what."

"I was trying to help you."

"Funny, I don't recall asking for it. In fact, *I specifically asked you not to help*." Turning on her heel, she marched to the bench but was too aggravated to sit down.

Nico marched up behind her.

"What was I supposed to do?" he asked. "You were putting your plans on hold because of the man. Was I supposed to stand back and let your dreams fall apart even though I have the ability to stop it?"

"Yes!" she hissed as she spun around to face him. "That's exactly what you should have done."

"You're kidding."

"No, I'm not. It wasn't your dream to save. It was mine."

"But you weren't doing anything. To save it."

"And that's my decision to make, too. I don't need you coming in and taking over."

"Taking over?" He looked stunned, as though someone had told him pigs could fly. "What are you talking about?"

He was kidding, right? They were arguing about his influencing a banker on her behalf and he was asking her to explain herself?

Then again, maybe he didn't understand. Taking over was so ingrained in men like him, they didn't know how not to be in control.

Louisa shook her head. When she'd found out about that damn staff meeting, she should have realized then, but she'd let him sweep her concerns away. Same as she did whenever she talked about going back to the palazzo. He need only touch her and poof! Her arguments disappeared.

Because nothing felt as safe and perfect as being in his arms.

"All I wanted was to help," Nico continued. "I thought it would make you happy."

"Well, it didn't," she said, sitting down. Kind of ironic they would be arguing about this in the same spot where they'd kissed a few days earlier. The harvest festival had been one of the most magical days of her life.

How much of those memories were real? "What else have you influenced without my knowing?" she asked. "Oh my God, the baptism. Did you ask your sister to make me Rosabella's godmother?"

"No. Of course not. No one tells Marianna what to do. You know that."

"Maybe. I don't know what to believe anymore." Other than knowing she'd created some of the problem herself, that is. Leaning on Nico came too easily. His strength made her feel too safe. What was it she'd said the day of the festival? *You'd rescue me.* From the moment the news about Luscious Louisa broke, she'd come to rely on him to catch her when she fell.

"I'll tell you what you can believe," Nico said. He was kneeling in front of her, holding her hands, his eyes imploring her to let him catch her one more time. "You can believe that I would never try to hurt you. I love you."

"I know." If only he realized, his saying he loved her only made things worse.

Suddenly, she understood why she'd been so frightened when he'd said those words earlier. Deep inside she knew that if she accepted his love, then she would have to acknowledge the feelings in her own heart. Nico was already her greatest weakness. Once she admitted her feelings, she'd lose what little power she had left. Before she knew it, she would be swallowed alive again. "I promised myself that would never happen again."

"What would never happen again?" he asked.

She hadn't realized she'd spoken aloud. Since she had, however, she might as well see her thoughts through. "I swore I would never let anyone control my life again," she told him.

"Control? What the…?" Nico sat back on his heels. "I'm not trying to control you."

"Maybe not on purpose," she replied. No, definitely not on purpose. "You just can't help yourself."

Same way she wouldn't be able to help herself from letting him.

"Goodbye, Nico." She pulled her hands free. "I'll pick up my things later on."

"I'm not Steven."

She was ten feet away when he spoke. The comment was soft, barely loud enough for her to hear. Turning, she saw Nico on his feet, hands balled into fists by his side. "I'm not Steven," he repeated, this time a little louder.

"I never said you were."

"Then stop running from me like I am!"

Didn't he get it? She wasn't running from just him. She was running from herself, too.

CHAPTER TWELVE

NICO STARED AT the vine-covered wall. Once upon a time, climbing to the other side meant escaping the turmoil that engulfed his house and finding tranquility. Too bad that wasn't possible anymore. Only thing crossing the wall would do today was make the pain in his chest more acute. Either because he didn't see Louisa or because he did, and she pushed him away again.

He was still trying to comprehend what had happened the other night. One moment he was declaring his love, the next… How had everything gone so horribly wrong?

"Signor?"

He forgot that Mario was waiting for an answer. They were scheduled to harvest the fields at the palazzo today. The final field of the season, Nico always saved it for last because the grapes took the longest to ripen. Mario wanted to know if he planned to check on the workers' progress. Thus the quandary over crossing the wall.

"You go ahead," he decided. "You can supervise on your own."

The young man straightened. "If you think so."

"I do." No need for the student to know that Nico was a coward, and that was why he didn't want to visit.

Besides, there was someone else he needed to speak with.

Marianna answered the door in a long floral dress, looking uncharacteristically tousled and unmade-up. Holding Rosabella on her right shoulder, she looked him up and down. "You look worse than I do," she remarked, "and I haven't had a good night's sleep in days. What's the matter?"

"I think I might have messed up," he replied.

"Messed up how?"

"With Louisa." As briefly as he could, he explained what had happened a few nights earlier, including what happened with Dominic.

"Tell me you didn't," she said when he finished.

"I was trying to help," he said. Why did everyone have a problem with him talking to the banker? "I gave my recommendation, same as I would for Rafe, or Ryan, for that matter."

"But we aren't talking about Rafe or Ryan—although it's nice to know you would speak on my husband's behalf—we're talking about Louisa. A woman who found out her husband had been lying to her about everything. And you went behind her back. Twice!"

"To help," Nico reminded her. "Steven Clark was a thief."

"Yes, I know, but surely you can see how keeping a secret, even a well-meaning one, would feel like a betrayal to her?"

Yes, he could.

"You owe her a very large apology," Marianna told him.

"If only the solution was that simple."

"You mean there's more?" The baby started to squirm, and she switched shoulders. "What else did you do?"

"Not me—her ex-husband."

"What did he do? Besides steal from all those people?"

Nico ran a hand through his curls. He'd already said too much. Having already broken Louisa's faith, he didn't dare break it further. "Let's just say he believed in holding the people he loved as close as possible."

"Oh. I think I understand."

"You do?"

"I think so. And if I'm right, then yes, you've messed up very badly."

"She accused me of trying to take over her life. I wasn't," he added when Marianna arched a brow.

"Not intentionally anyway," she murmured.

"Louisa said the same thing."

That his sister laughed hurt. "Poor Nico," she said, using her free hand to pat his knee. "It's not your fault. It's your nature to want to rush in and take over. You tried to with Ryan and me when I was pregnant."

"Great. So now you're saying I tried to control your life, as well."

"Don't be silly. I'm used to you. I learned a long time ago to ignore you when you start giving orders I don't feel like obeying. But I'm not someone like Louisa who is struggling to rebuild her life. I can imagine your interference would make her feel very powerless. Especially since you kept your actions secret. Why didn't you tell her?"

"Because I..." Because he knew she would tell him no. "I was trying to help," he finished, as if his intentions excused his actions. "I wouldn't have talked to Dominic if I didn't have faith in her."

"I know you wouldn't, but can you see how someone in Louisa's position might see things differently?"

Yes, he could. Especially someone who'd spent so many years trapped in a controlling relationship. Nico washed a hand over his face. So focused had he been on making Louisa happy, he'd let his desires blind him to what she truly needed. "I'm no better than her ex-husband, am I?"

"Your heart was in the right place."

Small comfort when life blows up in your face. He'd trade his good intentions for having Louisa back in a second.

At that moment, Rosabella started to squirm again, wriggling her tiny torso against Marianna's body. "I swear," his sister said, as she tried to make the baby comfortable, "this little one is part eel. Spends half her day squirming. Don't you, Rosabella?" She nuzzled the baby's curls. "You know what, why don't you hold her for a few minutes? Maybe Uncle Nico is what she needs to settle down."

Doubtful. He could barely keep *himself* calm at the moment. "Marianna, I don't think—" Too late. She deposited his niece in his waiting arms and he found himself looking into Rosa's big brown eyes. For the second time in his life, Nico's heart lurched.

"She's so little," he said, risking a finger stroke against Rosa's cheek. The baby responded with a sleepy blink.

"She likes you," Marianna murmured.

"Louisa said I'd fall in love," he whispered.

"Excuse me?"

"When we were talking about being godparents. She told me I would fall in love with Rosa."

He remembered every detail of their conversation, from the advice she gave to the way the sun crowned her head as he said goodbye. "She was right in more ways than one."

His heart threatened to crack open, the way it had every hour since Louisa had said goodbye. Struggling to keep the pieces together, he looked to his sister. "I love her," he said in a quiet voice.

"I know."

Neither of them had to say what they were both thinking. That finally after years without it, Nico had found love, only to chase it away.

"I tried to explain myself the other night but she wouldn't listen, and now she won't take my phone calls," he said. "I'd go to the palazzo, but I'm afraid she'll refuse to come out." Or send him away. Either outcome frightened him into inertia. "Tell me, Marianna. What do I do?"

"I don't think you're going to like my answer."

"If you're going to tell me there's nothing I can do, you're right. There has to be something I can do." Surely she didn't expect him to sit around and do nothing while the love of his life slipped through his fingers. "If I could only get her to talk with me."

"Why? So you can explain and try to charm her into forgiving you?"

Nico held his sleeping niece a little closer. "Is that such a bad plan?"

"I don't know. How well did charm work for her ex-husband?"

"I'm not him."

"Then prove it to her."

"How? How do I make her see that I don't want to control her?"

"You let her be her own person. And that includes letting her come to you for help when she's ready.

"What if she never comes to me again?"

He didn't realize his knee was bouncing in agitation until Marianna put her hand on his leg. "Poor Nico. So used to being in charge of the situation. Haven't you figured out by now that love isn't something that makes sense? If it did, our parents would never have gotten together."

Their parents. Despite his sadness, he had to smile at her comment. "Never were two people less suited for one another," he said.

"Or more meant to be," Marianna replied, squeezing his knee. "I think you and Louisa are meant to be, as well, but you have to be patient."

"I don't know if I can." Each day that passed without speaking to her made the hole in his chest a little wider.

"Of course you can, Mr. Viticulture. Think of it like a harvest. You wouldn't pick a grape with a poor Brix level, would you?"

"No," he replied. "But waiting on a grape is a lot less painful, too."

"You can do it."

He smiled at the woman beside him. His beautiful baby sister all grown-up and glowing with motherhood. "When did you get so wise?"

"Oh, I've always been wise. You just never bothered to ask me for advice. Might as well face it, dear brother," she said, "when it comes to love, you've got a lot to learn."

Yes, he did. He only hoped he'd be able to learn with Louisa by his side.

If space was what she needed to find her way back to him, then space was what he would give her.

His resolve lasted five minutes. Then the phone rang.

"After weeks of speculation, the Halencian royal family confirmed today that Prince Antonio and Princess Christina are expecting their first child. The royal heir is due to arrive early next spring. No other details have been released..."

The television screen showed a photo of Antonio and Christina dancing at their wedding. The same photo that had reignited the Luscious Louisa scandal. Nice to know news outlets recycled resources.

Clicking off the news, Louisa tossed the remote onto the cushions. She was happy for the royal couple. Really she was. They may have had some bumpy times at the beginning of their marriage, but the pair were very much in love.

Funny how that had happened to a lot of the people she knew in Monte Calanetti. The whole "love conquering all" thing, that is. Too bad it missed her. Then again, maybe it was her fault. After all, she'd loved Steven and love hadn't come in to conquer anything. What made her think the situation would be any different simply because she loved—

Oh God, was she really ready to admit she loved Nico?

She checked her phone for messages. What was a little salt in the wound when you were already miserable, right? Nothing. After six impassioned voice mails, Nico had stopped calling. Guess he'd finally gotten the message. Or lost interest.

Make up your mind, Louisa. What do you want?

Nico, a voice whispered. She shut the voice off. What she wanted was to stop feeling as if she'd been kicked in the chest. Nothing she did seemed to curb the ache. Every day she immersed herself in cleaning and home renovations, working herself to the point of exhaustion. There wasn't a piece of wood she hadn't polished or a weed she hadn't removed from the back garden. But despite collapsing in a deep sleep every night, she woke in the morning feeling the same emptiness inside.

The doorbell rang. "Go away," she called to whoever was on the other side.

"Louisa!" Nico bellowed from the other side of the door. "Open up. I need to talk to you."

Careful what you wish for. The anger in his voice could mean only one thing. He'd found out about the Realtor.

He pounded on the door again. "Louisa! You let me in this minute or so help me I will kick the door in."

Nothing like a threat to kill her self-pity. Anger took over and she reached for the doorknob. "If you damage so much as a speck of dust, I'll…"

Dear Lord, he looked awful. One of the qualities she'd noticed from the beginning was Nico's robust appearance. The man on her doorstep looked tired, his healthy color turned pale and sallow. His eyes, while flashing with anger, were flat and lifeless beneath the spark. He looked, to be blunt, as bad as she felt.

"Is it true?" Without waiting for an invitation or answer, he stomped inside, toward the main staircase. There he stood at the foot, arms folded across his body, waiting.

"Tell me you're not seriously thinking of selling your home."

"You got the call, didn't you?"

"But why?" he asked.

"Seriously, you have to ask?" He and Monte Calanetti were irrevocably entwined. How was she supposed to stay in the village and live her life when every corner she turned would present some reminder of him?

"I thought it would make things easier," she told him, walking into the living room. Maybe if she dismissed him…

Of course he followed. "For who?" he asked. "You?"

"Yes." And for him. He wouldn't be forced to share his hometown with an ex-lover as his neighbor.

Nico didn't say a word. Instead he crossed the room, to the cabinet where she stored the fernet. At first she thought he might pour himself a glass, but he put the bottle back on the shelf.

"Amazing," he said, shaking his head. "You do like to run away from your problems, don't you?"

"Excuse me?"

"Well, you ran away from Boston to Monte Calanetti. You wanted to run away when the paparazzi came and now you are running away from me."

Louisa couldn't believe him. "I'm not running from you," she said.

"Oh really? Then what are you doing?"

"I'm…" She was…

Starting fresh again. In a new place. Away from Monte Calanetti.

All right, maybe she was running away. Maybe she needed to run away in order to save her independence.

"What I do or don't do is none of your business," she snapped. "If I want to sell the palazzo, I will."

"Is that so? And here I thought I exercised such control over your actions."

Damn him. Who did he think he was, twisting her words? "If I am leaving Monte Calanetti, it's because you tried to take over my life, and you know it."

"I did no such thing."

"Oh yeah? Then what was calling Dominic?"

"A mistake."

A damn big one, too. She was tired of having this argument. As far as she was concerned, they'd already had it one too many times.

Unfortunately, Nico thought differently. "It was wrong of me to call Dominic without telling you. I was excited to be able to help you, and I didn't think about how my help might make you feel."

Louisa had liked the conversation better before. Anger was so much easier to oppose than this softer, conciliatory tone.

She stared out the window. The Tuscan hills were starting to turn. Shades of brown mixed with the green. In another few months, it would be a year since her arrival. Seemed like only yesterday she and Dani had met on the bus from Florence. And she remembered the first time she'd met Nico. He'd sauntered through the front door without knocking and demanded proof she owned the palazzo. *Here's a man who insists on being in charge*, she remembered thinking. Her insides had practically melted at the thought, and that had scared the hell out of her. Because she didn't want to be attracted to a strong man.

"Scared," she said, her breath marking the glass.

"I don't understand." He replied.

"Your going to Dominic. It frightened me."

"I made you feel powerless."

She shook her head. “No. You made me feel like I’d met another Prince Charming. Actually, that’s not true,” she said, looking over her shoulder. “I already knew you were Prince Charming. Calling Dominic made it obvious.”

“I still don’t…”

No surprise. She probably wasn’t making much sense. “I liked that you came to my rescue,” she told him.

“And that scares you.”

It terrified her. With a small shrug, she turned back to the hills. “I need to be my own person. When I’m with you, it’s too easy to give in and let you run the show.”

“Could have fooled me. In fact, I seem to recall more than one argument over my trying to run the show.”

His shadow appeared in the window. Louisa could tell from the warmth buffeting her back, or rather the lack of it, that he was making a point of keeping his distance. “Do you know why Floriana and I didn’t work?” he asked.

The odd shift in conversation confused her, but Louisa went along with it. “No. Why?”

“Because she was too perfect. I realized that just now.”

“If this is supposed to make me feel better…”

“Wait, hear me out,” he said. “Floriana… She and I never argued. She was always logical, always agreeable, always in tune with my thinking.”

“She was perfect.” While Louisa was the imperfect American who ran away from her problems. Both descriptions sickened her. “I get it.”

“I don’t think you do” was Nico’s reply. The warmth from his body moved a step closer. Not too much, but enough so Louisa could better feel its presence. “Floriana might have been perfect, but she wasn’t perfect for me. That was why I couldn’t truly love her. Do you understand?”

She was afraid to.

“I need a woman who challenges me every single day,”

he said. "Someone who is smart and beautiful, and who is not afraid to put me in my place when I overstep."

"You make it sound simple."

"On the contrary, I think it might be very hard. I don't know for sure. I've never been in love until you."

Until her. The declaration washed over her, powerful in its simplicity. Nico Amatucci loved her. And she... Panic clamped down on the thought like a vise.

"I know you are afraid," he said when she let out a choked sob. The anguish in his voice told her how much he was struggling between wanting to close the distance and respecting her need for space.

"I know that Steven left you with some very deep scars and that you are afraid of making the same mistakes. I am not Steven, though. Please know that no matter what happens between us, I will always want you to be your own person.

"So," she heard him say, "if you want to run away, that's your choice. All I ask is that you don't use me as your excuse." There were a lot of things Louisa wanted to say in response, but when she opened her mouth to speak, the words died on her tongue. In the end, she stayed where she was, afraid to turn to look lest she break down when she saw Nico's face. She heard his footsteps on the tile, the click of the front door, and then she was alone.

She'd said she wanted to stand on her own two feet. She also wanted Nico's arms around her. Desperately. What did that say about her?

That you love him. The words she'd been fighting to keep buried broke free and echoed loud in her heart. No amount of running away or lying to herself would make them disappear. She loved Nico Amatucci. She was *in* love with Nico Amatucci.

Now what? With a sob, she sank to the floor. Did she

continue with her plans? Move again and spend her life being haunted by two past mistakes?

Or did she stay in the village she'd come to think of as home and somehow find the courage to let her love for Nico grow?

Wiping her eyes, she looked out once more at the Tuscan hillside and the vineyards that stretched out before her. How much she'd come to love this view. And this palazzo.

She looked around at her surroundings. A lot had changed around here in nine months. If her ancestors could see this place now, they wouldn't recognize their old home. It wasn't the same crumbling building she'd found when she'd arrived.

Maybe she wasn't the same woman either. She certainly wasn't the impressionable young girl who'd fallen in love with Steven Clark. She'd loved, lost, withstood public scorn and found a new home. *You're a lot stronger than you give yourself credit for*, Nico had once said. Maybe it was time to start giving herself credit. Time to believe she *was* strong.

Maybe even strong enough to fall in love with a strong man.

"I asked Lindsay Sullivan if she would stop by the meeting, as well. It might be useful to get a professional event planner's input, even if she does specialize in weddings. Is that all right with you, Nico?"

"A wedding planner is fine," Nico replied. "Whatever you want to do."

"Whatever I...? All right," Rafe said, plopping down on the other side of the table. "What have you done with the real Nico Amatucci? Usually by now you would have rearranged the agenda items and brainstormed three or four new ones. Instead, you've hardly said a word. What gives?" Folding his arms, the chef tipped back in his chair and waited.

No doubt he found Nico's shrug an unsatisfactory response. "It's your committee."

"That I started with the full knowledge that you would take over. Honestly, I wouldn't have gone to all this trouble if I didn't think you would do the bulk of the heavy lifting."

"Sorry to disappoint you," he replied.

"Leave him alone, Rafe. He's nursing a broken heart." Walking past, Dani gave her husband a playful smack on the back of the head. "Remember how depressed you were when I left Monte Calanetti?"

"Depressed is a little strong. Ow!" He rubbed the back of his head. "I was joking. I was also trying to distract him from his problems."

"News flash. The playful banter isn't helping." Each quip was like salt in his already raw wounds.

"We're sorry," Dani said, taking a seat.

"No, I'm sorry," he quickly replied. "You shouldn't have to censor your happiness for my sake." Then, because he was clearly a glutton for punishment, he added, "I don't suppose you've heard anything?"

She shook her head. "Nothing. I called a couple of times, but she isn't picking up her phone. She's still in town, though."

"I know." He saw the lights on in the palazzo. Yesterday, while in the vines, he thought he caught a glimpse of her on the balcony, and he almost climbed up to join her. But since he was practicing patience, like his sister suggested, he stayed away.

"Do you think she'll go through with selling the palazzo?" Rafe asked.

God, but Nico hoped not. "It's up to her." He personally hadn't returned the Realtor's call. Probably should or else risk losing the property altogether. The idea of someone—anyone—other than Louisa living next door… Grabbing a fork, he stabbed at a *cornetto*. Far preferable to stabbing anything else. "It's her decision to make," he repeated, as much to remind himself as anything.

"Whose decision to make what?" a beautifully familiar voice asked. Nico looked up in time to see Louisa walking into the main dining room. She was dressed in a navy blue suit, the kind a banker might wear. The dark material made her hair appear more white than ever. Perhaps that was why she was wearing it pulled back in a clip. This, he realized with a jolt, was a different Louisa than the woman he'd left the other day. The woman before him carried herself with confidence and grace.

"Sorry I'm late," she said, setting a leather portfolio on the table. "Oh, please tell me that carafe is American coffee."

"Espresso," Rafe replied. He sounded as astounded as Nico felt. A quick look at Dani said she shared the feeling, as well.

Fortunately for all of them, Dani didn't have a problem saying something aloud.

"We didn't think you were coming," she said.

Pink appeared in her cheeks. "I wasn't sure I was going to attend either. I didn't make up my mind until last night."

"And the suit?"

"Confidence booster," she said, reaching for the plate of pastries that was in the center of the table. "I have a business meeting after this one."

"You do?" Nico sat up straighter. This was what he feared. She'd come to say goodbye. "You found someone to buy the palazzo?"

"No, someone to help me turn it into a hotel." Her blue eyes found his. "It appears I'm not leaving Monte Calanetti after all."

"You're not?" For a second, he was afraid he'd heard her wrong. There was a smile in her eyes, though. Would she be smiling if she was about to break his heart?

The rest of the restaurant faded into the background. Nico was vaguely aware of Rafe and Dani excusing themselves from the room, not that it mattered. He only had eyes for the woman in front of him. Everything else was background noise.

"What made you change your mind?" he asked.

Of course, her staying didn't mean she wanted him back in her life. He tried to remind himself not to get his hopes up. She'd never even said she loved him.

But she was smiling. They both were.

"For starters? A good long look at where I was." Her lip trembled, breaking the spell between them. She looked down at her pastry. "I realized I'd been stuck in the past. Not so much regarding what happened—although I was stuck about those things, too—but more like frozen in time. In my head, I saw myself as that same impressionable twenty-one-year-old girl. I forgot how much time had passed.'

Afraid she was about to beat herself up, he cut in. "Not so much time."

"Enough that I should know better," she told him.

She wasn't making sense. Confused, he waited as she got up from the table. Her high heels tapped out her paces on the terra-cotta.

"I should have known that the person I am today isn't the same as the person I was back then. At least I shouldn't be, if I let myself grow up.

"I'm not making much sense, am I?" she said, looking at him.

"No."

"I was afraid of that." Her small smile quickly faded away. "What I'm trying to say is that you were right. I was afraid of repeating the past. For so long I thought I was trapped in my marriage. Then the trial happened, and suddenly I had a second chance. Throughout the entire trial, I swore to myself I would never let myself become trapped again."

And along came Nico charging in to make everything better. Exactly what she didn't need. He'd heard enough. "It's all right, Louisa. I understand."

"No, you don't," she said, walking to him. "I should have realized that I can't make the same mistake, because I'm not the same person. I can make new mistakes, but I can't make the same ones."

Through her speech, Nico had been fighting the kernel of hope that wanted to take root in his chest. All of her rambling sounded suspiciously like it was leading to a declaration. Until he heard the words, however, he was too afraid to believe. "Are you saying…?"

"I'm saying I've fallen in love with you, Nico Amatucci. I started falling the day I arrived in Monte Calanetti, and I haven't stopped."

She loved him. "You know that I'm still going to want to rush in and fix things."

"And I'll probably get mad and accuse you of trying to take over."

"I'd expect no less."

The eyes that found his this time were shining with moisture. "Because no one said love had to be perfect."

"Just perfect for us." After days of separation, Nico couldn't hold himself back a moment longer. Jumping to his feet, he rushed to take her in his arms. Immediately, he felt a hand against his chest.

"I still have scars," she said. "You're going to have to be patient with me."

"I'll wait for as long as it takes," he promised. "There's no rushing the harvest. A long story," he added when she frowned. "I'll tell you about it later. Right now, I'd much rather kiss you."

Her arms were around his neck before he finished the sentence. *"Bella mia,"* he whispered against her lips. *Thank you*, he prayed to himself. All his dreams, everything he'd ever wanted, he was holding in his arms right now. Nothing else mattered.

As his lips touched hers, one last thought flashed across his mind.

No sweeter wine...

EPILOGUE

February 14, Valentine's Day

IF YOU ASKED LOUISA, the palazzo had never looked lovelier, not even when the place had hosted the royal wedding party. Standing in the ballroom doorway, she couldn't stop smiling at the crowd of people who were there to celebrate the opening of her hotel.

This weekend, the palazzo would only host a handful of overnight guests, mostly friends who had agreed to be guinea pigs and test the service. They would open to the general public on a limited basis next weekend, and she hoped to be fully operational by summer.

The crowd was here for the first annual St. Valentine's Ball. Billed as an opportunity to experience medieval romance and pageantry, the idea was the tourist development committee's first official success.

A flash of red sequins caught her eye. "Lindsay's outdone herself this time, hasn't she?" Marianna said, appearing by her side. "No wonder she does so many A-list weddings."

"No kidding." The room was a gorgeous display of roses and red tapestry. "We were lucky she offered to help, what with her schedule." But then, the woman had a soft spot for the village since it was where she'd met her husband. He was here with her tonight. A quick look across the dance floor found the two of them stealing a kiss in the corner. They were caught by Connor and Isabella, who'd apparently had a similar idea. Yet another couple who had found love here.

Monte Calanetti seemed to have a romantic effect on people.

"I overheard a couple talking in the lobby about booking a room for next year's ball," Marianna was saying. "I hope you're planning to take advanced reservations."

"Of course," Louisa replied. Talk about a foolish question. "My business partner would kill me if I didn't," Louisa replied. "Speaking of, where is your husband anyway?"

"He went upstairs to check on the baby and her nanny."

"Didn't you just check on them five minutes ago?"

"I did, but Ryan has to see for himself. Daddy's little girl, you know."

Louisa laughed. Sometimes she thought her two friends were competing to see who could dote on their daughter the most.

The idea of asking Marianna's husband, Ryan, to invest in her project had happened completely by accident. Literally. Louisa had almost knocked him over the day she had taken the palazzo off the market. As luck would have it, he'd been looking for a new start-up project. Neither Nico nor Marianna had any idea until the partnership was official.

Naturally, when he found out, Nico had teased her about going behind his back. In reality, he was excited for her. It was a sign of how good things were going between them that they could joke about that terrible night last fall.

A tap on her shoulder pulled her from her thoughts. "Nico told me to have you join him in the other room," Marianna said.

It never failed. As soon as she heard Nico's name, a shiver ran down Louisa's spine. The man would forever have that effect on her. "Did he say what he wanted?"

The brunette waved her hand. "You know my brother tells me nothing. I think he and Angelo are up to something. I saw them and Rafe with their heads together. Their poor, poor wives."

"You might want to include yourself in that category," Louisa reminded her. "Whatever they're up to, I'm sure it's only a matter of time before Ryan's involved, too."

"He'd better not be."

The two of them walked toward what was now the hotel lobby. Of all the changes that the palazzo was undergoing, this was the most drastic. What had been the plain entranceway was now a richly appointed lobby. Louisa had done her best to keep the structural changes to a minimum, although she did concede to installing a small built-in counter that served as both the front desk and concierge location.

The staircase remained the same, however. Richly polished, the stairs made a welcoming statement to everyone who walked in. It was in a group gathered around the bottom banister post that Louisa found her man. He was talking with his brother, Angelo, and Angelo's wife, Kayla, who had flown in from New York City. Rafe and Dani were also chatting.

Nico stepped to the side slightly, drawing her attention, and her heart stuttered. He sure could wear a tuxedo. Wasn't fair. Tomorrow he would be back in his T-shirt and jeans and would look just as sexy. Worse, she'd bet he would look just as good fifty years from now, while she'd probably end up with gray hair and a thickening waist.

So you think the two of you will be together in fifty years, do you? Nico caught her eye and winked.

Yeah, she decided. She did.

At her arrival, Nico leaned in and whispered something in Angelo's ear. His brother nodded. "There you are, *bella mia*!" he greeted. Wrapping his arms around her waist, he pulled her into a lingering kiss. Same as she did whenever Nico touched her, Louisa melted into his embrace.

Such an overt public display of affection surprised her. She chalked it up to the champagne and the atmosphere.

"I missed you," Nico whispered before releasing her.

"Down, boy. This dress isn't made for manhandling." She smoothed the wrinkles from the pink chiffon skirt before whispering in return, "I missed you, too.

"Is that why you wanted to see me?" she asked. Not that she would ever turn down a kiss, but again, even for Nico, the behavior seemed extreme.

"The kiss was merely a bonus. I was looking for you because I have a surprise."

"For me?"

"No, for my brother, Angelo. Cover your eyes."

Louisa did what she was told and seconds later, she felt Nico's breath tickling her ear. "I wanted to do something to congratulate you for everything you've done with the palazzo. Carlos, he would be proud. I know I am."

Warmth filled her from head to toe. She didn't need a surprise. Nico's respect meant everything. "Okay," he whispered. "Open them."

"Nico, I don't need— Mom?"

The silver-haired woman standing at the foot of the stairs offered her a watery smile. "Hello, Louisa."

"I—" She couldn't believe her mother was standing the lobby. "How—"

"Signor Amatucci flew me here. He wanted me to see what you've done. It's wonderful, sweetheart."

"Mom…" She couldn't finish the sentence. Instead, she ran and threw her arms around the woman, holding on to her as tightly as she could. "I missed you so much," she managed to choke out. Until this moment, she hadn't realized just how much. "I'm so sorry."

"No, sweetheart, I am. I let us grow apart, but I promise I won't let that happen again." Pulling away, her mother cupped her face like she used to do when Louisa was a little girl and had a bad dream. "Okay?"

Louisa nodded. This was the best surprise she could imagine. "Thank you," she said when Nico joined them.

"My pleasure," he replied before looking serious "You're not angry I went behind your back?"

"Are you kidding? No way." If anything, his kindness only made her love him more. A pretty amazing feat, since she already loved him more than seemed possible.

She saw the same love in Nico's eyes. "Good. Because a woman should always be able to share her engagement with her mother."

Her engagement? A warm frisson passed through her at the words. She'd be lying if the idea of spending the rest of her life with Nico hadn't crossed her mind during these past few months. Trying to imagine life without him was… Well, it was like staring at a blank wall.

Still, she wasn't about to let him know that. The man needed to be kept on his toes, after all. Arms folded, she lifted her chin and said in her most haughty voice, "There you go, taking charge again. What makes you think we're getting married?"

"A man can hope, can't he?" Nico said, reaching into his pocket. Louisa gasped when she saw the small velvet box.

Bending on one knee, he held it out to her with a shaking hand. "Louisa Harrison, my beautiful, haughty American princess, you are the only woman I will ever love. Will you marry me?"

There was only one answer she could give. Same as there could only be one man she would ever want to be with forever. "Yes," she breathed. "Yes, I will marry you, Nico Amatucci."

He pulled her into another kiss, and this time Louisa didn't care how wrinkled her dress got. As his lips slanted over hers and the crowd burst into applause, she felt the last ghosts of her life with Steven disappear forever. She'd found a new life, a new home, a new love, here, in the vineyards of Monte Calanetti.

And they were better than she'd ever dreamed possible.

* * * * *